# PRAISE FOR *TRA*

T0170877

"Gipe [is] the best of populists: generous of spi    ..ᴜ smarmy. There are some deeply flawed people in Dawn's circle (she's one of 'em), but they're never all bad, never unchangeable, but never unrealistically transformed. . . . To borrow from an old country song, *Trampoline* is ragged but right, and it builds to an effective blend of contrasting tones: world-weary yet hopeful, not too sentimental but . . . 'soft, like the sound a Christmas tree makes when you throw it over the hill.'"

—*The Star Tribune*

"*Trampoline* is that rare kind of book, a first novel that feels like a fourth or fifth. . . . It is a roaring tale that knows when to tamp its own fire—which is another way of saying that it is funny as hell but will hurt you too."

—*Electric Literature*

"A story that left my heart at once warmed and shattered, *Trampoline* rides the razor's edge of raw beauty. This is Appalachia shone with a light uniquely its own. I dare say Robert Gipe has invented his own genre."

—David Joy, author of *Where All Light Tends to Go*

"In 1980…John Kennedy Toole's classic, *A Confederacy of Dunces*, was published by the Louisiana State University Press. The following year it won the Pulitzer Prize in fiction. That may have been the last time a university press introduced a major American voice—the last time, that is, until now…. *Trampoline* is a new American masterpiece."

—*Knoxville News Sentinel*/Chapter16.org

"There are the books you like, and the books you love, and then there are the ones you want to hold to your heart for a minute after you turn the last page. . . .*Trampoline* is one of those—not just well written, which it is; and not just visually appealing, which the wonderfully deadpan black-and-white drawings make sure of; but there is something deeply lovable about it, an undertow of affection you couldn't fight if you wanted to. . . . Gipe deftly avoids every single cliché that could trip such a story up, which includes having a pitch-perfect ear for dialect and making it into something marvelous."

—*Library Journal*'s "What We're Reading"

"I fear this book. I'm in love with this book. I'm laughing out loud at this book. I am knocked to my knees in grief by this book. One of the most powerful works of contemporary fiction I've read in years. I'll never forget Dawn Jewell. I'll never escape Canard County."

—Ann Pancake, author of *Strange as this Weather Has Been* and *Me and My Daddy Listen to Bob Marley*

"Robert Gipe has produced a one-of-a-kind masterpiece. Here's a narrator, Dawn, trapped absolutely in an Appalachian Gregor Samsa kind of way, surrounded by loved ones [who are] at times difficult to love. Dawn is precocious, bighearted, and fearless—a mountaintop-removal-fighting Mattie Ross. I couldn't put this novel down."

—George Singleton, author of *Between Wrecks*

"Billboards. That's what we need. 'Dawn Jewell is queen' on one. 'Jump on this Trampoline' on another. All of them shouting how good this book is. Read it, everyone, read it."

—Jim Minick, author of *The Blueberry Years*

"Robert Gipe has the most original voice to emerge on the literary landscape since Lewis Nordan. Dawn Jewell is a delicious heroine, whether she's shouldering her way through a community conflict or a family scrimmage. Geographically anchored, yet universally relevant, *Trampoline* is funny, serious, dark, radiant, and honest, filled with rich characters and a culture wracked with contradiction and heartbreak, but also strength and resilience. An excellent debut from a gifted and insightful writer."

—Darnell Arnoult, author of *Sufficient Grace*

"I believe it takes a special genius to create a story that is hilarious *and* poignant *and* eloquent all at the same time, and Robert Gipe has done just that in his amazing debut *Trampoline*. Gipe's is a voice like no other and I guarantee you'll fall in love just like I did."

—Pam Duncan, author of *The Big Beautiful* and *Moon Women*

" . . . Quite possibly, one of the best books to ever come out of eastern Kentucky."

*Huntington Herald-Dispatch*

"*Trampoline* is a moving account of working-class Kentucky mountain people who live in an environment dominated by mountaintop removal coal mining. *Trampoline* is also the most innovative American fiction to appear in years. The story, the characters and the writing style are startlingly new, as in: original. *Trampoline* adds a fresh consciousness to the enduring conversation about the Appalachian region. Pathos and humor are present in about equal measure."

—Gurney Norman, author of *Divine Right's Trip* and *Kinfolks*

"Dawn Jewell is one of the most memorable and endearing narrators I have ever read. She's like a combination of Scout Finch, Huck Finn, Holden Caulfield, and *True Grit*'s Mattie Ross, but even more she is completely her own person, the creation of Robert Gipe, an author who has given us a novel that provides everything we need in great fiction: a sense of place that drips with kudzu and coal dust; complex characters who rise up off the page as living, breathing people we will not soon forget; and a rollicking story that is by turns hilarious, profound, deeply moving, and always lyrically beautiful. I think *Trampoline* is one of the most important novels to come out of Appalachia in a long while and announces an important new voice in our literature. I loved every single bit of this book."

—Silas House, author of *Clay's Quilt* and *Eli the Good*

"[Dawn's] authentic voice draws in the reader from the first page, and Gipe's naïve illustrations heighten the storytelling."

—*Louisville Courier-Journal*

Trampoline

# TRAMPOLINE

AN ILLUSTRATED NOVEL

## ROBERT GIPE

OHIO UNIVERSITY PRESS • ATHENS

Ohio University Press, Athens, Ohio 45701
ohioswallow.com
© 2015 by Robert Gipe
All rights reserved

To obtain permission to quote, reprint, or otherwise reproduce or distribute material
from Ohio University Press publications, please contact our rights and permissions
department at (740) 593-1154 or (740) 593-4536 (fax).

Printed in the United States of America
Ohio University Press books are printed on acid-free paper ⊗ ™

25 24 23 22 21 20 19 18 17 16 15    5 4 3 2 1

First paperback edition printed in 2015
ISBN 978-0-8214-2153-6

*Library of Congress Cataloging-in-Publication Data*
Gipe, Robert.
Trampoline : an illustrated novel / Robert Gipe.
    pages cm
Summary: "*Trampoline,* a debut novel by Robert Gipe, is set in the coalfields of
Kentucky. Its narrator is Dawn Jewell, a teenager who recounts the turbulent time
when her grandmother Cora led her into a fight to stop a mountaintop removal coal
mine. Dawn's father, Delbert, is dead, killed in the mines, leaving her mother, Tricia, a
grieving drunk. *Trampoline* follows Dawn as she decides whether to save a mountain
or save herself; be ruled by love or ruled by anger; remain in the land of her birth or
run for her life. *Trampoline* includes more than two hundred drawings that punctuate
the narrative in a unique, dramatic, and moving way and amplify Dawn's telling of her
story"— Provided by publisher.
ISBN 978-0-8214-2152-9 (hardback) — ISBN 978-0-8214-4524-2 (pdf)
1. Teenage girls—Fiction. 2. Dysfunctional families—Fiction. 3. Coal mining—
Kentucky—Fiction. I. Title.
PS3607.I4688T83 2015
813'.6—dc23
                    2014044397

# Contents

~~~~~~~~~~~~~~

### ACT I. ESCAPE VELOCITY

| | | |
|---|---|---|
| 1. | Driving Lesson | 1 |
| 2. | Smother | 17 |
| 3. | What Hurts | 34 |

### ACT II. RECKONING

| | | |
|---|---|---|
| 4. | Dead Cow in the Creek | 53 |
| 5. | Monster Birds | 78 |
| 6. | Waterlight | 106 |

### ACT III. BULLDOZER

| | | |
|---|---|---|
| 7. | Hominy Heart | 125 |
| 8. | A Thing Boils Up | 147 |
| 9. | Ignorant Girl | 165 |

### ACT IV. MEATSPACE

| | | |
|---|---|---|
| 10. | Raccoon Eyes | 191 |
| 11. | Fake Marshmallows | 207 |
| 12. | Mudhole | 227 |

### ACT V. SILVER DAGGER

| | | |
|---|---|---|
| 13. | The Mouse | 249 |
| 14. | Governor | 272 |
| 15. | Magic Yellow Pop Can | 290 |

| | |
|---|---|
| Acknowledgments | 313 |

*Dedicated to the memory of my father*

Robert Leroy Gipe

1934–1994

ACT ONE

# ESCAPE VELOCITY

# DRIVING LESSON

MAMAW STARED through the gray-gold wood smoke curling from a pile of burning brush in the front yard. I set a glass of chocolate milk at her elbow and sat down next to her on the porch glider.

"That's where they're going to strip," she said, nodding at the crest of Blue Bear Mountain. "They'll start mining on the Drop Creek side. But they'll be on this side before you graduate." She sipped her chocolate milk. "You watch."

Mamaw linked her lean arm through mine and told me about growing up on Blue Bear Mountain. Her stories smelled of sassafras and rang with gunfire, and the sound of her voice was warm as railroad gravel in the summer sun, but the stories flitted through my mind and never lit. I was fifteen.

That August, Mamaw signed her name to a piece of paper, a lands-unsuitable-for-mining-petition, the state calls it. The petition stopped a coal company from strip mining on Blue Bear Mountain. The coal companies told everybody Mamaw's petition would be the end of coal mining. Halloween, Mamaw got her radio antenna broken off her car. We never even had a trick-or-treater.

Mamaw didn't get her antenna fixed until the Saturday before Thanksgiving. That afternoon Mamaw came in my room. I was eating M&M's straight out of a pound bag, about to make myself sick. They weren't normal M&M's. They were the color of the characters in a cartoon movie that hadn't done any good and the bags ended up at Big Lots, large and cheap and just this side of safe to eat.

"Put them down if you want to go driving," Mamaw said.

I took off running for the carport. I was strapped into Mamaw's Escort a long time before Mamaw came out. She got in the car and turned to me, the keys closed in her hand.

"Put your seat belt on," she said.

"It is on, Mamaw."

"You know you got to keep your eyes moving when you're driving."

"Yes, Mamaw."

A pickup truck covered in Bondo pulled up and spit out Momma.

"Going for a driving lesson?" Momma's cigarette bounced in her mouth.

Neither one of us said anything. Momma jumped in the backseat. I closed my eyes and wished her gone. She was still there in the rearview when I opened my eyes. I started the Escort and backed onto the ridge road.

I WENT THROUGH THE CURVE TOO QUICK.

My cousin Curtis come flying the other way on his four-wheeler. Mamaw's Escort side-swiped the wall of rock on the high side of the road. The sound of the scraping metal felt like my own hide tearing off.

"Daggone," Momma said. "You're worser than me."

"Hush, Patricia," Mamaw said. "Dawn, are you all right?"

"Yeah," I said, my hands shaking.

"Get on home, then," Mamaw said.

When I pulled into the carport and shut off the motor, Mamaw and Momma got out and looked at the side of the car.

"Whoo-eee," Momma said.

They went in the house, left me sitting there breathing hard, all flustered. I turned on the radio. It was tuned to a station Mamaw liked. Most of the time they played old country music, but that night they had some kind of rock show on. "I'm about to have a nervous breakdown," a boy sang. "My head really hurts." The guitars sounded like power tools being run too hard. I'd never heard such before. I turned it up til the speakers buzzed. The next song was a country song, all slow and twangy. I was about to turn it off when the singer sang, "My head really hurts." The country song had the same words as the one before. At the end of the song, there was the sound of a throat clearing. The voice that spoke sounded like spent brake pads.

"That was Whiskeytown doing the Black Flag song 'Nervous Breakdown.' Before that we had the Black Flag original. You're listening to Bilson Mountain Community Radio. I'm Willett Bilson. This here next one is another record I got from my brother Kenny, by the band Mission of Burma."

Willett Bilson sounded about my age. He sounded like someone I would like to talk to. The power tool guitars started again. Willett played five angry, reckless songs in a row. My head got light. I started the engine and slipped the shift into reverse. The bands came on one right after another, rough and mad, and they carried me through curve after curve. It felt good, like riding a truck inner tube down a snowy hill curled up in my dad's lap. When I pulled into Mamaw's, rain pecked the carport roof, bending the last of the mint beside the patio. Inside, Momma was gone, and Mamaw set a bowl of vegetable soup in front of me. She didn't say anything about me taking the car back out.

The next day after school, Mamaw asked me if I wanted to ride with her to Drop Creek, the place where she grew up, to look at a man's house. I ran out of the house and started the Escort.

"You aint ready to drive to Drop Creek," she said. "You need more practice."

"Well then, I aint going."

"Yes, you are. Scoot over."

The house we went to had vinyl siding and set on blocks. The yard was neat and the gravel thick on the driveway. A little boy with a head like a toasted marshmallow bounced a pink rubber ball against the wall under the carport. When he saw us he hollered in the house. A stout silver-haired man came out.

"How yall doing?" he said. He told me how tall I was getting like everybody does. "Want a piece of pound cake?" People always fix pound cake when Mamaw comes to talk about their troubles with the coal company. We went inside. It was quiet and neat in there too.

"Look at that Christmas cactus," Mamaw said. "So beautiful."

"Thank you," the man's wife said. "It likes that spot."

The wife had a northern accent. She moved through the room making things straight. Mamaw and the silver-haired man set down at a table in the kitchen next to the wall. I stood at Mamaw's shoulder. The man showed Mamaw pictures he pulled from a drugstore one-hour photo folder.

"These was done before they started blasting." The man pointed at a picture of the block at the base of the house. "I took these the other day." He showed Mamaw a picture of a crack running up through the same block. Then he showed her a closeup picture with a thumb stuck up in the crack.

Mamaw said, "Did the state inspect?"

"Yeah," the man said, "they did."

"What did they say?"

"I keep notebooks where I write down when the blasts happen and how long they last. They looked at them said they'd look into it."

"That all they said?"

The man's wife set down a plate of sliced pound cake, a bowl of strawberries, and a tub of Cool Whip. Mamaw looked at the pound cake, then she looked into the man's eyes.

"They said subsidence was natural, could have caused those cracks," the man said.

"Oh, bullshit," Mamaw said. "When was this house built?" Mamaw put a piece of pound cake on a paper napkin, took a big bite out of it.

"Daddy built it with Granddaddy. Right after him and Mommy got married. Finished it a year before they went to Michigan. So, 1958, 1959. Something like that."

"And you aint never had no cracks before, have you?"

"No ma'am," the man said. "Not that I know of."

"Pure sorry," Mamaw said, spooning out strawberries and Cool Whip into a bowl. She crumbled the rest of her pound cake down on top of the strawberries and Cool Whip and mashed it all up with a spoon. Then Mamaw said, "What do you want to do about it, Duane?"

"Well," the man said, "I hate to see people get run over."

"You coming to the meeting Tuesday?"

"Yeah," he said, "I got a doctor's appointment in Corbin. But I should be back."

"Well," Mamaw said, "we could use you. You coming tonight to the planning meeting?"

"I'll be there," Duane said.

I went outside. Marshmallow boy threw his ball into a pile of leaves. A little black dog leapt in the leaves and disappeared. The rustling leaves looked like Bugs Bunny moving underground.

ME AND THE BOY LAUGHED.

Mamaw and the boy's daddy come outside, and the man showed Mamaw the cracks.

"The blast shook the whole house, throwed her china plates out on the floor," the man said. "They was stood up in a cabinet and they busted all over the place." The man shook his head.

Mamaw toed a weed in the gravel. The little dog ran up to me and the boy, dropped the ball, and backed off, its tail wagging. Mamaw told the man to thank his wife for the pound cake, that it was real good. Mamaw drove us back to Long Ridge.

The state scheduled a meeting the Tuesday before Thanksgiving for people to come and give their testimony about whether or not the company's permit to mine should be approved. Monday night Mamaw's group had a meeting in town at the library to talk about what they were going to say at the meeting on Tuesday. That's the way it was that fall. Meetings about meetings, and then a meeting on top of that. Again she made me go, and again she wouldn't let me drive.

I sat at the back of the room in the basement of the public library and looked at pictures of the USS *Canard County* in a glass case. It was a navy ship that hauled tanks and trucks to Haiti and the Persian Gulf and Argentina til the navy sold it to Spain.

THERE WAS A MODEL OF THE BOAT MADE OUT OF SUGAR CUBES SPRAYPAINTED GRAY.

The organizers that the statewide group sent came in carrying rolled-up maps and armloads of flyers and information sheets. The one named April wore a homemade sweater of purple yarn that hung big on her. The one named Portia had leather patches across the shoulders of her sweater, like she was on a submarine. They both had big wild hair. Mamaw said they looked like woolyboogers.

April and Portia talked awhile, and then different ones in the group said things. A man with a receding hairline stood up and said that they would use the same explosives on that strip job that blew up the building in Oklahoma City. A woman with short hair and a sticky-faced little boy said they used to eat fish out of the creek.

"You see what it is now," the woman said. "Yellow mud." She put spit on her thumb and used it to wipe her boy's face.

Mamaw said, "Duane, why don't you say what happened to yall."

Duane told what had happened to him, to his house.

April told them they had to practice what they were going to say, have their facts straight, if their petition was to stop any new strip mines on Blue Bear Mountain. They had to have goals, April said. She put paper on the glass case that held the sugar-cube battleship and made people make a list of goals. Portia put big maps on the case and showed them what lands would be protected.

When they took a break, a woman with a gray ponytail and trembling hands out smoking said the dust from the coal trucks was so bad she couldn't let her grandbabies play outside. April tried to get her to say she would talk at the meeting.

On the way home, Mamaw stopped at the Kolonel Krispy dairy bar and got a double fudge shake with brownies swirled up in it. We sat in the parking lot and watched the red light, and Mamaw said all strip mining ought to be outlawed. I asked her if I could drive home. She said I needed to practice more.

When we got home, Mamaw looked at a pile of mail on the kitchen counter. "Where's my check?" she said. Three of Momma's cigarettes were in the ashtray. Mamaw called my uncle Hubert's house and asked where Momma was. They said she'd gone to Walmart. When Mamaw caught up to Momma in the Walmart parking lot, Mamaw's face was solid red.

"You come here," Mamaw said, hard as a broomstick to the back of the legs.

Momma kept walking towards the store. I guess Momma didn't think Mamaw would do anything in the Walmart parking lot.

Mamaw caught up to Momma and got her by the arm and smacked her in the face. She stuck her hand in Momma's front pocket and pulled out a wad of money.

"You don't do me that way," Momma yelled.

"Watch me," Mamaw said.

Then they both went to yelling at the same time. I went in the store, looked dead in the eye of the people coming out, the ones who didn't know yet Cora Redding and her wasted daughter were having it out in the yellow stripes of the crossing zone. I went back to jewelry and asked my dad's niece who worked there to take me home. She said it would be an hour. I wandered through the store, through the Christmas candy and blow-up snowmen and stupid dancing Santas playing the electric slide and stupid reindeer socks. My cousin took me to the snack bar and bought me everything I wanted to eat. Pizza sticks. Two slushies. Then we went to the Chinese restaurant. I ate every fried egg noodle they had in there.

When my cousin dropped me off at Mamaw's, Momma and Mamaw sat at the kitchen table, hundreds of envelopes and flyers saying write the governor to protect Blue Bear on the table between them. Momma helped Mamaw stuff the envelopes like nothing had happened. I was so sick on cookies and pop and hot dogs and Chinese food.

But I didn't. I went to my bed panting like a black dog in August and swore to the ceiling I wouldn't never have a child. When I slept, I dreamed I was playing music on the radio with Willett the DJ.

The next day in biology, a girl from up the river sat behind me and talked to her cousin the whole class about whose chicken nuggets had better crust. "They got too much pepper on theirs." "Them others is too mushy." I was ready to kill her. I turned around and said, "There's more to life than chicken nuggets, you know." She looked at me like I wasn't there.

I told my friend Evie about the chicken nugget girl when we were out in the parking lot drinking beer at lunchtime.

"I whipped that girl one time," Evie said. "It wasn't fun at all."

I asked her why not.

"She's too stupid," Evie said. "It was like stomping a baby bird."

I told Evie about the band that played the nervous breakdown song. Black Flag. She said she never heard of them. She only listened to what was new. I told Evie about the radio station on Bilson Mountain. She said only old people and hippies listened to that station.

Mamaw picked me up after school. "I need to stop by Duane's," Mamaw said.

The sun peeped over the ridgeline and lifted steam off Duane's roof. In the shadows there was still frost on the yard. A dark pile of something lay in the carport. I thought it was a wadded-up shirt. It was the little black dog frozen solid. Mamaw knocked at the kitchen door and went in before anyone answered. I stood in the carport looking at the dead dog. It was going flat. Its tongue was out. There was no sign of the boy. The pink ball was up against the back wheel of Duane's truck. Mamaw came out of the house. "Let's go," she said.

"What happened, Mamaw?"

"Duane aint coming to the meeting."

"Why not?"

"Somebody fed his dog broken glass mashed up in hamburger."

The meeting was in a stone community building the VISTAs built on Blue Bear Creek back in the sixties. There must have been two hundred people there. Where Blue Bear had the state's highest peak on it, people all over were excited about protecting it. It wasn't just an ordinary mountain with ordinary people living on it. It belonged to the whole state.

Three people from the state—two men and a woman—sat in front of the stage at a table. Their powder-blue shirts had button-down collars and an embroidered patch of the state seal on the sleeve. Hair striped the top of one man's head. The other had a thick bronze helmet of hair. The woman's eyes were wide behind clear-framed glasses, cheap like they gave us for free at school. The three of them sat behind their table. They stacked and restacked their papers, took folders out of file boxes and then put them back in.

People filed in in clots of three and four. There were painted signs saying stuff like "SAVE BLUE BEAR," and "COAL KEEPS THE LIGHTS ON" strung out along the walls of the community center. People settled in, talking low to them they came with, leaning forward and greeting the people on their side with pats on the back and handshakes, smiling.

When time came to start, the man with the bronze helmet of hair leaned forward into a microphone. "Good evening everyone. This hearing is required by law, and pertains to mine 848-1080, amendment 3, a surface-mining permit application in the Drop Creek and Little Drop Creek watersheds in Canard County, Kentucky. Everyone who wishes to speak should have already signed up. All speakers will be limited to three minutes. If anyone has more to say, they may wait until everyone who has signed up to speak has spoken, and then we will go around again. I would remind everyone no decision will be made tonight. Everything said will go into the file and will be taken into consideration as the cabinet makes its decision. We will begin in three minutes."

After three minutes, they called the name of the first woman signed up to speak. The state woman brought her a wireless microphone. The first woman said she was proud of her husband, that she had married him because she wanted to be a coal miner's wife. She said she would not be ashamed of what he did and would not allow her children to be ashamed of what he did.

The second person to speak was also a woman. She said the state should consider all the trash that was in the creeks, how terrible a shape the road was in. All the dust from the coal trucks flying up and down the road was terrible. She couldn't even hang her clothes out on the line, she said, and when she said something to one of the drivers he was just rude.

The third speaker he talked about the ozone layer, how there was holes in it and how we couldn't go on burning coal forever, that we needed to think about the future, about what we were leaving behind for our children. He talked for a while longer, and the man from the state had to tell him his time was up. The speaker said he had more to say, and the state man said he could give his paper to him and he would attach it to what all else he had.

Then the man from the state said he wanted to remind everybody that they was only there to consider testimony pertaining to mine permit 848-1080 amendment 3 and that of course people could use their minutes any way they wanted to but that that particular permit application was what they were there for.

Mamaw sat stone still in her folding chair, and the speeches went on and on. Every speaker tried to talk people into believing what they themselves believed.

The fluorescent lights flickered. Four different ones needed changing. Out the high windows, the lights of coal trucks streaked past. The state people sat like prizes at a carnival game, eye wide and blank, stuffed pink monkeys, green hippopotamuses piled too close together. Every once in a while they would take a note, but not that often.

A woman I'd seen at Mamaw's meetings called the coal company out by name, said they'd told her mother they weren't going to strip mine her land, that they was just going to build a coal haul road across it and that they wouldn't be out there even a month. She said they'd promised to build a road out to her family's cemetery—widen it. And then when her mother signed her rights away they'd strip mined the shit out of it—that's what the woman said—and they'd mined right up to the cemetery and probably would've mined right through it if she—the daughter—hadn't come back from Georgia. There wadn't no way, that woman said, that company ought to be allowed to mine coal period, much less on Blue Bear. They ought to be put in jail, that woman said, everyone of them, and especially you, she said, and pointed to a man with a wire-brush moustache standing in the back spitting into a plastic pop bottle, his arms folded across his chest.

"Especially you, Mickey Mills that lived right here in this community and lied to my mother. You're a sorry excuse for a man," that woman said, and started towards him before her husband stopped her.

Then a woman stood up and said "You aint taking my husband to jail. You're just a busybody. You don't live here no more and don't deserve no say in what goes on here."

The man from the state got on the microphone. "All right. Order. Please."

The next speaker was a man in a sweater vest and a green plaid shirt I didn't know. He talked about the Indiana bats and the Turk's cap lilies and other plants and animals that only lived in Kentucky near the top of Blue Bear Mountain. I didn't know what difference that would make to anybody. Mamaw told me it did.

A thick coal company office man stood up and told how many jobs the company made, about their participation in the youth baseball leagues and their big ads in the high school gymnasium. Another company man talked about how that if they didn't approve these permits that it would likely mean the end of coal mining in Canard County and maybe all of Kentucky. He said people didn't know how the coal industry could fall apart at any minute, and then where would Canard County be? When he asked that question he spread out his arms and turned to the crowd, and it seemed to me that that was who he was talking to anyway. He finished up by saying that the state should approve the permit and get out of the company's way and let the good working people of Canard County do what they do best—do better than anyone in America—run coal. When he said that there was all kinds of cheering and whistling as he sat down.

The next person to speak was the woman with the pulled-back hair who had been at Mamaw's meeting, the one I'd swore would never have spoke. She was on the other side of Mamaw from me, her paper shaking in her hands. She put her other hand on the back of the folding chair in front of her, barely able to see over the frosted blonde head of the miner's wife sitting in front of her.

"My name is Agnes Therapin. I live on Little Drop Creek." Her back straightened when she said the name of the creek. "I am against this here permit. They's people that lives beneath these strip jobs. It aint out in a desert somewheres. It's up the creek from me. This here is the third time you have let them add on to this strip job. I wish you'd never let them start, but I don't know why you didn't just let them mine the whole thing to begin with. Then we wouldn't always have been a-hoping that maybe we might have a decent place to stay." Her hands beat restlessly on the back of the chair in front of her. The miner's wife leaned forward, turned to look at Agnes. "My mommy lives with us," Agnes went on. "She has a bad leg, and this dynamite has knocked her out of bed more than once. We thought you fellers—you come up here from Frankfort or wherever—and I guess I thought you was there to protect us. To protect our homes and our property. I thought that was what the law was supposed to be there for. To keep the peace. Well, you fellers need to know, and I don't know if you all have been up there or not, but let me tell you. There aint no peace on Little Drop Creek."

Agnes's neck was stiff. She arched her back like it hurt.

She stared at the state people. People were quiet, but the seconds passed and people started to rustle.

"Thank you, Ms. Therapin." The state man said her name wrong.

"You are supposed to protect us," Agnes shouted. "Surely they's laws against blowing up people's houses. People aint setting off dynamite at your house, are they? Don't reckon they come blowing yore people up do they? Where do you live?"

"Thank you, ma'am," the state man said.

"Where's your house at?" The state woman came to take the microphone from Agnes. Agnes jerked it away.

"Sit down, Ms. Therapin," the state man said.

"Maybe we ought to come set a couple shots off at your place." Agnes's neck was red as blood. "See how you like it."

"Agnes," Mamaw said, and covered Agnes's hand on the back of the chair with her own. Agnes sat down. Another woman across the room with "I heart coal" on her T-shirt stood up and faced Mamaw.

"Cora Redding, this wouldn't be happening if you weren't stirring everybody up. You don't live on Drop Creek. You moved to town. You wouldn't have no business, you wouldn't be sitting on your little pile of money, if it wasn't for the working people around here, people mining coal. You need to mind your own damn business."

"Anyone who cannot remain civil," the state man said, "will be removed from the meeting."

The woman stuck her finger out at Mamaw. "You need to keep your big fat nose out of things don't concern you."

I stood up. I pointed back at the woman.

I said, "You don't need to be telling my mamaw what her business is. You don't know my mamaw. You aint got no right to talk to my mamaw."

"Young lady," the state man said, "you are speaking out of turn."

I wadn't done. "What do you want us to say? 'Go ahead and tear up the world. We'll just get out of the way while you destroy ever thing our friends ever had? Here, take my house; I'll just live here in this hole in the ground. Yeah, go ahead and set that big yellow rock on our heads. We'll be fine.'"

"If I could ask the deputy sheriff—" the state man started.

"Dawn, sit down," Mamaw said. "Sir, she don't mean it . . ."

I sat down. A buzzing in my head kept me from hearing what was said after that. I wished I hadn't spoken. I wished I hadn't said a word.

Someone held up a jar of dirty water. Somebody brought in a bunch of kids carrying a banner. I'm not sure what side they were on. When it was over Mamaw had to shake me to get me to move. I dreaded walking out. I wasn't invisible anymore.

# 2

<center>~~~~~~</center>

# SMOTHER

WHEN WE were walking out of the hearing, a bald man in a hoodie and long shorts came up to me and said, "That was awesome." His face was right up in my face. His eyes swirled in his head like two Sasquatches penned up in a dog lot. I don't know where he was from, but it wasn't here. "You are one awesome chick," he said, stabbing his meat cigar finger right at me.

He had canvas bags hung over both shoulders. "Can I do a quick interview?" he said. "Just a quick one."

A miner's kid bumped into me and the bald man took me by the shoulder.

"I'm with a radio station. Bilson Radio. I don't know if you ever heard of it." His voice seemed to come from his crazy Sasquatch eyes.

"Mamaw listens to it all the time," I said.

"OK, OK. All right," he said, his head bobbing. "Is that you?" he asked sticking out a hand for Mamaw to shake. "I'm Kenny Bilson."

"Yes, that's me," Mamaw said.

"Now what is your name?" he said to Mamaw. She told him and he said, "Oh wow. Yes. You call my uncle's show all the time. Yeah," he said, bobbing his head, "I know yall. Yeah. Hey. Let me do an interview with yall. About this here tonight. Cause you and what you said. Yeah. It was right. Cataclysmic. Our listeners need to hear it. Yeah. And you, ma'am"—he pointed again at Mamaw—"they told me that I had to talk to you. That you are the main one"—people were starting to look back at us as they walked past—"the straw that stirs the drink for real."

Mamaw said, "It's getting late. I need to get this youngun home."

"Oh yeah, me too. Me too. I got the baby. Yeah." He thumbed back over his head. A baby in a black onesie sat in a carrier on a folding table two women were standing wanting to take down.

He took us in a little room off the big room. Dented folding chairs were stacked against a junk popcorn machine. There were broken lighting fixtures and moldy ceiling tiles piled everywhere. He set the baby down beside him in a folding chair with a bent leg. He got out a tape recorder, a microphone, a tangled cord and hooked them up. He put a cassette with no label in the recorder and asked us to tell him what happened, tell him how we felt about it, what we hoped would happen. He draped his arm across the baby carrier.

"Oh yeah, that's good. That's good," he said as I spoke. Mostly he said nothing, just sat smiling while we talked, like we were saying what he wanted us to say. When he finished, he closed up his recorder, tucked it back in his canvas bag.

"Yeah, we'll put you right on the radio. Hell yeah. Sorry, ma'am, but yeah. They's a little dude on the mountain he is so going to dig this, he's the one who edits all this stuff. My little brother. Willett."

"Yeah, you got to listen to it."

We walked out into the parking lot.

"Probably be around seven minutes, unh-hunh. Yeah. Have yall had supper? They say that dairy bar there has badass shakes, yeah."

"We had supper."

"OK. Yeah. But Dawn, man, you are awesome. Cataclysmic. Yeah. We'll call you when the show is gonna be on."

The baby started to stir. Bald Sasquatch Kenny waved a pirate rattle in the baby's face.

"Well," Mamaw said, "it was real nice meeting you."

Kenny said, "Yeah," and popped the hatch on his dented no-front-bumper Subaru. He put his equipment in. "Yeah. So do yall think you'll hear anything before Christmas?" He closed the hatchback.

"Honey, you don't want to leave that baby back there, do you?"

"SHIT! No. No. Yeah. Thank you all." Kenny opened the hatch and took the baby out. "OK. Well. Bye now."

Mamaw was in the car. She rolled down the window. "Dawn honey, do you want to drive?"

"Goodbye," Kenny said. "Great. Great to meet you. Yeah. Great."

I nodded. Kenny kept standing there. I got in the Escort. I sat there with my hands in my lap.

"Let's go, sweetheart," Mamaw said.

I started the car. We left the meeting.

"Them state people are just going through the motions," Mamaw said as we crossed the bridge at the mouth of Blue Bear Creek. "They know what their job is. They have their orders, and they don't come from us." Mamaw faced me as she spoke. Her eyes glittered like stones in a stream. "You got to change their orders. You got to change the people telling them what to do. You got to make *those* people feel the pinch." I liked to see Mamaw's eyes glitter, but I didn't know how she was going to do what she was talking about.

"Who gives the orders, Mamaw?"

"Really? The companies. But the governor," Mamaw said. "He can do some."

Mamaw twirled a toothpick on her tongue.

"About what you said up there."

"I don't guess I should have called that woman a heifer."

"No. Probably not."

"But she is."

"I don't like meetings," Mamaw said. "They just tear people apart. Our fight aint with nobody who lives here."

That didn't make sense to me and I told Mamaw so.

Mamaw bit down on the toothpick over and over. "They're being put up to it," she said.

We drove the rest of the way home without talking. Snowflakes twisted in the headlights.

That night I lay awake a long time. I thought about people who patted me on the back as I came out of the meeting. I thought I would get my ass whipped before I got to the car, but I didn't. I felt like Evie said it did when you got baptized.

Mamaw was stacking something in the kitchen. I heard the clink clink clink from my narrow bed in the front bedroom. It sounded like she was sorting bullets, shells, some kind of ammunition. Ghosts in bedsheets ran bulldozers through my dreams. I woke Wednesday morning wishing I could turn on the radio and hear my voice come out of it. I could smell the coffeemaker spit out Mamaw's thin coffee. I got up.

I WALKED out to the end of the ridge road to catch the school bus. The bus came up the back side of the mountain against a skim-milk sky. The bus was full of little kids,

They were afraid of spit in their ears, gum in their hair, knuckles to the base of their skulls. The bus stank of middle school B.O. and cooking grease. I sat down next to a little boy who wiped his nose with an infected finger. Hardly any of the kids who rode the bus had parents working at the coal mines. The ride was quiet.

When I got off the bus, Evie grabbed my arm and headed me out into the parking lot towards her car. "Did you say something at that meeting last night?"

"Yeah, I said something."

"Why?"

"Cause they talked bad about Mamaw."

Evie stood looking at me over the hood of her tan Cavalier.

"You don't think your mamaw can take care of herself?"

"I guess."

"You don't think she knows what's she's getting into?"

"Shut up, Evie. You're retarded."

Evie got in the car. So did I.

"You're the one who's retarded," she said.

I fooled with everything loose in that car. The lighter. The black rubber butterfly hanging from the rearview. The Missy Elliott air freshener. I was scared but wouldn't tell Evie. I wiped my eyes.

"We need to go," Evie said. "Get out of here."

"I have a French test."

"God Almighty," Evie said. "Yall have a test in there every day."

I opened the car door.

"Don't, Dawn."

"Aint nothing gonna happen," I said, not really believing.

"When's your test?"

"Second period."

"Don't go in til second period."

"You stay with me, Evie."

"I caint. Donnie's got a court date."

"What time?"

"Right now," Evie said. "You should just take a zero on that test."

A bell played over the loudspeakers. I got out of the car and started walking towards school. Evie's horn honked. She waved me towards her. I went to her window.

"You want a beer?"

I shook my head.

"You want a Xanax?"

"No."

She got a pint bottle out from under the seat. I drank an orange capful.

"Hope it comes out OK with Donnie," I said.

"It won't."

When I turned at the door of the school, Evie was still sitting there. I walked through the lobby and buzzed to be let in. My first-period class was at the far end of the building on the third floor, the longest possible walk. Two nerdy girls passed me on the steps, looking at a clothes catalog. The hallway to my history class was two hundred yards long. At every window in every door people rolled their eyes, lay with their heads on their desks, leaned into one another, threw punches into arms, tossed paper wads. Teachers peeped out doors as they spoke.

Everyone that could, in cell after cell, looked up to see what was passing. A door opened in front of me. My brother Albert stepped out into the hall. He lived with my uncle Hubert, and I never saw him, especially not at school. He was a senior and only came to school to sell pot. He had a hall pass anybody who looked would see was fake.

"What are you doing here?" I said.

"What are *you* doing here?" he said.

"I go to school here, douchebag," I said.

Albert grabbed hold of my shirtsleeve. "Momma wants you to come stay with us."

"Don't talk to me about Momma, Albert."

Albert grabbed hold of me again. Tighter. A year before I could whip him. Wasn't so sure I still could that day.

"You need somebody," he said, "to talk some sense into you."

"Who? You?"

Albert's rat eyes burrowed into me. I was the target of his arrowhead nose. He said,

MAMAW IS **LOSING IT,** DAWN.

MAMAW IS FINE.

GOING **WILD** AT WALMART? STIRRING UP **SHIT** WITH BLACK OAK?

SHUT UP, ALBERT.

YOU KNOW SHE'LL GIVE YOU **THAT HOUSE.**

I jerked away from Albert. I could see people in classes gathering up their stuff. The bell was about to ring.

Albert reached his left hand out to touch my cheek. I busted him in the face just as hard as I could. I meant to knock his eye clean out of his head. He staggered but didn't fall. Faces gathered at the narrow slits of glass in the classroom doors. Albert put his hand over his hit eye and stared at me with the other.

"You think Daddy would want you talking at them meetings?" Albert said. "He's spinning in his grave."

The bell rang and I stuck the crown of my head right in Albert's mouth with everything I had. He went down, flat on his back. I started stomping him. He grabbed my foot and I fell, but I landed on my knees right on his chest.

I beat him in the face with the spine of my French book, wishing it was hardback. He caught me by the hair, pulling hard, when two teachers got me under the arms and pulled him off of me.

THE SCHOOL suspended me. Momma took Albert to the hospital and Mamaw took me home. That night I lay in bed, grinding my teeth, swearing at the ceiling. I couldn't get my breath.

MAMAW GOT up real early Thanksgiving morning. There were three pie crusts in tin pans lined up on the counter by the time I got up. We were going to her brother Fred's house for Thanksgiving dinner on Drop Creek, and she was making chess pies. Mamaw moved like she was mad, everything short, sharp, and hard. Only thing she said was, "Store lard caint touch what we got ourselves."

We were supposed to be at Uncle Fred's at twelve, but Mamaw took her time and it was almost twelve before we left the house. Mamaw's sister Verna and her buckeye husband were in the car in front of us as we headed up Drop Creek. It was gray and dreary when we got out of the car at Fred's house. Verna hit her husband on back of the arm and asked did he bring the playing cards. He said he did.

We walked up the broad steps onto Fred's deep dark front porch. My cousin Kevin's little boys were shooting paintball at a target at the side of the house. The targets were stuck on Uncle Fred's woodpile, the biggest woodpile I ever seen.

When we walked in the front room of the house, all four of Mamaw's nephews were standing there in front of the television.

They looked at us like they'd been waiting, but they didn't say anything. Two were Fred's sons. The other two were Verna's. Verna lived in Cincinnati, but the boys stayed in Canard County. Mamaw's nephews all worked on strip jobs around Blue Bear or wherever they could get work. Uncle Fred's younger son Denny worked on the strip job Mamaw's petition was about.

We carried pies in the kitchen. Uncle Fred's wife Genevieve took them from us. Genevieve was round and nice, but whenever we went over there she said at least once what a pretty girl I could be if I wouldn't wear Halloween makeup all over my face.

"Dawn, you been sick?" Genevieve said as she took my pie.

One of my eighth grade cousins, a boy with a football jersey on, ran through. "She got suspended."

"Is that right?"

"Don't matter. We're on break anyway," I said.

Fred laughed at that.

Genevieve sat us down to eat at a round table off the kitchen. The dishes were white with flowers on them. Fred passed me a pan of rolls. Aunt Verna was filling a water pitcher at the sink when a hose came loose under the sink and water started flooding out all over the kitchen floor. Fred moved quickly, quietly, and turned it off. He was soaked. He smiled.

"Drownded," was all he said.

Genevieve left the kitchen and returned carrying a folded shirt, plaid and soft, a clean white V-neck T-shirt. Fred patted me on the shoulder as he passed behind on the way to the back of the house to change his clothes. Genevieve had the water on the floor mopped up before the bread got cold. Fred came back. He had a tan canvas coat on. He nodded at his wife and left.

"He's going to check on the mine," she said. "They have a new boy working the guard shack." We finished eating and cleared the dishes and pans from the table. Genevieve set a pound cake, a stack cake, a plate of cookies, and one of Mamaw's chess pies out on the table.

"Should we wait for him to get back?" Mamaw said.

"He'll be a while," Genevieve said. "Untelling." She stacked plates, piled silverware. I looked at Mamaw. She nodded at me. I rose to help.

"I'm fine, Dawn," Genevieve said. "Why don't you go out there and see what Denny's doing."

My cousin Denny sat in the living room slouched down in an armchair. A deer head hung above his head. He wasn't paying attention to the football game on the TV. He smiled at me and got up and went in the kitchen.

Denny brought me a Mountain Dew and sat back down in his daddy's chair. His mother passed through, got a big piece of Tupperware out of a closet. She went back in the kitchen and brought me a paper napkin. I had a headache. My skull felt like it was about to split in half.

"Denny," his mother said, "you get in some wood. Start a fire."

Denny lifted up out of the chair.

"Come on," he said. I didn't move. He tapped me on the side of the knee. "Come on."

We went out to the big woodpile. I stood waiting for Denny to pile my arms full of wood. He turned around and took a pint bottle of whiskey out of his jacket pocket.

"Where's your pop?" he said.

"In there."

He poured some of the whiskey in his red plastic cup. He handed it to me. I took a sip and was glad for it. One sip and the world widened out in my head.

I shook my head. It was enough. He took a sip.

Denny filled my arms with split oak. He waved me in the house and even though the woodpile was big as a trailer, he split more, long arching strokes with the ax. We went in the side door. There was a mud room, where their boots and work clothes stayed. I seen broken glass sitting on a Styrofoam tray like meat comes on at the grocery store.

"He making you pack that wood?" Fred was behind me. His eyes looked tired too. He took the wood from me and stacked it by the stove.

Everybody was sitting in the TV room when we went back in the house. One of the grandkids was in Fred's chair. The grandkid got up and Fred sat down. Mamaw and the other women came in and stood around behind the chairs and sofas.

Fred looked up at Mamaw. "How you getting along with the tree huggers, Cora?"

"Doing all right," Mamaw said.

"Well, I'm worried about you."

"Who's winning the football game?" Genevieve said.

"And I have to wonder what you're thinking getting that youngun mixed up in it." Fred said.

Nobody said anything. All those big men made me smother. I went out in the yard. There were six four-wheelers parked on the gravel. I took off on one.

The tires crunched against the frosted ground. The bark of the motor ran through the skeleton trees. I wound straight uphill, dipped across a dry creek bed and then up again. I came to the edge of the woods, to the mine the meeting on Tuesday night had been about. I turned the four-wheeler engine off. The strip job was quiet. A hawk circled far out above the grass on the reclaimed section. A security man came out of the guard shack into the sun. He sat down on a block of wood. He ate out of a plastic container, sopped Genevieve's yellow gravy with a dinner roll. The sun made long blue tree-trunk shadows, turning the stones at the edge of the highwall gold and orange. The light anyway was beautiful.

I walked away from the four-wheeler.

THE MOUNTAINS SEEMED EMPTY. BUT I KNEW THEY WEREN'T.

You walk on and on, thinking you're going deeper into the woods, deeper into the past, farther away from the bullshit of the world, and then you trip over the cable running from somebody's satellite dish, and then you see the trailer and hear the creak of the trampoline springs, and then it's oh well, welcome back. I wished I was warm, by the stove at Mamaw's, cutting pictures out of magazines, looking at winter through her dripping windows.

I walked the rutted mine road back towards the house. An owl swiveled its head high up in a poplar tree. Its doubloon eyes fixed on me. It flapped to another tree, deeper in the woods. I followed it. The owl moved to a third tree. I went after it, my eye fixed on the owl, and the ground beneath my feet broke in on itself, made a hole narrow and deep.

Once I was in, it felt like the ground closed up over me. It didn't; I could still see the sky, but the hole was deeper than I was tall. I tried to stand, but my ankle gave out on me, and when I fell I peeled back the skin over my shinbone on a wedge of sandstone. My pants leg bloodied up, and I rolled over on my back at the bottom of the hole.

# 3

## WHAT HURTS

I LAY at the bottom of the hole until the stars came out. Orion the hunter shot straight up into the moon. My dad first showed me Orion's belt. He showed me how once you saw the belt, the rest of him fell into place. He told me he liked the way it looked like the hunter was running and shooting. Like Rambo or something. I got lightheaded and I saw Daddy in a tree stand above me, bow season. Daddy lifted out of the tree stand and began to run across the sky. I hollered but he couldn't hear me.

The owl settled in a tree above me. I spit out little pieces of leaf.

My father built his own truck, put it together from the parts of other trucks—eight Ford Rangers lined up facing the road—eight Ford Rangers it took for him to get one to ride back and forth to work. Hubert gave people credit if they'd bring him a Ford Ranger, but they had to park them lined up straight the way Daddy liked them or it was no deal.

The owl hooted.

I would go out and sit in one of the Rangers the winter after Daddy died and Momma started grieving out of a Heaven Hill bottle. I thought about them trucks, and the night got colder and my leg hurt worse. I had to keep my wits about me. Of course you know I survive because I'm telling you the story right now. But you don't know I don't lose a finger, do you? Maybe I lose my foot. Maybe I lose my foot and grieve over it and become a drunk and then a drug addict like Momma. No. I wouldn't be like her. Not the same mistake. A different mistake. I lose my foot and get depressed about it and eat and eat and get so enormous, like six hundred pounds, I can't get out of bed, look like I melted into the sheets. See me, unwrapping a whole box of Little Debbie oatmeal creme pies, all twelve pies, so I can cram them in my mouth all at once to suffocate myself?

"Dawn?"

Momma stood before me, silver like the dull side of aluminum foil. Momma looked young and clean, her face smoothed out by the hunter's moon. She crouched at the lip of the hole. She wobbled and then steadied herself. She lay her hand on my cheek. Her fingers against my face didn't feel right.

A flashlight beam lit her from behind.

"Hubert," Momma said over her shoulder.

Hubert put the light in my face, his voice deep behind the shine. "What are you doing out here by yourself?"

Safer by myself than with you, I'd of like to said, but I didn't say anything.

"Put your hands up," Hubert said.

Hubert lifted me out of the hole and carried me up the hill. His hair was long and greasy. Stubble filled his cheeks outside his moustache and goatee. His miner's jacket opened on a wifebeater and smelled of burning plastic and the salve he put on his arthritis. He carried me to the mine road, to a coffee-colored Delta 88 he left in the yard with the keys in it in case somebody needed to move it. Hubert lay me in the backseat. Hubert and Momma got in the front.

"Where's Mamaw?" I said.

"She went the other way," Momma said. "Hunting for you."

Hubert and Momma headed up Blue Fork towards Virginia. They said they were taking me to the hospital there. Then they fell to talking about a man who pawned seven weedeaters for a friend. The weedeaters turned out to be stolen, and now the man who pawned them was facing a charge. They stopped at the man's house and he came out, three hundred pounds easy, cheeks and forehead full of acne, all red-rimmed craters and white-topped peaks. Wet strings of black hair cut across his face like the lines on a globe. He came to Momma's window.

"In the back, Cinderella," she said.

Cinderella got in beside me. He rubbed his raisin eyes with the heels of his hands and breathed like he was snoring even though he was awake. He cried over a lost girl.

"I don't care," I said.

"She was everthing to me," he went on. He began to moan, like you'd hope your mother would at your funeral.

"I don't see why," Momma said to Cinderella. "She told everybody you stole that church van. She parked it at your mother's house."

"I know," Cinderella said.

"She still gonna be your 'everthang,'" Momma mocked Cinderella, "when you go to jail over them weedeaters?"

Cinderella put his face in his hands and sobbed.

"Yes," he said.

Momma said, "I should have drowned you when I had the chance."

"When was that?" Hubert said.

"Seventh grade."

God kept Momma from telling that story. Thank you God. Momma opened a beer and handed it to Cinderella. "Here."

Cinderella nearly dropped the beer taking it from Momma when Hubert went too sharp through a curve.

"Goddam, Hubert," Cinderella said. Then he turned to me. "What's wrong with your leg?"

I didn't say anything.

"This girl is in shock," Cinderella said.

"She aint in shock," Momma said, "She's my daughter, dumbass."

"I'm in shock at how retarded you are," I said.

"Hey," Cinderella said, "You aint got no call to talk to me like that."

I said, "Momma, I'll give you a hundred dollars to put the radio on something good and turn it up loud as it will go."

"Loud don't make it good," Hubert said. "Good you don't have to turn up loud."

Hubert had been drinking too much. If he hadn't, he wouldn't have said that. He would have sat there still as a stone and not said anything, all John Wayne about it.

"Give me one of them beers," I said.

"I aint," Momma said.

"Give her one," Hubert said, "might make her nicer."

"Go to hell, Hubert," I said.

I hadn't been around Momma and Hubert for weeks. It made me sick how easy I fell into their way of talking. Momma handed me a beer. I drank half of it in one pull.

"Daggone, Hubert," Cinderella said, "who is this girl?"

Cinderella looked at me. His mouth smelled like he'd thrown up a bale of hay.

Hubert laughed through his nose at that, and I wanted to break it for him, take that nose and twist it to where the falling rain would drown him.

"Dawn, you need to settle down," Momma said. "Drink your beer. Take it easy. It's a holiday." Momma started to sing. "O come all ye faithful." There were new gaps between her teeth.

"That's a Christmas song," Hubert said.

"No it aint," Momma said. "It's a Thanksgiving song."

"No it aint," Hubert said.

"I think she's right, Hubert," Cinderella said. "I think she is." Cinderella nodded at me.

"Hey, Cinderella," I said. He looked at me out his raisin eyes. I said, "Give me your knife."

"I aint got a knife," he said. "What you want a knife for?"

"Cut my throat you're so retarded."

"Dawn," Momma said.

"Then what's the next line?" Hubert said.

"I don't know," Momma said. "Yall got me flustered."

"Oh come ye, oh come ye," I sang, and Hubert joined in on "to Bethlehem."

"See," Hubert said.

Momma shook her head.

The road wound past brokedown coal camp houses pressed against the blacktop, past the pipes and belts and rows of lights of the processing plant, past wide spots puddled in gray water, places that weren't anything anymore, weren't nature, weren't human, just places left behind. We started up the mountain. A curve snuck up on Hubert while him and Momma were singing some country song, and I got thrown up against Cinderella. The pain in my leg jumped up in my waist, and I hollered out right as I landed against him. He put his arms around me. I put the heel of my hand in his greasy face and shoved.

"Get your hands off me," I said.

He put his hands up in the air and I went back to my side of the car. Nobody said much the rest of the way to the dinky one-hall hospital across the Virginia line. When we got there, the doctor looked at me standing in the hall and said there wasn't nothing broke and that I could go on. Momma said she was worried about how I was hurting, and couldn't he give us something. The doctor sized Momma up and sent us on home.

Hubert was taking Cinderella wherever it was they were taking him and so Momma and I sat in the hospital front room waiting for Hubert. She looked all through her coat pockets for cigarettes, for her keys, for change for a pop, for her lighter, anything to keep from having to look at me. She found the lighter and rolled it over and over in her hands.

She said, "This is where they brought your daddy."

"Do what?" I said.

"After the accident. This is where he died."

There was a spot of color on my mother's cheek, just a spot of the way she was before Daddy died, seeping through like blood seeping through a rag. I wanted to wring my real mother out from the rag her body had become. I wanted to wring that rag out over a bucket, pour what I wrung out into some kind of mold, like a jello mold of my old momma, my good momma, and make her back into what she was.

Hubert came through the automatic doors, coughing and sniffing. Momma said to me, "Did your mamaw give you any money?" When the automatic hospital doors fell closed, it was like I woke up, never knowing I'd been asleep. The spot of color was gone from Momma's cheek. She looked like candle wax. I went out to the car. Cinderella was sitting in the front seat.

"What are they doing in there?" Cinderella said.

I got in the backseat, reached across the front, and changed the radio to the Bilsons' station. My own voice came out the speakers.

"I love this place," I was saying, "I don't want to see it tore all to pieces."

"These mountains are what we got," my voice on the radio said, "they are what holds us together."

"I aint never heard a girl preacher on there," Cinderella said, and changed the station.

When Hubert and Momma came back out, we took off into the darkness, headed for home. Hubert stopped at a place in the woods, a beer store had Budweiser NASCAR flags and the price of cases of beer in four-foot-high letters all over its outside. Hubert and Cinderella went inside.

They came out loaded down with cases of beer. Hubert and Cinderella put the beer in the trunk and got in the car. Hubert gave me a beer. I sat drinking it, and a car full of girls coming home from a night out pulled in. They were dark-headed and older, and their laughs were sharp as cat claws. Cinderella sat eating barbecue pork rinds and looking at the dark-headed girls. He rolled his window down. Icy air rushed in. The girls passed, trailing fake strawberry smell.

"Aint that something?" Cinderella said.

Hubert grabbed the pork rinds out of Cinderella's hand, got a handful, and dropped the bag in my lap.

"Where's your mother?" Hubert said.

I hadn't noticed she was gone. "I guess she went inside."

The girls came out of the store.

"You don't know what you're missing," Cinderella said to them through the open window.

The girls laughed. Cinderella got out of the car.

"Who you laughing at?"

"Cin, get back in the car," Hubert said.

"Hey," Cinderella said, and grabbed one of the girls by the arm.

"Goddamn it," Hubert said, and got out of the car.

My mother came around the side of the building. Snow began to fall. I jumped out of the back as a girl broke a wine cooler over Cinderella's head. Momma shoved her. Hubert grabbed my mother. I slid into the driver's seat and started the Olds. I backed out and drove off. Momma and Hubert, Cinderella and the wine cooler girls, they were all screaming—at each other, at me, at the cosmos.

The snow fell harder. I started home through Astor's Pass, a different way than the way we came. It wasn't til I came through a hairpin curve a third of the way up the mountain that I remembered hearing if there was any snow on the ground anywhere, not to cross Astor's Pass. I accelerated into a patch of ice on a steep stretch. The car stopped moving, and the wheels spinning sounded like the howling of the wind. The Delta 88 slid backwards and started getting sideways. The car skidded off the guardrail on one side of the road and missed the guardrail on the other side. I closed my eyes as the Oldsmobile began to roll down the mountain. When the car hit a tree and stopped, the ground was against my window. I felt my face for my glasses. They were gone. Tree trunks and branches crossed and recrossed in the headlights. Everything loose in the car, all the cups and unpaid bills, half a fifty-pound bag of dog food, piled on top of me. I was like the cowboy in the movie when he gets trapped under his horse, except instead of a horse I was trapped under a pile of my family's shit.

Snow fell on my head through the shattered passenger window. I closed my eyes.

I woke to the first blue of day, to the crunch and creak of the taped-up car seats. My breath clouded up in front of me and floated past my ear. I worked my legs loose from under the steering wheel, pulled myself up by the passenger seat belt. I stood, ankle throbbing, my head sticking out the hole where the passenger window used to be.

A voice came from above. I looked up through deep patches of snow.

"Hey there."

Daylight soaked into the edges of my cousin Denny's silhouette. He slid down the bank, stood eyeball to eyeball with me, close enough to be in focus. He stuck a finger behind his lower lip and hooked out his tobacco. He was so close I could see the hairs on his beard, clear and red, each one sharp in the morning light like he was on a high-definition television.

"Having trouble reaching escape velocity," he said, flinging the lump of minced tobacco to the ground. He rolled his tongue against his lower teeth.

"I guess."

"I thought I would make a good astronaut," Denny said, spitting out the last pieces of tobacco. "But I never could figure where the signup was at. Can you get out of there?"

"I don't think so."

Denny climbed up on the door. He put his coat around the broken glass edge of the window.

"Be careful now," he said, and pulled me up and out.

Denny stepped off the car onto the hillside. He lifted me into his arms. He was barely as tall as I was, and staggered as he leaned back. He got me up the hill to his truck and sat me down in the front seat. He stood with his elbow resting on the open truck door. Denny's breath heaved out of him. He rubbed his belly, put another dip of tobacco in.

"You are needed here," he said. Then, "Do you have anything you want to get out of the car?"

"What did you say?" I said.

His eyes were chocolate and ink. "I said, 'We need you here.' You and your mamaw. Telling the truth. Nobody can say so. But we do. Don't take it personal when people threaten you."

"Don't take it personal?"

The woods were snow quiet.

"So you want anything out of there?" Denny said.

Denny stepped away from me, went out of focus, and my chest tightened, like my foot when I was little and Mamaw would draw my shoestrings tight.

"That dog food," I said. "And my glasses."

Denny made his way down the side of the hill to the car. He cupped his hands to the windshield and looked in. He climbed on top of the car and lowered himself in. I could hear the crinkle of the dog food bag. I could hear him raking loose food into it, separating out the papers and the dirty clothes and the food wrappers. I panted like a black dog.

Denny's truck was running. I slid across the front seat, put it in gear, and swung it around. In the rearview I saw Denny scramble up the hill, grab for the truck bed, but I got away. I rolled down the Kentucky side of the mountain.

The truck radio was on an old rock-and-roll station. Molly Hatchet, flirting with disaster. I turned the knob, moved the blue number to Bilson Radio. I caught the middle of a song full of tingly guitars. Run run run run run, the singer sang. When I turned onto the state road, the truck roared like it hated that music. I stomped the gas again and made it roar some more. Escape velocity. A deep-voiced woman sang about all tomorrow's parties. Another truck, I think it was a Dodge, blinked its lights at me, blinked its lights at Denny, I guess. I got to the mouth of the creek, and the road widened again as I came into town. I drove past the bootleggers, past the tombstone marker for the old black school, past the tunnels where they moved the river out of downtown.

Willett Bilson came on the radio and told me I had been listening to the Velvet Underground, told me he had to go feed chickens and was going to play the whole album again. I pulled up at the stoplight next to the high-rise nursing home old folks apartment building. It crossed my mind to take Denny back his truck.

But when the light turned green, all I wanted was Willett Bilson. I turned left at the flood wall, and I roared past Walmart, the hospital, and out of town. I was on the new road, the bypass cutting through the land of one of daddy's friends, the one with the horses in a barn where he dropped the hay through the holes in the loft, strings from the bales of hay hanging on a whittled wood peg. I headed for Virginia. The singer said he was waiting for his man.

I was well into Virginia, on the river road that ran to the top of Bilson Mountain, when I ran out of gas. I pulled over, listened to the woman sing about the things she does to please. Just a little tease. Oh oh whoa. I leaned forward to see the ridgeline above me, made out the lights on the tower where the Bilson Radio signal came from straight in front of me, straight across the river, straight up the hill. People passed, their headlights blinding me. People going to Walmart, to the malls in Tennessee. Going to buy stuff. Right on schedule. Regular people. It was Black Friday. Willett went off the air, and a woman with a voice like Mamaw's came on.

"Well, we're gonna play this here news story again, about what's going on with our friends over in Kentucky," the lady said. "And then we'll have some Country Gentlemen for you."

The voice of Willett Bilson introduced the story about me, about the hearing. If I had gas, I would have gone up that hill and gone in that radio station and grabbed ahold of that Willett Bilson, pulled him in my lap to listen to that story with me.

My voice on the radio said, "They need to stop permitting these mines is what they need to do."

Denny said aint nothing gonna to happen to me. Said they need me to run my mouth. Said somebody had to say what needed saying. Said he and his daddy had my back, even if they had to say ugly things to my face.

Mamaw's voice came on the radio, said, "The governor needs to get involved."

I thought of Kenny's baby at the hearing, Kenny's hippie baby in the black onesie, and I wished I could live in a hippie place, like that baby did, a place where I could mix up in things and then run away when it got sticky. Go hide and listen to people play the bongo drums til it was time to go out and stir things up again. I'd like to live in a place where doing something righteous was a big party.

Mamaw's Escort pulled up behind me, and she got out in a green T-shirt with a frog on it and putty-colored walking shoes she ordered out of the Sunday magazine came in the Lexington paper. She got in the truck. The story about us was still playing on the radio.

"They's a right thing and a wrong thing," Mamaw said on the radio. "And they know which is which. Whether they'll let on like they do or not."

And that was the end of the radio story. There was ten seconds of nothing, and then some guy sang through his nose, "She walks through the corn leading down to the river. Her hair shone like gold in the hot morning sun."

I turned the radio off.

"Nice truck," Mamaw said.

I didn't say anything. Didn't have anything to say.

"Quite a night," she said.

The cars kept coming past. Come all ye faithful.

I said, "Mamaw, why do you fight the coal companies?"

Mamaw looked me dead in the eye. "I don't know. They just make me mad, I guess."

"We could be doing something else," I said.

Mamaw looked out at a field coated in frost. She said, "I used to think things could be different." An SUV slowed down to look at us and then went on by. "But I don't guess they could."

I felt the crown of my head where I butted Albert at school. It was tender.

"Nothing that won't clean up," Mamaw said.

She put her hand out and I put mine in hers. She closed her eyes and I closed mine. She said, "Let's go get you some gas."

We got in the Escort and went to the filling station where the river road hit the four-lane. She filled a gallon can with gas. When we got back to Denny's truck, I got out with her to put the gas in. She's so short, I had to help her balance the can. When she finished, she handed me two twenty-dollar bills.

"Go on," she said.

"What do you mean?" I said.

"Keep going."

"I don't have my license."

"I don't see no police."

"I aint got my glasses."

"You come this far."

Mamaw opened the truck door. I got in. She stood looking up at me. She looked like a doll, like her head was a dried apple.

I rolled down my window.

"What about Denny?" I said.

"Denny will be all right."

"I don't know where to go."

"You know I love you," she said.

I nodded.

And then Mamaw drove away. When she did, I didn't want to listen to Bilson Radio anymore. I didn't want the company of Willett Bilson. I didn't want anything. I drove out to where the river road hit the four-lane. There was no one behind me and so I sat there. Longer I set, harder time I had breathing. Before long I couldn't catch my breath at all. The truck got all hot inside, and my belly was popping in and out, and I started banging the window glass with the heel of my fist. It was like there was bad air in that truck cab.

Then a woman in an Astro van pulled up behind me, and she was talking to her baby in the backseat. I could almost hear her talking in my rearview. And I was all right. My breath came back. I scratched out, turned left across traffic, towards Kingsport.

Before I got to Gate City, I stopped at a restaurant in a stand of pines. It was an old place, all glass across the front. When I got inside, the place smelled more like a bar than a restaurant. I sat down in a booth. The waitress asked me if I wanted coffee, and I nodded. The sun broke through the window, and the ceramic cup she set in front of me steamed. Snow thickened on the pavement outside, and an old man in a felt hat fell right on his behind coming in. He picked himself up, but he left his hat laying in the gravel. On the wall between the windows at my booth there was a picture in a dime-store frame of an airplane landing in the straightaway in front of the restaurant. My brother and I sat with our parents in places like this many a night when we were little, trading punches by the light of a jukebox.

"What can I get you?" The way the waitress chewed her gum reminded me of every girl I ever hated.

I said, "I need another minute."

The waitress didn't smile when she said, "Honey, you all right?"

"Last night I was at the hospital," I said.

The waitress dropped her hands to her side, but her jaw kept working that gum.

"They had a TV bolted to the wall." I put my hands around my coffee mug and squeezed on it. The warmth, the squeeze, made me feel better. "They was an astronaut movie on." That was true. There was. "One of the astronauts was floating around outside the spaceship breathing through a huge long tube like a professional carpet cleaner uses."

The waitress sat down. "I seen that. The dude's tube broke loose from the spaceship and it flopped real slow like a water snake." The waitress showed me how the tube flopped with her arm. It was exactly the way it was.

I nodded at the waitress. "And the astronaut turned real slow away from the ship. Head over heels." I leaned towards the waitress. "Twisting out into the nothing."

"And they showed a closeup of his face," the waitress said.

"And he was smiling."

"It was so creepy," the waitress said.

"Yes it was."

The waitress stood up. She shook her head and popped her ballpoint open and touched the point of it to my page in her order book. She raised her chin like my time was up. She was wanting to be tough, but her eyes had a rattled look. Least I thought they did. I ordered chocolate chip pancakes and a chocolate milkshake. When the waitress went to put the order in, I went out to the truck and got in.

AND THEN I COME ON HOME.

ACT TWO

# RECKONING

# 4

## DEAD COW IN THE CREEK

I NEVER should have stolen Denny's truck. Not without my license. Or my glasses. And not if I wasn't going to steal it for real. But I had to get out of Canard County. I had to lay my hand to the cheek of Willett Bilson, put a face to the voice on the radio. And I almost made it. I got to the foot of his mountain, but I lost my nerve. So I come home.

I drove up Drop Creek to take Denny back his truck, but he was gone. They all were. I sat down on the swing on Denny's daddy's porch. Its chains creaked like a coffin lid. The snow came down in clods, piled up at the edge of the porch's unpainted boards. Denny's daddy had a pretty place. Grass gouged up through the snow. Stuff for the kids was strung all over the yard. Pine mulch lay thick under the shrubs. Nothing I wanted, but still. Denny's double-wide faced his daddy's place. It had a porch with red latticework underneath it. White Christmas lights dripped from the gutters and wrapped through the neat little trees and bushes in the yard.

I went in Denny's daddy's house. It smelled like cinnamon and coffee. I called Evie to come get me, but she didn't answer. I sat down on the couch. Without my glasses, the deer head over Denny's daddy's chair was all fuzzy.

I walked over and got up in its face. Its hard black eyes and too-shiny nose come clear. "Sucks to be you," I said to the deer head.

An old woman's voice came from a bedroom back down the hall. "Come here," the voice said, but it didn't sound like two words. Sounded like one, like this: "Kmeeer." It came in pairs too: "Kmeeer. Kmeeer."

I went to the back of the house. Mamaw's sister, the one lives in Ohio, lay on the carpet beside Denny's mommy and daddy's bed, flat on her back, drunk it seemed from how loud she was and the way her eyes played in their sockets. Her hair spun loose around her head like cotton candy.

"Kmeeer."

I did and she said, "You're Cora's girl," and I said, "She's my grandmother," and she said, "You know she took my man," and then she fell off to sleep, her head laid off to its side like a chicken ready for the ax. Mamaw's sister. Aunt Ohio.

When she talked she sounded mountain, which wasn't the way she talked normal. Normal she talked through her nose all buckeye about stuff like everywhere they ate on the way down here and what they had at each stop. She told us about every chicken nugget, every drop of honey mustard sauce. She was aggravating. I watched her sleep a while. Normal boring church pictures of Denny and his brothers and their wives and kids in flimsy picture frames crowded the tops of the chests of drawers.

I was chickenshit was what I was. That was why I was back in this shitty spookhouse county. Without the courage of my convictions, Mamaw would say. Aunt Ohio started snoring. I went in the kitchen, stood in front of the refrigerator looking at the Thanksgiving leftovers, the wads of foil, the piles of Ziploc bags. I took a pop and left in Denny's truck and come back to Mamaw's house on Long Trail.

~~~~~~~~~~~

"WHY'D YOU steal Hubert's beer, Dawn?"

It was hard to answer with my brother Albert's arm clamped around my neck.

"He said you drove off with his beer."

The night before I stole Denny's truck, I stole my uncle Hubert's Oldsmobile and drove it off the side of Astor Mountain. I rolled it at least three times and crashed it into the side of a hickory tree. Three days before that, I'd busted Albert's jaw at school. Beat him bloody with my French book and put him in the hospital for Thanksgiving. And this is what was on his mind when I got home—the beer in the back of Hubert's vehicle when I wrecked it.

THAT RIGHT THERE IS WHAT YOU NEED TO KNOW ABOUT MY BROTHER ALBERT.

Albert tightened his grip around my neck. I could feel his breath against the back of my ear. He was hunched up behind me, trying to hook his leg around mine, get me on the ground. I tried to reach back and get his hair, but they'd shaved his head, at the hospital I guess. I tried to grab him low, but he wouldn't let me get ahold of him. We spun round and round on Mamaw's patio, concrete all slushy. Albert finally got me down, drove my face into the snow in the yard.

"Where's it at, turd?"

He's so stupid. I couldn't tell him with my mouth full of snow. I had twenty pounds on Albert, probably thirty, so when he tried to pin my arm behind me, I threw him off and got on my feet. He grabbed at my ankle, and I turned one of Mamaw's steel patio chairs over on his hand. Edge of the steel caught him across the fingers, and I figured it cut a couple off, but he jerked his hand back and all his fingers come with it. Me and Albert had been fighting my whole life. Just like that, like crazy people. I was sick to death of it.

"It's just beer," I said.

Albert stood up. He raised his lip at me, showed his teeth like a dog. "Wait til Hubert gets out and gets ahold of you."

"Shut up, Albert."

"He aint gonna turn loose of you so easy."

I smacked Albert's finger out of my face.

"You better calm down," Albert said. He sat down in the patio chair.

I stood over him. "What do you mean, 'when Hubert gets out'?"

Mamaw stood on her tiptoes looking out the window over the sink at us.

Albert said, "Hubert's in the Wise County jail."

"What for?"

"Him and Cinderella got into with it some chicks over there."

Mamaw tapped on the window.

Albert said, "Give me a ride back to Hubert's."

"Come on, little mermaid. Let me ride in your new truck."

"Get there the way you got here, asshole."

Albert sat in the patio chair like the prince of winter. He belched and steam shot out his mouth. "Give me a ride, little mermaid."

With both hands on his shoulders, I knocked his chair over, left him laying there, and went in Mamaw's house.

~~~~~~~~~

"DID YOU make it home?" Mamaw said in a voice dry as flour, getting up from the kitchen table where she was reading coal mining permit papers.

I sat down, put my head on the table. The vinyl tablecloth was sticky with sugar. I could feel it against my forehead.

Mamaw said, "You want some milk?" She brought me a glass of chocolate milk and sat back down. She put her hand on my hair.

"Your sister's passed out in the bedroom at your brother's house," I said without raising my head.

"Do what?" Mamaw said.

I told her what I seen and where I seen it.

"Hunh," Mamaw said.

"What's she talking about, you took her man?"

Mamaw looked at me a minute. "Don't pay no attention to her. She's lost."

It didn't bother Mamaw to be alone. Maybe she was preparing me for the same. Mamaw got up from the table, went over to where she kept her papers stacked, come back, set my glasses down in front of me.

"Your cousin Denny brung them," Mamaw said.

My glasses had been cleaned, screws tightened. Shined up. Mamaw set back down to her business. Didn't say nothing, but she wasn't reading, just shuffling papers, waiting for me to say something. That was her being there for me. Hell with that, I thought. My leg was bouncing I was so mad. To calm myself down, I thought how Mamaw took me and Momma in when things at Hubert's got crazy. I thought how she took me walking in the woods when I was agitated. I got up and went out on the patio. Albert was gone. The air smelled of coal smoke from my papaw Houston's house back up on the hillside. I could see him in my mind, surrounded by his music, fire going in the stove, not like pioneer days, not that old feeling, but like something you couldn't find no more in the world today.

Everything was blue and gray out. It was so quiet I could almost hear Houston's fire cracking and popping. My cheeks were numb.

Kmeeer. Kmeeer. I walked towards Houston's. Halfway up the hill, I looked back at Mamaw's, light orange in the kitchen. I was starting to stink. Good time to go see Houston. Didn't matter how you smelled at Houston's.

<hr />

WHEN I pushed open the door, Houston sat in the front room baked by coal fire, glazed in his own grease, his face sawed open in a smile. A man on a 78 rpm record sang, "The cuckoo, she's a pretty bird, and she wobbles as she flies." An idler and a thief is what Mamaw called Houston, but I never seen him idle. He was always out trading with somebody or fishing goods out of the river. Or holding something up to the light to check on how clear it was. Clarity.

HOUSTON WAS FOREVER CHECKING ON THE CLARITY OF SOMETHING.

"Hey oh," he said when I come in the door. "Is it a haint? Or the darling Misty Dawn?" He leaned up on the heels of his hands in the armchair. "Get to the icebox, little sister. Fetch out a jar."

I set the jar and a glass with painted flowers on it down at my grandfather's elbow. Houston fixed a glass of the cold clear liquor and handed me the jar to put back in the icebox. I slumped in a chair across from him and fell off to sleep.

"Go back there and lay down on the bed," Houston said when I opened my eyes.

I did, between the birdblue electric blanket and the ancient brown chenille spread, the light fuzzy through the window plastic. I dreamed I heard Willett Bilson's voice, and I lay waiting for it to turn into a body. I wondered did Willett Bilson have chest hair and how it would be around my finger.

Houston's dogs whined and barked in my sleep. I woke annoyed, wishing Houston would make the dogs stop. Houston came in the room, said, "I reckon she's asleep" to the dogs. The dogs sniffed my face. It was dark outside. The yellow lamp lit the window plastic.

"Time to eat," Houston said. "If you want."

"I should go back to Mamaw's."

"Coming down pretty good out there."

A dog licked my hand. I said to Houston, "What did you do for Thanksgiving?"

"I was supposed to go to Kingsport to see daughter June, before all this snow."

The dog licking my hand was wet and missing an eye.

Houston said, "Nobody brought me nothing to eat."

The dog lay its head on my hand.

"I thought maybe that's what you was doing. Thought maybe Cora fixed me a little plate of turkey and dressing. Maybe some sweet potatoes. With them little marshmallows melted down over em."

"Nah." I stood up. The one-eyed dog crawled under the bed.

I don't remember Houston ever living under the same roof as Mamaw. When I was little he lived in a block building out in Mamaw's driveway next to the carport. Momma told me Mamaw and Houston used to have a photography studio together, used to spit and fuss together every day of their lives. But Mamaw kicked him out and kept kicking him til she'd kicked him up here on the ridge.

"Well then," Houston said, "you want some stew?"

The dogs trailed Houston out of the room. I followed. Houston browned meat and cut up carrots and onions and potatoes and put salt and pepper on them and poured soup out of a can into it. Houston sipped from a coffee cup.

"Your grandmother was a nurse. How I met her. She was taking care of my head. Where I fell out of the back of a truck."

"Hit wasn't moving. It was sitting in her driveway. At her daddy's house. Drop Creek."

A dog stood on a rag rug next to the stove and shook water off itself.

"So," Houston said, "you courting?"

Albert told me one time he heard Houston was fooling around with a woman come in their photo studio for some glamour shots and Mamaw almost beat her to death with a camera tripod.

"I better go, Papaw."

"I done called your mamaw. Told her where you was."

"What'd she say?"

"Said I could keep you. For the night, anyway."

Houston set the stove eye on low and headed back to his chair in the front room.

"Course I'd had my eye on her long time before I fell out of the truck. Your grandmother was real good with makeup. She didn't hardly wear none. But what she wore worked like a charm. Bright like a bird in spring. We took her picture, me and Daddy. I made me a copy, packed it around til one day it fell out of my schoolbook. My buddy found it and give it to her. Boy, was she mad. She didn't want nobody having no part of her. At the time I thought it was me she didn't favor, cause I wasn't no slight airborne woodland creature of bright plumage and easy means of escape like her. I was earthy. A salamander at best, but more like a grub, something beneath the bark of a tree, at home in soft wood, something a bird like her, with her sharp beak and bright plumage, would feed on."

HOUSTON TALKED LIKE THAT SOMETIMES.

He said, "I wore her down though."

"Didya."

"One May I thought I was possessed by the devil. I wasn't of course. It was just a kidney infection. But her preacher uncle convinced me it was the devil. He hollered and mashed my head between his hands til the spirit flew out in the yard and holed up in my Chrysler. Her preacher uncle dumped gas on that car and set it blazing. To get that devil out of it."

"Did it work?"

"Go see for yourself. It's still sitting up Drop Creek."

"Hunh."

"Your mamaw sort of took pity on me after that, and I got in there that way, you know."

I didn't quite believe Houston, but I ate his stew and stayed at his house that night. He left me alone, played 78 rpm records out in the front room, and when I slept, I slept like I was dead.

---

SATURDAY MORNING early, there was a knock on Houston's door. Houston never stirred. I got up and opened the door. It was Aunt Ohio with a bunch of food. Houston came into the kitchen as Aunt Ohio come in the house.

"Verna," Houston said.

Behind Aunt Ohio out Houston's door, the sun came out. Water dripped even across the length of the eave. The ground was solid snow, but shiny.

"How are you, Houston, honey?" Aunt Ohio had her hair done up tight. Her makeup was crisp as frosting on a cake in the glass case at the grocery store. She wore high-waisted jeans and shoes for walking. She set all them Ziploc bags and wads of foil from Denny's daddy's refrigerator on the counter. She had most of a ham. Half gallon jar of tea. Better part of a pie.

IT WAS A BOUNTY.

Aunt Ohio said, "Houston, what time you coming to see us? You know it aint Thanksgiving til you come out. Them boys love your stories. We all do." Aunt Ohio pulled Houston's head over, kissed him right on its top.

"Where's Gene?" Houston said.

Gene was Aunt Ohio's husband used to manage a metal garbage can plant in Ohio before things went plastic. Houston told me one time Gene give him a job. Said it was the best job he ever had.

"Down at Cora's," Aunt Ohio said. She went to the icebox and took out the jar.

"Verna, I don't know I'm going to get out to Drop Creek this year." Houston's Adam's apple bobbed up and down more than usual. "Gout giving me fits."

Aunt Ohio leaned on her elbows on the kitchen counter. She was trying to look appealing. On Drop Creek, she was the person knew the rules to the card games and didn't care to tell you. She was the one said the mashed potatoes weren't hot all the way through. She never tried to be appealing on Drop Creek. Aunt Ohio turned her smoky eyes on Houston.

I WISHED I HAD EYES LIKE THAT TO TURN ON WILLETT BILSON.

Houston licked his chops over that ham. I did too. Houston got a bag of white bread off the top of the icebox. He laid it on the counter, got the yellow mustard out. Aunt Ohio's smoky eyes followed Houston to the icebox, to the counter, back to the icebox. The air was filled with honey-glazed tension. A car horn honked. Aunt Ohio stood up. Houston pulled a slice of ham off the bone. Aunt Ohio moved to the door and waved at Gene. She turned.

"Goodbye, Houston."

Houston took two pieces of bread from the bag. "Adios," he said, pronouncing it "add-ee-ose." He laid the slices out on the counter and smeared yellow on both.

"Hope that gout don't get the best of you," Aunt Ohio said with a smile. She turned to me. "Dawn," she said. And then she was out the door, which slammed behind her.

The liquor set on the counter next to the mustard. Houston lay down his knife and tipped the liquor jar.

"Phwoo," he said when he set it down.

"What was that?" I said.

"You'll have to ask her."

Sunbeams leaned through the window. The dogs ganged up at the door, scratched the aluminum, dragged their noses across the glass.

"I'm asking you, Papaw." I walked to the counter and put the jar to my own lips.

"I have not always been the gentleman you see today." Papaw finished putting together his sandwich. He went to the cabinet, pulled a plate from a pile of plates, set the sandwich on the plate. He came to his chair. "I did not used to be so comfortable in my own skin," he said.

"Your own skin," I said.

"Let the dogs in," he said.

I did. They looked this way and that, set up underneath the ham.

"I used to get agitated," Houston said.

"Hunh."

"Used to lose my sense of myself. Had to go elsewhere to figure out who I was."

"Only so much a man can figure out at home."

"So who'd you love more? Mamaw or Verna?"

Houston chewed his sandwich, licked mustard from his lips, took a dreamy look.

"First one thing and then another," he said.

The dogs settled down around us. They wagged their tails.

Houston said, "There is a pain in watching others eat known only to dogs. They pretend to like us. But they are filled with anger at how unfair the world is." He put the last of his sandwich in his mouth. "You are too young for us to drink enough for me to tell you of my courtship of your grandmother and her sister. There are doors through which it is not yet time for you to walk."

NOBODY TOLD ME JACK.

My life was one long river of bullshit.

"I will say this." Houston put his knotty finger to his eye. "Fear men. Flee them. Give them nothing. They mean you ill. Their voices smack of honey and their words set off string music in the chambers of your heart. But mark my words: they will cut you down, chop you up, cook you over fire, eat only the pieces that suit them, and throw the best of you into the weeds for other beasts to rend and gnaw."

Houston pulled on his coat and went out into the snow, dogs on his trail in a barking wad. His yard was full of sunshine and puddles. I went back to bed.

~~~~~~~~~

WHEN I woke, clouds covered the sun. I lay there in a twist, thinking I wasn't nothing, and wasn't never gonna be nothing. Living was gonna be one long disastrous horrifying embarrassment.

Houston was the best man in my life since Daddy died and he wasn't for shit. I was eight years old when Daddy died. People say you can't be happy til you know what you want.

Right before he died we went to his momma's house in North Carolina, and he set at dinner and told a story about a boy named Jack tying death up in a sack, and I thought it was real. I never heard him tell a story like that, and my mouth hung open, and that's what haunts me, that every day I would have learned something new and good about what my daddy was.

I turned on Houston's portable radio with its rotted-off leather handle and red needle set on Willett Bilson's station. Two tobacco farmers were playing jazz records.

"Now that there was John Coltrane," one of them said.

"Hello there, Mr. Bilson," the other jazz farmer said. "How are you this fine morning?"

"Just dandy," said Willett Bilson. "Up with the chickens."

Willett Bilson made a clucking noise and the jazz farmers laughed. I don't know why I was taken with the voice of Willett Bilson. It didn't seem like something I would like. Too goody goody. I should have thought him stupid. But I didn't. I lay there in the bed and waited through a show-offy saxophone song to hear him again.

"Man, that was some playing," said Willett Bilson. "I feel taken away, transported, swept right up off of this mountain to the bustle of New York City. You are my wife. Goodbye city life. Heh."

There was a pause and the old jazz farmer said, "Well, that'll just about do it for us," and they signed off and Willett did a show by himself, playing music and announcing Christmas pageants and Santa Claus giveaways and a hog killing. He talked slow and appreciative about the beautiful morning—"the frost, friends, has created a jewel box out our window here."

I worked Willett Bilson up in my mind. I didn't think he would be super hot. But his reedy voice made him tall in my imagination. Maybe some kind of red hair. Maybe thick and curly. Maybe freckles. I drifted back to sleep, and woke when Mamaw called to say Denny was at her house looking for his truck.

DENNY CAME to pick up his truck with a guy from work. The guy wore a ball cap and looked at me hard. His look said, "I have a life and it is a good life, a life of laughing and closeness and fun, and you aint never gonna be a part of it, weirdo treehugger girl." Mamaw knew the boy. He had been to her house before. She had been to his. Mamaw had been a school nurse. People knew her that way besides her being a tree hugger. She had saved all kinds of people all kinds of money on doctor's bills. She had that going for her besides what she was doing trying to stop a strip job.

I HAD NOTHING GOING FOR ME BESIDES.

There wasn't any "well but" with me. I was a freak, soft and four-eyed, with black fingernail polish, a dead daddy, a drunk momma, a crackhead brother, outlaw uncles, and divorced grandparents who made trouble for normal people every time they come off the ridge.

Denny smiled at me with his eyes. He put his hand out, and I put the keys in it. He nodded and turned to get in his truck.

"That's it?" his friend said. "Just take the keys and go?"

"I reckon," Denny said.

"I'll be damned," his friend said.

Denny opened the truck door.

"What would you say," I said, "if it was your truck?"

"Dawn," Mamaw said.

Denny's buddy turned to face us. "Wouldn't say nothing," he said. "I'd a called the law. Had you put in jail. Lawless thing. Wouldn't matter if you was my cousin."

"Lawless," I said, "like when yall mine off your permit, and blast ten times more than you're supposed to, build ponds where you aint got no permit, lie on your water reports—lawless like that?"

"You need to shut your mouth," Denny's buddy said, "cause you don't know what you're talking about."

"What," I said, "break a law on a bulldozer and it aint a crime?"

"I work," he said. "That would be something you don't know nothing about, you truck-thieving little freak."

"Yeah, well," I said, "drug dealers work."

"I guess you'd know about that," he said.

"I'd be glad to go to jail," I said, "if they put me in right next to you."

He come around the truck, wanted to get up in my face. Mamaw put her walking stick between me and him.

"That's enough," Mamaw said.

"This aint a game, little girl."

I flipped him off. Mamaw knocked my hand out of the air.

"Let's go, Keith," Denny said.

"Yeah, go on, Denny," I said. "You pussy. I'm glad I stole your truck. You strip mining pussy with your pretty Christmas lights and your chrome-plated double-wide. Go the fuck on."

"Yall get on out of here, Denny," Mamaw said.

Denny didn't say a word, just got in his truck. His buddy tried to stare me down. He didn't have nothing to say. What was he going to say? What I said was true. He knew it was. I flipped him off again. Soon as I did that last flip-off, I wished it all back, like I had at the hearing, except this was worse. I had made it personal with Denny's friend. Way too personal. Denny and his friend left in the snow, sliding and slipping down through the gravel of Mamaw's drive to the blacktop.

"You been paying more attention at them meetings than I thought," Mamaw said.

"What's that boy's name?"

"Kelly. Keith Kelly."

My head spun. I wanted to be back at Houston's, old music playing.

"Reckon we'll see them again when this snow melts," Mamaw said.

"What are you talking about?"

"We're going up there and inspect that strip job."

"By ourselves?"

"State man go with us."

"Us who?"

"Me, you. Anybody we want to take."

"When?"

"Supposed to clear Thursday."

I walked over behind Mamaw's snowball bush. I put my hands on my knees to throw up. I coughed. I spit. Mamaw came over, put her hand on my back. I stood up.

I was cold and filthy from sleeping at Houston's. I wanted so to go in Mamaw's and take a shower, but I did not want to have to talk enviro-fighter strategy with Mamaw. I wanted to go somewhere and be clean and beautiful. I wanted to wear a dress. I wanted to have my picture made. I wanted to rest my hand in the crooked elbow of a boy who loved me. I wanted our favorite song playing. I wanted my head on his shoulder.

I tried to think where my mother was. The last I had seen of her, she was in the rearview mirror of the Delta 88, high, trying to break up the mess between Cinderella, Hubert, and the party girls. Did she have to go to jail with Hubert? I didn't figure she did. Albert would have said so. She was probably at Hubert's. How did she get back from Virginia? I left her there without a ride. Who would I ask? I did not want to ask Mamaw. She probably wouldn't know anyway. Hubert was in jail. Houston wouldn't know. I could ask Albert.

"Honey, come in from the cold," Mamaw called from the doorway. I saw in Mamaw's face how crazy I looked.

"Where's Momma?" I said.

"Come inside, Dawn."

When I got inside, Mamaw told me hadn't nobody seen her.

"She aint in jail?" I said.

"No."

"Then where's she at?"

"I don't know."

"Who does?"
"I don't know."
"You ask Albert?"
"I did."
"What'd he say?"
"He don't know."
"Shoo."
"I even asked Cinderella."
"You know Cinderella?"
"I do."
"What'd he say?"
"He don't know."

Out the kitchen window, Mamaw's Escort sat in the carport. Mamaw kept her car cleaner than her house. Clean. A slight airborne thing. It was Thanksgiving Saturday and the men would be back at Denny's house. The women might be doing their in-county Christmas shopping. The men were sitting around watching television, watching somebody beat the shit out of UK. Denny would be back with them in a minute. Him and Keith Kelly. My new enemy. Monday I go back to school.

Mamaw paused. "You scared to go back?"
Why did she have to put it that way? "No."
"Dawn?"
"What?"
"She'll be all right."
"How do you know?"

"I don't."

I turned from the window, looked around the kitchen, turned back to the winter light.

Mamaw said, "Want to walk with me? Clear your head."

I stared out the window. Mamaw looked at me a long time, like I was a dead cow in the creek she couldn't figure out how to move.

"You want some hot chocolate?" she said.

I shook my head. She stood there some more. Dead cow still in the creek.

"You don't have to do this," she said.

"Don't have to do what?"

"You don't have to be involved with this Blue Bear business. You don't have to go. You don't have to speak."

She knew it was too late for me to back out. I nodded. "Yall are right about what you're doing. Somebody's got to say it."

I thought Mamaw might move towards me. But she didn't. She put away dishes. She moved things from one end of the room to the other. She picked pieces of fuzz off her sweatshirt.

"Your momma's been living the way she's living for a while now," Mamaw said.

"I know."

"Aint there no other kids at school," Mamaw said, "feel the way you do about Blue Bear?"

"Not that I know of."

Mamaw nodded. "Well," she said.

I went in my room, changed my clothes.

"You gonna take a shower?" Mamaw said.

I put on clean jeans, a high-neck shirt, long johns, a hoodie, two pairs of socks.

"I'm going out," I said. "I can't think."

"Well," Mamaw said.

I stood at the kitchen door. "I'll see you."

"You want something to eat?" Mamaw said.

"Nah."

"You going up on the ridge?"

"I reckon."

"Here." Mamaw went to her coat pocket behind the door, got me her pipe, her tobacco pouch. I held them in my big hand, tucked them in the front pocket of my hoodie.

"Helps me," Mamaw said.

"Does it?" I said.

Mamaw tucked her chin and smiled. Mamaw was so strange. The house ticked like a clock. Tick. It was the heater. Tick.

"Mamaw?"

"Yes, honey."

"Would you rather I was alone?"

"Do what?"

"You wish I was by myself all my life? You rather I live that way?"

"Honey, no. I wouldn't wish that on a dog."

I bowed my head. Mamaw came to me. She closed me up in her arms. I was so much bigger than her. Big. A big girl.

Mamaw said into my ear, "I'm doing my best, honey."

~~~~~~~~~~

I WALKED out the door like I was leaving for good. That's always how I felt when I went out in the snow.

Houston wasn't at his house. I put a pint jar in my hoodie pocket and headed up on the ridge. The trees against the snow-white sky were like words on paper. I tried to read what they said. In a beautiful mystical nature language that no one could understand but me they said for me to kiss their ass. I am not a nature girl, see. Don't camp. Don't fish. Can't tell which animals are which by their poop. I just wander the woods. All. By. Myself.

The snow squeaked under my feet. I lost my breath when the way got steep. I sat down on a boulder and sipped from the jar. Corn liquor. Made by some ancient craft. The children I was gonna have or not danced at the edge of my eyes. When I turned my head towards them, they were gone. I didn't think about Denny. I didn't think about Keith Kelly.

"Til this year I thought you was a boy." That's what the only boy who ever said he liked me said the first time he got me by myself. I sipped from the jar.

"Mamaw," I said in my head.

"What?" she said in my head.

In my head I said, "Remind me what I'm missing doing home school."

In my head, Mamaw laughed. Ha. Ha. Ha.

I got drunk in the snow, on a narrow patch of land Mamaw owned. Hell deep. Heaven high. No divided mineral. Do you know what I mean? Fuck you if you don't. Do you remember what it was like to be fifteen? Do you know what it is like to grow up in Kentucky? Either you do or you don't. Aint no use explaining if you don't.

I moved through the snow. I wished I had a dog with me. I turned to see if one of Houston's dogs followed me. I took out the jar again so as not to think about what it meant that not one of Houston's dogs followed me.

Snow and trees gave way to snow and rocks as I climbed. Fresh, I said to myself. Everything was fresh. Maybe, the wind said to my face, maybe you should cut yourself off with that liquor. I sat on a rock at the crest of the ridge, exhaled. Everything to the north of us sprawled out in front of me. Cut yourself off, I said to the wind.

I took out the pipe and pouch. I did not have a lighter. I did not have fire. I stood up to kill myself. I looked down. There was a ledge ten feet below. I could jump down on that to practice kill myself.

# 5

~~~~~~

# MONSTER BIRDS

I FELL heavy off the north side of the mountain and landed on the rock ledge ten feet below. My first thought on landing was "I'm sorry. So sorry." My weight took me forward, towards the valley below. The great white of the sky turned in front of me, and as I pitched forward the stripped winter ridges rose up and then the road at the base of the mountain, and I closed my eyes to fall. Why close my eyes? I wondered. Why deprive myself of the last marvel?

Something took hold of my legs. I stopped moving. My ears filled with the sound of dripping water and a white pickup truck pushing through the slush on the road at the base of the back side of the mountain.

When I rolled over onto my side to see what had stopped me falling, the wet rock soaked me from my ribs to the bulb of my ankle. Aunt Ohio lay face forward against my hip and looked at me calm as if she were beside me on Houston's sofa, as if I had just asked for a cookie or for her to change a channel on the television.

Aunt Ohio squinted past me, and I imagined a winged monster bird coming in for a landing behind me. Aunt Ohio took the jar of liquor from me and said, "Shame we couldn't live right here."

I said, "What are you doing here?"

"I been coming here long before you was born, little darling," she said. "What are you doing out here flying around," she said, "scaring me to death?"

I sat up out of the wet. "I didn't know you were here," I said. "I wouldn't have scared you."

Aunt Ohio smiled. She drank off all that was in the jar.

Clouds diffused the light. Aunt Ohio was clear as a bell. There was barely enough wind to chill us. The snow was coming again soon.

I DIDN'T MEAN to KILL MYSELF, I SAID.

"Mother Nature," Aunt Ohio said, and scooted back under the overhanging rock. She pulled twigs from her pockets. She had branches piled for a fire. Aunt Ohio said, "I would give anything to be you." She took out her lighter and lit the little pile and bent to blow.

It was like a rocky bedroom there, and I wanted to sleep by the fire with Aunt Ohio and her smoky eyes.

"I don't have the energy to get stirred up," she said. "I don't have the stick-to-it anymore."

I didn't know what she was talking about.

"I couldn't steal nobody's man no more," she said. "I don't care enough to try."

MY STRANGE AUNT OHIO.

"I barely had enough to get up this hill," she said. "Not enough to fling myself off it. I mean," she said, "look at you. You jumped right off. Full of life."

I said, "I only jumped ten feet."

Aunt Ohio crawled to the edge of our little perch. She gathered up Mamaw's pipe and pouch.

"We are what we are," Aunt Ohio said. "Aren't we?"

"I guess," I said.

Aunt Ohio filled the pipe and struck her lighter. The tobacco flared. She smoked by her little fire, then passed the pipe to me. "I suppose this is your pipe to smoke."

I reached for the pipe and she pulled it back.

She said, "You didn't steal it, did you?"

"No."

"You didn't steal it from your grandmother?"

"No."

I snatched at the pipe. I did not like her treating me like some dandelion. She handed the pipe to me, its thin flat drawhole pointed towards me. I pulled at the pipe and coughed. The tobacco made me think of George Washington. So did Aunt Ohio.

"There must be some magic," Aunt Ohio said.

"Why?" I said.

I DID NOT THINK THERE HAD TO BE MAGIC.

Aunt Ohio took the pipe back from me. "We sit at the top of the world with a roof over our heads," Aunt Ohio said. "Magic enough in that, I suppose."

She drew on the pipe, and the smoke curled out in question marks.

"Come here," she said, and she moved over on her rock to make room for me. "Call me Verna."

"All right," I said.

"Not Aunt Verna," she said. "Just Verna."

"All right," I said.

"You can't be careful," she said. "You need to be careful. But you can't."

Birds flew by level with us. I would always like that.

"Don't worry about your grandmother," Aunt Ohio said. Her Ohio accent was back on full blast. I could hear her septum vibrating when she spoke. "You can't pay any attention to her."

"I like paying attention to her," I said.

Aunt Ohio searched my face. "Sure," she said. "Of course you do. I'm not saying don't. Not what I'm saying." She stared at me like I was her reflection in a window she was cleaning. She wrinkled her brow, looking for the spot she missed. I expected her to lick her thumb and rub the spot off of me. But she didn't.

"You must breathe," Aunt Ohio said. "There is no substitute. The air going in, going out. Focus on that." Aunt Ohio raised both her eyebrows as high as they would go. "If you do," she said, her raised finger like some twisted stick of Christmas candy, "there's no stop to it. Natural. It's what your body wants to do." Aunt Ohio pulled on the pipe. "It's like music," she said exhaling. "See," she said, "running her hand through the smoke, "like music." She lay her arm across her knee. She pointed the pipe at me. "What is the most magical thing you've ever done?"

"Well, think."

"I wished Albert would puke one time and he did."

Aunt Ohio turned to the swirling snow, and then back to me. "It's a start," she said.

I asked Aunt Ohio had she done something magic.

"I've been around," she said. She waved her arms, nearly hit me in the head. "Whoosh," she said. Pulling her arms back into her lap, she said it again: "Whoosh." She offered me the pipe. I didn't take it. She put her arm around me. "It's hard doing this," she said.

She left her arm around me, and the snow came harder, but no winged monster bird came and picked out our eyes. It got colder, and her arm around me may not have been magic, but it was magic enough to get me and her off that mountain in one piece.

~~~~~~~~~~~~

ME AND Aunt Ohio come off the trail where it met the highway. Gene had the Cadillac pointed off the mountain. Aunt Ohio hugged me, asked did I want a ride back to Mamaw's. I said I didn't. Aunt Ohio hugged me again.

Albert was sitting in front of Hubert's, and when he seen me he jumped on a four-wheeler and rode up to where I was.

I said, "Albert, I aint in the mood to fool with you."

He said, "You seen Mom?"

Even though Albert spent all his time with Hubert, the mainest source of Momma's problems—actually, I considered Hubert the total source of all our problems—I couldn't deny Albert cared for Momma. Albert was a walking menstrual cramp, but Momma brought out the sweetness in him. He tried to keep it hid. But everybody could see it.

"No," I said. "I aint seen her."

"You want a ride back to Mamaw's?"

I got on the back of Albert's four-wheeler. Albert was thin, not fleshy like me. He wore a dark gray canvas coat. From behind, him and Mamaw had the same bird skull. He wore boots too big for him, gloves too big for him. He sped up and the cold air pressed our faces. He brought me to Mamaw's carport.

"Where would Momma be," I said, "if she wasn't with Hubert?"

The four-wheeler seat creaked as Albert turned towards me. He shrugged. "You want to go look for her?" Albert said.

Mamaw come out in a hurry and got in the Escort.

"Mamaw," I called, but she acted like she didn't hear me. "Mamaw!" I called louder, but she pulled out of the carport. Albert hopped the four-wheeler in front of her. She stopped.

# WHERE ARE YOU GOING?

I SAID TO HER THROUGH THE WINDOW.

"Get in," she said back through the glass. I got in and she pointed at Albert. "You too."

Albert got in back. Mamaw took off, driving kind of crazy, which she does, but even more so than usual. When we got to town, people were looking at us funny, and Mamaw threw gravel turning onto the Drop Creek road. She passed coal trucks when there wasn't room. Me nor Albert said a word, not even to ask where we were going.

"They found your mother," she finally said.

"Is she all right?" Albert said.

"They said for us to hurry," Mamaw said.

"Who?" Albert said.

"Denny," Mamaw said.

And that was all was said.

When we got to Denny's, Denny and his daddy Fred and a bunch of others sat on four-wheelers. I was glad to see Keith Kelly wasn't there. There was two four-wheelers didn't have nobody on them, and Fred said something to Mamaw I didn't catch, and Albert and Mamaw got on one four-wheeler, and I got on the other. I felt strange on that four-wheeler by myself, all them other motors rumbling like men on the porch outside a funeral.

We took the path I'd taken when I stole one Thanksgiving. I wondered had Momma fallen down the same hole I had. I wondered had Momma fallen off the highwall. Had she OD'd or something like that, they would have taken her right to the hospital. The four-wheelers stopped. Mamaw was off hers first. She stared into the treetops. When I saw they was all looking up, I looked up too.

Albert yelled, "What are you doing?"

"What?" Momma said.

Momma looked crow-sized she was so high up in a poplar tree. I about got sick looking at her. Albert asked her again what she was doing.

"My business," she said.

We were scared for her, but her buzz brought a tiredness, an about-wore-out-ness to our worry.

"Can you get down?" Mamaw said.

"I don't want to get down," Momma said.

"Aint no way she could get down," Fred said, "not til she sobers up."

"Bless her heart," somebody said.

Mamaw rubbed her hand across her face. Albert walked up to the tree, sizing it up like he was going to climb up there after her.

"You stay here, boy," Fred said.

"We should get Hubert," Albert said. "Hubert could get her down."

Nobody said nothing to that. A bird sang, sounding happy like a bird can even though a bird aint got brain enough to be happy. We were within thirty yards of the highwall.

"What are yall doing here?" Momma yelled down at us.

"What?" Mamaw said, and Momma yelled her question again.

Some of my cousins looked at each other like they were wondering the same thing, like they were thinking maybe they would leave Tricia Jewell up in that tree and go back and watch the ball game or maybe even do some chore for their wives.

"Destruction!" Momma yelled. The sound hung in the air.

Somebody said, "How long you reckon she's been up there?"

"Where's her vehicle?" somebody else said.

"Maybe somebody brung her."

"We could throw her a rope," someone said. "I could go get a rope."

"Why don't yall go away?" Momma yelled.

"Pete's got one of them harnesses he wears to work on power boxes up on poles for the cooperative."

"Thought they used bucket trucks for that."

"We could rig up a rope like a zipline, run her down that way."

Fred said that could work. "What do you think, Cora?" he said.

"Somebody'll still have to go up there," Mamaw said. "Take her the rope, hook her up. Won't they?"

"I'll go," Albert said.

"No," Mamaw said.

Momma sang, "If the real thing don't do the trick, you better think up something quick . . . ooooh . . ." and then she trailed off.

"I'll go," Denny said.

Momma was a good thirty feet off the ground. She sat in a Y where the trunk split. A woodpecker laughed. My mind flashed to the time Momma's sister June took me to a movie in Kingsport had a Woody Woodpecker cartoon on before it. My mother looked out over the strip job. I wished I could see what she was seeing. I wished I knew what it was like to be on the level with a woodpecker's call. The sky screamed blue. The tree branches surrounded my mother.

She waved at me. Light flooded her from behind. In a way, I did not want her to come down. I was glad to see her so high up. She had not escaped, but she was closer. And she was not so detailed to me there in the tree. I could not see vomit crusting on her cheek. I could not see the red swirl in the whites of her eyes like peppermint candy. All I could see was her beautiful stick-thin body wedged in the Y of the tree, the gold at the edge of her hair.

Momma turned away from the strip job to look the other way. When she turned, she slipped and nearly fell. Too much weight hit on that ankle, turned it. Momma cried out "OH!" and Fred said, "Get up there and get her, Denny. Fore she falls out and kills herself."

Denny threw off his coat. His daddy and his cousin had to boost him. His crack showed as he pulled himself up on the lowest limb. Denny seemed too heavy to climb that tree. He hitched up his pants and up he went. I seen a bear climb a tree one time on Animal Planet. Denny climbing was like that. Big parts doing what they were supposed to do. Denny was our personal fire department, pulling me out of wrecked cars, climbing trees after Momma. His shoulders were big, powerful. He climbed in a T-shirt with a picture on back of all the American presidents who had been cockfighters. The backs of his arms turned red and splotchy. Up he went. The sun came piling through the trees, turned the back of my eyes green and spotty. I could not see Denny and my mother. My nose filled with the smell of molding wood, my ears with the pinging of the cooling four-wheeler engines.

I moved to where I could see Momma and Denny better. Momma reached for Denny like a baby waiting for its mother to lift it out of a stroller. The bark of the tree stained her cheek. Her skin was torn, and the bark mixed with her blood. I could not see it, but it did.

"That tree aint gonna hold," someone said. "They both coming down."

Denny got to my mother, and Fred threw a rope up to him. "We might as well bring it down, before it comes with them."

The men pulled on the rope, and the tree, which was already falling, came with their pull. The wood cracked and split. My other cousin walked in front of me. My nose almost caught on the side of his head.

"Put it over yonder," Fred said.

My cousins dragged an old trampoline, its springs half-busted. I backed up. The trampoline stopped and the rope went tight, and the spot where my mother and Denny were in the tree ended up directly over the trampoline, and my mother's legs come loose from the tree, and they dangled, like two strings, like the fringe on a cowboy shirt, and Denny's arms circled her ribs, and her shirt rode up and I could see her belly beautiful and rounded, like a perfect sausage, and Fred went, "There you go," and my mother come loose from Denny, from the tree, and she dropped to the trampoline, and my cousins, her cousins, moved towards her, towards the trampoline, and she bounced with an "Oh," and two cousins reached out to keep her away from the place where the canvas sagged from the broken springs. Denny yelled "Move her," and we looked up and heard the crack of the wood, and I grabbed my too-light mother by her ankle to make room for Denny to fall. When Denny fell onto the trampoline, the branches crashed on his back like water dumping out of a bucket. He bounced and rolled, and some of the branches smacked him in the face.

They tried to stand Momma up, but her ankle was broke. Denny didn't say a word as the wood rained down on him. Albert went to Momma. Fred and the other men went to Denny, looking up first to make sure nothing else was gonna fall, and then they reached in and threw all the wood off Denny, and he sat up on the trampoline, his elbows resting on his raised knees. Momma sat on a four-wheeler and asked one of the cousins for a cigarette, and he gave it to her, and she pulled out her own lighter and lit it. Albert put his arm around her shoulder. The woods were quiet then. There were eleven of us there in the room of trees, quiet and clear and calm.

"Jesus Christ, Tricia," Mamaw said. She did not walk towards Momma. She stood with her hand against the trunk of the tree Momma had been up in. Denny sat on the trampoline and got him a cigarette too. He did not get upset with Momma or anybody or anything else. I didn't know what to think, what to do next. I felt like maybe I ought to run off.

# BUT I STAYED.

Up in the tree where Momma and Denny had been looked like lightning had struck, looked like a lot more time had passed than actually had.

~~~~~~~~~~~~

"MOMMA, WHAT were you doing up there?"

On the way home from the hospital, I sat in the back of Mamaw's Escort with Momma. Albert sat up front. Mamaw drove. Mamaw always drove. Momma had her head in my lap and a cast on her ankle. Momma smelled of the tree. Her hair was greasy. She needed a bath. A long one.

"I care too," Momma said quiet.

"Do what?" Mamaw said.

"I care too."

Albert turned and looked at us. "About what?" he said.

"About strip jobs. About things getting torn to pieces."

Mamaw didn't say anything right off. Then when I thought she wasn't going to say anything at all, she said, "I know you do, Tricia."

~~~~~~~~~~~~~~~

MOMMA HAD her arm around Albert's shoulder as they made their way down the hall from Hubert's kitchen. The kitchen table and counters looked like bears had been in there, packages tore open, jars busted in the sink and on the floor, everything edible licked clean. My cousins ate Hubert out of house and home every time he got put in jail. I followed Albert into the room my mother kept for herself in Hubert's house. It was the only room without boards or cardboard or foil over the windows, the only room where you could see out. The rest of the house was sealed up tight.

DARK LIKE THE INSIDE OF THE
# REFRIGERATOR.

We set Momma down on a ratty couch somebody got out of a dump and Momma had cleaned and covered with a pink quilt. Albert disappeared, brung Momma back a glass of orange juice. Momma couldn't settle. She bent and stretched and twisted.

"Put some gin in that juice," she said. "So's I can settle."

I could barely hold my own head up. I closed my eyes and nearly fell over. I put my head on Momma's shoulder.

"You want to take a shower, Momma," Albert said. "Dawn, run her a bath."

I didn't think I had the strength to give my mother a bath, but I did. The bathtub was new, but cheap and plastic—and dirtier than she was. The water came good and hot, scalded the nasty off the sides of the tub. I rinsed it out, run more hot water. When it cooled a little, I picked Momma off the commode and set her down in the tub. I kept her bad foot out of the water. She smiled for me to touch her, smiled as I rubbed the soap on her. I ran the rag over the thin skin covering her ribs. Her chest felt like a pair of panty hose with a bird cage stuck up in one leg. At first I wished I'd just stood her up in the shower. I didn't want to be giving her a bath.

BUT I GOT USED TO IT.

Man voices refilled the kitchen. They came down the hall, beat on the door, but it was locked. They went back to the kitchen. When I finished giving Momma a bath, she pulled on a T-shirt of Hubert's, walked in her room, got in her bed, and turned out her light. I stood in the bathroom door and watched her across the thin hall. Albert come up from the kitchen where he'd been sitting with whoever it was come in.

"She down?" he said.

I didn't say anything. He went in the room and closed the door.

"Come here, Dawn," somebody hollered from the kitchen. "Come here, Dawn Jewell."

I didn't acknowledge. Whoever it was kept on, but I still didn't acknowledge. Finally they quit. Albert's hand shook when he closed the door on Momma. I followed Albert out on Hubert's porch. Albert slouched against the porch rail.

"Why do you come out here to smoke?" I said. "They all smoke in the house."

Albert squinted and didn't say anything.

"Momma will sleep now," he said half a cigarette later. "Be lunchtime tomorrow before we see her."

I didn't say anything. There wasn't anything to say.

"You remember when she first got in the cake business?"

OF
COURSE
I
DO.

"You couldn't get up before her," Albert said. "Couldn't go to bed after her. That woman could stir."

Daddy used to call her "that woman" the way Albert did.

"It aint getting no warmer, Albert," I said. I wanted him to take me home. Albert flicked his cigarette out in the yard. He moved like he had a bad back, like an old man. I followed him. We got on the four-wheeler. He started out onto the Trail, out towards Mamaw's. It was pitch-dark now, crystal sparkly dark night. A truck come up to us and stopped. The two men in the truck chewed tobacco. I could see their jaws working through the window glass. Big one driving rolled down the window. "What are you doing?" he said to Albert.

"Taking her home."

"Hey, Dawn."

"Hey."

It was Crater. I didn't hate Crater.

"You'ns should come over," Crater said. "Decent's coming."

Decent Ferguson was a big woman. Older. Gone to college back in the wild free days. She was gray-headed but still had freckles like a girl.

"You want to go?" Albert said to me.

"Don't matter."

Crater had Pickle Peters with him. Pickle Peters didn't have no neck. His hair came down his forehead even with his eyes. That's the way his momma cut it. Covered up the fact he had one eyebrow run clean across the front of his head. Pickle Peters was twenty-eight and never been to a barber shop. He raised his chin at me when he seen I was looking at him.

"We'll be up there after while," Albert said.

Crater pulled off without rolling up his window.

"Well," Albert said, "you don't want to go, do you?"

CRATER HAD a high house. When I got off the four-wheeler, I felt like the house might fall over on me. We walked the wooden steps up from the underneath-the-house carport, through the darker-than-dark dark. When we walked in Crater's house, Decent was on the edge of her chair, her arm reared back like she was fixing to throw something.

"I drew back the skillet," she said, "and let it sail. 'Whoopwhoopwhoop' it went. Skillet landed 'thunk,' right in the small of his back, and he went down like he was shot. I thought I'd killed him. Momma came out went berserk."

Crater's wife Priscilla covered her nose to keep snot from blowing out she was laughing so hard.

"Did you get your hamburger back?"

"Yeah, I did. He still had it in his hand. Knocked out cold and never turned loose of that hamburger."

"He was a sight," Priscilla said getting up off the hard chair she was sitting on. She went to the kitchen. "Albert," she said, "they's beer and pop in the cooler. Chili in that pan. Yall help yourself. Hey, Dawn."

Just as I sat down, Decent got up to smoke.

"Crater won't let us smoke in here no more," Decent said. "How about that? World gone wrong, aint it?" Decent hacked. "I need to quit anyway."

The men slapped Albert on the back. "What say, little badass?"

There was one other female there. She was drawn back into the sectional sofa, lost in her buzz. Bottle-white blonde hair and black-ringed eyes. Her smooth cheeks said she hadn't been running with this bunch long. They all looked at me. I had no doubt they knew about me stealing the truck and the car, but nobody said anything. Albert got up. Brought me a beer.

"How tall are you?" Pickle said.

"Five ten."

"You done growing?"

I twitched my shoulders.

"Put your hand up here." He raised his hand, and I put mine flat against his.

"God damn," he said. "That's a big old Sasquatch hand." Pickle held me by the wrist. "Where'd you get that big old Sasquatch hand?"

I tried to pull my hand away, but Pickle held on tight. I said, "I don't know."

Pickle said, "You play basketball?"

"Not really."

"You ought to."

"What are yall doing," Decent said, blasting into the room on a wave of cold air, "playing patty-cake?"

"I'se looking at this woman's monster hands."

"Turn her loose, Pickle," Decent said. "You aint got no business handling her like that."

Pickle reminded me of Cinderella, which I wish he hadn't cause soon as I thought of Cinderella, soon as the idea of him come on my mind, here come the real Cinderella tramping through the door.

Decent said, "We found this here going through your garbage cans, Crater."

"Shoulda shot him," Crater said.

"I wadn't going through nobody's garbage cans," Cinderella said.

"Look who's here," Pickle said. "Your old chauffeur."

"Well, I'll be goddamned," Cinderella said, "I ought to beat your ass or kiss you one, Dawn Jewell."

"Why you gonna kiss her? I heard she got you throwed in jail."

"She did," Cinderella said, sniffing down in the chili pan. "If I'd been home that night instead of in jail? I'd of still been in jail and not for no drunk and disorderly. They'd a jacked that jail up and throwed me under it."

Cinderella come sit between me and that other girl. Keith Kelly stood facing me. He must have come in with Cinderella. He shook his head looking at us. Keith Kelly and his wavy brown hair. He could barely keep it under his hat. When I looked at Keith Kelly my stomach tightened, like there was somebody standing on a tire iron screwing down the lug nuts of my guts. I tried not to look at Keith Kelly, but when I did, my eyes locked down on him like a ray gun.

He didn't say nothing to me, but I could tell he was feeling his power over me. Him and his wavy brown hair was feeling their power over me same way every square-ass schoolteacher, every girl knew exactly what everybody else is wearing to school that day soon as her precious feet hit the floor in the morning, every kid who had both parents at home, got what was on his Christmas list, slept in the same bed in the same house every goddam night of his goddam life felt their power over me. I narrowed my eyes at Keith Kelly, and he didn't do anything, sat there like a stone, like a clock, like a face on a campaign billboard.

"Hi, Keith," said that girl with the black-ring eyes, "How you doing, baby?"

Keith Kelly didn't say a thing, took in what that girl said like it was money somebody owed him. That girl settled back in the sofa and knocked Cinderella's hand off her leg when he tried to pet her with it. She hadn't quit on pretty Keith Kelly. She set looking at him like she would be making another

run at him before the night was out, like he best not turn his head. Pickle
Peters asked Keith Kelly for a cigarette. Keith Kelly said he didn't have one.

"Pickle, you don't smoke," said the black-ring girl.

That house was dark, too dark. Nobody could see I still had mud from
jumping off the mountain on my pants, still smelled of gas from the four-
wheeler ride back to Denny's, still had the smell of gauze in my nose from
taking Momma to the hospital.

"All is well. All is well." Priscilla was trying to quiet somebody down in the
kitchen who was going, "All is well. All is well." There was a wood box yawning
open like a drunk in church on the coffee table. Box was black-lacquered with brass
hinges, red velvet inside, somebody's dope box, a baggie full hanging out of it.

"Want to burn one?" bleary Pickle said to me.

I twinkled my fingers in front of Pickle's eyes, told him to get back in his
box. He raised his hands up in my face, hands like wood, and I got hold of his
mother-trimmed bangs, a fistful of his hair, and I slapped his grizzly cheek with
my other hand.

"You don't know what I'm feeling," I said to Pickle Peters's gape-mouthed face.

They all laughed and the lugnuts tightened again in my belly. I turned loose
of the front shank of Pickle Peters's hair. Nasty thick three-colored stuff like
straw. Not like hair. Not thing one.

My mother's hair was getting like Pickle Peters's hair. It wasn't soft like it was even two years before. I'd noticed that giving her a bath. There wasn't much softness in my life, wasn't much softness in life in that fuckpot county of mine, and it seemed then like the softness was going from it, fast and furious like smart kids leaving after high school graduation. Someone let a long wet fart, and they all laughed. They was wanting to laugh. They didn't care what at. Keith Kelly lit a cigarette. Pickle Peters set up like he remembered where he left a hundred-dollar lottery ticket.

"You told me you didn't have no cigarettes," he said.

"Hush, Pickle," Priscilla said.

Pickle said, "Boy, don't you remember?"

Keith Kelly blew out, waved the smoke and fart smell from in front of him.

"Boy," Pickle stood up, "tell me I caint have a cigarette now."

"God Almighty," Priscilla said, and hit Pickle in the eye with a cigarette. "Shut the fuck up."

"YOU DON'T SMOKE, PICKLE," that black-eyed girl said again.

I wished hard for my momma's soft hair.

"How'd you get mud all over you?" Cinderella whispered in my ear.

"Jumping off a mountain trying to kill myself."

"Why'd you do that?" Cinderella said.

"So I wouldn't be here having this talk with you."

"Boy," Pickle was still standing, "what's the matter with you? Can't you hear what I'm saying?"

They all knew then Pickle was going to go ahead and get redneck. Didn't matter if I'd just announced I'd tried to commit suicide or told them I was carrying Dale Earnhardt's baby. Pickle was out and gone.

"It's a Friday night." Pickle was rocking back and forth now. "And you don't need to be lying at no nice get-together like this."

"Pickle," Priscilla said, "that's the last time I'm telling you to shut up. You don't need to be a total asshole. Not every weekend."

"It aint me being assholish," Pickle said. "It's this Barbie doll motherfucker."

Keith Kelly gave Pickle a cigarette. Pickle tore it open and blew the tobacco back at Keith Kelly.

"God Almighty," Priscilla said.

"I been following you," Cinderella said to me. He thought he was talking low, but everybody heard.

"No, you aint," I said.

A pointy-eared dog, white with chocolate spots, come hopping out of somewhere.

"Yeah I have," Cinderella said. "Soon as I got out of jail I come right straight looking for you."

"What for?"

"Cause I wanted to see you again."

"How old are you, Dawn?" The room went quiet when Decent asked. Her eyes were two humming outboard motors pushing a boat across summer waters. I water-skiied behind her outboard motor eyes, rope tight pulling me across a rough glass lake under a paste-gray sky.

"Cinderella, you filthy pervert," Decent said.

"She's older than that," Cinderella said. "Look at her. She's a giant."

I looked at Albert. He grinned. Decent pulled me up and away from Cinderella. She put her arm around me. "Cinderella, you can't tell time. How you know how old she is?"

They all laughed. Decent turned me loose. I sat down on the far end of the sectional. Decent poured drinks all around, put beers in people's hands, sat down beside me. She kicked Cinderella's feet off the coffee table. "Play something, Pickle," she said.

Pickle strummed his guitar, warmed up his low voice. He sang that prison song about being tortured thinking about people moving on. Then he sang that one about falling in the burning ring of fire, and then Decent sang "Make me an angel that flies from Montgomery." The blonde girl got down off the sectional and curled up on the strandboard floor. Keith Kelly sang "Sam Stone." I glanced over at him out of the corner of my eyes. No hat on, brown hair wavy and full there on the couch with them other men.

"You act like you're her lawyer, Decent," Keith Kelly said.

"Who?"

"That one," Keith Kelly said pointing at me.

"I aint her lawyer," Decent said. "I'm the judge."

The blondie girl woke up off the floor, laughed—"HA!"—and fell back to the floor.

"That's what I say," Crater said. "Ha."

"You laugh," Decent said, "but I know them girls got Cinderella put in jail. Dawn was right to get out of there. Them women diseased."

"We didn't catch no diseases," Cinderella said. "They wouldn't have nothing to do with us. They was trying to kill us."

"That's what I'm saying," Decent said, beer bottle bobbing on her knee, "no point waiting on yall."

Everybody laughed. Pickle Peters elbowed Cinderella, made him spill his beer into the sectional.

"Goddam yall," Priscilla said.

"That don't make it right to steal a man's car, nor another man's truck," Keith Kelly said.

"She was just having her a Thelma and Louise moment," Decent laughed.

"Decent, what are you," Keith Kelly said, "some kind of lezzie?"

"Do what?"

"You heard." Keith Kelly rose up. "You aint her momma. You aint her friend. And it's obvious she aint normal. I think you're doing her your own self."

I had heard all this before.

MANY A TIME -

"Why don't you shut your mouth." Oh, dear lord. Albert speaks.

"Where's your man, Decent Ferguson?" Keith Kelly said. The sleeping girl sat up again, big grin on her face, eyes dancing to see what happened next.

"Strong woman," Keith said. "I'll show you strong." Keith Kelly was drunker than I'd thought.

"Will you?" Decent said.

"Decent, don't," Priscilla said.

"Yall need to settle down," Crater said.

"I don't care to show you," Keith Kelly said, "not one bit."

Pickle Peters dropped his guitar. The strings went "bonnnng" through the hollow wood body. I leaned forward.

"Dawn," a voice came from behind me. "Dawn don't look right."

My vomit splattered on the pointy-eared dog, rained all over Keith Kelly. I threw up again. Everybody scattered, except for Decent and Priscilla.

"Here, honey." The bottle blonde put a bucket in front of me. "Aim for that, doll baby," she said.

"How much had she had?"

"I aint seen her drink nothing."

"That girl aint right."

I heaved again. The vomit came in strings. I don't know what it was or where it came from, but it sure felt good.

"I aint never seen nobody throw up smiling like that."

~~~~~~~~~

I WOKE up at Decent Ferguson's place, in her quilt-thick bed at the back of her little house dwarfed by its big-ass garden plot. She sat beside me on the bed, looked right at me.

"Why don't you talk to somebody about what's going on?"

"And say what?" I said.

"Well," Decent said, "You don't think you need to talk about car stealing and jumping off mountains to somebody?"

"That don't mean nothing," I said. "Bad day."

Decent's lips flatlined. "You reckon?"

Decent's eyes was brown. Her lips was great big. Her hands was meaty, red rough and raw. She sat with one foot propped on the other. I looked around Decent Ferguson's place. I could smell her bad sulphur water. It was in the clothes piled at the end of the bed and in every chair. She had animals made out of painted gourds on shelves near the ceiling looking down at me. Folded quilts heaped up in every corner, and Loretta Lynn album covers were tacked all over the walls. Fist City. Don't cat around with the kitty.

"So who would I talk to anyway?" I asked Decent Ferguson.

"Well," she said, "Let me think about it."

"Can I talk to you?"

"You can talk to me," she said. She didn't mean it. I could tell.

"Why won't my mamaw tell me what she's thinking?"

"Have you asked her?"

"Why do I have to ask her? I'm supposed to be the kid. Why do I have to ask to be raised?"

Decent Ferguson said she didn't know.

"You just need to do what is best for you," Decent Ferguson said. "There aint no heroes, no oracles."

"What's an oracle?"

"Like a fortune teller."

The space behind my eyes hurt. I said, "You're not helping me."

"I'm sorry."

The clock clicked over to twelve, over to Sunday morning. I started to cry.

"It's crazy," Decent said, "that anybody would ask me for advice." Decent got up and dug through drawers, ran her hand behind the stuff on top of her refrigerator. "Shit," she said, going through the pockets of coats and sweaters on hooks behind the kitchen door.

"What are you looking for?" I said.

"Cigarettes." She found a pack in a sweater pocket. Two left. She lit one and said on the inhale, "Maybe your aunt June, maybe that's where you need to go." Decent exhaled. "You remind me of her."

"How?" I said.

"I don't know," Decent said. She drew again on the cigarette, looking at me. "Around the eyes." I had my glasses off. "You're dark. Your eyes are always moving too. June's eyes were like that. Are, I guess." Decent drew again. The smoke swirled again. Always smoke in the air. Always forest fire season. Decent wiped her nose on the back of her hand. "So you seeing anybody?"

My heart dropped when Decent asked that. Decent was freedom to me. Not chained by man nor kid. She rode her own personality like it was a horse. She wasn't good looking. Lumpy face, crooked smile. But in that moment I saw I had to have a boy to have something to talk about. I didn't want a boy.

Decent took the last cigarette out of the pack and looked at it. She lay it on the table, rolled her fingers back and forth over top of it. "That's all right," she said. "I don't blame you. Not one bit." Decent Ferguson coughed, waved her hand in front of her face like she was waving away smoke, or bugs, but there wasn't neither one in the air in front of Decent Ferguson's face.

Decent Ferguson sat up that night and talked to me. She showed me where her arm was burned pulling records and quilts out of her last trailer fire. She explained to me who was in the pictures on her walls. There were black men with guitars and tambourines and groups of people wearing baseball gloves and shirts that said SPAM on them. There were always men in the pictures. Decent Ferguson pulled out a sweater she had made. It was a great big sweater and a blue I didn't like. But it was homemade and I liked that, and she put the sweater in a plastic bag and gave it to me which I liked too. I thanked her and set out for Mamaw's.

The snow turned to rain. Plain old rain. I walked through it in Decent's sweater, which felt like it could hold it all, every drop. The road was slick but not shiny, the only light shot out as usual. The rain came so hard I knew nobody was going to look out their windows, much less come out. It was going to rain on me and nobody else. No vehicles, only rain coming down like bucket after bucket of cat guts.

My clothes got so full of water, and I was so tired I felt like maybe I had turned to water, that I should just lie down like water, stretch out on that cracked black asphalt and drain away to the creek, to the bottom of the mountain. If it had been one degree warmer, that is what I would have done—just laid right down and turned to water and flowed right off that mountain. But as it was, it was too cold.

# 6

~~~~~~

# **WATERLIGHT**

I STRIPPED off my wet clothes on Mamaw's patio, stepped through the storm door, and stood on the mat in my underwear. Goose pimples popped up all down my arms, jumped to my legs, covered me up. I stood by Mamaw's bed, watched her sleep. Her mouth gaped in the lamplight like a dead woman's. Her breath was wind through the trees, rain picking up, drawing back, picking up again. I watched her breathe til I was satisfied she'd be there in the morning and went to my room. I turned on the radio, and Willett Bilson played a hippie song, a man singing about his heart's delight and how the thought of her made him cry. I had a heart's delight, which was Willett Bilson, which I wasn't likely to attain, and which wasn't going to make me cry. Not a drop.

Willett Bilson said he wanted contact. Said people should call him on the air. Said he had an e-mail address and people could e-mail him. I didn't know what e-mail was then. He gave the radio station post office address, and I wrote it down in my book where I stuck my pictures. Willett Bilson talked about the winter night, about the stars, about the beauty of every season, about the reasons he liked the bands he liked. His voice whistled through his nose, and I could tell he'd taken beatings. I could also tell he felt safe on the air. The sound of his voice come close on my ear like we were locked in the trunk of somebody's vehicle together. I looked at a page in my book where I had pasted a picture of a truck in India had three hundred suitcases strapped on top of it. I drew a

picture of myself next to it saying "Too much baggage," and next to that I taped
a picture of schoolgirls with AK-47s, a hawk with a rat in its mouth flying off a
cathedral, and three women gold miners from back in the San Francisco gold
rush days. Willett Bilson said, "My musical pleasure has no measure." I wrote
that out next to the pictures, and drew a picture of me saying "More punk rock.
Not so many hippie bands." I folded the page up in the shape of an envelope and
addressed it to Willett Bilson. I went to sleep with his music playing in my head.
And that is how I survived the Saturday of Thanksgiving weekend.

SUNDAY MORNING Mamaw was gone. Bed made. Dishes rinsed off.
Counter wiped down. Stacks made plumb. Generally Mamaw kept things
pretty junked up. Heaps of paper grew like spring flowers beside her bed, on
the couch, everywhere. Her mind ran hot, buzzed like a blow-dryer, taking
in information, calculating, talking on the telephone. Slow down to clean the
house and the assholes would run roughshod over America. There wouldn't
be nothing left. That's what she said. But a day of pulling her daughter out of a
tree and a night of waiting for me to get back from first Crater and Priscilla's and
then Decent Ferguson's must have took it out of her. She'd struck a lick getting
the house shipshape and then lit out through a cloud of dollar store pine scent.

Another morning, another empty grandparent's house for me. Didn't
matter. I was glad to hog up the morning sun at Mamaw's house. Where
she was on the ridge, and the way her house was angled towards back up
the river, the sun came straight through the windows soon as it topped Blue
Bear. I sat next to the front window by Mamaw's curled-up withered-out
houseplants and let the warm catch my face before it scoured out the dusty
house. My face glowed, and I was a superhero, an extraterrestrial, drawing
strength from the rays of my home star.

I hoped I could sit til the sun got up on the roof and not have to fool with
nobody. Just be myself. Think about anything I wanted. Willett Bilson.

My brother Albert hanging by his nose from a tenpenny nail. Anything. I set out thinking, started with Momma. I thought about why she drank and smoked and run around like she did. She couldn't settle. She couldn't get something or another right. I wondered what it was, wondered what was off inside of her. She was scared of something, running like an animal from fire.

But maybe it was the opposite. Maybe she was chasing something, something she'd lost. Like when Daddy died. Maybe she was running to keep from thinking, wind in her face blowing the things she didn't want to think about out of her mind. I didn't know. How would I? I was fifteen, and more of a kid fifteen than a grown fifteen.

The light angled in on the floor. I lay down on Mamaw's magenta wall-to-wall carpeting. The sun was orange against the inside of my eyelids. What goes on in your mind, Momma? I wanted to go see her, but I didn't want to go to Hubert's house. So I stayed at Mamaw's. And the house stayed quiet.

I went into the kitchen to see what Mamaw had to eat. Nothing. I went in my room and got out the envelope I'd made for Willett Bilson. It looked stupid. I wasn't going to send it. I dropped it on the floor, said if it landed with his address showing, I would mail it. It landed back side up. I dropped it again, which made me know I was going to mail it no matter what side it landed on.

I wondered had Mamaw gone to church. She did, every once in a while. She said she went when she'd forgotten how much it aggravated her. I didn't go, not ever. Just never had.

I never thought much about what happens to you when you die. I never even thought of Daddy in heaven.

In a bad way, mostly, because he was just a memory, getting fainter all the time, like pictures in a magazine left on the backseat of a car. But sometimes he came to me as a spirit, and he'd tell me what to do.

When I was a little girl, I never had a thing to say. Not that I remember. I think of myself wanting to be around loud sounds—loud music and machinery. I think of myself standing under the eave of my father's house, watching thunder and lightning, weather rared back on its hind legs. Loud noise natural I liked. Loud noise machine-made I liked. Loud noise human I could not abide.

I looked for Mamaw to come in the house any minute. I was ready to know had she gone to church or was she gone to the woods. Ready for her to tell me one wasn't no better than the other.

~~~~~~~~~

MOMMA CAME busting in the house through the front door while I was lying there on the magenta carpet. Nobody came in Mamaw's through the front door.

"God Almighty, Dawn," she said when she saw me. "Scare me to death, why don't you?"

Momma's wet hair soaked her sweatshirt shoulders and clumped together in thick strings like it might freeze.

"I thought yall were gone," Momma said.

I looked around for something. I don't know what. Something to give
Momma, I guess. A pillow? She looked like a person needed a pillow. She had
bruises on her neck and her bumpy blue wrists.

"What are you doing?" Momma said.

I shrugged. I really didn't know. "Nothing," I said.

"I doubt that," Momma said. She took off her sweatshirt. She had on a
too-small wore-out T-shirt with holes where the rest of the shirt was pulling
away from the neck. She sat down on the edge of a chair stacked with
newspapers, pulled out her cigarettes, and stopped when she remembered
where she was. "I come looking for my coat," she said.

"What coat?"

"That long leather one Hubert give me."

"Mamaw sent that back."

"You sure? Did you take it to him? When was it?"

Questions come out of Momma faster than I could answer them.

"Albert took it back last week," I said.

"Hunh," Momma said. She popped up out of the chair. "Come out
with me and smoke." She went through the kitchen on the way to
the patio, and pulled one of Mamaw's work
coats down from the hook behind the kitchen
door. Chair I'd knocked over on Albert was
still turned over on the patio. Momma sat in
the other one. I stood looking at her.

"Cold," Momma said.

"Mm-hm."

Momma looked me up and down. "Let's
go to Mexico," she said. She smiled her
crooked teeth at me. I knew she was fooling.

"Be nice," I said. It would have been. Me
and Momma. Take a vehicle from Hubert's.
But which one? They was all pretty shitty.
Nobody went to Hubert's to trade up.
Always down.

"Where'd your mamaw go?" Momma said, her shoulders rolled forward towards one another, hands between her mashed-together knees.

"I don't know," I said.

"She's been acting weird," Momma said.

Momma talked to me more and more every day like I was her sister. "What do you mean?" I said.

Momma shook her head. "She don't follow no pattern. Can't count on her for nothing."

"She better not've gone to town. She said she'd take me to town."

"Aint you full of piss and vinegar," I said.

"Ask her," Momma said. "She'll tell you."

I said, "Maybe she got sick of us."

"Maybe." Momma drew hard on her cigarette, looked at me squinty-eyed. "When do you go back to school?"

"Tomorrow."

She kept looking at me. "Are you ready?"

"Not really," I said.

"You need to do something with your hair," Momma said.

"Why?"

"Show them," Momma said.

"Show them what?"

"Show them," Momma said, "they aint broke you."

I HAD NO IDEA WHAT SHE WAS TALKING ABOUT.

"Dye it green," she said.

"That don't sound like a good idea," I said, but a smile come on my face.

"See," Momma said, pointing two fingers at me with a cigarette between them. "See. You know I'm right."

"You aint right."

Momma jumped up. "Come on," she said.

"Where?" I said.

"Hubert's."

"I aint going to Hubert's."

"Yeah you are. That girl Jan has a bunch of hair dye stuff left from Halloween."

"God amighty," I said. But I went with her.

~~~~~~~~~

HUBERT'S KITCHEN was way worse than when me and Albert'd put Momma to bed the night before. For one thing, the lights had all been knocked out.

"Hubert aint back from Virginia," Momma said.

"Is he still in jail?"

"Hell if I know," Momma said. "I hope not."

The light come in through cracks around the foil and cardboard over the windows. Most of the light come in through one fresh-busted window over the kitchen sink.

"Where are we going to do this?" Momma stood with her hands on her hips. She turned on the spigot. "We'll have to bleach it first."

"Maybe we ought to bust out another window," Momma said, "For the light."

I said, "We don't have to do this."

Momma stacked the dishes in the sink on down the counter.

"What are yall doing?" Big Jan stood in the doorway, puffy-eyed.

"Nothing," I said.

"Dyeing Dawn's hair green," Momma said.

"Awright." Big Jan slapped her palms together. She rubbed them back and forth, and I swear it smelled like meat cooking. She went and got two miners' caps with batteries and lamps. "Here," she said, handing one to Momma, "So's we can see."

"Where'd you get these?" Momma said.

"In trade."

"Hunh."

Momma and Big Jan hung the red batteries off their belts. The cables run up to the lights on their hard miners' caps. They both shined their lights on me.

"I don't know I got bleach enough for all that hair," Big Jan said.

"Should we cut it?" Momma said.

"No you aint," I said.

"Probably," Jan said. Momma and Big Jan looked at each other. "I'll get the scissors," Big Jan said.

"Get the clippers, too," Momma said.

Big Jan laughed down the hall.

"Fuck," I said.

"Quit your bellyaching," Momma said. "It's going to look cool."

Big Jan run back up the hall with her scissors. That's how it was at Hubert's. You couldn't pay a person to run unless they had something sharp in their hands.

"Sit up there," Jan said, pointing with the scissors at the table. I climbed up on the table, and she laid into me with a comb. "God Almighty," Jan said, "don't you never comb this mess?" She tried with the comb one more time and said, "I'm just gonna whack it off."

AND SHE DID.

She was still going at it when Momma said, "Let me in there," and fired up the clippers. Their machine noise soothed me, but Big Jan laughed louder than the clippers. She walked barefoot through my falling hair and the crushed glass of the busted-out light bulbs from the night before. Momma run the clippers up my neck, got it all bristly. Then they put the bleach to me. It went on like birthday cake frosting and burned like the candles.

While we were letting it work, Momma said to Jan, "I heard Cinderella about got his ass killed."

Big Jan said, "He's crazy. Me and you might act crazy, but that man is crazy."

"Yall cut off way too much," I said touching the back of my head.

"You don't know," Momma said. "You aint even seen it."

"Don't get that bleach on you," Big Jan said. "It'll fuck up your clothes for real."

I DUG MY FINGERNAILS INTO MY THIGHS.

"Let's smoke a bowl," Jan said.

Momma's head snapped around, made Jan blink when the mining light hit her in the face. Momma grinned and nodded, the light bobbing up and down. The bleach stunk so bad, I took a towel and put it over my nose. Jan unfurled a baggie, sprinkled the dried green weed into a paper's crease.

"I heard you been doing some tree climbing," Jan said.

"That I was," Momma said, "that I was."

"What was that about?" Jan said.

Momma shrugged and covered her face with her hands, the beauty draining out of her fingers a little bit every day. The bleach caused my eyes to water.

"I couldn't even put it in words," Momma said.

"I couldn't get up in a tree to save my life," Jan said. She ran the loose end of the rolling paper along her tongue. She twisted the ends. "Got too big."

"You aint big as Denny," I said through my teary eyes. "He's the one got her down."

"Well," Jan said sparking her lighter, "aint he the American Dream."

"I seen things so different," Momma said, looking towards the hole in the busted-out window. "It was like I could see things growing back." Tinfoil wagged in the winter wind at the edge of the window hole, sparkled in Momma's lamplight. "I could see how it would be in a thousand years, in a hundred thousand years. Trees growing huge, new dirt layering in, rain coming in drops big as beer cans."

"Bullshit," Jan said.

"You could understand the words the birds was singing," Momma said.

Jan took a hit off the joint. "What was they singing?"

"I don't know," Momma said.

"I thought you said you could hear it," Jan said.

"I could," Momma said, "but, but I couldn't."

Jan took the joint back from Momma. "That's fucked up."

"No, it aint," Momma said.

I couldn't stop my legs twitching. The bleach was eating me alive. It was chewing the skin right off the top of my head.

Jan pushed me back down on the table. "I remember one time," she said, her eyes starting to pull closed, "when we was little, Hubert stole my brand new fucking bicycle, bent one of the wheels. I lit a Roman candle and started shooting at him and run his bony ass up a tree. He said he wasn't coming down til I got over it. So I got me a gas can and set the motherfucker on fire."

"You set Hubert on fire?"

"Shit no. The tree. I set the tree on fire."

"Good God."

I said, "Then what happened?"

"Hubert come down and put it out. And when he got done," Jan set the joint down in a mayonnaise jar lid, "I beat the living snot out of him. Yall want some cookies? Them church people left a bunch of packs of cookies."

"Where they at?" Momma said.

Jan left.

"My head's burning off, Momma."

"You ready to dye?" she said.

"Yeah," I said, "something."

She dropped my head into the sink, turned on the water. This sounds stupid, but it felt religious the way she rubbed on my head with them rubber gloves.

Momma said, "That's the tree Hubert and his mother hid in when his daddy got too crazy."

Jan come back in the room. "Tell me something else," she said, setting me back on the table, slamming two boxes of double-fudge sandwiches down next to me. Momma turned the blow-dryer on me, but I could still hear Jan when she asked Momma, "Why'd you climb the tree in the first place? You climbing trees all the time? This something we need to be aware of?"

The joint sat angled into the jar lid on the other side of me from the cookies. Smoke drifted up my nose. The hair dye felt so good after the bleach.

"I was thinking about her," Momma said, and her lamplight fell on me. I could see her pointing at me through the glare. "I was looking for that place she fell."

"What for?"

"I had a dream Dawn turned into an owl. I woke up, went out there hunting her."

Jan picked the joint up out of the lid. "That shit right there is why I love getting high with you." Jan passed the joint to Momma, but I stuck out my hand and took it. Momma painted the dye into my hair with a mascara brush, and I drew the yellow smoke into myself.

"It won't be no bright green," Jan said.

"Darker," Momma said. "It will be darker." Then they laughed.

"You patch things up with Cora?" Jan said. Cora was my mamaw.

"She don't know I'm in the world," Momma said.

My head starting getting fuzzy. I wished I had something to drink.

"Here." Jan handed me a pop. My hand come out from under the cape and took the can.

"My mother," Momma said, "is too hard."

Hard like a rock, or hard like arithmetic?

"She makes everything too complicated," Momma said.

Jan nodded. She rolled another joint.

"I'm supposed to go to school tomorrow," I said.

"I know," Momma said, "that's why we're doing you this way." She waved her hands through the air like monster birds was attacking her. "So you'll be ready."

Jan smiled, struck fire. "Ready, steady, go," she said.

Momma dried my hair, and I was glad for the noise. I threw off the cape, which was smothering me. My hair was dyed, and Jan and Momma sat back satisfied, like two jungle cats after they've eat their fill of wildebeest. They sat there smoking cigarettes, eating missionary cookies. I stood up to leave.

"Where you going?" Momma said.

"You look like a guy," Fat Jan said as I was going out the door.

The night air hit the back of my neck for the first time in years. The night had warmed up, or the dope had warmed it up. I was out in the yard when I heard Jan say, "She aint never." Jan and Momma's cackles tore through the open door, through the hole in the window.

~~~~~~~~~~~~~~~~

I DIDN'T go back to Mamaw's. I decided to walk til my hair grew back long.
I turned off the road, down into the woods, towards town. Further I walked,
more I got scared I would run into Hubert in the dark. I tried to walk quiet.
I had picked up the smell of meat off Big Jan. I was sure to draw predators.
Hubert would drop down out of the low clouds, the winged monster bird I
had feared all weekend, gouge my eyes out with his beak, plunge his talons
into the meat of my shoulders, carry me off to tear to pieces and laugh over. I
knew that was dope talking, but knowing wasn't enough.

I wanted to be in school. Not my school. Some other school. A school
that was all pencil necks pushing glasses up their noses, sniffing their fingers,
smiling to see me come in the room, smiling to see me safe.

The road curved into my path. I stepped down into it. I passed into the
darkness of the big rock overhang. I felt someone lead me, an iron band, a
dog collar round my neck. But of course there wasn't. I felt someone jerk a
chain and draw me along. But of course they weren't. In the darkness of the
rock overhang, I coughed. Nobody answered. The road steepened down,
and my feet slapped against the blacktop. It did not feel late, but the houses
were dark.

When I stepped off the road again, the mountain swallowed me up.
Put the Jonah on me. The snow had melted. The tree limbs were wet and
heavy, the leaves underfoot wet and heavy. I went down the mountain a
way I had never gone. An owl hooted. The woods dripped. There was

light in the woods, but I couldn't tell where it came from. It seemed it
came from the water in the mountain. The total amount of water in the
mountain began to freak me out. I did. I freaked out about the water.
Stupid. I sat down on a fresh-fallen log. The wind crackled through
the leaves clinging to the limbs. Sounded like a clutch of old women
whispering at the back of a cold, empty church. The light was dwindly and
low, and I wished you were there.

Who?

Ha ha. I want you to know what it's like.

Maybe it wouldn't be Hubert I'd see. Maybe it would be ghosts. Indian
ghosts. Packing meat. Or ghost Indian braves moving fast and empty-handed,
running from some stupid massacre. Or maybe it would be some scared Civil
War boy ghost out there running. Not sure which side is which, only sure he'd
took a shot at somebody.

I stood up and every manly story I'd ever been told rushed through me.
I drew breath and sat back down on the fresh-fallen tree trunk. The train
on the tracks at the foot of the mountain sounded like a piano playing in a
cowboy movie saloon. I wanted somebody to tell me everything. Any of
them would serve: Decent Ferguson, Aunt Ohio, Mamaw, Momma, Jan. Sit
me down and lay it all out. The air went out of me, and I imagined a dog's
nose against the underside of my arm. I imagined my father, a big red hunting
dog, lying down at my feet.

I began to walk again and directly came into a backyard. A dog barked, and I heard a child talking excited, too late for a child. I veered into the woods and come to an eight-foot drop down to the old road into town. I skirted the rim of the drop until I come to a creek coming off the mountain same as me. I got down in the gulley and come under the road through a four-foot culvert. On the other side I knew where I was even though I couldn't see. A field opened out in front of me. It was the last beautiful bottom in Canard County, the last place to see how it was for the first white people, the last pocket pasture with its deep dark dirt, the last one that wasn't road, wasn't trailer park, wasn't cigarettes for sale, wasn't fucked-up mining equipment piled all archaeological. But this last one was going to be our new high school football field. I crossed the field, climbed the horse fence that bound it, thinking how if you, if I, had been a Cherokee, a Shawnee, we would have dreamed to see buffalo, to see elk, on that field and would have thought a farmer's field no better than a car wash.

I crossed the field, done thinking I could see my happiness by the wee hour waterlight.

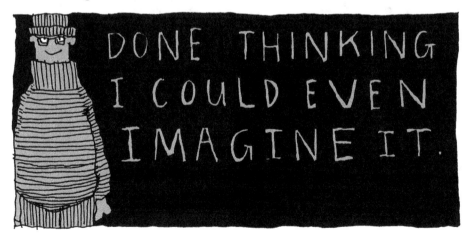

I come up on the halogen freakout of my glass-box high school, my shoes caked in yellow clay mud from the churned-up football field. I come across the twinkling black glass river on the Canard County version of some Paris bridge I'd seen in the fog on the television in a black-and-white movie I couldn't understand. I come up on the part of the parking lot where the buses brought kids from all over the county and set them out. There, in one of the long parking places marked off for buses, I fell flat on my face and slept, my arms spread, the pavement soft, my fingernails digging into the yellow paint.

# ACT THREE

~~~~~~~~~~~~~~~~~~

# BULLDOZER

# 7

~~~~~~

# HOMINY HEART

WHEN MY father said, "Take it like a man," I couldn't tell where his voice came from, face down like I was. The pavement pressed into my cheek, and the sun blistered my neck. I rolled onto my side, and my father squatted beside me, his beard loose and curly.

"I'm not a man," I said. "I'm fifteen. And a girl."

A cloud covered the sun, and his face came clear. His eyes were tired, the way they always were. "Don't give up," he said, reaching for my chin. "You hear me?" I nodded, and then I woke up. My father, of course, was still dead, and the only light stood on silver poles like low stars all through the high school parking lot. I put my head back down on the pavement and fell asleep. When I woke, it was still dark, but headlights moved above me, and a maintenance man, a fat one with a broad leather belt curled at the edges, stood over me with his hands at his side. He had no broom, no mop, nothing to do with, just biscuit in his moustache and the name "FURL" stitched on his dull green shirt.

"You want coffee?" he said.

An empty bus passed. Over top of Furl's boots, the treeline took shape in the morning light. "Yeah," I said, "coffee."

Furl said, "You want it out here?"

I got up, moving like my grandfather Houston when the liquor was gone.

"I seen you around here," Furl said. "They say you're smart. They say you do good on them testis." He rooted a bandana out of his back pocket and wrung runny winter snot out of his nose.

"I'd rather have hot chocolate," I said.

Furl put the handkerchief back in his pocket. "OK," he said, ducked his head, and waddled at a tilt towards an unmarked door. "You graduating this spring?" he said, turning the key in the lock, pulling the door open by the key.

"I'm a sophomore," I said.

"Well," he said, and went through the door, down a hall with a stripe of scraped-off paint halfway up either side. Inside the double door at the other end of the hall, a radio sounding like it had pie pans for speakers played "Love Is a Battlefield" by Pat Benatar. We are young. Heartache to heartache. A skinny man sprawled in a wheelbarrow blended into the rake handles and weedeaters. He was younger than Furl, and stared at me like he wanted to handle me, like he was already handling me with his ballpoint eyes.

He said, "What you brung us, Furl?"

Furl moved to the utility sink, ran water into a coffee mug, and put it into a nasty microwave oven. Furl locked eyes on the skinny man while the mug turned.

"Well," the skinny one said, tipping forward out of the wheelbarrow, "I'd say A.J.'d be needing me bout now fore he screws them heaters up totally." The wheelbarrow crashed back into place. I jumped and Furl poured gray-brown powder into the hot water. The skinny man eyed me on his way out.

"Here you go, Swiss Miss," Furl said, handing me the cup.

"Why you call me that?" I said.

Furl pointed at the chocolate packet, and I was embarrassed.

Furl got another mug off the shelf, poured him a cup of coffee, then stirred in hot chocolate powder. "You sleep out there all night?"

"Most of it," I said.

"That's the kind of thing I used to do," Furl said. "When I was drinking." Furl pointed at my green buzz cut. "Where'd you get that?"

"From my mom."

"Your mom got green hair?"

I looked at Furl to see if he was fooling. He grinned and stirred his coffee. I smiled too. The principal, Mr. McCarty, come in.

"Ms. Jewell," he said. "No students in the building til seven."

"It's—" Furl started.

"Ms. Jewell, please excuse us."

I stepped into the hall.

"I told you last time," McCarty said. "It was your last chance."

"Who—" Furl said.

"Don't worry who," McCarty said. "Get your things."

"Mr. McCarty, you don't have no idea."

"I'll meet you out front."

I was still standing in the long hall when Furl come by slow as church. McCarty came to the door.

"Not exactly coming back on the right foot, Dawn," McCarty said.

I walked after Furl, dropped my chocolate. When it hit the floor, the chocolate sounded like when somebody busts a blown-up paper bag. When I stepped out the door, the skinny one stood there smoking, doing nothing.

I said to him, "Rat."

"I might be doing you a favor," he said.

"Don't do me no favors, pencil dick."

He stubbed out his cigarette, said, "Least it's sharp," and went laughing through the door.

The night before I wished I was back at school, and there I was. I sat down on the curb and made a note to myself: no more wishing. Daylight came, dusting its gray-blue quiet lovely on the parking lot and the trees beyond. A shame, it seemed to me sitting there breathing hard in the cold, a shame a person had to go inside to school. What I wished was some mountain man in a fur coat for a teacher, who would take us out and teach us something—us, this grim parade of fatties and candy eaters, girls with brittle hair and green eyelids, mouth-breathing boys bent to the screens in their hands—I wished some grizzly beast would come take us out and show us the true facts of life—subject us to the elements, test us.

I was grinding my jaw over these things, no better than the rest of them bouncing off the buses like beachballs with bookbags, when a doughboy ninth grader Mamaw was trying to teach to read, a kid with a head like a green grape and wiry blond curls, came out of breath off my bus and set my bookbag down in front of me and stood there, gap-mouthed and weaving, wore out from the strain of packing my bag the four steps from the bus.

"What?" I said.

"Nothing," he said sniffing. "Cora sent you that."

I said, "You tell her thanks."

He tucked his chin into his neck, tilted his head, and said, "You tell her. You live with her."

"Get out of my face," I said.

He kicked the bookbag and walked towards the school. I turned to see him pull up his drooping pants, which fell straight back soon as he let go of them. A dog with no more going for him than that I would hit in the head with the back of a shovel, put him out of his misery, never think a thing of it.

A motor revved and Belinda Coates's pink Camaro ran straight over my bookbag. I cut through the parked cars to where she was circling through. She laughed in my face through the open window. Dirty nasty teeth. Belinda Coates thinks cause she has big titties and leaves them hanging out she don't need to take care of her teeth. I busted her right in the side of the head with my bookbag. Knocked that smile clean off her face. That was plenty satisfying, but the force of swinging my bookbag made me fall, and Belinda Coates circled again and come up behind me, and this time I just barely had time to throw the bookbag at the front of her car as she passed. "Treehugger," Belinda Coates said as she went by. I got up and flipped her off with both hands. Of course from there, it was back to McCarty's office with its giant "Friends of Coal" stickers and a lecture about how I was pissing away my talent. He thought if he said "piss" it would get my attention, I guess.

~~~~~~~~~~~

WHEN MCCARTY let me go, I sat in French class and drew a picture on my desk of me pushing Belinda Coates off the top of the Eiffel Tower until one of Ms. McKamey's flunkies handed out a quiz. It was multiple choice and over French words for food, mostly meat. **Boeuf. Canard.** Stuff like that. The name of our county meant "duck." And our school nickname was "Eagles." The retardation around here staggers the mind. Asshole Belinda Coates finished fast because she answered a-c-d-c over and over because AC/DC is her favorite band.

Evie Bright, my best/only friend, turned and asked me, "What's number seven?" I looked to Ms. McKamey. She was staring at her computer. I edged my paper to where Evie could see it. She pushed my arm away and moved my paper to her desk and copied all my answers.

After school, I was sitting waiting for the bus when the puffy frosted-blonde school counselor Ms. Cleek came by and said, "Scholarship interview day after tomorrow, Dawn."

"Do what?"

She said, "Thursday at ten, Dawn. Don't forget. If you really do want to go to art school, you need to be there."

I nodded and didn't look back at her shaking her head like I was some kind of waste of time, like I was a fool for wanting to go to art school. You should do something more practical, more *realistic,* I could hear her saying. Fuck her. Fuck you, school counselor, wherever you are tonight. Fuck you.

I fell asleep on the bus without anybody putting anything in my hair, a blessing, thank you Jesus, and when I went home, Mamaw didn't say anything, another blessing, thank you Jesus, and I went in my room and fell asleep drawing, a yellow pencil dragging across paper as I went unconscious.

---

NEXT DAY, Ms. McKamey handed out the graded French tests. When Evie got hers, she hollered, "ZERO?" because Evie didn't care what people thought. Evie's paper had a long note written in red and French. "What does this say?" she turned and said to me.

"Says you cheated and she knows it. Says I should tell you not to cheat off me."

"What'd you make?"

I showed her my zero. I looked at Ms. McKamey smiling a sad smile. I wanted to punch Ms. McKamey even though she used to like me. I wanted not to care she thought I was a redneck cheater. Belinda Coates cackled on the other side of the room. "Forty better than you," she said, holding up her paper with its 40.

Ms. McKamey looked up from her papers and said, "Dawn, Evie, I need to see you after class." The bell rang and the black-eyed hen Belinda Coates cackled. Evie didn't stay after class. She headed straight for the door. "Evie," Ms. McKamey said.

"You can tell her whatever you was going to tell me," Evie said, and slammed the door shut.

"You don't have to carry her," Ms. McKamey said.

I didn't say anything.

"Do you hear me?"

"Can I go?" I said, and then, "yes." I thought Ms. McKamey would take my hand, but she didn't. She just nodded. I went out Ms. McKamey's door and ran straight into some football team quitters. They pulled back like they was scared to touch me. My ears rang. I went back to my locker, and even though the hall was packed I sat down, my back to the locker. I got out my math book, worked a geometry problem right in the margin.

"Witch."

I looked up and there was Belinda and two of her cronies. The second one said to Belinda, "She looked at you."

"Better shut up," the first one said, "or she'll witch you down in that pop can." They all three laughed.

In that moment I had a vision, and in my vision I waved my hand and the school doors locked and chains weaved through the door handles. Combination locks flew shut on the chains. I waved my hand again and Belinda's pink Camaro flew up out of the parking lot and landed on its T-top in the river. I waved my hand and I was on a broom laying napalm down the halls of the school. I dropped my cigarette and the school burst into flames. Belinda and her friends screamed and I flew off on my broom, laughing my head off.

When I came out of my vision, Belinda was up in my face, her eyes red, her eyeliner blue. Belinda licked her lips. "Freak," she said. I was ready to go on and get into it. Another suspension wouldn't mean much. Stupid girls. One of the girls was redheaded. Her shirt was too small, and her belly showed underneath her jacket. "Go die, freak," she said. Belinda stepped toward me. That other girl, who had real stressed blonde hair, came at me too. The redheaded girl fell in behind me. I was a head taller than all of them, but I couldn't figure out how to whip all three at once. "I aint like yall," I said.

I had my fists balled up ready to go when Evie came tearing down the hall behind Belinda and put the flat of her hands between the blondheaded girl's shoulder blades. Blondie's hands flew out in front of her, and she went down on her face. Kids walking down the hall veered out of our way. Some stopped to watch. "Get your asses away from her," Evie said. She shoved the redheaded girl into the lockers. Evie held her hands out from her side, like a gunfighter. She looked dead at Belinda and said, "What are you looking at, cow?" and when Belinda didn't say anything, Evie added, "Fucked up stoner cow."

That was enough for me. I was over it, ready to get on out of there. "Come on, Evie," I said.

Evie shoved Belinda in the chest. "Fight her, fight me." She shoved her again. "Cow."

I pulled at Evie's arm. "Come on."

Belinda smiled. "That's right," she said. "Go on. Go on, lesbian witch skanks."

Evie jerked her arm loose from where I held her and buried the tips of her fingers in the underside of Belinda's chin. Belinda's chewing gum flew out of her mouth. I had to laugh. Belinda gagged and doubled over. Evie got a handful of her hair and twisted it, and Belinda's knees bent and her head turned to keep Evie from tearing her hair out. Evie walked Belinda down the hall like that, and every time Belinda tried to rise up, Evie jerked her hair, give it a twist, and Belinda would holler and give. I saw what Evie was going to do. She was going to throw Belinda down the stairs. I said, "Evie," and ran to her. I threw my arms around her. My arms were still around her when McCarty clapped a hand on our shoulders. Belinda sloshed onto the floor like spilled mop water.

~~~~~~~~~~~~

"YOUR BROTHER going with anybody?"

When McCarty kicked us out, me and Evie went back up behind the school where kids went to cut. There wasn't anybody there, and we sat in broken lawn chairs patched with beer cartons. There was a fire pit filled with burnt aluminum cans. Evie was trying to start a fire with sticks and the chapter on the Depression out of her social studies book.

"No," I said.

Evie shook her head and poked the fire. Her thin fingers ended in yellow smoker's nails. "I hate them girls," she said. "They can't stand it when people don't give a shit about them." She poked the fire some more. "Damn cows." She threw down her fire-poking stick. She took up a topic she'd raised on the way up the hill. "Why don't you like vampire movies?"

"They're all right," I said.

"I love them."

I hated them. I threw some twigs I'd been fiddling with into the fire.

Evie said, "You see that one where the woman's husband don't know she's a vampire and tries to talk her into having a kid?"

I put my hands out to warm at the fire. "How come vampires can't have kids?"

Evie stopped poking the fire. "Uh, because they're dead."

"Then how come—" I didn't finish.

Evie said, "I always get kicked out of school on Thursdays."

"Why?"

"Don't know. Just do."

I said, "You don't do it so you can have a long weekend?"

THURSDAY IS MY BAD DAY, SHE SAID.

Evie's fire began to crackle. She fed it from her pile of sticks. The school made a buzzing sound, and kids came out punching and shuffling, papers flying loose and pop cans clattering on the pavement. The buses pulled away, and the people on the sports teams straggled back to school to practice. When Evie's hand touched mine, all I could think to say was, "What do you see in Albert?"

She rubbed her thumb across the back of my hand then let it go. "Nothing, I don't guess," Evie said. Evie's fire got bigger, like something in Hawaii, huge pig-roasting hula-girl fire. Evie dragged a pallet over and threw it on, wood not meant to burn. The pallet snuffed the fire a little bit, and the cold on my back seeped into my arms.

"Albert don't never get tired," Evie said.

"Cause he don't do nothing," I said.

"Yeah he does," Evie said.

The pallet caught, the sparks rising into the trees.

"Then why you holding my hand?" I said.

"I don't know," Evie said. "Cause you need somebody to hold your hand."

I thought to say, "Who told you you know what I need?" but I didn't.

"Jesus," Evie said. "Aint no point in getting all weird."

"I don't know."

"Yeah you do," Evie said, standing up. "We're gonna get the Samson twins from Slope and beat the shit out of Belinda and them."

The flames danced like a carnival ride. "I don't think I am," I said. I was tired of it, tired of fists up. Tired of no talking til yelling. I wanted murmur-by-the-fire talking, whisper-in-the-cold talking. Evie got a box of oatmeal creme pies out of the truck and set it between us. She handed me a pie. I didn't want it, but I ate it anyway. We sat and talked until the sun dipped into the treeline and its rays came long and low and lit our faces like candles. Evie got a pint of vodka and poured it into a half bottle of Sunny D, and we sipped on that easy and slow until we laughed. The fire burnt down to embers, so we kicked dirt on it, got in Evie's Cavalier, and drove away.

NEXT MORNING, I sat in Mamaw's kitchen staring at the sticky plastic tablecloth the color of baby food peas. My eyes felt like balloons. Mamaw came down the steps in new yellow sneakers.

"You ready for your scholarship interview?" She passed behind me, smelling of menthol rub.

"I can't go," I said.

"Yes you can," Mamaw said. She set the skillet on the stove eye.

"No I can't," I said.

Mamaw cut a wad of butter into the skillet. The butter began to sink. "Why not?" she said.

"I got suspended."

Mamaw turned to me, a jar of hominy in her hands. "For what?"

"Fighting."

Mamaw emptied the jar into the skillet. The hominy sizzled and popped in the skillet. When it settled down, Mamaw slid a spatula under it, laid it out on a plastic plate, and set it in front of me. Then she went out to smoke. I shook black pepper out on the hominy. Mamaw came in and kissed me on the forehead. She ran her hand through my stiff green hair. I didn't want Mamaw's hand on me. I didn't want the apple smell of her pipe tobacco up my nose either.

"I'm going up on the hill," Mamaw said.

I nodded.

"You fold the clothes," she said. "All right?"

"Yes, ma'am," I said.

Mamaw pulled the door shut behind her. There were three straight pins lying on the table. I used one to flip a piece of hominy out on the cloth.

I said, "That's your eyeball, Belinda Coates." And I struck a straight pin in the loose piece of hominy.

I said,

I stuck another pin in the hominy. "Laugh with two pins stuck in your eyeball." I stuck another pin in Belinda's hominy eye and went back to eating, blind Belinda's screams music to my ears. When I got done, I went down in the basement. I took our clothes out of the dryer and folded them on the washer. It was cold and damp in the basement, and it made my head hurt worse. I hate winter. To tell you the truth, I don't have a favorite season. Don't have a favorite month. Don't have a favorite day of the week. I heard something sounded like thunder, and then a pecking sound. I went upstairs. Hubert shifted his weight through the clear crystalline contact paper over the windows in the kitchen door. I opened the door. Hubert had shaved since last I seen him.

"Hello there, Dawn."

I let Hubert in Mamaw's house. He crossed in front of me. His clothes smelt sour and slept in. Hubert leaned back against the kitchen counter.

"I see you, see," Hubert said. He put his finger to his eye and then pointed at me. "I see you." I thought there must be some kind of new drug out. Hubert's heard about it at jail and gone out and got him some. "I want you," he said and I got stomach sick, heaved like I was gonna puke.

"Not like that," Hubert said. "No. God no. Not like that."

Crazy thing was I got offended by the way he said, "God no."

Hubert said, "I need you to work."

"No, Hubert."

"You need to work. You got a head for it. And you got the nerve." He ducked his head so I had to look him in the eye. "Grand theft auto," he said, the gaps in his smile showing. He pointed at me again. "You are a part of this," he said.

I'm not.

"Besides," Hubert said, "you owe me. You wrecked my car."

I said, "That Delta 88 was junk and you know it."

"Yeah, but they was thirty-eight cases of beer in the trunk."

"Then go get it."

"I did. It froze."

"Then go get you some more."

"I figure between the beer and the car you owe me seven hundred dollars."

"Well, that's too bad." I thought a second. "It's what you get for kidnapping."

"We was taking you to the hospital."

"Law me then. I'll tell the judge you tried to make me have sex with Cinderella."

Hubert smiled and Mamaw rattled the door coming in.

"Well," Hubert said, "I'll tell your mother you said hey." He nodded at Mamaw. "Miz Redding."

"Hubert," Mamaw said as Hubert slipped out the door. Mamaw stood at the kitchen sink, watched out the window as Hubert pulled out. She shook her head. Then Mamaw squirted dish soap on the skillet and said, "The little hen said, 'Who will help me hoe the corn?'"

I stood at the table and jabbed a stray piece of hominy with my fork. I thought to myself that right there is Hubert's heart, soaked in poison til it cracked, puffed up, turned pale. I took a pin out of Belinda's eye and stuck it in Hubert's heart, picked it up by the pinhead, and held it to the window light. I closed one eye. Hubert's heart floated next to the back of Mamaw's head.

"You all right?" Mamaw said.

I sucked the piece of hominy off the pin. I ground my teeth and swallowed. It hit me it was my heart, not Hubert's, on the pin. Mamaw turned and looked at me like she didn't have no idea what got into me.

Who will help the little hen harvest the corn?

Not I.

The phone rang and Mamaw picked it up. When the call was over, Mamaw walked out of the kitchen. She came back in, got her pocketbook, and opened the door.

"Where you going?" I said.

"Betty seen your momma at Walmart." She tapped on the doorknob and looked at me like a woman in a play who can't remember what her line is. "I'll be back," she said.

When she was gone, I wandered the house. I pulled an envelope packed thick and hand-addressed to me out from her mail pile. It was a letter written in the most sprawled-out handwriting I had ever seen. The letter was fifty pages long.

~~~~~~~~~~~~~~

Dear Dawn,

Thank you for your letter. You asked me a bunch of questions, which I greatly appreciate. Curiosity is a dying art, and it gives me heart to see one such as yourself reach out to another human being known unto them only as a voice on a radio. I have decided to set down on paper my answers even though I am increasingly a digital man. In order to achieve proper flow, I will start from the beginning, even if it means telling you things you already know. If this does not seem a fit way to proceed from your perspective, you are well within your rights to stop reading now, or at any time during the following narrative, and I will understand.

All right. Still with me, I see. Then onward:

My name is Willett Bilson. I live in Kingsport, Tennessee. Kingsport is known as the Model City, because it was built with a plan. The plan is hard to see now, especially if you haven't been told about it your whole

life. Kingsport was built around the time of World War I. The people
with the plan laid out the city right before the railroad came through.
They recruited a bomb plant and a paper mill and a chemical plant for
everybody to work at. And even now today we still have a bomb plant
and a paper mill and a chemical plant. Some plan!

My mother grew up in Kingsport. My father did not. He grew up
across the line in Virginia. His father was a storekeeper. My father works
at the chemical plant. It's the biggest of all Kingsport's plants so people
just call it "the plant." My father has cancer and is off work at times,
sometimes for a long time. He works in the warehouses when he is
able. My mother's father worked at the plant. He was an office man. My
momma's daddy made plenty of money at the plant. Plenty, my daddy
says. Momma's daddy got my dad his job at the plant.

When I was in high school, I was on the basketball team. I was the
manager. I kept the scorebook, the statistics. And then I went away to
college. My mother saw to that. She wanted me to to maximize my
potential. One day when I was in high school, she came home from her
women's meeting and came in my room. I was listening to music and
straightening out my scorebooks, refreshing my memories of important
games. She said I was going to make myself deaf with the volume so
loud. I said, "What did you say?" Ha ha. My little joke.

She told me one woman's girl was going to this one school. This other
woman's boy was going to that other school. And this other one's girl
applied to fourteen different schools. She told me I had better get busy
or I wasn't going to have any options. She told me if I didn't get on the
stick, I was going to get left OUT!

On the stick, what does that even mean? I thought about that while I
was sitting on the commode, where I always end up after one of Momma's
advice sessions. I have a troubled colon. When I got out of the bathroom,
Momma had websites pulled up of different colleges and she asked me did
I like this one, did I like that one? They all looked fine. The people on them
all looked fakely happy, so it was hard to know. They should sneak up
on people when they take pictures for those websites. Then it would be
easier to tell what the places were really like for people.

I don't know if I was smarter than the children of my mother's
friends, but not a one of them made better grades than I did. People
always used to look off my paper when we had tests. I acted like I
didn't care, so I wouldn't get pounded and made fun of quite as loud.
Sometimes the teachers would catch us cheating and I would get
separated from the people cheating off me, but I would always get to
stay where I was and the people cheating off me would have to go sit

by the teacher. Which seemed strange to me, because if the teacher moved me, that would have stopped more cheating. But the teachers never did move me.

One night a man with a bow tie came to our house after supper. He had gone to high school with Mom. He was a lawyer and had wavy hair, and he set me up a scholarship interview at the college he had gone to in North Carolina. My mother smiled and said, "What do you say, Willett?"

I said his college was third in the ACC that year, which I meant as something good. But my mother said, "Willett!" and I knew I had missed that question, but the man still set up the interview in three weeks, and in that time Mom worked hard to help me not breathe through my mouth so much. I had to use a nasal rinse five times a day every day those three weeks. She said I didn't look too smart sitting there with my mouth hanging open. Which I understand, but I have a hard time thinking when I don't get my oxygen.

The day of the interview the air in the room was full of oxygen, and so I got my scholarship and the next year I went to college. I was excited when my parents drove off and left me, mostly because of music. Mom never let me go to shows or concerts or things like that when I was in high school, so I was ready to rock and roll. To par-tay. I thought the music would be good at college. But it wasn't. And the other thing was everybody there wanted to be popular and not look too different than anybody else. Which was not an option for me. And then the school wasn't much bigger than my high school, and most of the uncool people were all smiling and Christian. And people seemed to have so much money. I wasn't poor, and I didn't have a car, but long as I kept my scholarship Mom would send me money if I asked for it. But I was going crazy because I couldn't find people to be with. I couldn't get started.

Then one Friday afternoon I was sitting in a room in the student center with big sleepy chairs and barely anybody in there and this awesome music was playing. I'd had seven pork chops for lunch, fat and all I ate, and so I was sitting there burping and letting off steam so to speak, and they were playing some kind of ska punk and I was so happy. My head started rocking back and forth, and pretty soon I forgot about my unfortunate colon, but then somebody somewhere changed the music to some superbland "rock." Made me so sad. I started feeling rumbles in my gut and I thought well, I'll just go sit in the bathroom for a while, the bathrooms in that building were in the stairwells, green and quiet. I stood up and somebody yelled, and I quote here, "FUCK," and I turned around and there was a blackheaded girl in a chair with her back to me and she was almost as fat as I was and she stood up and said, and again I quote, "WHAT THE FUCK??" and she had an L7 shirt on, which is a good band from the 90s, and she stomped out of the room, out into the front hall of the building, and by the time I got to where she went, she had climbed up on the information desk and lay down and said she wasn't moving until they changed the radio station back and that that was the student station it had been on before and the girl at the info desk said, "Well, I'm a student and what they play on the student station sucks." And the other girl rolled over on her back, laid out on the information desk, and shook her legs and shoulders, messed up all the flyers for free movies and prayer groups and hiking clubs, messed them up good, and then rolled off the counter back there on the other girl's side and stuck her finger in the information girl's face and said, "What sucks is you—sorority suck girl—suck is you. Suck. Is. You." What she said didn't make any sense—unless you liked that music that was on before they changed the station. And if you did, what she said made total sense.

Then the fat girl climbed back over the counter, and I don't mean to call her fat, that was just the difference between her and the other girl, and she stopped in front of me. "What's the matter with your lip?" she said to me.

I pulled my lower lip in. I hadn't realized how close I was to drooling. "Nothing," I said.

"Where'd you get that shirt?" she asked me.

I had on a Smiths shirt. "Knoxville," I said.

She looked me up and down. "Do you have your license?" she said.

"Driver's license?"

"Yeah, doughboy. Your driver's license."

"Yes."

"You want to go to a show tonight?"

"Yes."

She took me to this little house place in Greensboro. Everyone there was weird and I know they didn't go to my school. And the band that played was so good. They were younger than us, than me and Brittany, that was the girl's name. They were young, but their hair was caveman long, and they swung it in spirals and never cracked a smile, never took a break, never said foolish things between songs, never took a guitar solo. They were just real good. And I wanted to call my brother Kenny and tell him about where I was, wanted to call him so bad, but I knew he would just tell me to live it up and so I banged my head and when Brittany jumped in the mosh, I did too.

I had the best time of my life. I had got to where I wanted to be, and Brittany took me there. And September October November of that year, she did all the drinking and created all the commotion and I didn't have to do anything but drive and she figured it all out for me. And so it was hard when Brittany told me she was changing colleges right before I went home for Christmas. And when I got back from Christmas she was gone. But she had changed me, and I could do for myself a little better it seemed.

The week of Thanksgiving my sophomore year, Momma called me home early. She cried on the telephone. Dad was taking chemo and was real sick again. She thought I should come home. She didn't say so, but she wanted me to come because she thought it might be the end. I was on my radio show when she called. By that time I was assistant student manager of the student radio station, the same one brought me and Brittany together.

I came home on Monday night. My dad had been sick like he had been before, but this time it was worse. Five rounds of chemotherapy, six more to go when I got home. I didn't have to do anything when I got there, just be there. My dad was a supervisor in a warehouse. They stored and shipped filter tow, which is the raw material for cigarette filters, which they shipped to the cigarette factories in the town where my college was. Was. Where my college was. I never went back to college after that time my dad got sick. He got better, but I never went back. I took some classes at the community college, but I never went back to North Carolina. Never finished college. That year and a half in North Carolina seems like a dream now. It seems like I never went.

My father had two sons with his first wife, my half-brothers Kenny and Ray. They grew up in Virginia and live there now. Kenny, he drives down every day to work in in a production unit at the plant, runs an extruder, Kenny does. He is my total idol. I love my dad, but Kenny, he was in bands. He was/is like a rock star. When I was little Kenny was still in high school. He played all the sports and he was my idol because of that too. I would sit in his room in the attic of the house he grew up in in Virginia—and I would listen to records with Kenny and he would try to figure out how to play the songs on his own guitar and it was just the best.

Kenny tore up his knee during his senior football season trying to stop a boy a hundred pounds heavier than he was, and that was pretty much the end of his sports career. He was a mess for a while after that. He turned sour. When he would come home from college, Mom really didn't want me hanging around with him, but there was a lot of times he wouldn't even come home for Christmas or whatever, but when he did he would always have lots of records and tapes. Tapes mostly. It was the 80s. And sometimes he would bring guys from his bands and they would hang out with my papaw before he died. Because my papaw, we called him Pap, he played music. Old music. "It's a world of wonders," that's what my pap always said. Pap always wanted Kenny to play the old music. "Pick it like Mother Maybelle," Pap always said.

Pap was already dead when Dad got sick the first time and Kenny came home to stay. When Kenny came home, he did something him and Papaw talked about doing a hundred times, talked about doing for as long as I could remember. Kenny started a radio station. Up on Bilson Mountain, where Pap's people had been for 150 years.

Dad survived the treatments and is even working some, and so I am kind of at loose ends. I started sitting with Kenny on his radio shows, and then I would do shows of my own mostly late at night, and a lot of times when I did that I would just spend the night over at Kenny's house he built on the big bald on the top of Bilson Mountain where he had grown up and Dad and Papaw had grown up.

So there it is. I came to the radio station, and there's where I heard you, and you heard me, and now we are writing to each other. I suppose this seems like way too much of a letter, but since you have read this far, I will just tell you, devil may care, caution to the wind: I love the sound of your voice. "Fuck you"—you said it in that interview you did with Kenny. I think you thought Kenny had the tape recorder off. "What I'd like to say to them is, 'Fuck you,'" is what you said. I was transferring that tape to the editing tape and I heard that and I about lost it. It sounded so good. I know it will sound weird to say, but I was like, man, I'd like to hear her talk to me like that. That's the kind of girl I get on my mind, that I have imaginary talks with, and I can't get them off my mind. I guess maybe I'm still hung up on Brittany. But anyway. Do you ever come to Tennessee? Do you have e-mail? It would be easier for me to write more if you had e-mail.

Anyway. I will let it go at that. That is plenty to put out. Which is what she said. Ha ha.

Your friend (hopefully),
Willett Bilson

PS: My email address is punkrockwarlord@netscape.com

I DECIDED TO GET A CAR AND GO SEE THIS WILLETT BILSON.

I took a job at Kolonel Krispy, which is where everybody in Canard County goes for milkshakes and fried chicken and doughnuts and such. The last day of my first week was a Sunday and a lady about forty with gentle eyes and straight hair was training me how stuff went in the freezer when Momma walked in and sat down in a booth back where the plumbers and carpenters smoked and ate their biscuits. Momma waved at me to come sit by her. I shook my head no. She waved again. The woman training me said it was OK to go.

Momma said, "I need the car." Mamaw let me use her Escort to go to work.

"So do I," I said.

Momma lit a cigarette, drew on it with slitted eyes, exhaled, waved the smoke from in front of her face, and said, "Give me twenty dollars."

"No," I said. Momma pounded her hands on the table, cussed me, slapped the salt and paper shakers on the floor. She slapped her hand on the table.

"Give me them keys," she said. And I did. That night, at the end of my shift, the boss lady paid me, thanked me, and told me it might be best if my mom didn't come to see me at work anymore. I went out into the dark and looked at my check. Seventy-nine dollars. I folded it up, stuck it in my pocket. I went back in the restaurant and called Hubert to come get me.

I walked across the highway to the supermarket. When Hubert got there, I went to get in the cab, but he had three other guys in the front seat. They were one big wad of hairy arms and ball caps, so I climbed in the back. We pulled out in a cloud of exhaust, and I lay down in the truck bed, trying to keep from freezing to death. When we got back to Hubert's place on Long Ridge, we bounced into the rutty, rocky yard, and the men piled out and bumbled in the house. I was so cold I could barely move. At least a dozen men were crowded onto the porch staring at sausages grilling on a sawed-off drum. I slid through them, trying not to touch them, and stepped over a man in coveralls passed out on his stomach inside the front door. I walked down the hall to the room where Hubert kept his computer. I started it—Windows 98. Hell yes. While the modem chirped and pinged, the front door slammed and men and women yelled. The door slammed twice more. Everybody in the house came running down the hall past where I was sitting and out the back door. Two sheriff's deputies came down the hall, guns drawn. When they saw me, they turned and went back to the front of the house. They left, taking the passed-out man with them. I started my e-mail program. Hubert and the rest filed back in. Momma was with them. I ignored her. The pictures Willett sent me of himself made me smile. He was a lot cuter than I thought he'd be. I typed, "That's a good picture."

Willett typed back, "Thanx."

We typed back and forth and the most relaxing calm came over me. Hubert walked past, looked in on me. Then he went into the bathroom across the hall. That trailer was so small it felt like he was in the room with me. Hubert's brother Filbert hollered from the front of the house, "Hubert! Tell Dawn her turn's over."

Momma yelled from the other end of the trailer: "You leave her alone. She's doing her homework."

The door to the bathroom was still open. Hubert was sitting on the commode with his pants down. "You be off of there by the time I get out," he said, and pushed the bathroom door shut.

I typed to Willett, "Is that the real Chewbacca in the picture with you?"

"One of them," Willett typed back.

Filbert come huffing and puffing up the hall. "Hubert, Dawn's using up the Internet."

"Goddammit, Filbert," Momma hollered from her room. "Watch one of your goddam videos."

Hubert came out of the bathroom and kicked over a pile of CDs. "Get off," he said.

"Don't do that," Willett typed.

"Filbert," Momma yelled, "Why don't you go get something real?"

"Why don't you come sit on my face?" Filbert said.

Hubert left the room, went back to where my mother was. "Can I poison their dogs?" I asked Willett.

"Don't do that, either," he typed back.

Filbert came and gouged a Phillips head screwdriver in my ear. I took a swing at him without ever taking my eyes off the computer screen.

"Just save your money," Willett wrote.

Filbert gouged again. I swatted at him. Then I balled up my fist and punched him in the arm.

"Buy you a car," Willett wrote.

"If I had a car," I wrote, "I could run over them."

Filbert kept on gouging. I kept on swatting, still wouldn't look at him.

"If you had a car," Willett wrote, "you could come here."

I snatched the Phillips head from Filbert. "If I came down there," I typed, "would it be just you and me?"

"Just you and me," Willett wrote, "and my action figures."

Filbert came at me, and I stabbed him with a sharp downward motion, drew some meat, and flung the screwdriver down the hall after his retreating ass. "That," I typed, "sounds like heaven."

Momma laughed loud and unpleasant. I told Willett goodbye, logged out of the e-mail program, and left Hubert's house.

~~~~~~~~~~

MAMAW WAS asleep when I got back to her house. I came through the kitchen and went down the hall to my room. I took the check out of my front pocket and got down on my knees in front of the closet. I dug through a pile of shoes and clothes and picked up a basketball shoe. It smelled terrible. I pulled up the insole and stuck my check under it. I picked up a notebook and flipped through the pages. The notebook was going good, filling up with drawings and collages of stuff I cut out of magazines. I turned to a blank page. I found a pencil and drew two heads. Momma's laugh from the back of Hubert's rang in my head. She used to have a pretty laugh. I scratched out the two heads. I closed my drawing book, turned off the lights, and lay back on my bed. The past came in on me like the smell from a busted sewer line. I fell asleep thinking about the day Dad died. I woke when I heard Momma rooting in my closet. The lamp came on and Mamaw was in my room. Momma was holding my check. I sat up in bed. "Momma?" I said.

"Put that down," Mamaw said. "And get out of here."

Momma closed her hand on the check and tried to bull past Mamaw. Mamaw clamped down on her arm and snatched the check away from her.

"Please, Momma," I said.

Momma's face was gray and damp. "You don't care," Momma said to Mamaw. Mamaw stared at Momma and Momma stared back. Momma blinked. "Fuck you," Momma said. "You fucking bitch. You never cared."

"Momma," I said. "Stop."

Momma said, "You don't care if I die out there."

That's when I started sobbing. Mamaw looked at me, and Momma snatched the check from her and ran out the door. Mamaw grabbed Momma's arm and Momma knocked her hand away.

"Stop," I hollered.

Momma knocked Mamaw to the floor and ran out. I ran to the bathroom and locked myself in. I rocked on the commode and cried.

Mamaw said, "Don't cry. Darling, don't cry. That aint your mother. It's that dope."

I wailed so loud the pictures on the wall rocked in their frames.

# 8

~~~~~~

# A THING BOILS UP

ONE TIME when I was eight years old, back when Dad was still alive, I drew a giant baby eating pickup trucks like they were candy. The people in the pickups screamed, and the baby smiled. The day I drew that, Momma was leaning against the kitchen counter. It was May, and Momma was on the phone. She moved the phone from one side of her head to the other, pushing strings of hair behind her ears. Her voice sounded like tennis shoes going round and round in the dryer. I loved that sound.

I was lying on my stomach between Momma and the front door. My sock feet swung in the air. Momma hung up the phone and grabbed hold of my ponytail. "Come on, Dawn," she said. "Time to pick up my flowers."

"What flowers, Momma?" I said.

Momma rooted through the spark plugs and mustard greens on the kitchen counter until she found the truck keys. "I won that contest at the hardware store," she said. "Hundred dollars of flowers for a prize. Aint that something?"

I changed crayons. "When did you enter a contest?"

"I didn't," Momma said. "Hubert entered me."

I was only eight, but I knew that didn't sound right. "Uncle Hubert entered you in a contest?"

"Come on," Momma said from the front door. "Hubert said he'd help us plant tomorrow if we went tonight."

I pushed my glasses up my nose and put on my tennis shoes. The pickup was running and Momma was wearing out the horn as I came down the trailer's cinder-block steps. I knew Momma wanted me to get excited, but I was like Dad. I didn't get excited. I climbed in the truck, and before I got the door shut, Momma was bouncing down the ruts in the yellow-clay drive onto the gravel road. The steep hillsides off either side of the road flashed in the gaps between the dark green tangle of the woods. The truck twisted along, past houses with roofs standing even with the road—one here with a hula hoop on it, one there with dandelions in the gutter.

"A hundred dollars," Momma said. The truck picked up speed going downhill, and Momma jerked the wheel to avoid the deeper ruts. She stood on the truck's brake pedal when the ridge road met the two-lane blacktop that led down the mountain to town. "God Almighty." Momma jammed her foot down on the gas pedal and darted in front of a gravel truck. The truck's horn wailed. "I want me some hollyhocks," she said. "Big old irises." Momma beat her hands on the steering wheel. "It's gonna be beautiful."

I lay my forehead on the truck window, stuck my tongue out at a church. "Too late for irises, Momma. Mamaw said so."

"You got to help me water. You big enough to help me?"

"I'm eight," I said, nose against the glass.

"So you will?"

"Yep," I said, breath fogging the window.

The truck motor boomed when we passed through cuts in the crumbled sandstone. I hung onto the door handle for dear life when Momma swerved past houses hunkered in hollers, piled up together like gossips.

I said, "You're driving awful fast, Momma."

"I know," Momma said. "I'm sorry."

The truck's tires spit gravel as we spun onto the four-lane towards town. A Delta 88 trailed a cloud of blue smoke in front of us. Momma pulled into the left-hand lane behind a half-ton with nine refrigerators strapped on its bed.

"Don't close," Momma said. "Please, please, please don't close."

"Blow your horn, Momma," I said.

She turned off the bypass onto the winding main street of town. The truck idled at a red light next to a convenience store. Inside the store, coal miners stacked cakes and candy bars, cigarettes and pop on the counter. They pointed at fried brown things in stainless steel bins lit by heat lamps. My stomach growled. The light changed, and I asked what would happen if we didn't make it.

We passed a car dealership turned pet store turned place to buy security systems turned payday loan shop. We rolled past a storefront church named in vinyl letters dripping vinyl drops of blood. The street turned left and crossed the ditch where the river used to be. I asked Momma what time the hardware store closed.

"I don't know," Momma said, "but we're gonna make it."

I looked at the clock in the truck dashboard. It said twenty til seven. It said twenty til seven my whole life. Momma pulled into the hardware store parking lot. She grabbed my fist and ran into the store. She slapped her hands on the counter and told the man standing there, "I'm Tricia Jewell. I won that drawing and I'm here for my flowers."

The man behind the counter wore both belt and suspenders and put the end of his pencil to his tongue before he wrote on his pad. He shook his head. "Don't know what you're talking bout."

"They told me they was a jar, had all these names in it. Told me they pulled my name out and now I'm spose to get a hundred dollars worth of plants. They told me whatever kind I want."

"They told you wrong," the man said. He hammered a lid onto a paint bucket with a mallet. "What else can I do for you?" People in line behind us scuffed their feet and cleared their throats.

I said, "He is the devil," and stomped out of the store.

"She aint talking about you," I heard Momma say to the man behind the counter, "she's talking about Hubert."

Out in the parking lot, a van's tires screeched against the blacktop when I stepped in front of it. "Dawn," Momma shouted, and when the van passed, she grabbed me by the arm. I shook loose of her and a guy from the store, a young one covered in sawdust, came up behind Momma.

"Ma'am?" he said.

I sat down on the truck bumper. The guy was pushing a buggy full of plants. He wore a brown knit shirt faded to tan stretched tight over his stomach. He looked like a sawdust doughnut. He stood in front of Momma, his eyes skimming over her, from the blue blood vessels visible through the skin of her high forehead to her hand, every finger with a ring on it, trembling in its grip on her purse strap. Momma's hair lifted in the breeze and waved like the streamers on the handlebars of a rich girl's bicycle. The young man's mouth hung open. I couldn't tell if it was from Momma's beauty or if he had a breathing problem.

"What is it?" Momma said.

The man handed Momma two trays of impatiens from the buggy. He said, "These been here too long to sell. You can have them."

"Really?" Momma said.

"Rootbound," the man said. "You can have this stuff too," and waved his hand over the rest of the wilted flowers in the buggy. The man put the plants in the floorboard of the truck. There were so many, some had to go in the back.

When he was done, Momma said, "You won't get in trouble?"

"Don't matter," the man said. "Quitting Friday." His eyes swam in his head as he looked Momma over one more time, and I decided he didn't have a breathing problem. It was like this with Momma. Some people, like the man behind the counter, couldn't see her at all. Some, like the boy with the flowers, had to stare at her from every angle, like she was some fancy salamander or butterfly. The staring made me proud, but

On the way home, I sat with my feet on the seat to keep them out of the plants covering the floorboard.

"That worked out good, didn't it?" Momma said.

"Yep," I said.

"Think Hubert will help me plant?"

"Nope."

"Bet he will," Momma said. "But if he don't? Who cares?"

I turned and looked through the back window of the cab at the plants rustling in the bed of the truck. I wished this flower business had never come up. "It sure is a pretty bunch of flowers, Momma."

"It sure is," Momma said.

When Dad got home from the mines that night, I told him what happened. "Hubert lied to Momma. Made us drive clear to town for nothing."

Dad stroked his beard, opened his lunch bucket, and gave me an oatmeal creme pie. "So where'd all them flowers come from?"

"This boy give em to us."

"What boy?"

"Some boy."

Dad turned to Momma, who was sitting on the couch with Albert. "Hubert going to help you plant?"

"Too busy," Momma said.

"You know what he done today, Dad?" Albert said.

I climbed onto one of the high stools at the counter that separated the kitchen from the living room. I got tired of Albert's Hubert stories. Hubert lifted the front end of a truck off the ground all by himself. Hubert got free HBO cause he run a line from an old woman's house without her knowing it. Hubert killed a twelve-pointer with a .22. Hubert sold moonshine to a man from the governor's office. Hubert. Hubert. Hubert.

Hubert's diesel pickup rumbled in the road below. Dad went down the hall to the bedroom. I sat on the stool and ate my oatmeal pie. After while, Dad came out, left the trailer, walked down the hill across the road to the house where Hubert stayed.

"Yall get to bed," Momma said, running her fingers through my hair.

~~~~~~~~~~

MOMMA WAS already out in the yard when I got up the next morning. Dad sat at the kitchen table eating eggs and fried baloney. I sat down next to him and stared at the side of his head. He didn't look up, but he smiled. He kept chewing and reading.

"What are you doing?" I said.

"Reading the instructions for how to put your trampoline up." Dad got me and Albert a trampoline the fall before in an end-of-summer sale. We'd had it for months, but Dad hadn't put it together yet.

WHAT FOR? I SAID.

Dad had four brothers who lived on the ridge—Hubert, Colbert, Filbert, and Prestone—who were forever in their yards putting something together or taking something apart—deer stands, four-wheelers, backhoes, ditch witches, swingsets, come alongs—forever hooking stuff up—propane tanks, washing machines, water heaters—and I had never seen them read instructions. There were loose parts and old sets of instructions everywhere gathering dust on top of the refrigerators, getting sticky behind toasters, piling up like leaves in the gutter under furniture.

"I don't know," Dad said. "They was just sitting here."

I knew Dad was fooling me. He was the one who read instructions. "You gonna put it up today?"

"Hope to."

"That'd be good." I lay my head on the table. I hoped Albert would sleep all day. I imagined how much happier we all would have been if I were an only child. Dad whistled as he rinsed a bowl for me and poured the last of the milk onto my Lucky Charms. Hubert's diesel pulled up next to our house.

"How come you walk to see him and he rides to see you?" I said.

Dad set the bowl of Lucky Charms down in front of me. He rubbed the top of my head. "You're gonna wear yourself out thinking." He squeezed my shoulder and went outside.

I took my bowl of Lucky Charms to the window. Hubert got down out of his truck. Momma was setting out plants on her knees in a circle of dirt in front of the house. Hubert stood at the truck with his hand on the rearview mirror, shifted his weight off his bad hip. He said something to Momma, something I couldn't hear through the glass. Hubert was not as tall as the other Jewells, but he was tall enough. He was powerful built, biceps and calf muscles like roofing nails in paper sacks. His skin looked like roasted potatoes beneath the flecks of black hair that covered his body. I knew I would be taller than Hubert if I made it to full-grown, but when I backed up from the window, my reflection fit over Hubert's form in a way that made me sick. We had the same high forehead—except Hubert was balder—same wide-set eyes on the same deep shelf of cheekbone—except my eyes were gray—same hammy shoulders, same birdy legs, same sausage fingers.

Hubert backed the truck next to Momma's circle of earth, sprang out of his vehicle, and opened the tailgate on a truck bed of mulch he'd collected from a debtor with a sawmill. He raked the mulch out on Momma's bed. I could not see Dad standing on the trailer's porch, but I heard his voice. Hubert stopped, knee-deep in mulch, nodded at what Dad said, and went back to spreading mulch.

I chewed my Lucky Charms with my lower jaw pushed forward. Hubert and Dad's other brothers made liquor, grew marijuana, came and went at all hours of the night in their sedans with chewed-up mufflers and their pickups with smokestack exhaust pipes.

He drove a plain truck and worked in the coal mines ever since Albert had been born and he'd married Momma. The law didn't come to our house. There wasn't glass breaking and loud laughing all night long at our house. All that stuff went on across the road.

Momma took another impatiens plant from the plastic cup it came in. She picked at the roots delicate as a bird and set the flower in a hole. She troweled dirt in over the plant and patted it. Momma's hands moved like spider's legs over the flowers, the dirt, her tools. I would cut off my foot, I thought, to have her hands.

Albert came around the back of the house. Momma had Albert's hair cut short, but it was still sticking up every which way. Albert was eleven then and a mystery to me. He was made skinnier than I was, and I never could get ahold of him, never could catch him. He wasn't a honeybee, either—sting once and die. He was a yellowjacket. Sting over and over. He'd rap the top of my head with his knuckles on his way out the door and push me over when I came out of the house chasing him. Pour ice water in my ear while I was sleeping. Spit in my food. Break my crayons. Dad and Momma punished him every time. Didn't even slow him down.

Albert stopped in the yard in front of Hubert's truck. Dad came off the steps and stood in front of Albert, put his hand on Albert's shoulder. Albert got in Dad's truck. Dad came in the house and headed for the kitchen.

"Where you going, Dad?"

"Get pop."

"Can I go?"

Dad stopped on his way back to the door. He was the youngest of the Jewell brothers and had the softest face. "You stay here. Keep an eye on things. OK?"

I nodded.

"You're the boss til I get back."

I nodded like the whole bunch were zombies me and my dad had hypnotized to do whatever we told them to do. I wished they were, cause if they were, soon as Dad got out of the yard, I'd snap my fingers and make them all squawk and scratch like chickens. Dad went out and got in the truck. Momma ran towards the truck and leaned in Albert's window, rising up on one foot to kiss him goodbye. When she got around to the other window, Dad's arm was out, reaching for her. Momma and Dad kissed what seemed to me a real good kiss. Dad and Albert left, and when Momma got back to the circle of earth, Hubert had pulled up some of the plants and put them other places. Momma stood with her hands on her hips. Hubert pointed with the trowel, explaining what he thought she ought to do. When he finished, he put his hands on his thighs and looked up at Momma. Momma smiled, nodded, fell to her knees, and went back to work on the opposite side of the circle of earth from Hubert.

My bowl of Lucky Charms was all soggy. I sat down on the arm of the chair beside the window in the front room of our house and held the bowl of sweet pink milk to my lips, my mother's rumbly voice coming from outside.

Already in those first eight years of my life I had seen my mother's parents split up. My other grandparents split before I was born. I had been to the emergency room seven times I could think of for one or another of my dad's family. Been to the courthouse at least that many times for the same reason. I had been to Tennessee four times to see my momma's sister. I had been to the beach once, to Dollywood once, and to see my dad's momma in North Carolina once. I had set on Dad's knee in the unemployment office and my mother's at the food stamp office.

Things were quiet that morning in the single-wide, the television off, the heater off, the fans off, the murmur of my mother's voice in the front yard, laughing, telling a story. I wanted to go back to bed and dream what would happen next, dream a place quiet all the time, sunny pink and yellow, me drawing, people pulling up in the driveway of my house looking out over the ocean, the pictures I'd drawn piling up in a basket and a man with a black moustache, a woman with a gumball bracelet, coming to pick up the drawings— "Aren't you something" and "These are spectacular," they would say, and "Well, we'll leave you alone" as they slipped out, leaving food and grocery bags full of money by the door and me by myself in the pink-and-yellow room, drawing, everything taken care of, everyone a stranger, the ocean in and out.

The storm door jerked back with a squeak. The front door flew open and bounced off the wall. Albert shot through the room, put a fist in my shoulder—"Wake up, Fatso"—and was gone down the hall. The chunk-chunk-chunk of heavy metal guitars found its way to the front of the house through the trailer walls. I stared into my bowl at the blue marshmallow moon vibrating across the pink sweet milk. Surrounded by kin, nestled in the bosom of family, I exhaled. Then breath, heavy with the scent of hardwood mulch, diesel, and fried baloney, filled me again.

~~~~~~~~~

A WEEK later, three weeks before my ninth birthday, my father's father, Green Jewell, sat at his kitchen table and tore up a playing card. "I need more room. People bringing in cars and I need more room."

Dust swirled in the morning sunlight behind Hubert in the new section of the kitchen where plastic sheeting stretched between pine studs, translucent in the morning sun, a blond cage.

Hubert said, "I don't know, Dad."

"Sippett set a load of gravel at Delbert's. Get up there and spread it." Green tore the playing card again. Green never wrote anything down, but he always kept playing cards held by a rubber band in his shirt pocket. Every card stood for something needed doing. When something got done, he tore up the card. Green wiped his lips with the back of his hand and prowled through the new section of the kitchen, stepping around buckets, over sheets of plywood, picking up nails, dropping them in his pocket. The bigger kitchen was Green's new wife's idea. Green began to growl. I followed Hubert out of the house to the bulldozer.

"Go on," Hubert said. "Get out of here."

"You aint the boss of me."

Hubert had on shorts. Dad said Hubert wore shorts because he didn't like being hemmed in. Claustrophobic, Dad said. Green came off the porch and went around to the back of the house. Me and Hubert watched him go, an old man with a shock of white hair standing straight up off his head, black-rim glasses, body thick through the middle. Green passed the houses where my other uncles lived and went into a building made of corrugated metal. He pulled the door shut behind him.

"Get out of here," Hubert said again.

"I aint."

Hubert smacked me in the face. "Get."

Hubert had never hit me before.

"Go on, Dawn."

I stepped back to where I could get away from whatever he did next, but I didn't go away. A thing boils up, I thought.

Hubert turned away from me, and I touched my face. Hubert got on the dozer, started it, crossed the road, and went up my driveway. He lowered the blade into the gravel. I followed, and raised the back of my fist and then my middle finger at Hubert, but he didn't see it.

When I got inside our house, it came on my mind not to tell on Hubert. The thought of keeping Hubert's smack secret scared me, but I couldn't get around it. The television was up against the front window turned up loud. Albert lay on the floor in front of Dad's recliner. The curtains were drawn, and it was dark in the room. The light from the television played on Albert's face. I stepped over Albert on the way to my father's chair. Albert shoved me in the side of the knee without taking his eyes off the television, and I fell into the chair.

"Butt," I said.

Albert gave me the finger. He was watching a wrestling video. The crowd was full of people screaming at fake fights. Their anger was real, a smiling laughing anger they'd paid hundreds of dollars to let out. The dozer cut off, and Hubert came in the kitchen, took a glass from the shelf, ran it full of cold water. The door opened again, and Momma came into the TV room. Red splotches spilled down her neck. "Albert, where's your daddy?"

"Working a double," I said.

Momma went in the kitchen. She stood with one hand on the kitchen counter. "Hubert, you got to tell him." Hubert smiled, his chin tucked into his chest. Momma stamped her foot. "Colbert can't come in the store no more. Not while I'm working."

Back then, Momma worked in the bakery at the grocery store down the mountain in town. She was the best they had. She did cakes for the wives of lawyers and judges. She did the wedding cakes for coal operators' daughters. I turned towards the kitchen, towards Hubert and Momma. I hated my uncle Colbert worse than I did Hubert. Hubert was a snake, but Colbert was a monstrous black cloud of stupidity and destruction.

"Turn it up," Albert said. When I didn't, Albert rolled over, grabbed my foot and twisted my ankle.

"Ow. Stop it," I said.

Albert sat up on his knees, grabbed the remote control out of my hand, and hammered my fingers against the chair arm with his free fist. When Albert turned back to the television, I kicked him in the ear.

"Hubert, you could. He's your brother," Momma said.

"What am I supposed to say to him," Hubert said, spreading his arms. "It's a free country, aint it?" Hubert sat down at the table and took a piece of cake out of a clamshell box.

"Hubert, he was so drunk he peed on the eggs."

"When did he do that?" Hubert said.

"Today." Momma put her hands on her hips.

"What time?"

"What?" Momma was nearly panting.

"What time of day was it?" Hubert said.

"I don't know," Momma said. "Four."

Hubert shook his head. "I don't think it was him."

"They got him on the store cameras," Momma said. "He's gonna get me fired."

"You need to start your own business anyway," Hubert said. "Then you wouldn't have to put up with shit like that."

Momma stood silent.

Hubert said, "You need to let me help you."

Momma picked crumbs from Hubert's beard. I walked on Albert's hand on my way outside. Two boy cousins younger than me were on the trampoline.

"Get off of there," I said.

"No," the fat one said.

"Tell you where Albert hid his BB pistol."

They stopped bouncing. "Where?"

"Under the couch in his room."

The boys rolled off the trampoline and tore past me into the house. I pulled myself up on the trampoline. When I bounced I could see into the tree branches of the remaining oaks in the grassless yard. My hair rose and fell as I bounced. I wished I could see a black-and-white photograph of Hubert at the top of an obituary, blurry in a baseball cap, stunned or pissed or spoiling for a fight when the camera flashed. I jumped higher. I swore I'd see all my Dad's brothers that way, their names under each other's pictures, surviving, preceding, until they were all preceding, the last one dead. Then I would sit in the tree that rose and fell in front of me with a .22 and pick off their boy children one by one whether they had been proven Jewells or not. No Jewells left. None but my dad. I bounced until the sweat was pouring off of my face. I was still bouncing when Hubert came out and started up the dozer. I bounced with my back to him until he was gone.

"Dawn, come get your supper," Momma said from the trailer door.

My knees buckled and I collapsed in a heap. I was hot and dreaded going back in the trailer. "I aint hungry," I said.

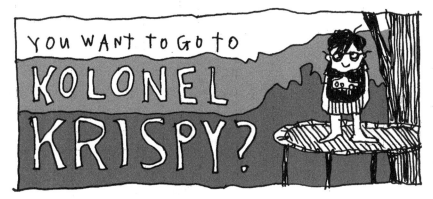

When I was little, I loved Kolonel Krispy better than anything. Momma went inside, came back with Albert. We loaded up, drove into town. The Kolonel Krispy had once been a dairy bar where people walked up and got their fried chicken and doughnuts, burgers and fries in white paper bags, from workers leaning through a sliding glass window, but they closed it in, built a dining room huge and smoky as an Indian cave. Momma took us through the drive-thru. Momma said, "Get whatever you want." We all got hotdogs and fries, and cherry pies. I got a large pineapple milkshake, Albert a drink full of antifreeze-blue slush. Momma got a hamburger with extra pickles. We all smacked our lips in fevered expectation, pulling fries from the bag while Momma parked the car. Crumbling concrete stairs led down to the river, and we ran to the broken pavement at the river's edge. Momma set the bags on a picnic table chained to a tree in a muddy flat spot while Albert skipped stones and I stood staring at the food. Momma unwrapped the wax-paper squares and lay them on the table. She set the packets of fries on the corner of the bags. She called to Albert. Albert ran to the table, gathered his in his arms, and ran back to the river. He ate his fries a half dozen at a time, throwing rocks at a duck with his free hand. I settled in close beside my mother. She set my food in front of me and I ate, feeling better with each bite of hot dog, each handful of fries, each sweet, chunky sip of the pineapple shake. Momma elbowed me, and I looked up. Momma had a pickle covering each of her eyes.

I always loved that. We sat eating, watching Albert. He threw a rock so hard his pie slipped out of his hand and fell into the water. I laughed, and when Albert stuck one foot in the river to rescue his pie, Momma said, "You fall in that river and you're walking home." I was feeling much better when Momma said, "Hubert told me what happened. Told me he hit you." My hot dog turned to rubber in my mouth. "Told me he felt bad about it."

I asked Momma what she said to him.

"I told him if he did it again I'd kill him."

I got up from the table and stood at the edge of the water, away from where Albert was. It gave my heart a jump to think of my mother killing Hubert. I wondered how she'd do it. Blow his head off with a shotgun. Maybe an ax. Ax would be good. She'd probably do something quieter, like put poison in a piece of cake.

which would be fine.

Albert stood at the point where the two forks of the river came together and ran on down the valley. Albert poured the pale slush, the blue juice drained from it, into the river. Then he threw the plastic cup hard as he could. It caught in the breeze and did not go very far, dropped into the water, spun and disappeared. Water doesn't care what goes in it. It just keeps going downhill. I sat down on the weedy riverbank.

Momma sat down beside me. "Daddy used to bring me and June down here, feed us doughnut holes, tell us stories." Momma's sister June lived in Tennessee. Momma plucked up a blade of grass, held it between her thumbs, blew on it to make a buzzing noise. "He said the old people say the forks was brothers. The brothers piled up where Albert's standing, and went on adventures downstream—stealing out of people's gardens, scaring up the fish. Done everything together, thick as thieves. And you know those high rocks down on the county line?" I nodded. "The river splits there, don't it?" I nodded again. "People say that's where something broke them brothers up."

"What?" I said.

"Some say they was fighting over a woman. Some say a piece of land. Some say over which their mother loved best. But whatever it was it split them brothers up." Momma sat humming. Even then I got all mixed up by my mother, all mixed up about how to feel, whether to go whole hog trusting her or not. I let the flow of the river fill my eyes, the caramel-colored water natural and unnatural at once.

"Which doughnut holes you like best, Momma?"

"Coconut." Momma handed me her milkshake.

"I like coconut, too."

"Looky there," Momma said and pointed a painted fingernail at letters carved in a tree. "JR + PR" the letters said. "June Redding. Patricia Redding. We done that."

"When?"

"When we were in high school. I think your daddy was swimming in that river over there that night."

"Was you on a date?"

"No. Not then. We weren't. Him and June may have been."

"Him and Aunt June dated?"

"Nah, not really."

I ran my finger down in the grooves of the letters. Aunt June lived by herself, older than Momma, but no husband, no kids. Albert said she liked girls. Albert didn't know anything. Albert didn't have a thought in his head. He just repeated what Hubert and the others said.

"Gonna get dark here in a minute," Momma said. "Where did Albert go?"

He wasn't throwing rocks in the river anymore. He wasn't anywhere to be seen. The frogs croaked like old scolds, and I felt guilty. No idea why. Feelings came on me all that day I had no way of explaining. "I want to go home, Momma."

"You want to go draw?"

"Yeah."

Momma wrapped her hands around my head, pulled me to her, bent my glasses. My hair caught in Momma's rings. Albert come up behind us, kneed me in the back, and ran towards the broken concrete steps hard as he could. He tripped three steps up and caught himself, never stopped running. I turned to the river, imagined the forks a brother and a sister, couldn't wait to get to the county line where some rocky thing would split them apart and run them separate plumb to different oceans, never together again til Antarctica and by then so mixed up with other water it wouldn't matter.

When we got home, Hubert called and asked did Albert want to go sit with him at the store. Momma said she didn't care, said, "Albert, you want to go to the store with Hubert?"

Albert was out the door before she finished saying it. Momma sent me to take a bath. She shampooed my long black hair. Her fingers moved across my scalp like the big soapy brushes at the car wash. After I bathed, I stood on the mat. Momma sang songs without words while she dried my hair. The rough rubbing of the towel knocked me off balance, but I was happy.

"What you gonna draw tonight?"

"I don't know," I said. "Something."

I got my pens and crayons out from under the bed. They were in a cigar box I'd got from Mamaw. I got out the big pad of paper Momma brought me from the missionary salvage store. Eleven inches by seventeen inches. Big paper. I crawled into bed and opened the pad on my propped-up legs. I put a black pen in my hand and waited for my mother to get there to start. After a minute I put the cap back on the pen.

Momma came to the door. She had changed out of her blue jeans into dark orange cotton shorts and a light orange tank top. She got into bed and put her arm around me. She had taken her rings off and felt soft and perfect to me. I took the cap back off my pen.

I said, "How do you draw a penguin?"

"Well," Momma said, "they got a little round head, and they aint got no shoulders."

I put the black pen back in the cigar box and got out a pencil. I drew a penguin with my pencil and went back over it with the black pen. I colored in its beak orange. Then I sat feeling my mother's rib cage rise and fall.

"Now what?" Momma said.

I turned to a new piece of paper. "What did you and Aunt June look like when you were my age?"

"Scrawny. But June was way prettier than me. She had eyes like yours, gray like polished gravel. But she was backwards. Nose stuck in books. Her big treat was to go to the library and look at old magazines. Them things made me sneeze. Summer Momma would leave us there and I'd wander the streets."

I drew two skinny stick bodies. "You weren't scared somebody would get you?"

"Wasn't like that then. Nobody wanted another kid." Momma squeezed me close. "One time June cut up a Sears catalog and a bunch of *National Geographics*, pasted the pictures together, and made a story out of them. Had people in Africa with gold bands on their necks talking to women in girdles, except they never showed the faces of them women in girdles in the Sears catalog, so she'd glue somebody up, like a man in his hunting cap, and she'd have that half–hunter half–girdle wearer talking to that African woman."

"That sounds cool."

"It was cool. Your Aunt June is cool."

I drew June with a pile of books under her arm and a pair of scissors in the other hand. I drew in my mother's head.

"Put me in a football jersey. I loved football jerseys."

"What number on it?"

"Sixteen. Joe Montana."

"What color?"

"Red."

I drew Momma with her arm around her sister. I erased out the scissors and put June's arm around Momma's shoulder, too. With her other hand, Momma held a knife. I drew a tree with June and Momma's initials on it.

"That looks good," Momma said.

"You want it?"

"No. You keep it in your book."

I wanted my mother to stay there with me til I fell asleep. When Momma tried to shift out from under me, I pushed my head into her shoulder, tried to hold her in place. Momma got up to go. "Your daddy be here in a little bit." Momma stood and turned off the overhead light. The little lamp next to my bed was hardly enough to draw by, but I kept on, moving a yellow pen in empty spirals. I was wanting to put a machine gun in the penguin's flippers, draw a penguin army with belts full of bullets across their penguin chests, ready to fight to keep people they didn't want off Antarctica. But I didn't draw that. I didn't want to scare my mother. I fell asleep by the dim lamp, my paper and pens all over me. When I woke up, my dad was dead, crushed by a cutting machine in the mines.

# 9

## IGNORANT GIRL

MY TENTH day working at Kolonel Krispy was the day Hubert took Momma to the dryout hospital. Hubert and Momma, my uncle Colbert and his lunatic girlfriend came to see me at work on their way out of town. I signed out on break and sat with them at the pressure-treated picnic table outside. All of a sudden, Colbert said, "Oh!" and ran out in the middle of the road, blocking the way of Sidney Coates's Firebird.

It had been seven years since my dad died in the mine when the arm of a cutting machine swung around and pinned him against the rib, broke his back. Colbert still believed a boy sniffing cocaine off the deck of the cutting machine hit a button caused the machine to kill Dad. Colbert said Sidney Coates sold the boy the cocaine. Sidney Coates's cousin was the sheriff, and the story was the circuit judge owed Sidney something he never could quite get paid off. All that is to say only idiots messed with Sidney Coates.

Colbert spread his arms wide and walked up to the passenger window and put his elbows on the roof of Sidney's car and leaned in the window. Traffic backed up behind the black Firebird.

"Hey, you fatass piece of shit," the boy driving the Firebird said. "You better step the fuck off."

"Language," my manager said. Hubert used his lower lip to clean the milkshake from his moustache.

"Why don't you fellers move along," Colbert said, "or come out of there and suck my dick."

"Language," my manager said, a little louder than the first time.

Sidney, his thick lips dry as stones in the sun, stared at Colbert. Without taking his eyes off Colbert, he pumped his pointer twice towards the windshield. The Firebird pulled forward. Colbert stepped out in traffic and flipped the back of the Firebird off with both hands.

Hubert sipped from his milkshake.

Colbert's girlfriend said, "You better hope I don't tell him you said that." Colbert's girlfriend's eyes were dull as social studies, and she had no idea men had been to the moon.

At the end of my shift, the manager said it didn't seem to be working out for me at Kolonel Krispy, and asked me not to come back.

WHEN HUBERT got back from taking Momma to rehab, he told Colbert to stay close to the Trail for a while. But Colbert and his girlfriend kept running the roads. Two nights later somebody let Colbert off at the top of the driveway. Colbert's pupils were two little inner tubes in a vast red sea. He was grinning and past language and lucky to make it to Hubert's couch before his legs gave out. Colbert didn't move from Hubert's couch for sixteen hours. Hubert threw a sheet over him, and I sat and watched him out of the corner of my eye while me and Albert watched television. Every once in a while he would stir under his flower-print sheet.

"Where's your woman?" Hubert said when Colbert finally sat up.

Colbert's head crashed back to the sofa, and he slept another seven hours.

Right after Colbert fell back to the sofa, I got up and went and looked out the window over Hubert's kitchen sink. At woods edge in the small backyard there was a spot where the briars and the blackberries broke. I put my shoes on, crossed the muddy yard, stepped through the break, and made my way into the woods. Two, then three, then four motors sputtered behind me. The sound of them began to move in circles. My head got light, and I drifted down the barely formed trail, dark in the middle of the day. Mud covered the tops of my shoes. I came to a little clearing where the mud rared up in truck tracks. I followed the truck tracks deeper into the woods. The front of my head felt like it emptied out, and I couldn't see for a minute. When my sight came back, a pearly-green head rose up out of the viny mess beside the truck-tracked road. Dirt fell off the T-shirt hanging on Colbert's girlfriend's shoulders. Her lips and eyes were red as a clown's, and when she reached out her arm to me it was covered in cuts and bruises and blood.

I took off running back through the woods. When I got to Hubert's, I ran up the drive, across the Trail, and back up the hill to where I had lived when my dad was alive. I climbed up on the trampoline and sat on its edge. The sun broke through the wiry lattice of wood that hemmed us in, but it wasn't warm at all. I pulled off my gray-mudded shoes, and sat on the edge of the trampoline and rocked. After while, Albert crossed the road with a pop. He reached it to me, water beading on the outside and curving down the sides of the bottle. I shook my head, still breathing hard.

"She's gonna be all right," Albert said.

I nodded, rocked a little.

"Who did that?"

"I don't know," Albert said.

"Colbert?"

"I don't know," Albert said. "Maybe."

I rocked some more. My brother climbed up next to me, put arms around me, tried to still me. Within a minute, he was rocking too.

~~~~~~~~~~~~

I WENT back to Mamaw's, took a long shower, and went to bed. When I came to, I decided to ask Hubert to loan me money for a car. I went to his place, marched right down the hall and into his room. I shut the door behind me. He was sitting up on the bed, and when I seen him, I decided he didn't have enough money to get me where I wanted to go, so I started backing out of the room.

He said, "Where you going?" and I just looked at him, and he said, "Girl, you need to be talking," and God, that flew all over me.

I said, "Talking about what?" and he got quiet and I hated that room, hated how dark it was, how dark it all was, and I said,

The bed was my mother and father's from when I was little. It was the bed I went to during thunder and lightning; bed I went to when girls at school called me Big Bird, Stork, Marilyn Manson, Freak Interrupted; bed of Momma's pillowcase tears; bed of Momma gone to Hazard all night; bed Mamaw caught Albert having sex with a missionary girl in; bed Hubert packed off to his house the day he took Momma to the dryout hospital; hand-carved black walnut bed Daddy made in the carpenter's class he went to when he tried to get out of the mines so he would be able to see us, see me and Albert play ball, see us do nothing, see us just sitting watching television, but Dad took too long with things, took too long to make any money being a carpenter, never enough money, and so he went back underground, and now he's dead, cause he wouldn't be no outlaw, not like his daddy, not like his brother Hubert.

I wouldn't look at Hubert, but I heard him, heard Dad's bed creak when Hubert leaned up on one hip and the chain on his wallet tinkled like a bell on a cat's neck, and I didn't look when his wallet come out and he said, "How much do you need?"

I said, "That aint your bed. You aint got no business with that bed."

Hubert sucked his teeth.

"You aint got no dental hygiene neither," I said, mad at myself for being so mad. I stepped to the door, said, "Nasty greasy thing." Tears come up in my eyes. "I hate your . . ." I didn't know what to say. "I hate your teeth."

"You're too excited," Hubert said.

"Why am I here?" I said. "This is stupid."

The roll of Hubert's shoulders sitting on the bed looked like Dad in his johnboat fishing, me sitting there with him, fingers dragging in the warm lake water, smile about to break my face, air purple and green with the sun behind the mountain, me free to smile big as I want in the dimming light.

Somebody whistled at the other end of Hubert's trailer. Somebody turned on Aerosmith loud. Somebody flung a garbage bag of bottles out in the yard. I heard the bottles scatter. The tears broke loose from my eyes, and I turned to hide them. I forced my hands to be still, so they wouldn't go to my eyes, wouldn't give me away.

"You like that boy talks on the radio," Hubert said. "I hear you laughing at him."

I stayed facing the door. "I do not," I said. I wanted to lay my neck open with the knife on Hubert's dresser, bleed out on the floor of Hubert's room.

"What's his name?" Hubert said, "William? Wilson?"

"I need eight hundred dollars," I said to the door.

HUBERT PUT me in harness. He sure did, the very next Monday, while I was still suspended from school for fighting Belinda Coates. There was a pipe come out of the mountain in a curve on the road to Hazard. On the back side of the mountain, there was lots of people didn't have water where their wells had gone bad. People would pull up to the pipe and fill milk jugs all day long, however many jugs they could fit in their vehicle. They'd draw water to bath, do dishes, make beans, whatever people use water for. Hubert had a store right across from the pipe, sold cigarettes and lottery tickets, and the worst toilet paper ever was.

Hubert also sold liquor out of the store, which was illegal cause our county was dry, and this man Hubert didn't back was sheriff, and so it had been hot for Hubert, and he couldn't just be handing jars of liquor across the counter, so he'd gone back up in the mountain where the water ran into that pipe and he'd put a splitter on it, and then he'd run his own pipe up the hillside to a spot that looked out over the store, a little rock-hidden spot where a person could sit and when Hubert flashed a light in the store window that person would turn a valve and the water would stop running out of the pipe. Then the person would open a second valve and empty one of the liquor jars stacked in the back of a pickup truck into a galvanized bucket Hubert had rigged up with a hole in its bottom that led into Hubert's pipe, and then the liquor would run into the water pipe at that splitter and on into whoever's water jug was waiting down at the road at the other end. And when the jug got filled, the person on the top of the hill would turn them two valves, and water would start running out the pipe at the road again. And the person at the top of the hill would sit there doing nothing until Hubert flashed his light again. And so Monday morning after our little bed talk, the person waiting for him to flash his light was me.

~~~~~~~~~~~~

NINE O'CLOCK Thursday morning, the day my suspension was over and I was supposed to be back in school, I was still up on the cliff above Hubert's. After my first liquor jar of the day drained into an old woman's Wisk jug, I turned on my little radio to listen to Willett on the radio. He played the song "Muscles for Brains" by Gang of Four. He liked old music and so did I. A man in a Geo without a hood pulled up, and Hubert flashed his light. I didn't see it cause I was banging my head, dancing around up there at the cliff's edge, mostly to stay warm, but also to be with Willett Bilson. Hubert kept on flashing his light, at least he said he did after, and then the gunshot shocked the birds off the phone wire and the bullet exploded my radio and killed the Gang of Four.

~~~~~~~~~~~~

HUBERT SAID, and kicked pieces of the radio off the rock edge. The radio parts made a thin clatter against the blacktop below.

I said, "From the money tree, I reckon."

The flat of Hubert's hand landed against my cheekbone, and the milk crate I was sitting on jerked out from under me. My shoulder hit the rock first. I scrambled to get up before Hubert could hit me again, but he put his hand in my shoulder and pushed me back down.

"Stop it," I said.

Hubert pointed at the galvanized bucket where I was supposed to pour the liquor. "That's where money comes from." He pulled the silver flashlight with its ridges down its shaft, too many for me to count, out of his back pocket. He shoved the light in my face. I knew the flashlight was going to break my teeth, and I flinched. He turned on the light, an inch from my face. "This is where money comes from, you ignorant girl."

Mad blinded me and I stood up and threw my shoulder into Hubert's chest. He made a sound, a little one, the puff of a grunt a man can't help but make when he gets out of a car or bends to pick up something he's dropped. I knew Hubert was most likely to knock me clean off the mountain, but I stepped to him, taller than he was, my mouth at his eyes, and said, "I aint ignorant."

Tires crunched in the gravel below. "Then show me you aint," Hubert said, onions and tobacco on his breath. He went back down the trail to the store.

Directly, Hubert's light flashed. My head still rang from his slap. I knew what I had done wrong. I shut off the water, opened the liquor valve, got a jar out of the truck, and spit down the pipe. I poured the liquor down after it and swore never again to tell a man what I need. Then I lay down on the cold truck seat and closed my eyes to sleep.

~~~~~~~~~~~~~~~

NOBODY ELSE came for liquor that day, and I slept on and on, face stuck to the hard truck seat on the hillside above the store. When Hubert woke me, it was a cold waking. He touched my shoulder and said, "Let's go."

"Where?" I said.

"Back," Hubert said, "back to the ridge." And so we went, Willie Nelson singing about the redheaded stranger in Hubert's last good truck. "You still wanting tomorrow off?" Hubert said when we pulled into Mamaw's carport.

"Yes I am," I nodded. "Yes I am wanting off."

Hubert nodded and I got out of the truck. Dark and cold it was, dark and cold. The stars were drops of oil in a black coffee sky. Dogs barked out on the ridge. No snow, only hardwood freeze. The rings in the trees drew close together in the bone-cracking night, and I didn't care if I never went back to school, didn't care if Jesus came tomorrow with me not knowing the Pythagoras theory. I was not ready for the house, and so I went out on the front porch, which I could barely find because the booger light was out and so were the lamps in the front room, and so with my hands I found the glider on Mamaw's porch, and there I sat and let my eyes adjust, and the light from the stars grew brighter and my bottom numbed against the winter steel of the glider, and I wished for fire, fire against my bottom, fire to warm me inside out, and there came a chink and a spark and the whistle of air through tobacco in a wooden bowl, and Mamaw and her pipe sat waxy in the shadows like an unlit candle.

"Hello." Mamaw's voice came out of the smoke, and the smoke bore light.

"Hey Mamaw," I said.

She said, "Why don't you ask me for money? Why do you go running to him?"

I said, "Say what's on your mind, why don't you?"

And Mamaw said, "Too cold not to."

The night sky sparkled, and I said, "You reckon the star of Bethlehem is still out there?"

Mamaw's profile was like chiseled rock at the edge of the porch. She bent her neck back, lifted her chin to the sky, and said, "I reckon it is." Then she turned to me. "Do you seek the newborn king?" she said.

I said no.

"Kings," Mamaw said with a hiss, and put the spark to her pipe again. The smoke left her nose and lips and the wooden bowl and drifted towards me, sideways across the porch.

ANSWER MY QUESTION, SHE SAID.

"I don't know," I said. I made the glider squeak. "You don't want me working for Hubert, do you?"

"You know I don't," Mamaw said.

"Then why don't you stop me?" I said.

"Why don't you stop yourself?"

And then the night and the cold and the smoke came between us again, and I wished for alcohol, for my own pipe running down my own throat.

"Men," Mamaw said, loud enough to make me jump. "Men are scared. Men are a bunch of rabbits—a bunch of rabbits who woke up one morning with sharp teeth and thought that made them lions. But it don't. They can tear up the whole world with them sharp teeth, and they still won't be nothing but rabbits." Mamaw stood up and took hold of the porch rail to steady herself.

"Mamaw," I said. I thought she was drunk.

"You going with me tomorrow to look at that strip job," she said, and she wasn't asking.

"Yeah, Mamaw," I said, "I am."

"All right then," she said. "Don't forget to go to bed." And with that she knocked the fire out of her pipe and slid into the dark house.

By then I could make out the ridgeline of Blue Bear across the valley, and my mind grew still in the face of its broad silent dark. Then the mountain began to laugh. It wasn't my mother's scary high person laugh, and it wasn't my father's easy-rolling laugh. It was a laugh I'd never heard before. It was a laugh like something was actually funny, something that would be funny to everybody, and not mean. And even though I didn't know who was laughing or what they were laughing about, my bottom grew warm against Mamaw's glider. I rose and went into the house, and when Mamaw woke me in the morning I felt rested and we ate bacon and pancakes at the Huddle House and met the organizers and went and looked at the mine and what the rabbit's teeth could do, and I was strong and free for a little while.

~~~~~~~~~~~~~

WHEN WE finished the strip job inspection, the last of the mist lay in the mud lot filled with pickups where you come off the job. The state man thought if he made us come early, wouldn't be so many show up. But there was five of us—me and Mamaw, Otis who used to be a miner, and the organizer girls, April and Portia. The organizer girls had been partying the night before, and they made such a racket complaining, I stood away from them at the edge of the cliff drinking my pop. Something flashed in the parking lot. It was lit up green, green like a traffic light, but not really, more like I don't know what—a funny green, like from a dream green, but it was something I knew and I couldn't think from where.

"You people seen enough?" the state man said, his crew cut flat on top as the strip job and his voice dull as a city man's pocketknife. We got back in the van, and he drove us down to the muddy parking lot. When we got out, Otis said goodbye and drove off in his pickup. The organizer girls stood with their expensive notebooks covered in bumper stickers and wrote down what Mamaw and Otis told them they seen. I walked over to where I'd seen the green light. I bent down and pulled it out of the mashed down gravel and yellow mud. It was a one-hit pipe, with the space alien from the Flintstones on it. The Great Gazoo. When you'd draw on the pipe, the Great Gazoo's head would light up green. I knew what it was cause I got one just like it for Momma one time. Weird. I looked in the truck window next to where I'd found it. There was a pair of panties on the seat. They were mine.

"Dawn, honey. You ready to go?" Mamaw's breath stood in the cold winter air, the tip of her nose red as a cherry Tootsie Pop. "Shut your mouth," she said. "What you doing standing there slack-jawed?"

Would you have told *your* grandmother a pair of your panties were on the front seat of some truck you never seen before? Well, I didn't. I closed my mouth and followed her back to Portia's little car. It was bright midday when we pulled back onto the Drop Creek road, the sky so blue it was almost UK blue. The skinned trees stood gray and clear like old people talking, no word wasted.

"We need to follow up on those water test records," April said.

"I wrote it down," Portia said. "I'll call EPA when we get back from the gathering."

I was wracking my brain. Black Ford F-150. Who drove a black Ford F-150?

"I should have made them take us over on the Oat Creek side," Mamaw said. We went by a house with a live gazelle in the yard. I knew the man owned it. He had a beard long as last year. "That's the way they do," Mamaw said. "Wait you out. Make you beg. Make you figure it out."

"Burden of proof, right?" Portia said. They all shook their heads.

April turned smiling to look at me in the backseat. "That was great what you said, Dawn."

"What did I say?"

"About the rock getting pushed over the side of the hill," April said. "That is a violation."

"I didn't even look at what that guy was doing," Portia said. "I couldn't get over his hair."

I said, "I hate that guy."

"Who was it?" Portia said.

"Why do you hate him?" April said.

"Boy named—" I started. Oh my God. That was Keith Kelly's truck. I heard Denny say one time how vain Keith was about his black Ford. Keith Kelly was one of them tiresome assholes thought Fords were everything and GMs no good. Who gives a crap? But it was his truck with my drawers in it. Why, I thought, is Keith Kelly stealing my drawers? Pervert. Then I remembered the Great Gazoo one-hit pipe. It wasn't Keith Kelly stealing my panties. Momma got into my underwear all the time when she didn't feel like washing her own. That *was* Momma's one-hit pipe. *She'd* been with Keith Kelly.

"Dawn," April said. "Are you all right?"

"Dawn," Mamaw said.

"Don't feel good," I said.

"I'm sorry," Portia said. "Is it my driving?"

"Dawn don't get carsick," Mamaw said.

Maybe Momma didn't go with Keith Kelly on her own, I thought. Maybe he kidnapped her. Motherfucker. He did. I would kill him.

"Dawn, do you need to stop?" Portia said.

"I want to go home," I said.

They were quiet then. For a minute. Then they started talking again about overburden and permit boundaries and Indiana bat surveys and the agenda for the next meeting of the group. I got them to let me off at Hubert's. Albert was watching TV in the front room.

"Who's this girl Evie calling me, Dawn?" Albert said.

"I don't know," I said. "Where's Momma?"

"I don't know," Albert said. "At rehab, I guess."

"No she aint," I said, and when a banging came from the other end of the house, I said, "Who's that?" Albert shrugged, and I went thumping down the hall, cheap-ass trailer making me feel fat like usual. Momma was on the phone, her door cracked open.

"Yeah . . . No. I aint like that. What?" Momma laughed, "Tee hee hee. Maybe," she said.

I knocked the door open. Momma didn't even look at me, just turned and hunched into the wall at the head of the bed. She tee-heed and mumbled a while longer and then finally turned and said, "I got to go," and hung up. I looked at the clock. It was past three. Shift change.

"He aint working a double?" I said.

"Who?" Momma said grinning, bullshitting like somebody my age.

"Your boyfriend," I said.

"I don't know what you're talking about."

"What are you doing here?" I said.

"They cured me," Momma said.

I said, "Then let's smoke a little dope. Me and you and the Great Gazoo."

"Get out of here," Momma said. "Mind your own business."

"What?" Momma said. "Such a what?"

"Nothing," I said.

"A slut?"

"No."

"What then? Say it, Dawn."

"No," I said. "Leave me alone."

"Leave *you* alone?" Momma said, red and twitching. "That's a good one. That is rich, Cora Junior."

My breath went out of me worse than it ever had, because she saw it as meanness to compare me to Mamaw. "That don't hurt my feelings none," I said. "I'm glad to be like her."

"Good," Momma said. "Then why don't you run cuddle up with her and leave me the fuck alone."

"Fine," I said, but I stood there, and when nothing happened I said louder, "FINE," and slammed her door. Albert had the TV on mute, and it was weird quiet when I walked past him. He looked at me droopy-eyed like he was sad for me, lips tight like a line underlining what he was thinking—that I was wrong to stir things up.

"No I aint," I said to him, and run flush into Hubert coming in the door. He caught me up in his arms, and I almost collapsed crying, then I stiff-armed him in the chest, but my elbows give and my face did touch his just for a second.

"Watch where you're going there, hoss," Hubert said.

"I am," I said. "I am watching where I'm going. And I don't like it. Not one bit."

"What's she talking about," Hubert said to Albert.

I didn't even look to see what Albert did. I was out the door, out into the cold. And glad I was of it, too. I knew Mamaw would be back at her house wanting to talk about the strip job trip, quizzing me about what I saw and what it meant and what was legal and illegal about the operation, and I wouldn't know and I didn't care. Hard to feel anything for a pile of rocks and dirt when your mother's off running around with every no-neck dumbass that will buy her a cup of coffee and when she acts so stupid she ends up in the nuthouse she don't even stay a week.

There was a young dude in a sleeveless T-shirt and tattoos all up his neck out stringing Christmas lights through the scraggly little sticks of trees in front of the long blue trailer next to Hubert's. I didn't have anybody to go Christmas shopping with me. I could have gone with one of my cousins, but such a trip would turn into a shoplifting charge or a fight in the parking lot or the endless depression of listening to my cousins talk about everybody's problems. I was too tired to keep up with who had an EPO out on who; who'd ratted on who and got their check cut off; who'd wrecked whose vehicle. I got behind the wheel of one of Hubert's clunkers, a blue Cavalier with the paint peeled off the bumper showing the yellow underneath. Hubert came out and sat beside me on the front seat.

"You want to go get something to eat?" he said.

WE COULDN'T go to Kolonel Krispy because of idiot Colbert, even though idiot Colbert and his idiot woman had run off to Michigan out of fear of Sidney Coates. But we were still banned from Kolonel Krispy, so we sat in the truck and ate baloney sandwiches from the gas station downtown. The sun was out and leaves chattered across the parking lot, and the only sounds in the truck were the Merle Haggard cassette playing on the stereo and Hubert clearing his throat. After we finished our sandwiches, Hubert said, "You want anything else?" and I shook my head. Hubert wiped his forehead as he went in the store. He was sweating like it was summertime. I let the window down and thought about my schoolwork. I hadn't learned anything in a long time.

Hubert came back with a big bag of spicy hot pork rinds. He pulled it open and offered it to me. This is my body broken into strips and fried to a crisp for you. I took some and ate them. I asked Hubert for a sip of his pop. It was grape. I hate grape.

"Why don't you take me to the library?" I said.

Hubert said, "Do what?"

"Take me over to the public library and wait for me while I go in and learn something."

Hubert ate some more of his pork rinds. "All right," he said. "Spose to be a storm tonight."

"I'll walk," I said.

Hubert curled out his lower lip and nodded. "I'll be there when you're through."

I walked up the block to the corner by the fish store. I went back to Hubert's truck. He rolled down his window. "Thank you," I said.

"It's all right," he said.

~~~~~~~~~~~~~~~

THE LIBRARY wasn't much bigger than the houses turned lawyers' offices that sat next to it. When I walked in, the man behind the counter said the library was closing in eleven minutes. I walked past him to where the art books were. I walked down the aisle waiting for something to tell me to take it off the shelf. I saw a red book called *The World of Titian*, and it was in a box and full of art from the island city of Venice, which was built on wood sticks and threatened by the sea and kept from silting up and turning into a swamp by the sea, and so the bigshots in Venice, the men, would every year go out in a boat and drop a gold ring in the water and marry the sea, so the sea would keep getting them rich in trade and plunder and not drown them all in their sleep. That book also showed how in olden days, painters would put forty layers of paint down on every painting. Forty layers!

"Five minutes," the library man said.

I sat staring at a picture of a woman, floating on a cloud held up by a gang of babies. She was dressed in red and blue and reaching for a man looked like her daddy held up in the sky above her like an angel. She was the mother Mary, Jesus's momma, and below was all these beardy guys, looked like the bunch on Hubert's porch in a Nativity play, and they was reaching for Mary, trying to get past them babies to grab her and pull her back down.

The library man said, "We're closed now," and when I looked up from the rolling stool where I was sitting, the fluorescent lights looked like a rectangular halo over the library man's head.

Hubert came up behind me, and I put the art book back on the shelf where I'd found it and went with Hubert the way he had come. I looked back, and the library man was checking to make sure I'd put the book in the right place. He had his finger on the spine of *The World of Titian.*

Outside, Evie and Albert leaned on Hubert's truck, smoking. It was the first time I ever saw them together.

"What are you doing?" Evie said.

Albert said, "We need to find Mom."

"Blondie Kelly is hunting her," Evie said.

"That churchy bitch aint gonna do nothing," Hubert said.

"Her brothers might," Albert said. Blondie and Keith's brothers used to bust out TV picture tubes headbutting them. They say the younger one survived drinking a bottle of lye. The other one time swallowed a live baby snapping turtle. When they showed up, it was like it started raining washing machines. Things got broke.

Dark gathered in and the wind turned cold and the library man looked at us hard as he went past to his little car, looked hard again as he unlocked the car door. Lights came on in the pretty windows of the deep porch houses of town.

Hubert said, "Yall go back up the river, hunt her up near Coates's." Evie and Albert nodded. "Me and Dawn will go see what Cinderella knows."

~~~~~~~~~~~~~~

WHEN WE went to Cinderella's, his woman said Momma was with him, but she hadn't seen them since early. She said they might be at this man's had a pool table in Needle Creek, and so we went up there and Cinderella wasn't there, but they told us he was on up the creek at this man's kept a yard full of fighting chickens. When we got up there, Cinderella and this man sat in the kitchen writing bloodlines on eggs. Hubert asked them had they seen Momma.

"I seen her," Cinderella said. "She went off with Terry."

"Terry?" Hubert said, and Cinderella shook his head and give us directions.

Terry lived way up in the head of a holler in a trailer with holes from shotgun pellets all around the front door. "You stay here," Hubert said, and went to the door. I sat in the truck, and moony faces came by in the dark, peeking in on me on their way to the trailer, and they scared me.

I was glad when he came back, and the sound of Merle Haggard as we got out of there and headed up Drop Creek towards Virginia was a soothing sound.

~~~~~~~~~~~~

TERRY AND them told Hubert Momma went to a place below Queensbury on the Virginia side of Donnybrook Mountain. It was quiet and warming as we crested the mountain. By the light of the Rhubarb School we could see the sky hanging low. You could tell a big snow was coming.

"Which house is it?"

"They said it has a big cobra painted on the side of it. And a Confederate flag flying over it."

We found the place. The flag flapped in the wind. We heard it better than we could see it. I hate rebel flags. Ooooh, you're a rebel. So what? The cobra house was full of people more stoned than I'd ever seen. Their eyes were glassy and their faces red, and they were piled around a heater. It was none too warm in there, and they were in shirtsleeves. There were only like two beer cans and one wine bottle. People weren't even smoking. People nodded by the dim heater light.

When Hubert said, "Find your mother," he sounded like he was in an outer space monster movie and we had landed on the wrong planet. We stumbled through the drafty freak show Nativity scene of the cobra house party. Hubert tried to ask a couple of them about Momma, but they looked right through him and didn't answer. When Hubert said "Let's go," he didn't have to say it twice.

Outside the winter night closed on us like our heads were under the bed covers. Clean snow filled the ditch line and coated the trees. Snow makes you realize how many places there are that we never go, places we never set foot.

"You ought to keep a better eye on your mother," Hubert said.

I said, "That's my job?"

"Whose is it then?" Hubert said.

"What was that in there?" I said.

Hubert shook his head. "Quaaludes? I don't know. Some kind of monkey dope." Hubert spat. "Where do you reckon your mother went?"

I chewed on my lip. It began to bleed.

"Let's get out of here," Hubert said.

"No." I looked around, looked for some reason why no. None to be seen. Just snow falling in the orange booger light.

"I done crossed state lines hunting her," Hubert said, lowering his chin to look at me. "Maybe time for her to come to us."

"Maybe," I said. The snow fell thicker. I did not want to leave.

"Do you want to drive?" Hubert said.

"No."

The snow touched Hubert's shoulders, his combed-forward hair, and disappeared. "She's probably at his house."

"Whose?"

Hubert said, "Wavyhead." Keith Kelly.

I could see her there, snuggled down in his pay-by-the-month black pleather sectional. I started towards the car.

Hubert said, "You sure you don't want to drive?"

"We got to stop this," I said.

"Good a time as any to learn," he said.

I stopped walking to the car.

"You don't get in a hurry," Hubert said. "Slow things down. All there is to it really. Use your head."

"Where's the keys?" I said.

"In it," Hubert said.

I got the car up the hill before the snow covered the road. We got back down in Kentucky to the big tipple right as second shift came out of the mine. "You're doing good," Hubert said, "doing good." I got in the middle of the trucks coming out of the same mud parking lot where I found out Momma had been riding with Keith Kelly, the parking lot at the mine we had inspected. All them men roaring out in the snowy road tried to show one another how scared they weren't, how they could go fast in the snow in their high-off-the-ground trucks and their headlights flashing right in my eyes. The motors roared, and their tires howled through the curves back and forth on the gathering snow. "God Almighty damn," I said. The car heater got hot and made me sticky and pinched underneath my seat belt. Hubert smelled like cough drops and potato grease, and I thought I was going to be sick.

"Get out of this," Hubert said.

"What am I supposed to do?" I said. Old angers, inherited angers I had never seen born, welled up in me.

"Pull over down there at the church," Hubert said.

"Where?" I said. I didn't know anything up there.

"Right around this corner."

I pulled onto the lot next to the Lower Dogsplint Baptist Church. I let all those pickups rumble past. Directly it was quiet again. I spun my wheels pulling back onto the road.

"You don't have to gun it," Hubert said. "Nice and slow. Nice and slow."

We came through Shifters Mill quiet as thieves. We didn't have the radio on. We didn't talk. The heater blew through the Escort. The snow dashed at my lights like a thousand tiny suicides, and my eyes locked into the flow of flakes. Hubert grabbed the wheel. "What?" I said, because we were still right in the middle of the road, safe as could be. "What?" I said again.

"Pay attention," Hubert said.

I wanted to turn on the radio. I wanted to fly out the window, become a summer bird making a nest in my mother's hair, singing from a branch of the tree I imagined my father had become. Tweeta tweeta tweet tweet tweet.

Lost bird. Lost summer bird. My jaw hurt from grinding it.

Keith Kelly fell in behind us when we passed the old Drop Creek School. He came bearing down on us in that black Ford, and it was snowing too hard for me even to be mad. I just wanted out of that mess. Keith Kelly banged into the back of the Escort.

"Lord have mercy," Hubert said.

I thought maybe Keith Kelly's brakes were messed up or something, but Hubert said that wasn't it. We come sloshing through the tight curve where a Sugarberry man sold sex toys out of a Quonset hut below the road and the guardrails had already been torn out by numerous other wrecks. The snow was packed down and slick. "Where's the salt trucks," I said.

"They should've been here," Hubert said. "That's a fact."

Keith Kelly bumped us again. They always salt the coal-haul roads first, but not that night. I wanted to lay my head down. Strange a woman getting knocked off the road by a mortal enemy would be getting drowsy, but I was, sure enough. Hubert slapped me, but it didn't do any good. I had hoped it would, but it didn't, snow coming straight at the windshield like in a spaceship movie.

Keith Kelly rammed into us again. I was like, by God, this is going to get finished right here and now. I jerked the wheel sideways, pulled it to the left just as hard as I could pull it.

"Ohmygod," I heard Hubert say, all quick and together in one word, and I felt the whole left side of that Escort lift up off the ground, but it didn't flip. We got sideways, then backwards, then sideways in the other direction. The Escort ended up broadsided across the road.

I heard Keith Kelly go into a skid behind us. He swerved and clipped us, our front end spinning towards his back end, and we smacked into him and his vehicle, which was almost off the road anyway, slid back end first into the shallow ditch. If he'd gone off the other side, he would have free-fallen twenty-some feet and probably burst into scorching flames screaming, "Allllllll," and dying a horrible closed-casket death. But that didn't happen. His truck just rolled up on its side, passenger door against the bottom of the ditch, roof of the cab wedged up against the rock wall. My front end was off the road far enough to where my back wheels raised up off the ground. The Escort hung on the lip of the road, the asphalt black against the snow gouging into the undercarriage just past where the back door met the front.

"You stay here," Hubert said, opening his door to the snow, which come in the cab like a gang of hungry kids through a kitchen door. The bank was steep, and Hubert slipped. He steadied himself and climbed out of the ditch and walked around our vehicle, never touching it, his balance sure after the first fall. He opened my door, which gapped with a creak, and put one hard hand out to me, red and wet in the falling powder. I let him lead me.

Keith Kelly's truck was quiet as the snow and dark except for the dashboard scratches of green and orange light visible through the steamy windows. I dropped Hubert's hand as we angled along the ditch, but took it back when I saw Keith Kelly. He was slumped sideways towards the passenger side, hands loose, blood blooming black against the side of his head. Hubert climbed onto the road, nearly level with the truck door. He stepped onto Keith Kelly's truck. The truck rocked under Hubert's weight enough to cause him to bend his knees for balance.

"Be careful, Hubert," I said.

Hubert tried the door handle of Keith Kelly's truck, but it was locked, and Hubert crouched to say "Son of a bitch" and figure what to do next. He stepped off the truck and back onto the road, shuffling through the new snow to Mamaw's trunk. When he called, I brought him the keys, and he rustled through the trunk til he found the tire iron. He climbed back onto Keith's truck. The iron smashing the glass startled me. Hubert ran the iron around the edge of the hole in the glass until it was big enough to stick his arm through and unlock the door. The door opened up into the air like a hatch on a submarine, and Hubert grabbed hold of Keith Kelly's seat belt—which I was surprised to see he was wearing—and pulled Keith Kelly towards him with both hands.

"Is he alive?" I said.

Hubert strained to move Keith Kelly, but he finally got him close enough to wrap his arm around Keith's shoulder. I could see blood bubbling in Keith's nose. Hubert was on his knees above Keith, straining to hold him in his arms. Hubert managed to slide onto his belly without dropping Keith. Hubert breathed through his nose, deep distinct breaths. I could hear the snowflakes land on his canvas coat over the "ding ding ding" of the open door.

"Make that noise stop," Hubert said, and I got on my knees on the road next to them and stretched out across the gap between the road and the car and pulled the keys out of the ignition. I stood back up.

Hubert's feet began to work, his boots like a duck's feet under water. He pulled himself forward on his elbows until his body covered Keith's. I knew he would not be able to hold that position long.

"Do you need help?" I said, and started towards him. He raised up on his elbows. "Let me help you," I said.

With a long low moan, Hubert grabbed Keith Kelly's head with both hands and as Keith's body fell back across the cab of the truck, Hubert twisted Keith Kelly's face towards him. Keith Kelly's neck made a sound like a pop bottle coming open, and when it did Hubert turned loose of his head and Keith's body slumped into almost exactly the position it was in when we found it. The snow swirled into my brain.

. . . I said over and over, louder and louder til Hubert raised a finger marked with Keith's blood.

"Shh," he said, finger to his lips, "time for quiet."

My breaths came so fast there was no way to count them.

"Help me get him out of there," Hubert said.

I stared at the road. I dropped the keys into the snow. Hubert pulled Keith Kelly up by the seat belt again, a horror show rerun, quicker paced now, and got him first by one arm and then the other and got him out of the truck. Keith Kelly lay face down on the road, his arms above his head like he was diving into something.

"What have you done?" I said to Hubert.

"He was already dead," Hubert said.

"No, he wasn't," I said. "I don't believe you."

Hubert put in a dip of snuff. "Good thing you aint the coroner," he said. I stood there staring at Hubert with my mouth hanging open. The snow fell on both of us. I stood there thinking: if it wasn't Hubert killed Keith, it was me.

"He was going off the road anyway," Hubert said. "Wadn't nothing you done."

The snow stuck to my nose, my eyelashes. I turned from Hubert and stuck out my tongue. The snow stuck to it too. When it snows here, things get very quiet. There is no school; cars don't go out. Nobody out in their yard. No four-wheelers. No hammering. Nobody on a grinding wheel in the driveway. A lot of times a tree or a bunch of trees will get loaded down with snow and fall across the power lines and knock out all the electricity. So there is that—the sound of the tree cracking, and the transformer going "pop." But mostly there is nothing. Nothing but what you see—the snow falling from bushes in clods, hitting the snow on the ground without a sound, or maybe just the slightest sound.

Standing on the road with Hubert, Keith Kelly's body cold and getting colder, it was all that—quiet and dark, like a pretty Christmas card a hippie would send, something simple, light and dark, printed with a woodblock, so you can feel the dent in the card where the ink went on. The picture is a fallen log or a stand of trees, and it makes you feel you are right there in the scene, the printer's woodblock straight from the spot in the forest that's in the picture. And everything is safe, and you are looking at the Christmas card, and someone you don't know hands you a cup of something that smells of those spices you only have in stuff at Christmas and sometimes Thanksgiving. And the cup is steaming, and you hold the cup up and the steam curls in front of the Christmas card when you close one eye and a log pops in the fire, and it is warm, and you don't even want a present.

ACT FOUR

# MEATSPACE

# 10

~~~~~~~

# RACCOON EYES

"ME AND the wife heard the noise."

Mamaw's Escort stood on its grill in the ditch, and Keith Kelly lay face down dead in the snow, his arms stretched towards Love World, the sex toy shop below the road on Lower Drop Creek. Furl, the maintenance man they just fired at my high school, stood over us in sweatpants and unlaced workboots. "The wife sent me up here to see what happened," Furl said, staring at Keith Kelly's F-150 turned up on its side. Furl's eyes followed the blood in the snow where Hubert had dragged Keith Kelly out of his truck. Furl squatted beside Keith Kelly and turned his head sideways to look into Keith's face.

"Nice truck," Furl said. Hubert spat into the snow. Furl stood up with a moan and said, "Is everybody all right?" When we didn't say anything, Furl said, "Except for him, I mean," waving his hand over Keith Kelly. Hubert walked back to the Escort. I was afraid he would come back with something to kill Furl. Furl stepped past me, got between me and Hubert. "You all right, Dawn?" Furl said to me, but kept looking out into the darker place Hubert had gone.

I said, "He come up behind us, lost control."

Hubert's sneakers crunched in the snow. "You got a phone?" Hubert said to Furl.

Furl nodded and waddled back towards his house, us behind. "Nothing good can come of this," Hubert said when Furl was far enough away.

"Come of what?" I said.

"Calling the law."

I stopped walking towards Furl's house. My breath clouded out in front of me.

"Can't get no fair shake," Hubert said. "Law's got us buffaloed." Furl stopped and looked back at us. Hubert walked towards him.

"I don't know," Hubert said.

"Then why did you ask to use the phone?"

Hubert shook his head. "He didn't need to be doing no more looking."

I hurried up next to Hubert. "So what are you going to do when we get in his house?"

"You go back," Hubert said to me, stepping into Furl's yard. "Make sure nobody don't run over Keith."

When I got back, the snow had covered Keith Kelly. I got on my knees beside him and put my hands under his ribs. I lifted and kept sliding my hands under him until I got him flipped over on his back. He landed with a "chink." He had a small flask, stainless steel, in his shirt pocket. There wasn't snow on Keith Kelly's front side. I could see the shine of blood and the orange stripes from his miner's clothes under his coat by what little light come from the houses across the road. Coal dust caked around his eyes and down his gray cheeks.

I pulled the flask out of his pocket and drank the last of Keith Kelly's bourbon. I put my hand on his wavy brown hair, the thing my mother found so beautiful about him. I ran my fingers through it. It was nice hair. I rolled Keith again and got him off the road. I leaned against his truck and wished for coffee and a better life. It's not a thing I'm proud of, but I didn't wish Keith Kelly back alive.

Twenty minutes later, blue lights filled the narrow curve. One police car set up below and another above me and Keith. A state police with his stiff hat pushed forward on his brow walked towards me in his shiny shoes and his state police winter coat. He asked me what my name was and if I was all right. When I told him, he wrote down my name and looked over the scene. When he got to Keith Kelly, he felt of Keith's neck, looked at his watch, and wrote in his book. Then he waved up the man in the other car, talked to him, and went back to his car.

When the man came back he said, "Tell me what happened here."

"We was driving—"

"Who was driving?"

"He," I said, pointing at Keith Kelly, "come up behind us."

"Ma'am. Who was driving?"

"He banged into us three different times."

"Ma'am—"

"I was just trying to drive."

"You were driving?"

"Yes," I said.

"And how old are you?"

"Almost sixteen."

"I need to see your permit," he said. And then he leaned in. "Have you been drinking, ma'am?"

"Yes," I said.

"She don't know what she's saying," Hubert spoke at my shoulder. "I was driving."

They separated me and Hubert, took us to either end of the two crashed vehicles.

The young police said to me, "So you were driving."

I stood a long minute. The young police didn't have any hair showing underneath his hat. I bet he had a wife, and I bet she had a lot of hair. I looked over in the direction where Hubert and the other state police had gone. The snow fell thicker. The big police flashlights drove out all other light.

"Miss," the police said.

"Hubert," I said. "Hubert was driving."

"You're sure of that?"

"Yes," I said. I wanted to make up a big story how I had started off driving and how we had changed drivers at the Lower Dogsplint Church, but one time I heard Hubert say don't get cute. Don't be thinking you're smart.

"Because you said earlier," the police said, "you were driving."

I looked over to where Keith Kelly was, imagined Momma crying over his body.

"I took this out of his pocket," I said, and held the flask out in my flat open palm.

"Where'd you get that?"

"When I was rolling him," I said.

More cop vehicles showed up and these guys got out and looked at all the skid marks. They got out cameras and set up lights and strung yellow tape said "Do not cross." They reminded me of computer boys at school who thought they were cool because they had carts with tools on them nobody else knew how to use. They were cop AV.

"You gonna arrest me or not?" I heard Hubert say.

The state police asked me a bunch of other questions about Keith running up on us, about who crashed into who, and I mostly told him I didn't know, that it all happened fast. Then the two state police come together and talked for a while, keeping me and Hubert apart. Hubert stepped into the weak light from the pole at the corner of Furl's place. He was dull gray, like the light off a pencil lead. Then the scene-reconstruction guys turned on their lights, and the whole place lit up like daytime. The older state police said to Hubert, "You're free to go, Mr. Jewell."

"Let's go, Dawn," Hubert said.

"Ma'am, we need you to come with us to post."

"What the hell for?" Hubert said. "She wasn't driving. You see she got her liquor off of him."

The younger police said, "You're free to go, sir."

"I got a right to be with her," Hubert said. "I'm her uncle."

The older state police said, "Are you her guardian, sir?"

"Hell yes, I'm her guardian," Hubert said. "I'm her daddy's brother, and her daddy's dead."

"Where's your mother," the police said.

"That's who we was hunting," I said.

"Who do you stay with?"

Mamaw's name was on my lips, and then I looked at Hubert and said,

The two police looked at each other and then at us. "We have your contact information, Mr. Jewell," the older one said. "Thank you for your cooperation."

The young police got me behind the arm, started walking me towards his vehicle. The other one got in his vehicle and took off.

"It's gonna be all right, Dawn," Hubert said. The young police pressed me down by the top of my head into his vehicle. "You stay calm," Hubert said. "I'll be down there soon as I can." Hubert walked up to the window glass. The young police asked him to step away from the vehicle. "Calm," Hubert said. "Don't get excited."

~~~~~~~~~~

WHEN I got to the state police place, they set me in a room by myself in a metal chair. A raccoon-eyed woman came in, looked drunker than anybody I'd seen all night. She didn't look like state police. She was a case worker or something. When she asked me what happened, I told her Hubert was driving and we had a wreck and a man got killed. When she asked me did I get in fights in school, I told her about breaking Albert's ribs between first and second period, and I told her about whipping Belinda Coates after French class. She didn't seem too tore up about it.

Raccoon Eyes asked me about Hubert, asked me about Momma, asked me about Keith Kelly. When she ran out of steam asking, she told me she had to call a judge and see whether to keep me overnight and left the room.

About that time Hubert showed up. Hubert seemed to know everybody at the state police post, seemed to know how everything was supposed to go. It made it easier to breathe to look out and see Hubert talking close to Raccoon Eyes with his hands pressed together in front of him.

Raccoon Eyes disappeared, and I waited for Hubert's eyes to find me. I knew they would even though the glass rectangle in the door wasn't very big. When his eyes met mine, I couldn't remember the last time I had seen him in such bright light. Probably never. He looked like somebody in some low-ceiling white-light don't-give-a-shit-how-bright-things-are church. Had he raised up a rattlesnake above his head and started speaking in tongues I wouldn't have been surprised.

When Raccoon Eyes came back, she asked me was I still suspended from school. I told her it was Christmas vacation. She got a look on her face like she had time-machine eyes and she was trying to drive me backwards in time by looking at me.

"The judge says he's not going to keep you overnight," she said. "In a few weeks you'll get a letter telling you when and where you need to go. All right?"

"Yes."

"Dawn," that woman said, "you've got yourself in a bad place."

"Do you want us to call your grandmother?"

"Can I go home with my uncle?"

Raccoon Eyes gave me the time-machine look again. "Is that what you want?"

"I guess," I said. "Don't matter."

~~~~~~~~

A COAL train slipped through the mist and pearly light of town and stopped me and Hubert going home. The clanging of the bells at the railroad crossing was the same as it had always been. The train wheezed and squealed like it had forever. The moon looked back at me from the top of the sky, hazy and wakeful. There was no talking in town that night, only snow and the tossing of old men in their sleep, lights on all through the night, hopeless dogs breathing hard in dark corners of stale houses.

"Is this what you thought life would be?" I asked Hubert.

"Pretty much," Hubert said.

~~~~~~~~

HUBERT RATTLED Mamaw's beat-to-death Escort into the carport and walked back to his place. Mamaw didn't wake up as I came through the dark house, and it wasn't til I was in bed—the sheets cold and starchy—that I thought of Momma. I still didn't know where she was. She might still be setting at Keith

Kelly's house for all I knew. I got out of bed and stood over Mamaw's phone and thought, "This is too weird." And I went back to bed. I knew we hadn't heard the end of it. Me and Hubert would have to account for the death of Keith Kelly. I thrashed around in bed, pretty sure that was the way the rest of my life was going to be—never a decent night's sleep because I was a killer, a murderous killer, just another Jewell, just another one of my daddy's outlaw kinfolks.

The next morning was snow quiet, snow deep, and Mamaw's shuffling and banging in the kitchen was like any other of ten thousand days. If she had come to the room to see about me, I would have told her everything. I swear I would have. But she didn't. I got up and went in the kitchen. It was hot as blazes in there.

"Sit down," Mamaw said, not hardly looking at me, and I thought she'd found out, but she just set a plate of hot eggs in front of me, eggs scrambled hard.

I said, "These are the way you like eggs, Mamaw. These are your eggs." And she said, "Hush now. You're going to wake your Momma."

I said, "Do what?"

And she said, "Your momma's upstairs."

---

WHEN MOMMA came downstairs, the first thing she said was, "Let's go to Kingsport. Let's go Christmas shopping."

"How?" I said.

"Hubert gave me a wad of money," Momma said. "We got to get for the whole family."

I sat blinking like a fresh-born baby.

"Do you want to go or don't you?" Momma said, drumming her fingers on the back of her cigarette pack.

IS MAMAW GOING?

I SAID.

Mamaw came in the kitchen. "I got to see the governor," she said.

"Do what?" I said and looked at Momma, but Momma had stuck her nose in the refrigerator.

Back in the early fall, back when the leaves were still on the trees and the governor's reelection didn't seem so up in the air, his Tahoe pulled up at the Civic Center down in town, and he went in and gave a speech. Mamaw was there in her putty-colored shoes and her Roy Orbison sunglasses, and she and the organizer girls, and those retired coal miners, and those people whose house foundation had been shook by the blasting on Blue Bear held up signs asking the governor wasn't he worried about history's judgment, wasn't he ashamed to stand by and watch the state's highest peak get strip mined. When the governor left the building, he bowed his head and didn't say anything. Then later when Mamaw and them got a lawyer, the governor said he didn't have no power, didn't have no say-so in matters like this, and the newspaper editorial writers (back then the newspaper was still big and wide and people still read their editorials) said:

And the governor he called Mamaw's lawyer and said we got to talk about this, we got to get something settled. We got to get folks like Mamaw quieted down, the governor said to the folks beside him, until we can get this election done, and so Mamaw and them and the governor's people started talking to the company people, and that got the governor calmed down a little bit, but then Mamaw and them filed their lands unsuitable petition, which is federal, and it started looking like maybe Mamaw and them might win and stop *all* the mining on Blue Bear, and people wrote letters to the governor by the thousand—letters on real paper like the newspaper was then, with real stamps on them—telling the governor he needed to do right, and so he said again, you coal companies and you putty-colored mamaws, yall need to sit down and figure this out once and for all, and so they set a meeting, and so Mamaw couldn't go Christmas shopping with us on the Saturday before Christmas in 1998. She had to go see the governor.

That left it to me and Momma to go to Kingsport to get Christmas presents for the family. I didn't tell Momma or Mamaw what had happened to Keith Kelly. This was before cell phones, before Facebook, and a person not knowing what happened the night before was possible, particularly if a person is up early and about the business of getting out of town, and so it was that me and Momma ended up on the strange sunny day after that big storm, sliding off the mountain headed to Kingsport in Hubert's big green truck.

When we got on the road, I said, "When did Hubert give you this money?"

Momma said, "He come over before light, left me the truck keys and an envelope of shopping money."

"Left it where?"

"On Momma's kitchen counter."

"You saw him?"

"Well, no," Momma said, "but I heard his truck."

Meaning the truck we were then sitting in, massive and green and high above the snow, crunching gravel with tire treads like rubber dinosaur teeth. I wondered that day in the blinding brightness of the sunshine on the fresh-fallen snow, the sky a burning blue, what happened to the cuss-word way Momma talked to me last time we had been together, before we lost her the night before. I dreaded to ask her what brought such a change or where she had been while the snow fell. I feared what she might say, be it the truth, or worse, a question that might cause me to have to tell that me and Hubert had killed her new boyfriend.

"So Albert and Evie are courting?" Momma said.

"I reckon."

"Can't no good come of that," Momma said.

I didn't think much good could come of Albert period, but I said anyway: "Why do you say that?" cause I liked Evie.

"Shoo," Momma said, ripping past a little-car man, passing him in his own lane in a cloud of blue smoke, causing cuss words to pass his Sunday school liver lips. "Evie won't give Albert a minute's peace. Spindly little hen. 'Cluck, cluck, cluck,' scratch, scratch, scratch."

Momma was wound up. "Got you kicked out of school, didn't she?"

I said I could go back if I wanted, which was true, thinking of the fire and the Little Debbies that had passed between me and Evie.

"What should we get Hubert for Christmas?" Momma said.

Out loud I said I didn't know. Hubert's truck sailed through the slush. The cliffs in the curves glittered and dripped.

Momma said, "I'd like to get him a big gold ring, all pimpy, to wear on his little finger." Momma's big laugh showed where she had had her side teeth pulled. We skidded coming out of the curve. "Whoa," Momma said. The truck straightened out. "We might have to buy a tarp," she said, "to cover all the presents we're fixing to get, and bungee cord to hold it down."

My mother used to love getting people things. Her fingers shook on the wheel, and the smoke coming off the end of her cigarette trembled like the needle on a lie detector.

"I been begging Hubert to build Albert a wrestling ring," Momma said. "Out in the old man's shed. I think if he'd just eat he could be a wrestler. Don't you?"

"Yeah, Momma," I said. "He's just a suflex looking for a place to happen."

Momma gunned it through a yellow light and turned left onto the main drag of Pennington Gap, Virginia. She slammed on the brakes for a gray string of a family crossing the road in front of us. The sun shone bright on the pavement as they straggled from the permanent yard sale at the old car wash to the drugstore. Momma's cigarette hung on her lip like a two-by-four about to fall out the back of a moving pickup truck. She punched the gas again as the last of them cleared the road. She started mashing buttons and turning knobs on the dashboard. A school bus coming the other way blew its horn, and Momma jerked the truck back in her own lane.

"What are you doing?" I said.

"What's *he* doing?" Momma said. "There aint even school today." She took out her cigarette and coughed. "Find me a radio station, Dawn."

I got the radio going as Momma jerked through the stop sign at the other end of town, and we cleared Pennington Gap. The radio was set on country, and I turned the dial to the left and Momma wished out loud for Aerosmith, and I kept twisting the dial and for some reason tears came to my eyes, and I got the knob twisted to Willett's radio station, my wrist turned over, my elbow pointed up in the air. I almost leaned and put my head on Momma's shoulder, but she started clapping her hands to the song, which wasn't something I'd thought she'd like. It was a synthesizer dance music song about feeling fascination, and I had to grab the wheel, or at least I thought I did, to keep her from driving Hubert's truck into a shaley bank or the winter-green river. She didn't have neither hand on the wheel, but she said, "Dawn, you leave that wheel alone. Aint but one Santa can drive the sleigh, and that Santa is me."

Once upon a time my mother would have made a hot Santa, but she was dropping weight and getting too bony—drawn about the cheek and eyes—and looking like she needed a good night's rest. All in all riding with her didn't feel like Christmas. Felt more like a scary biker Halloween party.

"How you like your new hairdo?" Momma said. She reached out to palm my green buzz cut.

Momma said, "Let's get you some big red hat, or a red sweatshirt. No. Candy canes. Get you some candy-cane tights. Make you into a humongous Christmas elf." And then she started beating on the steering wheel with both hands laughing. I was glad she had hands on the wheel, but I didn't care much for her elf vision.

Willett Bilson was talking on the radio. It made me happy to go to Kingsport because somehow that might lead me to him, and me and him might talk face-to-face, and who knows it probably wouldn't but it might—it might end up with me having an actual guy friend.

"He sounds like a pussy," Momma said.

"Who?" I said, because Willett was playing David Bowie, who I kind of think sounds like a pussy, and if that's who she was talking about, then I could agree with Momma.

"That DJ," Momma said.

"No, he don't," I said before I thought, and with a voice too hot.

"Ohhh," Momma said, dragging out the word, "That's him, aint it? That's your little heartthrob."

"No," I said. I was in a fix because I didn't like to talk about my business, not with my mother nor anybody else, but I wanted Momma to have her mind on something other than Keith. I was hoping for a nice calm day of Christmas shopping and that Momma had already bought Keith Kelly something.

"Look at that," I said, and pointed across Momma at a pink Ford Pinto wagon had a bunch of young boys in it. "Aint seen one of them in a long time," I said.

"Oooh," Momma said, "that dark-headed one is hot," and I was like oh no. She was getting sex on the brain. I swallowed hard and said, "Why do you think Willett sounds like a pussy?"

The song on the radio ended and we come under a railroad bridge, and the sun poured through the windshield and Willett said, "Fall into it, children, fall into it. Fall into the rich, buttery goodness of the world. Spread your arms wide, abandon concern for your personal body odor and fall into it. Ahhh, the world is a swimming pool full of Cool Whip, with marshmallows stirred all through it, marshmallows of various hues and the size of throw pillows."

Willett played "Holiday in Cambodia" by the Dead Kennedys. Momma pulled her chin in, raised her eyebrows and said, "How old did you say he is?"

"Eighteen," I said.

"He sounds younger than you," she said.

"He's been to college," I said, "in North Carolina."

"Well," Momma said, "there you go," and we both fell silent.

I said, "This is where people get stopped speeding a lot."

"That right?" Momma said.

"What Hubert told me," I said.

"Your daddy and I used to go to North Carolina," Momma said. "To see his mother."

I remembered one trip there, right before Dad died. I remember his mother liked me, but she was strange and old-timey.

"I am going to get Keith," Momma said, "a leather jacket. A leather jacket and a fifth of liquor and a bottle of cologne that makes him smell like a jungle beast."

I sat and stared out my window, wished I was one of the cows standing on the gentle knobs of the leveling-out hills of Virginia, hills more mellow than the walled-up rat maze of mountains where we lived.

"I want you to start being nice to Keith, Dawn," Momma said. "You hurt his feelings."

"How could I hurt his feelings?" I said. "I don't even talk to him."

"Well, you do, you and Momma both. You hurt his feelings talking bad about strip mining."

"I thought you was against strip mining too," I said. "That's what you told us when you was up in that tree."

It was too hot in the truck cab. Momma had the heat turned up, and the sun made everything bright white. I started feeling pukish. Momma's top lip hairs had sweat in them. She looked like my mother again, like she hadn't for a long time, her flesh golden-brown in the sunlight, a dark glow coming from inside her. Maybe the glow was just me needing her, because I was scared about what we'd done to Keith.

She said, "Dawn, you got any money you could kick in on a leather jacket for Keith?" My mouth fell open, and Momma said, "I know you got money, Dawn. All that work you been doing for Hubert. Aint no need for you to be so stingy."

I said, "Keith Kelly is dead," just like that, flat as a piece of paper, and Momma didn't take her eyes off the road and she said, "That's not funny, Dawn. You know better than to joke with me about stuff like that." Then she looked at me. "I am still your mother."

A van cut in front of us, and I didn't care if we had a wreck. Momma stomped the brakes, said, "Son of a bitch," and laid on the truck horn. The van sped off.

I said, "You don't believe me, ask Hubert."

Momma said, "You better not be fucking with me, Dawn," and when I sat there she said, "I'm serious. You're not too damn big for me to not still beat your ass."

I was still looking out the window, so I know she couldn't see it, but I was crying a little. She pulled over to the side of the road under a billboard said if you get your GED they could get you NASCAR tickets, and Momma said, "Look at me," and I did and Momma turned off the radio and Willett was gone and his old music was gone and my mother's face was alive in front of me, both eyes wide open and human with wet in her black-painted lashes, all dolled up for the trip to town, and now the tears rolled off my face hot and steady, and my mother took my glasses off, put her thumbs to my tears, and said, "What happened, Dawn?"

And so I told her how Keith Kelly died and how I thought it might have been my fault the way I jerked the wheel in front of him. I put it out there because I wanted to put my head on my mother's shoulder, bony like it was there by the side of the road in the white winter sun. She stared out the windshield like she was trying to see things she wouldn't never see again, and I said, "I'm sorry." She started the truck and pulled back on the highway in front of a flatbed and said, "What is he thinking? He thinking if he can make me miserable with everybody else then I'll go back to him?"

I wanted to be a part of what my mother was going through, but I was too young. There were simpler games I should be playing, games that wouldn't make my stomach hurt so bad. I felt like I was watching a show people my age weren't supposed to be watching, except that the show was my life, and I was watching by myself.

Outside, it was a nice day. Flocks of birds lit and picked at the green grass showing between the sparkling patches of snow. Hubert's truck was big and loud as a Tarzan movie jungle drum. Momma didn't say anything to me the rest of the way. She muttered to herself and worked herself up into such a mad you could see her eyeballs vibrating. When we pulled up at my aunt June's house, she jumped out and ran in without knocking even though she hadn't been there, as far as I know, in years.

I STAYED in the truck when my mother ran in June's house, which set across the street from a long, straight stretch of railroad track. It was one of a string of little houses facing the chemical factory, small and old and town-looking. It had a small porch with iron rails made into the shape of twining vines holding up the awning. I imagined my mother in there crying into June's shoulder, June in some pretty color you couldn't get at Walmart, and my breath grabbed up in me in the cooling truck cab and I tried to gag, but couldn't.

I was in the town where Willett Bilson lived, and I imagined his shoulders, even though I couldn't really, didn't have sense enough in my mind what his body would have been like. All I had in my mind was the picture of him with Chewbacca. His shoulders were broad and sharp, like he had a coat hanger still in his shirt. But he was nice and tall, tall as Chewbacca. The sun was bright, but in the house shadow in June's narrow driveway I stayed cold. The chemical factory plumed out white smoke from a dozen smokestacks in the dim green light of Hubert's rearview mirror, and I could smell their stinks layered one on top of another—the strongest stink like the poop of a cat that's been living on molded popcorn for a month. I had just come to name that smell when Momma ran up to my window. She tried the door handle, but it was locked, and before I could get it open, she hollered through the glass, "Get out," and when I opened the door, the cold clean winter air rushed in, and she squeezed me at the elbow and said, "Come on," rough as a cop.

I said, "Where am I going?"

She said, "June will tell you," and soon as I was clear of the truck, she stomped over to her side, jumped in, and started the engine. My door was still open and she said, "Here," pushing my bag towards me.

I said, "Where are you going?"

"Home," she said.

I said, "What about Christmas shopping?"

She said, "Shut the door."

When I did, she put the truck in reverse and left me standing in June's driveway, the eaves dripping snow.

<hr>

I HAD not seen June since she came to my grandfather Houston's birthday back in September. Their birthdays are three days apart. Generally June didn't come home. I wondered how long I would be at June's. People tell me all the time I remind them of her.

When I turned to look, June stood at the front door, her fingers white and clean against the cast-iron ivy vine. She stood there with a black T-shirt on under some orangy-pink shirt, and she seemed lighter than anyone in the family, even birdy Cora, but she had Mamaw's square-set jaw and Houston's Santa Claus eyes. June sighed and waved at me.

"You want something to drink?" she said, her fingers clung to the porch rail.

"Where's she going?" I said.

"Home, I reckon."

"Is she coming back?" I said.

June came down the four steps and stood beside me, put her arm around me. "You used to like hot chocolate," she said. I put my head on her shoulder, and she walked me up in her house.

# 11

~~~~~~~~

# FAKE MARSHMALLOWS

JUNE'S FRONT room was dark and golden, like a pirate treasure cave. There were posters on the walls for hippie music shows and works of art that were funky and done, you could tell, by people June knew. There were quilted and woven and crocheted things, and it was hard to imagine anybody ever throwing up on any of it or anybody ever flinging a chair at somebody in that room. Everything looked like it had been sitting there forever with its perfect chair angles and fat art books on low tables, chilling out until the guy from the magazine got there to take the picture.

"Make yourself to home," June said. I could hear nervous in her voice. I sat down on the sofa. June stood looking at me like a bird lost its flock, scared to fly off with me. Beautiful bird.

June went in the kitchen. The refrigerator opened with a soft pop. A pan hit the stovetop, and a cabinet door opened and closed. A spoon came out of a drawer with a tinkle and a rattle, and my breath came easy, and the stove eye went "unnnnn," circling up orange on the cat-black stovetop. The wood spoon against the bottom of the saucepan was gentle, like the lap of water against a pier in the summertime at a lake house. June hummed over her saucepan of hot chocolate, maybe to calm herself, maybe to calm me. I don't know. Maybe she didn't even know she was humming. Maybe she just hummed—like the stove eye hummed, like the stars hummed.

Directly June set a mug thrown by somebody she knew (of course) down in front of me on a piece of tile with a picture of a dog painted by a child, and then she plundered through a pile of CDs, one at a time, careful like she was picking apart a snowball. She turned to me and said, "Do you want to listen to something?" She stood straight and beautiful, like an unwrapped candy bar before anybody's taken a bite out of it.

Tears filled my eyes.

She went to the kitchen and came back with her own mug of hot chocolate and sat down beside me with her knees together. A car slished by on the street outside. Cotton-white smoke boiled out of the factory stacks, and finally June said, "How are you?"

It all came out. "I don't know," I said. "I don't know how I am. Crazy. I'm crazy. I quit school. I wrecked a car and a truck and a four-wheeler and another car. I killed a man. Stole a bunch of stuff. Drove my mother off the deep end. Everybody hates me cause I'm a treehugger. I want to strangle about ten different people. I'm a crazy dangerous person liable to go off at any minute."

I wanted to knock everything off June's peaceful coffee table, but I didn't because I was afraid she would kick me out. I clenched up my fists and went "URRRRRRR" and put my hands to my head and tried to pull out my hair, but it was too short to grip. I grabbed at it until June put her hand to mine and laid my hands in my lap and left hers there on top of mine. We sat there for a bit, and I settled down some, and June said, "Yeah," soft as rabbit fur. She was a good deal smaller than me, but she pulled me toward her, and as I fell into her, I knew in my heart I was not dangerous, and that I did not want to be, either. My head landed in June's lap, her hand on my hair, and I just breathed and breathed in June's pirate cove.

"It is not too cold out," June said, "doesn't seem like."

"No," I said, "it wasn't too bad."

"How's your chocolate?"

"Good," I said. "I like that the marshmallows aren't fake."

June said, "You mean like those little hard ones that come in the packets?"

I nodded.

"I hate those," June said.

"Me too," I said.

I rose up out of June's lap and sipped at the mug, my heart like one of those movies where they take a picture of a flower every day and run the pictures back fast and it looks like it's blooming all at once.

"You want some more?" June said.

"I'm all right."

June put her hands between her knees, looked down, and then around the room. "I'm sorry it's so quiet here," she said.

I shrugged my shoulders. I said, "You like it here?"

"Here in this house," June said, "or here in Kingsport?"

"Don't matter," I said. "I was just wanting to hear you talk."

June looked at me fluttery. "I think this house is right for me," she said. "Not too big and not so small I'm always tripping over myself."

I said, "You got a lot of stuff."

"I do," she said, and laughed a watery laugh, water like comes out of a fountain at a shopping center.

"Where does it all come from?" I said.

"Don't all come from one place," she said. "People bring me stuff."

"You got a lot of friends, I guess."

"I guess," June said.

"Momma says you been everwhere."

"What does she say?"

"Nothing. Just that you been a bunch of places."

June chewed on the pinky nail of her left hand.

I said, "What did you do to your finger?" June had four Band-Aids on her left hand pinky.

"Cutting up a chicken. Do you like curry?"

June nodded.

"Why aren't you at work?" I said.

"Christmas break," she said. I sipped chocolate. June said, "Why have you stopped going to school?"

I looked around June's front room and wished music was playing. June's eyes were gray like a shepherd dog's, and I felt like a sheep, my urge to stray destroyed. June looked at her hands in her lap. "I should spend more time with you," she said. "That's my fault."

"No," I said.

"Cause if I did," she said, "I would know why you left school. I would know."

I thought she was going to cry. "Kingsport seems OK," I said. "All my teachers like it," I said. "Guy teachers especially. They say they like it better when their wives shop here. They say it's easy to get in and out of the stores in Kingsport."

June smiled. "You get to know people," she said. "They're really nice. Mellow. And invisible weird."

One time Hubert took me shooting, told me how you had to relax your face and eyes to see the animals moving in the woods. I looked out June's front window, tried to relax my eyeballs so I could see the invisible weird in Kingsport, flat-chested little factory town.

June got up and went in the kitchen, and came back and put the radio on Willett's radio station. I wanted to hear a strong woman sing, some liquor-drinking, cigarette-smoking woman who knew exactly what she wanted to say. Maybe she didn't know how to run her life, but at least knew what she wanted to sing, what she wanted people to hear, and when she got done singing, the crowd would cheer like a video poker machine hitting jackpot, gold coins spilling out on me and all the other tin-ear suckers cut loose in time.

But Willett wasn't on the air, and they weren't playing strong-voice women. They were playing music like Houston had in his music room, 78 rpm records. They played one where different musicians played different little bits of old fiddle songs and banjo songs and harmonica songs, and then they would pretend to drink moonshine, and one of them talked, giving a lesson on how things go in the country, and I thought in that moment how recreating a thing, making a thing seem like the same thing later, was stupid, was impossible.

I said, "Fix me something to eat, Aunt June."

June popped up like an actress I'd picked to be in a movie and said, "Come on in the kitchen." She got out a pottery bowl, a pretty thing didn't look like June used because she had to wipe the dust out of it and rinse it off.

"I love these bowls," she said.

June handed me the bowl, and I held it while she spooned brown rice from a saucepan and then dippered me out some green-yellow chicken stew from an iron pot. I said, "Where do you want me to sit?" and she reached out her hand towards the table, fingers delicate and white as Virginia Slims. June's hands danced over a stack of cloth napkins folded in an oak split basket. I put a spoon into the bowl of chicken. She lay a napkin down beside my bowl. I could hear the house creaking. June set down across from me. I ate the stew fast, bite on top of bite, and it wasn't so bad.

~~~~~~~~~~~~

THE DRESS June slipped over her head that evening sparkled night-blue. She said we were going to a party.

"What kind of party?" I said.

"A dancing party."

"Why?" I said.

June said, "There will be all kind of people there who will want to meet you because of what you and Cora are doing on Blue Bear."

"I don't have a dress," I said.

"Do you want one?" June said.

"No."

June swept her hair up on top of her head, pinned it, sprayed it. Then she stuck plastic flowers and wire strung with tinsel stars in it. She looked at me. "How about we put some glitter on your face?"

I said, "I don't know, Aunt June."

She sprayed glitter on her own face. She looked at me smiling and bright.

"You look like a fairy," I said.

"You want some?" she said, her eyebrows dancing.

"You make glitter sound like some kind of dope," I said.

"Glitter is a kind of dope," she said. Then she said, "HA." And then: "You don't have to if you don't want to."

I took the can and sprayed glitter on my face.

"That's some Christmas cheer, right there," June said.

I looked at myself in the mirror. I looked like I could grant myself wishes.

"Willett Bilson might be there tonight," June said.

I looked at myself again. "I don't guess you'd give me a sip of something would you, Aunt June?"

"No," said June, "I don't guess I would."

~~~~~~~~~~~~~~~

WE DROVE an hour getting to the party place. It was dark and a way I'd never been. We pulled off the blacktop onto a rocky road, and the car bounced until we came to a gate where a young boy with a red beard covering the front of his shirt sat. He smiled and pulled open the cattle gate. The road on the other side of the gate was rougher than what come before, and I asked June, "What is this place?"

We passed three people with angel wings carrying liquor bottles coming up the steep grade towards us. "Everybody out here owns their own house," June said. The road went down steeper and steeper. "But they own the land in common." We passed a house that was all weird angles and porches. We passed a house on stilts with three VW vans underneath. We passed more houses, all covered with unpainted wood and decks running around them and lots of potted plants. Houses built as an idea. Book-smart people houses.

June turned onto the grass, down a meadow towards the river. There were cars parked all down the meadow, back ends covered with bumper stickers for the earth and women and peace and banjos. There were so many bumper stickers. June parked and we got out, and we passed people with more hair, and bowties and sandals with thick winter socks. The men called each other "dude." We came to a barn. The door swung open, and an older man with little round glasses and cups of beer in each hand said, "Aw right. Merry Christmas. Praise Allah. Disco Duck." June hugged the man, and I stepped through the door. A band played at the other end of the barn, raised slightly above the crowd. They had electric guitars and buck teeth and played "Mustang Sally" with their heads bowed. The people dancing hollered, "Woooo!"

The dancing was either jerky and reminded you of drowning people or slow and almost not like dancing at all. Everyone seemed anxious to let everyone else see how happy they were. There were people above looking down from the barn loft, people standing leaning against rough lumber rails. Hay trailed down from above when they scuffed their feet.

"Are you OK?" June was in my face, like the glitter on both our faces was magnetized.

"Yes," I said.

June introduced me to a white-bearded lawyer and a woman with uncombed hair said she was a doctor. She introduced me to a professor of this and a person making a film about that. A fat man with black sideburns asked June to dance, and I followed somebody up a ladder to the loft. I did not see anybody close to my age. I did not see Willett Bilson. The music was loud and not so bad, and I wished I had something to drink.

A bald man who looked like he owned a business that used to do a lot better than it is doing now said, "Well, hello there." His whiskey breath made me light-headed. The man's forehead was the rind of a white watermelon, disappearing into his ski cap, and I wanted to thump it so bad. It made me sick when he said twice, "You got a feller?" I tried to set fire to him with my eyes. He looked like he was made out of marshmallows. I imagined turning his cheeks a beautiful golden brown, and then his whole face, and then his whole head flame and then ash, flattening like a poor kid's birthday wishes gone to nothing.

"Cause I," he said, "can dance. And I," he said, "can fix a sink. And I," he said, "will remember your birthday."

"I don't care," I said, "for you to even *know* my birthday."

"Do you care about this?" he said and jingled the worn keys to some kind of Chrysler in my face. "Three payments ahead," he said, and raised his eyebrows and rocked forward on the balls of his feet, which were in low brown shoes with rawhide laces, and his thumb pushed loose a cup from the stack of red plastic cups in his hand. "You want a drink?" he said. "You look thirsty," he said.

My aunt's hippie party swirled below. They were all elbows and earrings down on the dance floor while me and this man with his bubblegum lips and his pitcher of milky-green something stood up above in the barn loft, amplified hippie music about cowboys and drugs and cars that got poor gas mileage knocking loose the hay at our feet.

"Me and you should think about getting married," he said.

I said, "You got any ice?"

"How old are you?" he said as I took the cup and he poured me some of what he had. I didn't give an age, not until I got me a cup full, and when he stopped pouring, he went to put his arm around me, and I spun out from under him and spilled some of what he gave me, and then quick I drank the rest. He raised his eyebrows like he was the witch in *Snow White* and that cup was the apple.

I said, "Don't you touch me," and he just raised his eyebrows again.

"Where's your feller?" he said, and he tried to pour me some more to drink, and I moved my cup and the green poured out on the boards, dripped through to the stalls below. "Wasteful," he said. "Waste not, want not," he said.

I said, "I got me a feller. And he's a good man."

"Well, where's he at?" that moonheaded man said, his eyes shrunk up inside his thick eyeglasses. "A fortune," he said. "I made a fortune in the seventies." He pointed as he spoke, his cup in his pointing hand. "Everybody wanted coal when the A-rabs cut off the oil. We all had helicopters and cocaine, and everybody wore big gold chains." He touched the hair over his collarbones. "By God, a man could fill a coal gon with rotten wood. Put coal across the top. Sell it for a hundred and fifty a ton. The only time they ever treated us like they ought to."

I started moving away. He grabbed my wrist.

"You need a man man," he said, "somebody not afraid to be a man."

"I got a man," I said, but I trailed off saying it, cause I didn't know what I had, didn't know if Willett Bilson would ever show up, and what would show up if he did.

"You aint got no man," the marshmallow said, "because you don't know how to appreciate."

His grip was tight and I wasn't sure I could whip him. And I was in the wrong spot to knock him out of the barn loft. His belly was causing his shirt buttons to pull his button holes wide open. His pants was cinched so low didn't look like he had a behind.

"You're a man?" I said.

"That's right," he said.

I said, "You sure? You look like you're about to have a baby to me."

His eyes flashed with fire, but a smile come on his face. "Ride 'em, cowgirl," he said.

And he said, "Aint nobody trying to scare nobody." But his eyes stayed burning hot, and he still had hold of my wrist.

I didn't know where I was at except I was over my head. I knew I should just hit him, and somebody would stop him before it got too bad on me. But I just didn't know. I was too far from home. Anything could happen. Things I hadn't seen before. And so I stood there, staring at the creases in his forehead, the red plastic cup in my free hand like a play telephone on a string pulled tight and me with no idea who was at the other end.

The marshmallow man said, "They're gonna start a fire here in a minute." When I turned to look at the dance floor, he said, "Down by the river." He moved his thumb back and forth on my arm. "You want to go down there?" he said.

"No, she don't," said a voice behind me. Decent Ferguson grabbed me by the elbow with one hand and took my cup with the other. "Come on, girl," she said. "There's somebody I want you to meet." Decent dumped out my cup when we got away from the bald man. She said, "Welcome to the party, little girl."

Decent took me outside. The night sky was clear and cold. Decent was bare-armed, had on an emerald-green satin spaghetti-strap thing and cowboy boots. "Shit," she said. We went to her Bronco. It was still cold there, but she didn't start it, just threw on her coat, took a brown-bag bottle from between the seats and poured it into my cup, swigged straight from the bottle and handed me the cup. I took a swallow. It was sweet and peachy, and Decent looked at me with slow-down eyes. "Go easy, honey. Go easy," she said. I nodded and sipped slower.

"Heard you had a wreck."

"I did," I said.

"June will take care of you," she said.

"What are you doing here?"

"I been coming to this for years," Decent said. "This is my tribe."

I said, "Who was that guy?"

"Up in the loft? They call him Billy Goat Gruff. He was fixing to propose to you. That's about all he does—drink and try and get women to marry him."

"Hunh."

"Hey listen," she said. "How's your momma doing?"

"I don't know. I aint seen her."

"I heard she was cutting a swath. Heard she tried to run over Hubert in his own truck."

"Tried?"

"I don't reckon she killed him. I hear she came at him twice, but he got in the truck bed and wouldn't come out til she gave him the keys. I guess she messed up his paint job pretty bad."

"Hunh," I said.

There was a tap at Decent's window. She cracked it open. "Hey baby." The woman at the window opened the back door and got in. "How's it going in there?" Decent said.

"Good," the woman said. "No broken bones yet." Her hand reached over the seat to me. "I'm Sarah."

"Hello," I said. Sarah had short hair and—like everybody else at the party—round glasses.

"You're June's niece."

"That's right."

"What's your name?"

"Dawn."

"Welcome, Dawn."

"Sarah's house is right up through there." Decent pointed with two fingers up the hill.

"Have yall got a place to stay, Dawn?" Sarah said.

"I guess," I said. "Back in Kingsport."

"We've got a room here," Sarah said. "A bed and everything."

The snow kept coming, and the other back door opened and two dudes got in. One of them was Willett's brother Kenny, the one who interviewed me after the hearing right before Thanksgiving. "There she is," he said when he saw me. "Me and this dude was just talking about you." The other guy sat nodding like a bobblehead doll.

"How's it going?" Bobblehead said.

"Oh man, Willett is going to be bummed he missed you," Kenny said.

"He aint here?"

"Nah," Kenny said. "Went with his dad to a ball game in Knoxville."

I turned my head and stared out my window.

"Yeah, he plays that interview with you all the time. He's got to where he does a pretty good impersonation of you."

"What do you mean?" I said.

"He repeats what you say on that tape all day long."

"Hunh," I said.

"You heard anything about the petition?" Kenny said.

I said no.

"That would be awesome if that got declared unsuitable," Bobblehead said. "Aint never been one upheld."

"Least not that big," Kenny said.

"You'll be up there with the immortals," Bobblehead said. "Widow Combs, Preacher Dan Gibson, Hazel King."

"Your grandma is already up there," Sarah said. "She stood up to to strip miners before there was federal law. She was pre-SMCRA."

"What's 'smack-ruh?'" I said.

"The Surface Mining Control and Reclamation Act," Sarah said. "It's the federal law that regulates strip mining."

"They need to teach you your history, youngun," Kenny said. Then they told me how the Widow Combs sat down in front of the bulldozers, how Dan Gibson held them off his son's land with a single-shot .22 while his son was in Vietnam, and how Hazel King got the first strip job shut down using SMCRA after SMCRA passed in 1977. "I never heard of none of that," I said when they finished.

"They need to teach that stuff in school," Bobblehead said.

"How is your aunt June anyway?" Kenny said.

"Don't tell him nothing," Decent said. "Make him find out for himself."

"Come on, now," Bobblehead said, "don't make a man in love suffer worse." I looked at Willett's brother. "You love my aunt June?"

"There's a lot there to love," Kenny said and looked out the frosty window. "Plenty," he said.

"Tough nut to crack," Bobblehead said.

The women laughed.

"She likes things quiet," I said, remembering how rambunctious Kenny had been when he was at the hearing. There was a quiet in the backseat.

"Yeah," Kenny said. "I'm screwed then."

They laughed again. "You aint without your charms," Decent said.

"C'mon, Bobble," Kenny said, and the two men left.

"I guess I better go back too," Sarah said. When she left, we left with her. When we got to the barn, the dance floor swallowed up Decent. Sarah got caught up in a conversation about grants and jobs, and I saw a pack of cigarettes on a wooden rail, lighter under the cellophane. I picked it up and slipped out of the barn.

<hr />

PEOPLE LAUGHED and burning wood cracked and popped down towards the river. I walked sideways away from them. The meadow was broad, creamy blue in the snow, simple and new, like a painting in a book June would have. I felt like I was walking in a poem. On the far side of the meadow was a little woods. I ducked into it, far from the party, alone. A path angled to the riverbank. The river was dark and noisy and took the falling snow like a fat kid eating Skittles. The talk in Decent's Bronco got my mind off Keith Kelly, got me off the bad feelings I was having about everything. I felt good about what we were doing on Blue Bear.

A big tree had fallen into the river. I climbed its roots to sit on its trunk. I could see the meadow through the bare woods, the barn blazing with Christmas lights. I could hear the music and the laughs and whooping. I was glad those people were there, glad they were having a good time. They seemed so not hurtful to me. I tried to imagine myself a regular part of them. I tried to imagine myself walking across that meadow in each of the four seasons. I put myself on a tractor, mowing the meadow. I put myself in a room full of women, women like Sarah, working on a quilt and talking about smart stuff and feeling like things were getting better because all the people closest to me were working to make things better.

I made out a figure coming towards me across the pasture, walking in my footprints. I imagined it was Willett, traipsing towards me in snowshoes and a hat with earflaps, carrying an ax, a pipe in his mouth, a gentle giant with apples for cheeks and pockets full of cornbread hoecakes. When he got to me, we would turn our own circle of blue fire-orange in the winter woods, everything frozen melting, potatoes in the ash roasting, black and crusty and perfect, the roasted perfect of the past that only lasts a bit, a bit imagination blows on, like a fire with life still in it, needing a little air. The light in Willett's pipe, coming towards me, was a moment of the perfect precious past meant just for us.

<hr />

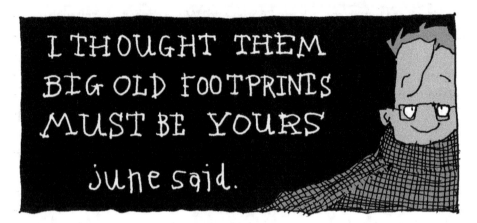

I THOUGHT THEM BIG OLD FOOTPRINTS MUST BE YOURS June said.

I WAS glad enough to see June. We are always glad to see something beautiful, even when there is something about them or it that makes us nervous. June did not have on shoes for snow. She had on soft leather boots dyed summer green, and I said "Watch your shoes," but she didn't seem to care and clambered up beside me. She'd been drinking a little bit.

"What do you think?" she said.

"It's cool," I said.

"You really think so?" she said.

"Yeah," I said. "Pretty much."

"Has everybody been nice to you?"

"I guess so," I said.

The sound of broken glass floated up the riverbank. June shook her head. The sound of the water made me want to pee. June's body shook in the cold. I put my arm around her. She put her head on my shoulder.

"Do you think you'd mind living around here?"

"It would take some getting used to," I said.

June said, "Getting used to people treating you decent?"

"That," I said, "and just missing things." I wondered did June even remember what she missed.

June said, "I miss all the racket people made when they got together. Everybody talking at once. Everybody jammed up together on the porch or in the front room, the kids all keyed up."

I said that's what I'd miss the least.

"Yeah," June said, "all that's why I left. Why I built me a fortress of solitude. But anymore it's what I miss."

We let the sound of the river do the talking for a minute. I said I'd miss our lay of the land, the way the mountains at home pitched up in your face, didn't lay around polite and easy, willing to work with you, the way they did in Tennessee and Virginia. More laughing and glass-breaking came from the party, rising and falling behind the river sound.

"So what is this business with Keith?" June said. "What happened?"

"I don't know, Aunt June. Even what I thought I knew I'm not sure I know. My mind is all muddled up."

"You ran him off the road, right?"

"I guess we did."

"And your mother puts it all on Hubert?"

"I reckon."

"Doesn't give you much credit, does she?" June said.

"Guess not," I said.

June said, "Hubert never can quite get the hang of it."

I said, "Hang of what?"

June was quiet a second and then said, "Living. No wife. No kids. Precious few friends. Hardest on the ones he loves the most."

I said, "Which is who?"

"You and Tricia and Albert," June said, "according to my calculations."

"Not according to mine."

"Who do you think he loves most?" June said.

"Himself. Then maybe Momma," I said. "Then everybody else in a tie for last, a tie for not-at-all."

"Maybe so," June said. "But I doubt it."

"Why don't you live with us, Aunt June? Cause it sounds to me like you sit out here figuring out what to tell us, figuring out what we need to hear."

"I don't have to figure it out, Dawn. I just have to remember."

"Well, then. What do I need?"

"You need somebody to clear the path for you to come up with all that you're going to come up with."

"You think I'm going to come up with something?"

June said, "I think you're going to come up with something amazing."

I said, "Maybe I don't want to come up with something. Maybe I just want to be."

June said, "How does that make you feel when people talk good about you and Cora slowing down the coal companies?"

"Because you're scared?" June said.

"No, not because I'm scared," I said. "It makes me want to run so I can think about it. Hear my thoughts."

June let the sound of the river come back. She raised up off my shoulder. "Do you need me to leave you alone?"

"You're all right," I said. And she was. I didn't mind her being there. Except I didn't want her to be cold.

"So have you figured it out?" June said.

"What I think about Blue Bear?"

"Unh-hunh," June said.

I slipped my arm out of my coat sleeve and pulled June inside my coat. "I figure it don't make much difference. Half of everything electric comes from coal. Half them Christmas lights on that barn yonder, half the juice for the lights in the offices of all the hippie enviro fighters, half of all of it. One mountain saved don't mean much. They can give us one just to shut us up, so we can think we done something. But they can't let us think we can get one whenever we want, or we're liable to think we can have all of them." I pulled June tight. "Seems to me it's taking too much energy in the asking. I can see it wearing down Mamaw."

"Can you?" June said.

"I can. There aint enough on our side. Aint enough people to fight all the time. So as long as it's a big fight, Mamaw and her kind will have to pick their spots, and them people over there at that party—they'll treat Mamaw and them like heroes—which they are—but they aint won."

I stopped talking, and the black river kept on and on. The hooping and hollering at the barn kept on and the laughing at the fire down the bank—it kept on too.

"Sounds like you've found somewhere to think," June said.

"I'll tell you another thing," I said. "It makes sense that yall at this party would need your get-togethers like this, away from things, where everybody has the same bumper stickers. But I wonder—what would happen if yall won? I'm not sure they could handle it."

June laughed. "Always be something to be stirred up about, I guess."

One more time we let the water music play through our heads, and then I said, "Aunt June, I believe I'm going to have to go back."

"To Kingsport?" she said.

"To Kentucky," I said.

"Well," June said, "OK."

I jumped down off the tree trunk and wiped my wet rear end. I helped June down.

"How does fifteen act?" I said. "Older than me or younger?"

"Kind of both," June said.

"Probably why I don't know if I'm coming or going."

I crossed the meadow and found Decent Ferguson in the punch-bowl-and-beer-keg area, talking and poking a grinning young boy in the chest. I said, "Decent, where you spending the night?"

She said, "I don't know. Where do you want to spend the night?"

I said, "I'd like to spend it at my mamaw Cora's house."

"Well, baby doll," Decent said, "that is right on my way. When do you want to leave?"

"Don't matter," I said.

"Give me twenty minutes," Decent said, "to get this Tennessee trash here lined out, and we'll go."

I nodded and turned away. The night air and the peach stuff Decent gave me to drink softened my opinion about the dancing, which had only gotten to be more of what it was earlier. When a guy asked me to dance, I let myself be pulled onto the floor. I couldn't hardly hear what he was saying, but his name was Bill and he was also from Kentucky and he had heard of me. When the song was over he said, "I heard you were younger than you look."

"I'm fifteen," I said.

He said his family had a newspaper and I should tell my grandmother he would like to talk to her sometime, and I said, "Why don't you want to talk to me?"

He laughed and said, "They don't raise em scared in Canard County, do they?"

"That's right, youngblood," Bill said. "Give em hell." Then he said he'd be glad to talk with me and my grandmother both, whenever it suited us. He slipped back into the crowd as Decent said in my ear, "You ready to go?"

The hippies swirled and shimmied, lost their balance and hugged together in a big gob, and I told Decent Ferguson I was ready to go.

~~~~~~~~~~~~

JUNE'S KISS goodbye was still wet on my cheek when Decent's Bronco started tear-assing out of that hole. I prayed there weren't any more hippie angels on that hill, cause Decent sure would have knocked them flying.

"Did you have a good time with my hairball friends?" Decent said, whipping the Bronco wheel back to the left as we come sailing over the rise down to the gate.

"I reckon," I said. "It aint gonna be the last fun I ever have, is it?"

"You're fine," Decent said. "I been down here a hundred times."

The gate boy flew into action soon as he saw Decent, his eyes big as a slaughterhouse cow's, and we passed him a millisecond after the gate gapped wide enough for us to pass. I turned to see him wiping his brow as he got back in his stickered-up Subaru.

"Did you see him pulling his britches up?" Decent said. "He had his little woman in the back of his vehicle. Getting him some." Decent accelerated into a sort of straightaway. I couldn't believe there weren't any cops, but we never saw the first one, and before I knew it we were almost to Pennington Gap.

Decent got into her music and spent most of the trip singing in a voice that was good-hearted and strong, but not easy to listen to, which was just as well, cause I needed to think, and when I did, I realized there were more things I should have said to June in our talk beside the river. Things like this:

Blue Bear wasn't just about winning a fight. Everything I could see from Mamaw's porch, every place I had run through on a four-wheeler, every birdsong and spring flower, every ferny frond that come up beside a yellow muddy trail—all that kept me alive sure as if it was air I was breathing. The trees and the roll of the earth held me up like the ridge holds the cloud from passing so it can pour down rain. The vines and the rabbits and the squirrels and the orange lizards out on the rocks after a storm—all those things I'd forget when people dragged me down—I needed them close and always, where I could get to them quick when Albert was crazy on some new dope, when Momma was out of her head, when Mamaw pulled back into her groundhog hole of nothing for me, when Hubert made me want to blow his head clean off—there was only the mountains could talk sense to me. Winter, summer, spring, and fall. Didn't matter I couldn't understand what they were saying. It was like if my best true friend were from Africa or Russia or something, and they didn't speak English, but they had a look in their eye or a sound in their voice made me calm down, made me look up, look out, instead of just letting my eyes go burning blank with panic and mad at the world.

When this reason for fighting came into my mind that night riding home with Decent Ferguson, the faces of my cousin Denny and his daddy rose up before me. Those coal miners who had been so good to me, who had loved me through my tree-hugging ways, needed mountains and woods more than any of us. They loved it here, and they had to tear it up to stay. The full hard hardness of their lot came down on me that winter night, and I knew maybe not them but other coal-mining people would be mad at me, would hate me, but after that night, I never was mad at them, not the ones who lived here with me, not the ones taking their own sorrow and joy from what was left of these trees, these rocks, these rustling waters.

# 12

## MUDHOLE

THE WIND sent garbage cans sailing down Long Ridge, and iron clanged against iron back towards the highway. Tree limbs clacked in the air. Mamaw wasn't breathing. I screamed into her face: "Please, Mamaw. Tell me." Last thing she said was: "Girl, you ought not to be scared of nothing like that."

"Like what?" I hollered. "Please. Tell me what." My spit spattered her face. I shook her by her shoulders, and her chin bumped against her breastbone.

I held her up by her hair, and her eyes rolled back in her head. I heaved her up over my shoulder and backed out the kitchen door. The wind threw

the storm door against the base of her skull. I put my hand over the crown
of her head, too late for the storm door, too late for her coming bump bump
bump down the stairs as I came in from June's hippie Christmas party. I don't
know what she was doing upstairs. Probably snooping after Momma.

"Hold on, Mamaw," I said. "Hold onto me." I got her out to the Escort
and set her on the backseat. I wished I'd put her up front with me, where I
could shake her and try and keep her awake.

What I hated most about living on Long Ridge was Daddy's people out
everwhere—but where were they that night? You'd of thought with a howling
snowstorm coming, a person could find them, but it didn't work out that way.
Just as well. I could hear my uncles' stupid women in my head—"I wouldn't
have carpet on my steps" and "She don't need to be living there by herself."
I hated my uncles' women—acting all smart when they put Dr. Pepper in
their babies' bottles and couldn't make change for a dollar if you put a thirty-
aught-six to their heads. But I needed somebody. "Daddy," I said, like I do
sometimes when I'm pulled out thin.

"Fooooooo," I said, started the car and rolled down the hill, turned right
toward the highway, but soon as I turned, I slammed the brakes, skidded in
the gravel, Mamaw going thump against the back of the front seat. A vehicle
turned sideways blocked the road, white door smashed, trim down the side
hanging loose and rusty. Chains and men's voices rattled across the pavement.

"Mamaw," I said. "Mamaw, Mamaw, Mamaw." She had fallen into the
space between front and back seats. I put the car in park, reached over the
top of the seat to try and pull her up. I climbed into the back, crying, breath

lost, squealing like a train wheel. Panic poured down over top of me like coal into a gon. My knees pressed into the backseat and I got up under Mamaw's armpits—like when Hubert pulled dead Keith out of his truck. "Mamaw, please," I said, and when I give her one more big jerk, "Unnnnh," she went, sucking air. Her eyes rolled back down, all glazed like Chinese food by the car door lights, and I could hear her breathing light as feathers, and I knew she was losing stuff out of her mind every second. I set her against the door and climbed back up front, got the car turned back to the left, went the longer way off the ridge, into the no-light-at-all fire-scarred woods, road wrapping back on itself like a snake Mamaw'd chopped in half with a hoe, trail of blood, twisting forwards and backwards all at once, trying to escape the fall of the blade.

"Breathe, Mamaw, breathe." Curves come quick, and I couldn't look back at her. Do and I'm off the road, gone over the edge into some homemade dump, tangled up in busted garbage bags, soggy mattresses, God knows what. "Pay attention pay attention pay attention," I said.

I come blind around a curve and felt mud against the doors, against the bottom of the car, grinding against the metal beneath my feet, and then sizzling around the Escort's spinning wheels. The Mudhole. The Mudhole took the whole left-hand side of the road for sixty yards on the crest of the mountain. The Mudhole was deep enough to baptize in. Nobody could figure out why it never dried up, but it never did. I was mired in it up to my hubs.

The car tipped, the driver side headlight submerged in the mud. I slid up and out the passenger side. The other headlight shone in the faces of two men and a woman walking towards us. I didn't know them, but I knew who they were. They were Keith Kelly's kinfolks. Come all the way from Drop Creek with their fists balled up around the end of four-foot roof bolts.

"We know you killed Keith," the woman out front said. "You and that dry heave Hubert."

I rubbed my eyes. The chickens had come home to roost. I could feel their talons clinching down on my eyeballs. Mamaw was laid out on her face across the backseat. If I'd had a gun I would have shot all them Kellys right on the spot. I swear I would have. "I aint got time for this," I said. "My grandmother aint breathing."

"Neither is Keith, you cocked-up little witch."

My first thought was to grab the woman by the throat and drown her in the Mudhole. She was big, but she was soft—blonde and thick. My second thought was to drown myself—just fall down and start swallowing Mudhole water, start swallowing and trust one of these Kellys to hold my head down and make sure I died. The men fell in line behind the woman. Their hands hung at their sides, roof bolts dragging in the gravel. The men's lips were parted, and the wind blew their hair, which was long and clung together in syrupy ribbons. They did not look at all like Keith Kelly, prettier face-down dead on the Drop Creek road than these two were with their blood all up and vengeful.

"It wasn't enough, was it?" the woman said. "It wasn't enough that you and your busybody kin was gonna cost him his job, get his mine shut down. Wasn't enough that your skanky mother come sniffing around. You and your crook uncle had to run him off the road and kill him on top of all that. You couldn't be satisfied. And why? What had he ever done to you? I tell you what he done. He hadn't done nothing."

"My grandmother is going to die," I said. I didn't say it to the blonde woman. I said it to the ground. But I said this to the blonde woman: "She didn't kill your brother. She is a good person."

"Like hell she is," the woman said. "We know your crook uncle fixed it with the law. So we come on our own."

"We like to never find you," one of the men said.

"Shut up, Arthur," the woman said.

I started to pant like a dog hemmed up in a room too warm and close during a thunderstorm. The men moved towards me. The first one got within arm's length, and I busted him right in the face. His nose flattened out,

He went staggering back, kind of whining, like a baby. The other one grabbed me before I could do anything else and pinned my arms back. I

stomped one of his feet. He clamped down on me with one hand and raised up that roof bolt with the other and was fixing to club me with it when another hand flew out of the darkness and stayed the Kelly man's hand. The Kelly man turned to see what stopped him busting my head, and when he did another man come out of the shadows and wrapped him up. The two other men had stripe work clothes and hats with patches on the front said the name of the coal company mining on Blue Bear.

"You need to settle down there, big boy," the one who grabbed him first said. "Didn't nobody come out here tonight to kill nobody, did they, Blondie?"

The man I punched turned to look at the thick blonde woman, Keith's sister Blondie Kelly, to see what kind of fight she was wanting to put up. The wind come up the gap colder, and run over top of the mountain. Blondie said, "Johnny Ray, what you come up here for? What'd you set that truck in the road for?"

The man she called Johnny Ray had a big red moustache, no beard, and a stone rose face, but with eyes warm and blue as a pilot light, like my father's. He turned to me in the light of the Escort. "We come up here to talk to your grandmother, Dawn, about what she's costing us. We didn't care to scare her, but . . ." A truck come up behind me, and then past me, slowing for Johnny Ray to take a set of chains out of the back, and Johnny Ray hooked the chain to the truck and then to the Escort's frame, then the truck moved forward and the Kelly men and then Blondie Kelly had to back out of its way. When the Escort got closer to the edge of the Mudhole, fanning through that fudgy water, Johnny Ray sloshed out into it, opened the back door against the water's weight, and said, "I'm going to pull you out now, Cora." And then my grandmother was floating in Johnny Ray's arms.

I didn't know Johnny Ray, but I remembered him from the hearing. His wife yelled at Mamaw in front of the state people who had come to hear what people thought about whether or not the state should protect Blue Bear Mountain from strip mining. Johnny Ray's wife had cussed Mamaw, said Mamaw was taking the food off her children's plate, said her man had never not worked a day in his life, said who did Mamaw think she was, said she said she was from here, but was she, really? I remember the people clapping and Mamaw just standing there in the dim blue-gray community center fluorescents.

"We'll get her to the hospital, Dawn," Johnny Ray said. "We won't let her die."

I watched Johnny Ray take my grandmother to the truck's red lights, then the darkness, then the door, and I moved towards the truck and unhooked the tow chain from it, patted the tailgate, and the brake lights blinked twice, and the truck pulled away, blue smoke piling out, and the exhaust giving a hollow rattle. The truck skirted the Mudhole, picking up speed, and then was gone around the curve, leaving me holding a chain caught beneath the burning headlights of a banged-up Ford Escort, and the glare of a thick blonde woman.

Blondie Kelly said,

I said, "Fight, I reckon."

"Well, come on," she said.

"Why you so sure you can't trust the law to fix us?" I said.

"Don't know a thing about the law," Blondie Kelly said. "All I know is Keith is dead and you and Hubert hated him and you and Hubert was right there when he died, right there on that road he drove every day for the last ten years."

"How do you know it wasn't him trying to kill us?" I said.

"Keith wasn't going to kill anybody," Blondie said.

"He sure was doing some weird shit," I said.

"He had been acting kind of loco," one of the guys said.

"Hush," Blondie Kelly said.

I walked up close to Blondie Kelly, close enough for her to hit me if she wanted. Up close, all I could see was her hurt. Her eyes were the eyes of a mouse stuck on a glue trap.

"We didn't want to kill your brother, Blondie. It was an accident."

Blondie Kelly looked at me for a long time, I think to see if I was going to change the way I was acting. I don't believe she thought I could stand there and act like a normal person who didn't mean her harm. Finally she said, "The only thing makes sense is you and Hubert got it in for us."

"Well," I said, "We do think Keith's a dick. But you can't wish every dick dead. You can't kill all of them."

"Lord knows," one of the men said.

Blondie Kelly's shoulders fell, the wind died, the clanging metal stopped clanging. A dog barked one bark and quit. "Yall come here," Blondie said.

I looked at the two dudes. Then I looked at Blondie Kelly. "Take my hand, Dawn Jewell," she said, "and we'll pray together."

The dudes took off their hats and joined hands, and the tall one he took Blondie's hand, and the other one reached out for my hand. Blondie reached out her free hand for my free hand. I didn't take hold of them Kellys right off. I stood there and wondered were they fixing to pull my arms out of my sockets and leave me squirting blood out my shoulder holes into the mud. That dog barked another bark and went quiet again. I looked into them Kellys' eyes. I wanted Mamaw to live.

I took their hands, and in the light of Blondie's Yukon holding hands in a circle, Blondie said, "Sweet heavenly Father, thank you for bringing us together under the stars of your heaven on this beautiful winter's night."

The shorter dude said, "Yes."

"Thank you for staying our hand," Blondie went on, "and not allowing us to shed no more blood. You're the one says, 'Vengeance is mine,' and if there is any to be had, we are reminded Your will be done. Til then, Lord, welcome our beloved Keith into Your blessed loving care, and move on the hearts of Hubert and Dawn Jewell to be truthful and mindful of the path You would have them walk. And Lord, please be with the law. Guide them towards the light of Your truth, so that justice might be done in the case of Your precious servant Keith. And Lord, be with Cora Redding. If it be Your will that she might recover from her fall, please let her better serve You. Thank You, Lord God our Father, for hearing our prayer. And keep us in Your loving embrace and grant us traveling grace as we strive to get off this godforsaken mountain. In Your blessed son Jesus' name, amen."

"Amen," said the dudes.

The four of us piled into Blondie's Yukon and made a long, slow, quiet trip off the mountain. The snow started falling again, and the only thing said was when the shorter dude asked me did I want a piece of bubble gum, which I took, and was still chewing when Blondie and them set me out at the emergency room at the hospital in town.

"I hope your mamaw will forgive us," Blondie Kelly said before she rolled up the window.

I stood in the salt-melt slush, and said I thought she would.

The short dude said I should come to church with them sometime as he switched to the front seat and gave me some more bubble gum for later.

WHEN I found Mamaw's room, Momma was already there and Mamaw looked at me spry as could be. "What you got in your mouth?" Mamaw said.

"Bubble gum," I said, and asked Momma how long she'd been there.

"I was here when they brung her in," Momma said, and showed me the casts on both her feet. "We was in beds next to each other."

"Jesus," I said. "What happened to you?"

"I fell off the roof," Momma said.

"What roof?" I said.

"Mine," Hubert said from where he was sitting behind the door.

"I was trying to drop a cinder block on him," Momma said, "and I slipped."

"Jesus," I said.

"You all get out of here," Mamaw said. "I need to talk to Dawn."

Hubert helped Momma out the door. When they were gone, Mamaw said, "Push the door shut." When I had, she said, "What are you doing here?"

"What are you talking about, Mamaw?"

"Why didn't you stay with June?"

"Aint you glad," I said, "I came back? You'd of been dead if I hadn't. Lord have mercy," I said. "Wouldn't kill a person to thank a person before you crawl up their ass, Mamaw."

"'Crawl up your ass?' Is that what they say now?" Mamaw stared at me. "Come here." Mamaw raised the back of her hand into the air between us. "Come here," she said, bending her fingers. I came to her bedside. She grabbed my arm just above my wrist, like it was a hoe handle or a baseball bat. "I will call you," she said, "or I will get Houston to call you, when it is time for you to go to court. All right?"

"Yes, Mamaw."

"You don't have to stay here, do you?"

"No, Mamaw."

"Well, then don't. You go to June. You stay with June. June needs taking care of. You want to take care of somebody? Take care of June. You do for her and some good might come of it. Do you understand?

"What about Blue Bear?"

Mamaw looked into my eyes. I was worn out with everybody looking at me so hard. But I looked back at Mamaw just as hard as she looked at me. "If there's anything about Blue Bear you can help with," Mamaw said, "I'll get word to you about that, too." She held tight to my arm, like she thought I was going to try to get away. "All right?" she said.

I nodded.

"What?" she said.

"All right," I said.

Mamaw nodded and let go of my arm. "All right," she said. "Nothing to be afraid of."

~~~~~~~~~~~

FROM OUT in the hospital lobby I called Evie and said did she want to drive me to Kingsport.

"I don't reckon," she said.

"Why not?"

"Me and Albert's going to Tennessee."

"Not that Tennessee," she said. "We're going to the lake."

"You are not," I said. "It's too cold to go to the lake."

"Well, we're going bowling then."

"Evie, please."

"I don't know, Dawn. Dangerous riding with you."

"Meet me someplace nobody will see you."

"Behind the drugstore?"

"Across the highway?"

"By the dumpster."

"All right. And Evie?"

"What?"

"Don't bring Albert."

"All right."

~~~~~~~~~~~~

THE NIGHT had cleared off. The leftover clouds glowed gray against the starry sky. The air felt brittle, like it was about to break. I put my hands in my pockets and pulled down my hat and crossed the bypass. Hubert's green pickup sat under a light in the drugstore parking lot. There were two heads in the cab—Momma's long thin one and Hubert's square one. I didn't want them to see me and so I snuck up on the cab. When I got to Momma's window on the passenger side, Hubert's mouth was hanging open, dead asleep. I was about to tap Momma's window—she was awake and the light was on in the cab—when she leaned forward and snorted up a line of white powder off the dashboard. It was the first time I ever saw her do something like that.

Evie's Cavalier turned off the bypass, and I went running towards her. She rolled down her window. "Aint that Hubert?" she said.

"Open the door, Evie."

"Why don't you get him to take you to Kingsport?"

"Unlock the door, Evie."

"It aint locked. It's broke. Let her in, Albert."

"Dammit, Evie. I told you not to bring him."

"You want me riding back from Kingsport by myself? Sides, he says he'll take us to House of Pancakes."

"I don't want to go to House of Pancakes, Evie."

"Why don't you get Hubert then?"

"Evie, there aint nobody in there."

"Yeah there is. Here." Evie started to blow the horn.

"Evie, stop it. Let me in the car, Albert."

Albert said, "'Hello' would be nice, little sister."

I put my head on the roof of the car and started to cry. The roof was so cold.

Evie said, "What did you do, Albert?"

He said, "Nothing."

"You done something," Evie said, "or she wouldn't be crying."

"Yeah, she would," Albert said. "She cries all the time."

"Fuck you, Albert," I said. "I do not."

"Yeah you do."

I busted Albert in the ear through the rolled-down window.

"Albert, open the back door," Evie said, and Albert reached over the seat and my door creaked open.

They couldn't get the back window closed. The winter air blew in on me, and it was the worst ride ever. I curled against the door and pulled my coat up over my head. Cold air beat against my back, blew down my crack, but I got enough privacy to feel like I was crying alone, and whether they knew I was crying or not, Evie and Albert didn't bother me in the back of the icebox Cavalier, and I slept.

~~~~~~~~~~~~~~

I WOKE up in Virginia, about halfway to Kingsport, and Willett was on the radio. Albert was snoring like an old man, and I asked Evie to turn the radio up. Evie must have stopped while I was asleep, because I had a greasy blanket over top of me and the window was up and I was almost comfortable. Willett played lots of live music, guitars guitars guitars, sort of soft and rolling, and when he came on to talk he talked about going to the ball game with his dad, the one he'd gone to while I was at the party down by the river.

"Friday past," Willett said, "me and my dad went to Knoxville to see the Big Orange play in their holiday tournament. Dad scheduled his radiation treatments for the same day, to save a trip. As most of yall know, Dad has lymphoma. Cancer of the lymph node system. We went down 11W, hurrying because we were late, because Dad had to take a bunch of returns to Belks for Mom because her thirty days were up and the return lady had a big long line because she was also doing gift certificates and catalog orders and a couple other things. The point being Dad wasn't in too great a mood by the time we got out on the highway.

"My father," Willett went on, "does not like to be late for anything, not for a doctor's appointment, but especially not for a ball game. His nostrils were flaring, and he was saying unkind things about what I had on the radio. We were past Bean Station, bearing down on Rutledge, when the car stopped running. Dad got it off the side of the road, cussing hard now. He knew it was something about the alternator running down the battery. I don't know. I got out with him, and he got his tools out of the trunk, and he wrenched loose the battery and told me to get the towel he uses to wipe his dipstick out of the back, and I did, and he said, 'Hold it open,' and he lifted the battery into it, said, 'Pay attention' and 'Don't drop it,' and when the battery was wrapped up in the towel, he locked the car and said, 'Come on,' and we started walking towards Rutledge, my dad thumbing.

"It wasn't too long," Willett said, "til a farmer picked us up and took us to Rutledge to a garage that charged our battery and a man at the garage took us back to Dad's Tercel and got the battery back in, and we went on down the road and were late for Dad's radiation—he'd called from the garage and told them we would be—but he had allowed plenty of time, and so really everything was fine and there hadn't been any reason to be agitated or in a hurry."

Willett's voice was soft,

LIKE THE SOUND A CHRISTMAS TREE MAKES WHEN YOU THROW IT OVER THE HILL.

"Later I looked at my father when we were sitting in the arena, watching the first game, which didn't involve Tennessee, sitting there behind the goal, eating our Arby's, and I thought if my mother had been there she might have suggested to my father if he had gotten a new alternator when his mechanic in Kingsport told him he needed one, he wouldn't have been out hitchhiking, nor would her only begotten son have been out hitchhiking either.

"I thought," Willett said, "to bring these things up to my father, who I enjoy aggravating, but when I looked at him in profile, chewing roast beef, keeping it off the sores in his mouth, sores he got from his treatments, his skin pale, his hands on the edge of cramping, holding his sandwich, watching the Brigham Young Cougars running their offensive set, watching LaSalle's transition defense take shape, I could not do anything but love him—love his ability to focus on living, to care so deeply about a game, to focus so completely on watching it, analyzing it, noting the degree to which the game was being played well, the degree to which the players were paying attention, were sound in their execution, were tuned in to what one another were doing—and the chance that my father might actually die became so real to me that I put my arm around him, and he cast a glance at me and then looked back at the court and said, 'That number thirty-four couldn't guard a post. He's killing LaSalle.'"

Then without saying anything else, Willett played a song by an Englishman playing an electric guitar by himself, and when it was over there was a caller on the line, a man who had lost his little girl to leukemia, and he was crying, and as Willett started to cry the phone rang again, and Willett said he had to go, that the next DJ was there. And Willett said he was going home, going to his parents' house to hang out a few days, and so wouldn't be on the air, not until after Christmas. And then he was gone, disappeared behind a song with an accordion on it.

I sat up in the backseat of Evie's Cavalier. Light came into the sky. I looked in my bag for the picture of Willett and his long wavy hair, tall like me, tall Willett with his sensitive heart and his brown eyes. I had called June from the hospital, told her I was coming back, but I decided to go to Willett's house first, and so I told Evie so.

"What about pancakes?" Evie said.

"Yall go on without me," I said.

"Fine with me," Albert said.

I looked out the window.

Evie said, "You know what you're doing."

I kept looking out the window.

"What kind of name is Willett?" Evie said.

"What kind of name is Evie?" I said without looking at her.

"Shoo," Evie said. She turned up the radio. The Virginia ridges, the knobtop cemeteries, the cows stepping along the stony hillsides, the farmhouses, the train trestles, the trailers and their trampolines, the angles of shadow, the blocks of colors ran past my window. These sights gave way to the stores and restaurants on the broad street at the edge of the city, the head shop and hamburger stand, the hardware store and the padded-booth restaurant still wrapped in chrome. We came to a stoplight at the end of the road, faced the smokestacks of the city.

"What do I do now?" Evie said.

"Go left."

Evie huffed and turned left. The Cavalier headed down a wide, busy city street.

"I hate Kingsport," Evie said.

"Have you ever been here?" I said.

"No," Evie said.

We came to Willett's street. It was lined with giant trees. We sat in the car in front of a brick house.

Evie said, "How you know that's his house?"

"It is," I said.

"Well," Evie said,

MIGHT AS WELL GET ON WITH IT.

I got out of the car. I leaned down. Evie rolled the window halfway down.

"You don't want me to stay?" she said.

I shook my head.

"Well," Evie said. She started the car. "Bye." Albert waved.

I waved. Evie drove off. I walked to the door of Willett's house. I knocked. A woman answered. She had lots of gray in her pushed-up hair and smiled like she practiced. "May I help you?"

I said, "Is Willett here?"

Her eyebrows crashed together. "Yes," she said, and stood there. "Just a minute." A wiener dog came yapping up behind her. "Would you like to come in?"

"That's OK," I said, and stayed where I was.

A chunky boy with curly thinning hair came to the door. His face was sticky and he had on baggy, shiny shorts. He was not the boy in the pictures. At first he didn't recognize me. When he did, his face lit up.

"Hey! I know you. How you doing? Come in."

My mouth fell open and I said, "Who the fuck are you?"

"What? Oh. I'm Willett." The dumb monkey just stood there grinning. "I can't believe it's you." He spread his arms, I guess for a hug. I stepped back.

"Get away from me."

"Come on."

I closed my eyes, then opened them. "I am so retarded." I turned to leave. "Wait."

I walked away.

"You're not retarded," he said.

He run after me, which running isn't his best thing, and grabbed me by the arm. I wheeled around on him, shook him off.

"Don't you touch me. Don't you ever touch me. You liar. You phony. You fake phony . . ." I couldn't think of what to call him. " . . . fucker."

"Dawn." His soft face got softer. "Give me a chance."

"I gave you a chance. I . . ." I turned and walked down the hill.

"Dawn."

I crossed out of Willett's neighborhood with its big houses to June's
section. I walked up the steps, and there were three beer bottles next to the
porch glider. I stood outside the storm door looking into June's front room.
I tried to open the door, but it was locked from the inside. When she heard
the door rattle, June looked up from her seat at the desk at the far side of the
room. A dozen picture frames sat on the desk, all pictures of me and Albert.
June got up and came to the door.

"Hey," she said. "Come in. What happened?" June said, looking out the
door. "How did you get here?"

I paced back and forth in June's living room, clinching and unclinching my
fists. When I ran out of steam, I sat down on the sofa.

"He's such a liar," I said.

"Who?" June said.

"He aint no different than none of the rest of them," I said.

"Who?" June said.

"That Internet boy," I said.

"Willett?" June said, and I nodded. "You saw him?" June said.

"He sent me fake pictures," I said. "He's fat as a hog. And his face was all
sticky." I sat down next to Aunt June and sobbed like I'd never shed a tear in
my life.

"Hunh," June said.

I said, "I don't know why I didn't whip him. He's soft as butter."

June said, "You want something to eat?"

I said, "I wish I had my own car."

"You can borrow mine," June said. "Where are you going?"

"Alaska."

"Oh. Well," June said. "You want supper first?"

I had to smile at that. "I reckon."

"If you can stay for dessert," June said, "I got chess pie."

~~~~~~~~~~~~~~~

THAT NIGHT, after pie, I lay under the covers in June's guest bed, my
drawing pad against my knees. June came in with an armload of magazines.
She asked me was I still doing my collages. I said I was. June sat down on the
edge of the bed, set the magazines beside me.

"Maybe you ought not be so quick to run," she said.

"You did," I said.

"I know," June said.

"You had a scholarship," I said.

June said, "You have things I never had. You can do things I never could."

I said, "I aint got nothing."

"I'm just saying," June said, "it's hard to go it alone."

"I aint going back," I said, and started flipping through a magazine. June picked one up too.

"Look here." June pointed at a picture of a painting of a woman in red and blue floating amongst winged babies hung from the clouds. Below her a crowd of men reached for her, and above her was a white-bearded man. It was the painting I'd seen in the Canard library when Momma went missing. "I dreamed about this painting last night," June said. "That's Mary ascending into heaven. And these are Jesus's apostles. I seen the painting when I was in Italy. It's fourteen feet high."

I said, "You saw that in person?"

"Mm-hm," June said. "In my dream I had that painting tattooed across my back."

"For real?" I said.

"In the dream," June said, "I was looking at my back in the mirror. I was flexing my back muscles, and when I did Mary moved toward heaven. I would flex one way, and Mary would move up toward heaven. I would unflex and she would go back down."

"Like she was on a trampoline," I said.

"Like one of those 3D pictures where Jesus's eyes open and close when you go past," June said.

I said, "Mamaw has one of those in the hall in her house. Scares me."

"Me too," June said. She ran her hand across the page. "Day before I saw that painting, a sheriff's deputy was in Momma's kitchen trying to get us to tell where Tricia was. Next day I'm in Italy staring at Mary going up to heaven. I remember thinking how could a person take brush and paints and turn them into something as beautiful as that?"

"Are you religious?" I said.

June said no.

"Do you wish you got married?" I said.

June said she didn't know.

I asked June if I should go out with Willett.

June said, "Maybe."

I said, "He started on a lie."

I sat there flipping through the magazine. I tore out a few pages. June said, "Maybe you should give him another chance. It's just a picture."

I didn't think it was just a picture. I was needing something more than another liar.

Aunt June said, "Online, it's not real life."

I came to Kingsport to find somebody wasn't all the time trying to run some game on me. All this felt like a hustle.

Aunt June said, "I know his family. They are good people. Willett has been raised a good boy."

I was not looking for a boy. I was looking for something I could lean on, something deeper rooted. Aunt June picked up the scissors I had been using to cut out magazine pictures. She picked up the picture of Mary bouncing on God's trampoline. She cut out the men, the disciples below Mary. June held the cutout men up below her eyes, like a veil across the bottom half of her face. Her eyes looked like two moons, rising up over them. The disciples marveled at my aunt June's eyes.

"Aren't you going to talk to me?" she said.

I took up the scissors and cut out Mary, cut her away from the absent men, away from the babies shoving her to heaven, away from the bearded daddy God waiting for her in the clouds above, cut her out until she wasn't part of nothing else. And I took her, her pretty hands out, looking up at God knows what now, and rubbed the glue stick across her back. I stuck Mary on the lampshade, and she lit up with the words that were on the page behind her. And Mary was alone.

"You know what I wish?" I said.

"No," said Aunt June.

"I wish I had a dog," I said. "A dog with nothing to do but hang out with me."

"Dogs are good," said Aunt June.

The room Aunt June had me in was painted purple. I lay my head on the pillow and stared at the ceiling. "Why did he do that?" I said. "He knew I was weird, that I wouldn't care what he looked like."

June lay down beside me. "What is it you like about Willett?"

"He's goofy," I said.

"And you like that?" June said.

"I do."

June said, "What else?"

I peeled the Virgin Mary off the lampshade. I held her up in the air above me. I closed one eye looking at her. "I like that he wrote me. Just to me he wrote that long letter. No way he sent that exact same letter to other girls."

"What else?"

I wished my cutout Mary was bigger. "I thought I liked the way he was built."

"So you have that in common," June said.

"What?"

"Yall have the same idea of what looks good to you."

I said, "Why are sticking up for him? You think he's the best I can do?"

June didn't say anything for a good while. I thought she might've gone to sleep. Then June said, "You can do what you want to, Dawn. But that boy is all right."

June kissed my forehead and left. I cut out pictures. There was one of Chewbacca. I fished in my bag and took out the picture of phony Willett and Chewbacca. The printout was tinted pink, where it came from a computer printer missing an ink cartridge. Peeking out from behind Chewbacca's shoulder in the pink picture was real Willett, fuzzy and smiling. I hadn't noticed him before.

# ACT FIVE

~~~~~~~~~~

# SILVER DAGGER

# 13

## THE MOUSE

WILLETT BILSON told me to meet him at a Chinese restaurant on a wide street near the mall in Kingsport. When I opened the door, the smell of bleach and grease filled my nose. The belly of the waitress on the pay phone stretched her maroon kimono wrap blouse. When she closed her eyes, her red-and-blue eyeshadow made a pair of tiny perfect desert sunsets. "You have to let your Lord love you," she said into the phone.

I sat down at a booth next to a window. The blinds were raised. It was cloudy out. When the waitress hung up, she asked did I want the buffet. I said I was waiting on somebody. She batted the menu against my shoulder and said, "Aren't we all?" I sipped the pop she brought til Willett come sliding in the opposite side of the booth in a white-fringed green satin cowboy shirt not big enough for him. He also had on baggy black punk rock pants covered with buckles and chains.

Willett grinned, his frizzy hair flattened down dark and sticky-looking. The waitress brought him a tall red cup full of Mountain Dew. It flashed on my mind Willett Bilson met all kinds of women in that restaurant, not just me. It flashed on my mind he was a player, and dangerous, and he would slip me drugs and carry me off and I would live dirty and tattered in a basement until he chopped me up into tiny pieces and mailed me to every president and king in every country in the world in his mother's tampon boxes wrapped in plain brown paper.

The waitress brought Willett a bowl of yellow soup without him asking. "Would you like some soup?" she said to me, "or maybe an egg roll?" Willett looked at me like I was about to tell some big buried treasure secret. The waitress poured more pop in my cup, and I said, "Egg roll." I never stopped looking at Willett, and I couldn't stop worrying about the brutal atrocities he was going to commit against me even though all he talked about was how great I was because of what me and Mamaw were doing to protect Blue Bear Mountain.

"You're going to save the world," Willett said. "You're hero material."

Willett slurped up noodles. "But you're so good. You know exactly what to say. It just comes out of your mouth."

"All that makes me sick to my stomach," I said.

"I get sick to my stomach," Willett said. "All the time."

I asked him what made him sick. "Is it people?"

Willett said, "I think it's more like food. Where I don't stop eating until I get sick."

"Why don't you stop?" I said.

"I should," he said.

I asked him was he really just eighteen.

He said he was.

"But," I said, "you've already been to college and back."

He said he graduated high school a year early.

"You must be smart," I said.

"You don't have to be that smart," Willett said. "You just have to be smart enough. And hate high school."

I pushed hot mustard with the butt of my egg roll. "I got the second part down."

"People gave me a hard time at high school," Willett said, "because I have poor saliva control."

I asked him what that meant.

"I slobber a lot," Willett said.

I nodded. "We have a kid like that at our school."

Willett sucked at his cheeks. It made a sound like worn-out windshield wipers. "Boy or girl?" he said.

"Boy," I said.

"Does he have a girlfriend?" Willett said.

"He doesn't come to school much," I said. "I think he switched to the Jesus Academy. I don't know. I haven't been going to school much lately."

"Why not?" Willett said.

"I have poor fist control," I said.

"You get in fights?" Willett said.

I nodded.

"Wow," Willett said. "Like, you start fights?"

I nodded.

"Wow," Willett said. "I've never started a fight."

"You should try it," I said. "It's great."

"Oh. O-OK," Willett said, and looked down at his totally clean plate.

"I was joking," I said.

"You seem real smart," Willett said. "Way smarter than me about mining and stuff."

"I'm just a parrot," I said.

Willett scratched above his eye with his fork. "But you can read and stuff, right?"

I looked at him. His smile looked like a baby gets when it first gets a couple little teeth. He didn't mean nothing by what he said.

We went back and forth for a while, and then Willett started talking about something I didn't even understand what the topic was. And he kept talking. After while, my eyes wandered out the window. Across the restaurant parking lot, a man pushed a lawnmower down the sidewalk through the snow.

I lost track of what Willett was saying, but was happy to be there with him. Willett got my attention back when he started choking on his yellow soup. I moved to the other side of the booth and hit him on the back with the flat of my hand, and when I did, I could see us together old. The vision surprised me, and when Willett stopped choking, I left my hand on his back.

Willett said, "You see what I'm saying? You see how something like that could happen if we don't take steps to prevent it now?"

I patted him on the back and said, "I do."

Willett wiped his nose on the back of his wrist. "What kind of ice cream do you like?" he said.

I said strawberry.

"Have you ever had lemon?"

I told him no. Willett said he liked lemon. I was still patting his back. "Is that right?" I said.

Willett nodded. "Daddy's people made homemade lemon. That's what they made on the farm."

"That right?" I said again.

Willett nodded.

I said, "What do you want to do now, Willett Bilson?"

"We could look at Christmas lights if you like to do that. Do you like to do that?"

I nodded.

~~~~~~~~~~~~

WILLETT POINTED out the car window. "Look at that," he said. We were pulled up in front of a house on a curving city street, not far from June's, a house small and square like all the rest on its street. The yard was boxed in by a cyclone fence and packed with light. Thousands of tiny bulbs blinked and ran in corded paths. Some were red and some were blue, but most were golden-white. I had seen plenty of Christmas lights in my time, but there were more squeezed into less space than I'd ever seen, and the sight burned a cube of light into my head. Willett rolled down his window, and I could feel the heat coming off the lights, and there was a little red wiener dog walking among them, and Elvis Presley sang Christmas songs low and quiet. The yard throbbed and pulsed like a cut finger, and the wiener dog didn't bark, a miracle if you know anything about wiener dogs.

"Hey boy!" a penny-headed woman said from the porch. Beside her
smiled a man with a high forehead and hair in dark stripes across the top of
his head. The woman, way shorter than the man, hopped like a bird down
the steps into the yard. Power cords criss-crossed the walk. Willett got out
and picked his way through the cords like a child crossing a creek. The old
woman followed him up the porch steps. The man reached behind her, untied
her apron strings, and she gouged him in the ribs. The man came to the car,
opened my door, and said, "Kentucky" as he put his hand on my shoulder and
laid the other palm up at the end of his straightened-out arm, showing me the
way into the house.

The house inside was blue-green carpet, silver lamps, silver picture frames,
silver pulls on the drawers of creamy white furniture, pearly-green and blue
wallpaper. It reminded me of pictures of icebergs. But the house was hot,
Willett's face already glistening. The woman was bare-armed and in a blouse
like I'd seen in pictures from when Cora and Houston moved to Florida for a
little while with Momma and June. In one of those square little Florida pictures,
Houston and Momma and June stood in an orange grove. A boy stood
between squinting June and frowning Tricia. He was burrheaded and smiling,
and in his five-year-old arms were at least a dozen beautiful oranges. And at
that moment for the first time, I realized the little boy was Hubert.

The man laughed. Then he raised his eyebrows and laughed again,
bigmouthed to where I could see silver fillings in his back teeth. He said,

They all three turned to look at me.
"Do what?" I said.

"What kind of pie do you want?"

"I don't know."

"But you do want pie," the woman said.

"I guess," I said.

She said, "I got blueberry and peanut butter, and key lime, and coconut cream, and two chess pies—that's Paul's favorite—and a little bit of chocolate."

"There aint no chocolate left," the man said.

"Paul," she said, and smacked him with a dish towel.

~~~~~~~~~~~~

"HERE'S YOUR pie," Paul said, and put a dinner plate down with a pale green piece of key lime next to a piece of chess next to some mess of something with chocolate chips shot all through it. Then he turned a fork in the air in front of me. The fork caught the light from the yard through the sheer curtains. I took the fork from Paul's hand, and the woman turned on the lamp.

"We knew you were coming," she said.

Willett sat down beside me on the couch. He was warm as the beach. I used the side of the fork to cut a bite of pie. I looked at Willett as the pie went in my mouth, and he smiled, and the sweet beauty creaminess of the pie ran to the four corners of my mouth. It was good pie.

"You like that?" the woman said. When I nodded, she said, "Well, we got plenty." I nodded and the man laughed.

He said, "I wasn't much older than you when I first had one of them. Strawberry rhubarb, the first one."

I kept eating, and the woman patted my knee. She settled down into an armchair. The fat of her legs came circling out of her gardening shorts. "You want some ice cream with that?" she said.

"No, ma'am," I said.

"Butter pecan," Paul said. "Whole tub of butter pecan."

Paul told us he was a man of science. He made bombs and explosives that never went bad. He smiled at me gentle. "Kentucky," he said, and put his hands on the arms of his chair, tipped his feet up in the air, and a footrest rose to join them. He pointed at his wife. "Pretty as a picture," Paul said, and her eyes softened. "Go look at the snakes," Paul said, eyebrows arching.

Willett took my hand and led me down a hall filled with plaques and certificates and a dozen framed pictures of a boy who got younger as we walked up the hall. We went into a green-lit room. Willett reached behind a line of aquariums, and they lit up, gold against the green light. Willett's face glowed like a child in front of a fire.

We stood holding hands in front of a glass box with a black snake in it. A mouse sat scared in the corner of the tank. The snake coiled around the mouse and squeezed it. Killed it in front of us, and then worked its jaw open and began swallowing the mouse.

"No shit," I said.

Willett put his hands in his pants pockets. I lay my head against the top of his. I heard a laugh I thought was my mother's. I turned around. The man was there holding a pie covered in foil. He held the pie out.

"Take it," he said. "It's apple."

Willett took the pie. "I'm ready to go," I whispered into his ear. We left the snake room, walked to the front door.

"Merry Christmas," the man said.

"Yall be careful," the woman said.

"WHO IS that?" I asked Willett when we got out on the sidewalk. "Are they kin to you?"

"His name's Junior," Willett said. "And everybody calls her Mrs. Junior. He works at the plant."

We stood in the street, opposite sides of ourselves lit up by the pie-house Christmas lights. I asked Willett why we had to go in the pie house. He took my hands in his.

He said, "It was good pie, wasn't it?"

I told him I thought it was. Willett nodded and kept nodding.

"There are good people in the world," Willett said. "Good people who make bombs."

I didn't know what to say to that.

"That's in you, too," Willett said. "Isn't it?"

"Isn't what inside me?"

Willett's smile cracked the dried pie on his face. "Good," Willett said. "You have good in you. And also the ability to make bombs."

This boy is strange, I thought to myself, and he has ahold of both my hands. I thought about Keith Kelly's funeral. I didn't know when it would be or what it would be like.

"I'll be damned," I said. I moved my fingers in Willett's hands, which were not as soft as I thought they'd be. Not as wet. When I saw real Willett for the first time, and I was repulsed and ashamed, I also thought—I bet he has wet hands. But they weren't.

"I'll be damned, too," Willett said.

In my mind, I saw Keith Kelly waxy and gray in his coffin. I said to Willett, "You know I'm only fifteen, don't you? Eighteen and fifteen—that's not that good."

Willett said, "I know what you're saying."

My thumbs rubbed Willett's hands some more. Out of all of it, holding hands is the best.

"Just so you know," I said.

Willett said, "Do you want to go home?"

I saw Blondie Kelly's lips, moist, pink, and thick as raw pork chops on Keith's candle-wax cheeks, her tears splashing into the grooves of his face. I said to Willett,

Willett took me to the Kingsport Kolonel Krispy. We sat at their glassed-in picnic patio. Willett had a trayful of hot dogs in front of him. He had been talking again, for ten minutes maybe.

"It was a nasty sunburn. Just nasty. Scary is what it was." Willett took a hot dog out of its little bag, peeled back its little paper tray, and shoved most of it in his mouth. "I couldn't move a muscle without excruciating pain. I couldn't lie down. I couldn't sit up. I won't lie to you. I screamed when Mom sprayed that stuff on me, that sunburn relief spray. That stuff with the dog pulling the little girl's bathing suit down on the bottle? It hurt." He shoved the last of the hot dog in his mouth and said, "It did."

"I hate it for you," I said. I put the edge of my hands to the window glass and my eyes up against my hands, and I looked out the window of the picnic pavilion at Kolonel Krispy, past the neon Kolonel Krispy sign, with its winking doughnut-eyed army officer. A paper plant rose up out of the night a block away, its aluminum siding rising a hundred feet into the air, logo of a Canadian paper company big as a pin oak on its side in an open field. Behind it, sawdust lay heaped against the sky, a blowaway pyramid. I ran a French fry through the smear of ketchup on the wax paper on the stone table in front of me.

Willett said, "Are you bored?"

"Yeah," I said, and took a sip of Willett's milkshake. "But it's nice to be bored for a change."

Willett looked into my eyes. "Can I have a fry?" he said.

I slid the wax paper across to Willett.

~~~~~~~~~~~~

WILLETT LIKED for me to drive. So I was behind the wheel of his mother's car when we left Kolonel Krispy. He showed me where he used to be a patrol boy and belched. He groaned; he farted. He said, "Oh."

"What?" I said.

Willett said, "Pull in there," pointing.

"Where?" I said.

"Up there," Willett said. "That shopping plaza."

I turned into the plaza. The smells that went with Willett's noises made my eyes water. "You want me to stop?"

Willett's eyes wrinkled up. He bared his teeth. "Grocery store," he said.

I pulled up in front of the grocery store, and Willett jumped out of the car, ran for the door, turned around and ran back to my window. I rolled it down. "I have a troubled colon," Willett said, and ran back in the store.

I parked and went into the store. I looked for Willett in every aisle and could not find him. I stood beneath the raised platform of the grocery store service desk and stared up the dog-food aisle to the back of the store. There were double doors at the back of the store, leading, I figured, to the restroom. The stringy-headed girl working at the service counter popped her gum.

I'm in love with a boy with a troubled colon. I said this in my mind to the stringy-headed girl up in the check-cashing booth at the grocery store in Willett's town in Tennessee. I didn't say it out loud. I said it in my mind. What I said out loud was:

And that girl said "Yis" through her nose and turned and walked away like she couldn't bear to watch me using her phone. But it wasn't her phone. It was the store's phone. I called June, said, "What are you doing?" She said, "Nothing," and I said, "This boy is strange. He talks all the time and he ate too many hot dogs and too much pie and he's been in the bathroom a half hour." June said, "Is he OK?" and I said, "I guess," and turned around and Willett was coming up the dog-food aisle with toilet paper stuck on his shoe. I heard that girl in the check-cashing booth snort, and I knew to stay on the phone or I would have had to whip her stringy-headed Tennessee ass right in the middle of her snotty Tennessee store.

I could tell by Willett's face he was going to come up to me and start talking like each of my ears has its own brain, like I could understand what he is saying with one and what June is saying with the other. Sure enough, he said, "If we had a house, what would you want in it?"

I said, "I have to go, Aunt June," and she said, "Wait," but the phone was already hung up. Willett stood in front of me, breathing through his mouth, and I wanted to squeeze his big soft head. The feeling was new and strange,

and I had to go to the front of the store, towards the light on the other side
of the giant glass windows. The buckles and chains on Willett's punk rock
pants made a racket, and I could hardly hear him when he said, "Know what
I'd want?"

I stopped. My mind was all mixed up, and I didn't know where I was at. I
put my hand on a buggy and said, "What?"

"I'd want me one of them power-flush commodes like they have in
stores." I just looked at him, and he said, "Can you imagine that kind of power
in a domestic setting?" And then he said, "WHOOOOOSH."

I put my hand on his cheek and squeezed. I said, "How is your stomach?"
and he said, "Better." I squeezed his other cheek with my other hand and said,
"Do I make you nervous?"

He got a piece of candy out of his pocket and put it in his mouth. Then
he took another piece of candy out of his pocket and offered it to me. All
this with me standing there holding his cheeks. I shook my head. He put the
second piece of candy in his mouth and said, "Everything makes me nervous."

I squeezed his cheeks between my fingers a little and said, "How nervous
do I make you compared to everything else?"

"Way less," he said, chewing. "Way way less."

I said, "You aint gonna hit me."

Willett shook his head.

I said, "You don't hunt."

Willett shook his head again.

I said, "You aint never cussed out the law."

Willett shook his head a third time.

I said, "You aint on drugs."

"An inhaler," Willett said.

"Do what?" I said.

"I use an inhaler," Willett said. "For my asthma."

And I kept squeezing his cheeks between my fingers, and he kept
chewing, and I was fine with a boyfriend who aint likely to slap me, aint likely
to sell pills, aint likely to terrorize woodland creatures nor cuss out the law.
And I was glad to have run off from home and quit school, and when that
stringy-headed heifer from the check-cashing booth walked by, smartass grin
on her face, I held onto Willett's cheeks and did not knock her down though I
easily could.

YOU WANT TO TAKE ME HOME? I SAID.

Willett said, "I can't go to Kentucky tonight."

"I'm staying at my aunt's," I said.

"Oh. Yeah," Willett said. "I'll take you home."

"Good," I said.

"How do I get there?" Willett said.

I let go of his cheeks, and we walked out of the store. "I'll tell you," I said.

Willett stopped in the middle of the parking lot.

"Draw me a map," he said.

"On what?" I said.

"On the back of my hand." He pulled a black marker out of his pants pocket. I took the marker, pulled off the cap, and took his hand.

"So if here's the park," I said, drawing a big rectangle near Willett's knuckles, "then June's house is nine houses down this way." I drew nine small squares, the last up near Willett's elbow with an X through it

"Right on the road?" Willett said, "Next to the railroad tracks?"

"Mm-hm," I said.

"Put the road and the tracks on there too," Willett said.

I dropped Willett's arm. "No," I said.

"Why not?" Willett said.

"I aint drawing all over you."

"Go ahead," Willett said. "Just a little more."

The skin on Willett's arm was white and dry and had a grain like good paper. I drew a line for the road and then a line for the railroad. I put hatches across the railroad line. Willett stood still, the ink catching in the hairs of his arm.

"There," I said. "Think you can find it now?

"I think so," Willett said. "Yeah. That should help."

I twisted Willett's wrist, turning up the fish-belly white underside of his forearm. "Want me to draw the plant on this side?" I said.

Willett smiled. "Sure."

I dropped Willett's arm. "Let's go. You drive."

~~~~~~~~~~

WHEN WE got to June's house, Willett came with me to the porch. There was a note on the door. June was gone to Virginia. She probably wouldn't make it back, the note said. I was surprised she would leave such news on the door for any sneak thief to see.

"Where's your aunt?" Willett said.

"Out," I said. Willett looked at me with the eyes of a puppy left out on the road. My stomach jumped like frog legs in a skillet. "You want a pop?" I said. Willett nodded and we went in the house. We stood facing each other in June's living room.

"Keith Kelly?" Willett said.

"You know about that?"

"Some."

Willett's eyes were like plastic baby pools. Full of innocence, and you'd have to try really hard to drown somebody in them.

"Would you draw on me some more?" Willett said.

I said I would. The light in the room was warm and golden. Willett took off his shirt and dropped it next to the television. I pointed and Willett picked up one end of the coffee table with its laid-out art books. I got the other end, and we moved it towards the couch to make more room. Willett lay down on his stomach. His back was a hillside made of meat, his skin the color of eggshells and peppered with moles, freckles, and pimples.

I left the room to get my pens and things, and when I came back Willett had his legs spread. I got down on my knees between Willett's legs. His smile was calm, but his breathing seemed off, rushed. I leaned over Willett's back with a felt-tip pen in my left hand. I sketched out Mary from Titian's *Assumption*, and then the apostles, and the baby angels, and then finally God up above. I worked quick, with short strokes of the pen. Willett laughed to himself and didn't say a thing.

In the quiet, my drawing came to life. Mary's face turned into Evie's face without me putting pen to it. Then her face became Momma. The apostles turned into Hubert and my other uncles and cousins, dressed up like the whole thing was a Nativity play. At first I thought it was Willett that was moving, but it wasn't, it was the figures I had drawn.

I heard laughing, not coming from Willett, and I looked over my shoulder. But the laughing came from the picture. Hubert and them were laughing on Willett's back. Laughing and complaining. They were grabbing hold of Momma, even as God and the baby angels tried to pull her into heaven. She was bobbing up and down, like a fishing lure. They pulled at her so hard I thought she was going to be pulled to pieces. And then Momma, Mary, turned into me.

"Let me see," Willett said. I came back to reality, and the drawing on Willett's back was just a drawing again, not some freaky psychedelic cartoon. Willett got up and looked at himself in the mirror June had up over the door to the bedroom. "That is so cool," he said.

I fished around in my big Ziploc bag full of pens, erasers, and stuff.

"Finish it," Willett said, and got back down on the floor.

I got up and put on some music. A woman with a big nose and a smoky voice began singing about sex over saxophones and a cheesy organ. I got back between Willett's knees and put colors into the picture, colors I remembered from the pictures in the books, and colors of my own, colors based on what pens I had. As I colored Hubert and them came back to life. Mary was Momma again, and she floated up in a burst, and almost made it, and the baby angels had her by the hand, and Keith Kelly jumped out of the apostle pile and got her by the ankle, like a lost kite caught. I pulled an X-Acto knife out of my bag and cut off Keith Kelly's hand. Momma floated loose, but another man got ahold of her, and so I took the knife and started cutting the throats of Hubert and the rest of the Apostles.

Willett screamed, and the blood ran from the slits I'd made in his back. Willett tried to get up, but he was easy to hold down, like pressing a half-filled beach ball underwater. I could do it with one hand and keep cutting throats on his back. Willett kept screaming.

"Dawn," a voice said. "Dawn!"

I looked up and June stood at the storm door, calm as a barber. She smiled like a woman selling something on television.

I looked at Willett's back, and it was the same pimply knob it had been when I started, only with my lame drawing of Titian's *Assumption* all over it. No cuts. I don't guess he ever screamed. He was snoring, actually. I stood up with a head like a get-well-soon balloon, silver and wobbly on its string.

"Looks like yall are having fun," June said. The phone started ringing. A man on the stereo sang, "I don't have much in my life, but take it, it's yours." Willett slept on, and I did not know what to feel.

"Dawn, it's for you," June said.

When I said hello, the voice on the other end said, "Hey-oh. The darling Misty Dawn." It was my grandfather Houston.

"Hey Papaw," I said.

"Your grandmother beckons you to history's stage," he said.

I said, "Do what?"

"The governor and Cora want to see you in Frankfort," Houston said.

"Not me," I said.

"You," he said.

I turned to June. She put her hand on my cheek. She smiled a Mother Mary smile. Willett stood with his shirt off in the doorway. I stared at him even though I wanted to close my eyes. He smiled. "I don't need you," I said. "Go on home." I don't know why I said that. But I did.

"Dawn," June said, her voice like the bell on an elevator going down.

Willett kept smiling, put his shirt on, and left.

~~~~~~~~~~

NEXT MORNING June brought me home in her dark red Honda car. My head was still balloon-light, my vision swimmy. My night with Willett was too much of being with someone. Truth be told, it was the *wanting* to be with someone that was too much. I don't know. I wasn't in the mood to be loved. Not the way Willett might've, not the way June would've, if I'd let her. It's weird and strange to say, but I was looking forward to falling back in with Hubert. Simpler.

On the ride to Mamaw's, June didn't say anything. She fiddled with the knobs, the windows, the mirrors in the car, but she didn't say anything. She wasn't like Momma. She didn't have to spill it all out there. I chewed on my bottom lip. We did not play the radio. It was just us in the blue-white morning light. Our faces were chalk floating in milk. We floated away from each other, far away from the way we had been by the river the night of the hippie Christmas party.

"So what's this about Kenny Bilson loving you?" I said.

"Who says that?" June said.

"He says it himself."

June pushed in the cigarette lighter. She didn't say anything til it popped back out. "When did you talk to him?" June said.

"At the party."

June lit her cigarette, cracked the window. "He shouldn't trouble himself," she said.

"You don't like Bilsons?" I said.

June smoked the better part of her cigarette. "I like them fine," June said.

"What then?"

"I'm closed," June said.

"Closed," I said. "What does that mean?"

"Means I aint looking right now."

"Hunh," I said.

"Not for him, anyway," June said.

"How long you gonna be closed?"

June pushed her cigarette butt out the window crack. "Not much longer," she said.

~~~~~~~~~~~

WHEN WE got to Mamaw's, Hubert's green truck was there. June and me both sat and looked at it. Evie's Cavalier was there too.

"Let's go back," I said.

We sat some more. "I may not go in," June said.

A black dog with white feet sniffed June's wheels, hiked his leg, and peed on her tire. Hubert came out on Mamaw's patio.

"We're all fixing to sit down."

~~~~~~~~~~~

MAMAW'S KITCHEN table was full of people. I hadn't seen it that way in a long time. Stranger than that, though, was Mamaw sitting at it. Houston was the one fussing at the stove.

"Ho, ho," he said, wiping his hands on a towel. "Santy couldn't have done no better than to send you two."

Eating around a table with a big bunch of family wasn't something I'd done much of and wasn't really something I missed, but when Mamaw, who was facing me from the far side of the table, pushed out the chair next to her, I slipped past my aunt and through the others and sat down beside her.

"June," Houston said, "Set these on the table," and handed June a pan of biscuits. "Yall get some and hand me back the pan."

Everything was calm. Maybe things could be in my family, I remember thinking, like they were on the hippie farm.

"Yall missed the blessing," Momma said. She made a big show of moving her feet with their casts on them.

Me nor June said a word back to Momma. Sausage and bacon chattered in one skillet, potatoes in another. Pancake batter spread on an electric skillet. Houston cut grapefruits Aunt Ohio had sent from Florida, like she did every year.

June said, "Momma, you look good."

Mamaw didn't disagree, which she normally would have. Houston poured coffee all around and Evie and Albert leaned into each other in their own private world. I wished Willett was there, not because I was jealous of Evie or to show Albert I had somebody too, but just to make everything whole and rounded. But then I remembered how I left it with Willett and my mouth went sour.

People started to eat. The potatoes had green peppers and onions cut up in them. Houston laid pancakes right off the griddle onto people's plates, and Hubert sang a little. The whole thing was like a TV happy ending. I wanted to ride the camera as it pulled out through the roof and left the family there and THE END came on the screen and the names of who all made the show went rolling over the perfect picture family. But our show went on, and spoons clattered in jelly jars, and plates filled with food passed through the air, and people rattled their silverware, and chairs scooted in, and we ate, forking it up and in, and then came the moment where in normal houses somebody would ask somebody about some good news something, but since it was our house, Albert looked up, jelly on his face and syrup on his sleeve, and said, "So. How was Keith's funeral?"

We all looked up. Mamaw picked up the bowl of potatoes. "It was nice," she said. She spooned potatoes onto her plate and said, "Yall need more potatoes?" Hubert put his hand out and Mamaw passed him the bowl, setting the spoon to where it would be easy for him to reach.

"You didn't need to be going to no funeral," my mother said. "Not so soon after your fall."

"Old people fall down all the time," Mamaw said.

"Momma," June started.

"Well," my mom went on, "It was nice Dawn happened to be around today. Never know when she's going to be in the area."

I said, "You're the one dumped me in Kingsport."

"I see you come back," Momma said, pointing at Mamaw, "when *she* needs you." Momma put a wad of pancake in her mouth. "Maybe you think you'll get on the radio or something."

"Tricia," Hubert said.

"You leave her alone," Evie said.

"I just don't understand," Momma said, "how people can be out fanning their tails all over creation when . . ." Momma's eyes burned holes in me. "I just don't understand."

And then the only sound was the black dog barking outside and Albert scraping the last of the scrambled eggs out of the bowl. That day at the table was the end of some part of me.

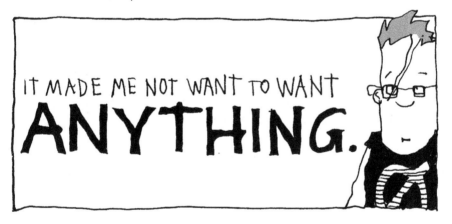

I got up from the table. My tongue was so swollen in my mouth I thought I'd eaten something bad, but I hadn't. I hadn't hardly had a bite of all the nice stuff Houston fixed. I slid out from behind the table and out the door. I thought about walking up to the jumping-off place, not to jump off but just to be there at the edge of things.

Instead I went to Houston's. Nobody came after me, and I set in Houston's front room, which was cold and greasy like pork in the refrigerator. I got the jar out of Houston's icebox and went outside and sat behind the wheel of Houston's junky truck. It was a Ford and hadn't run since I was a little girl. Houston mostly drove an old Cutlass that didn't have room for anybody else it was so full of old records and empty Pepsi bottles and such. I threw a crate of wood scraps and a box of drinking glasses and plastic Jesuses and water wells and fake flowers out of the truck's front seat, and made a place for myself—made me a nest there with my jar and my aggravation.

The liquor was buttery and easy to drink. The sun came out bright and warmed the truck, and when it did the smell got funky. The sweat on my lips and the sides of my head felt good. I was overcome by wanting to burrow down into the truck cab, let the sun pour in, and let the outside world pass me by. There is so much junk nobody ever sees it. It never gets moved. It just is. To be down in it, to *be* it, seemed not so bad. They would all walk past me like I was a junker pickup, ignore me so they wouldn't have to deal with me. I could sink down, burrow in like an animal, too hard to get at, too small and gristly to be worth eating, not worth fooling with—

That's where I was when Agnes Therapin came up to the truck window.

"Your granny can't go with us to the governor's," she said. "Says she's hurting too bad. Says she's addleheaded."

"She aint addleheaded," I said. Agnes stood beside the truck looking at me til finally I said to her, "Why you telling me?"

Agnes said, "Cora said we should take you, said you know more about it than her. She said you got a young spongy brain."

"Agnes," I said, "aint you heard? I'm practically a high school dropout."

Agnes took a sucker out of her dress pocket, unwrapped it, put it in her mouth. She slipped the sucker in her cheek and said, "A lot of smart people drop out of high school."

I shook my head.

"Your momma's taking good care of Cora," Agnes said.

"That right?" I said.

"Better than a lot of them said she would," Agnes said.

Agnes pulled her sucker into the O of her lips and then, with a slurpy swallow, slid it into the other cheek. Then she stood there, like a scarecrow, except not all crucified out like a real scarecrow, but her man sweater had holes at the elbows and frayed cuffs like a scarecrow's would. Agnes was suffering. She didn't want that blasting to come back. "It's getting on my last nerve, Dawn," she said when I said something about it.

"I know it," I said. I looked away from her when I said it.

Agnes said, "If don't nothing come of this, I'm going to my daughter in South Carolina."

Willett came over the rise with Evie Bright. They walked up and stood beside Agnes. "What are you doing?" Evie said to me.

"Nothing," I said. "Sitting here talking to Agnes."

"Well," Evie said. She looked at Willett and then lay her hand palm up towards me. "There she is." And then Evie Bright walked away. I hated to see her head drop out of sight when she walked down Houston's grassy drive.

"Hi," Willett said to Agnes Therapin.

Agnes nodded at Willett. "I better go, Dawn," she said.

When she spoke, Willett's eyebrows lifted and he said, "I know you." Agnes looked to me and Willett said, "I've edited your voice."

Agnes looked at me again and said, "I'll see you, Dawn."

When Agnes slipped over the rise after Evie, I said, "What are you doing here, Willett?"

"I don't know," he said. "I have come to pursue you."

LIKE A CREEPY **STALKER?** I said.

"It seemed more romantic in my mind," he said.

I sipped from my jar.

"Do you think I'm a creepy stalker?" he said.

Willett's questions were stressful. I didn't care much for him being there in my grandfather's yard, far out on the ridge, what should have been my fortress of solitude.

Willett said, "I missed your hands."

I looked out over top of Willett's head at the wide gray-white sky. Grateful I was to that sky for not telling me what to do, for not trying to get me to think anything, to feel anything. I tucked the jar between my thighs and raised both palms to Willett. I held them there and when Willett didn't say anything, didn't do anything, I put them down in my lap.

"Cora said I could stay at her house," Willett said.

I narrowed my eyes down at him. It took everything I had not to let my mouth fall open in shock. But I didn't say anything, just gave Willett Bilson my best gray-white sky face. I turned away from him, faced forward, and stared at the woods through the windshield. Willett went and sat on the back bumper of the pickup. It was muddy back there, and I knew it must be getting on his shoes. The bed of the truck was full of roof shingles and soggy cardboard boxes filled with rusting metal parts that hadn't been part of anything for a good long while. Willett settled down on the bumper like a dog had nothing but time to wait for its human.

And there we sat. I'd lost my peace and quiet and put in its place Willett sitting on the back end of my grandfather's truck. Out the rear window I watched him, the back of his head like a massive pine cone. He scratched his cheek. He rubbed the top of his head. Even after I had blown him off, talked to him like a dog, there he was. The glare of the sun made him look flat, like he was ironed onto a piece of cloth.

I stared at him through the glare and let him get less real in my mind. Then he raised both hands to his face. He rubbed them up and down. He ground the knuckles at the base of his thumbs into his eyes. I wondered what was going through his mind. I wondered what it was like for your daddy to die slow. I wondered if that would be better than having him die sudden.

I couldn't get his thoughts to come clear in my mind. But I felt them—his thoughts—close. I almost could tell what he was thinking. That was what I wanted—to know what he was thinking, to know what was on his heart—but only if I could do it without having to ask him. I was afraid of the risk. I was afraid of being wrong. Afraid if I spread my arms and put my chest out to him, open and pink, that from somewhere a bullet would rip right through me, and I would be gone.

I turned around, facing forward, and sat down in the truck seat. The steering wheel was cracked. I put my finger down in the crack, that dark human crack, and I cried. The tears seemed to come from the base of my spine, the roots of my teeth, the bottom of the holes in my head where my hair took root. I let the tears come without moving, without making a sound, and I was a water tower, a head without a body, servant to a place with no idea how I came to be full of water, water leaking out through my rusted seams.

Willett opened the door, pulled me out of the truck. I almost buckled when my feet hit the ground. Short, boneless Willett put everything he could into holding me up, but I still went to my knees, ready for the Kellys and the law to have me, ready to fail completely, ready for the buffalo to come back from the dead and stampede down Long Ridge, vengeance in their humongous hearts for waste and nearsightedness and the sheer mean stupidity of me and everyone else who ever claimed to be human.

I let go, ready to fall on my face in the soft ground where my grandfather's truck sat and let those snorting, angry, beautiful beasts grind me to meat, but Willett held the half of me still upright out of the mud, and I heard the sound of buffalo hooves as they went past us, and I looked into Willett's plastic baby pool eyes, his hands clamped to my shoulders, and I could tell he was trying to think of a song to sing to me, something funny and perfect and unexpected, and I felt the muscles in my belly turn back on, and I put a finger to Willett's lips, and I thought the song would be that one goes real slow: "You. Are. So. beautiful . . . to meeeeeeee." And I tried to mark in my mind so I could ask him later if that was the song, but at the time all I did was take my finger from his lips and kiss him. Gave him a kiss to keep.

# 14

## GOVERNOR

SO. ME and Willett kissed. It wasn't bad, but it was too cold in the mud outside Houston's to do it again, and I wasn't sure where to go with him. Mamaw's would have been OK, but Momma was there. Houston's would have been fine. Houston would have left us alone if we wanted, or he would have kept us distracted if we wanted. We could have gone there.

The truth of the matter was even though I liked the kiss and I pretty much wanted Willett around, what I really wanted was getting close in baby steps. So I told Willett that in a way I hoped wouldn't sound mean. I said, "Baby steps," and put my head on his shoulder and let him hold me tight, and I wasn't sure if he'd got what I said because he patted me on the back with both hands like I was a bongo drum, but more sweet and nice than that. Finally I said to him, with my head still on his shoulder, "Why don't you go on back to Cora's?"

He said, "Are you coming?"

I told him not right off. I told him I needed to stay and think a little bit.

"Out here?" he said.

"Yes," I said.

"Do you want me to build you a fire?" he said.

"How many fires have you ever built?" I said.

"Three," he said. "No. Two."

And Willett went. I got back in the truck. It was still early, not even lunchtime, and my mind was as jammed up with stuff as was Houston's truck. There didn't seem no way to sort it all out. What seemed most important? Was it Blue Bear Mountain and saving the land, protecting the earth forever and ever so that little babies not even thought up would have mountains to look on and scamper around in? Was it saving my own skin, somehow getting past what happened to Keith Kelly, getting shed of Hubert and crazy outlaw ways? Was it finding a way to patch it up with my mother, to stop our relationship from falling apart faster than a secondhand trailer? Was it finding a way to make my proud grandma Cora proud of me? And maybe I should think about high school and, like, graduating from it like so many young people way dumber than me did. And now also I had to think about love and figuring out what it would mean to care for somebody I didn't have to—somebody I wasn't obliged by blood or history to stick to.

Why did I have to think so much? Why couldn't I just be an animal? Why couldn't I just enjoy the kiss—the whole wonderful nerve endings all afire dirty book joy of it? Why couldn't I just enjoy fixing that dickhead Keith Kelly's wagon once and for all? Why couldn't I be like Mamaw and the organizer girls, glad to be in a fight for something good, throw my fists in the air and go YEAH! whenever we won the least little thing off the coal companies? Why couldn't I just party like June's friends—go WOOO! and dance around like a Roman with kudzu in my hair?

I took a pull off Houston's jar. How in the world was I going to make eighty years old? I took another pull off the jar and wondered what the governor's office looks like. How much difference could somebody like that make? Is somebody like that really high up? I got to thinking about law and order. Is there really such a thing? Order. Was there an order to my life? Was there an order to life in Canard County?

My head spun. You hear people say that—"my head was spinning"—but I felt like mine really was. Spinning like the earth. You have to decide, I said to myself. There really was deciding—people decided this and things were different than if they had decided that. I thought of Agnes Therapin. I thought of the explosions that knocked her mother out of bed. I thought of the men who set the shots that knocked her out of bed. I thought of their dinner buckets, and I thought of my daddy's dinner bucket and the oatmeal creme pies that come out of it—all those oatmeal creme pies I ate by the time I was eight years old that come from my daddy's hand, come from a coal miner's dinner bucket, the world spinning, me bouncing up and down on a trampoline.

I got out of the truck and walked down to Mamaw's and told her to tell Agnes I'd meet her at the Kolonel Krispy in the morning and we'd go to Frankfort. Then I sat down on Mamaw's couch beside of Willett Bilson and ate out of a giant bowl of cheese doodles and stared at where Mamaw should have had a TV set, and Willett told me the story of some dumb movie he'd seen where a man gets saved from the gallows by a woman who needs him to dig in her pipe dream gold mine. I told Willett I was sorry I'd been bad to him that night at June's.

I said, "I didn't have no call to blow you off that way when I decided I was going home."

"It's all right," Willett said, "Getting through bad feelings with a new friend is very important. I'm glad to have had the experience."

Willett wasn't looking at me when he said this. He was picking something off of his tennis shoe, scraping something poop-looking with his thumbnail. When I didn't say anything, he finally did look up. He smiled. He was a boy in a bubble. I felt like he might need slapping silly. I thought I should tell him to grow up and go wash his hands. But I didn't. Instead I said, "That's right," and he pushed the corners of his mouth down and pooched his bottom lip out like he wasn't used to anybody agreeing with him, and he shoved a handful of cheese doodles in his mouth and looked away from me, looked straight ahead to where the television should have been and said with his mouth full, "Well, all right then."

When he finished chewing and swallowed, he said, "Where are you staying tonight? Cora gave me your room. She thought you were staying with Houston. Maybe since you're here she'll just say it's OK for you to stay in there with me. Or maybe she'll just turn her head and not pay attention to what the sleeping arrangement turns out to be."

Willett rolled one cheese doodle between his thumb and pointer. I stood up. "I reckon I'll just stay with Houston," I said.

Willett looked up and his mouth fell open. Then his mouth closed and he said,

And I kissed him on his sticky forehead and left my mamaw Cora's house.

WHEN I stepped out Mamaw's kitchen door, Hubert stood silhouetted by Mamaw's booger light at the rail that held up the patio's corrugated roof, staring out into the frost like he was cut out of plywood. I went and stood beside him.

"Where you going?" he said.

"Houston's," I said.

"You going to see the governor?"

"I reckon," I said.

Hubert nodded. "You remember Sidney Coates?"

"He was behind the dope in the man that killed Daddy," I said. "And he fucked up Colbert."

"Him and Blondie," Hubert said, "is in cahoots. They're going to get our liquor operation busted. Case done made."

"What evidence?" I said. Hubert never sold to nobody he didn't know.

"Somebody's always got a weakness. And Sidney knows how to pick them off."

I asked Hubert were they going to get me.

Hubert said, "Maybe."

"How come," I said, "aint no more been said about Keith?"

"They're waiting on his labs."

"Where's your truck?" I said.

"Felt like walking," he said.

My breath out in front of me made me feel like I was smoking with Hubert.

He said, "I'm sorry I got you into all this, Dawn."

"Don't matter," I said. I started walking toward Houston's.

Hubert stepped off into the darkness with me. "Did you see your mother in there?"

I told him I didn't.

"I seen you sitting in there with that boy," he said. It was weird having Hubert start all the talk. He usually just responded to other people unless he was telling somebody what to do. "He seems pretty soft," Hubert said.

"So?" I said.

"We get past this," Hubert said, "you should go live with June. Get out."

"You think so, too, hunh?" I said.

"Some things is obvious," Hubert said.

We walked with our hands in our pockets down the little piece of road before you cut uphill to Houston's.

"We used to play that governor's high school in football," Hubert said.

I said, "That right?"

Hubert said, "I played against his little brother. He was dirty. Get you in a pile and put his thumb right in your eye." Hubert stopped walking. "But I got even—kneed him in the nuts so hard he squeaked like a rusty hinge."

I asked Hubert who won the game.

"They did," Hubert said. "Their field, their refs."

I asked did Daddy play.

"No," Hubert said. "He was just a freshman. Didn't even make the trip." We were in the dark place right before the light pole in front of Houston's house lit up the grassed-over driveway. I stumbled in a washed-out rocky place. Hubert caught me up by the elbow and hung on even after I had my balance. Hubert said, "Your daddy would be proud of what you're doing tomorrow."

I looked at Hubert's tangled hair drooping close to his red-rimmed eyes, and all I could see was all the things I'd done that would have shamed my daddy.

"I'll see you, Hubert," I said.

The barking of Houston's dogs covered whatever Hubert said, and it was just as well. The light over Houston's door came on, Hubert slipped back into the night shadows, and I went in the house and went to bed.

～～～～～～～～～～

COME FIVE o'clock the next morning, Mamaw gave me a ride down to Kolonel Krispy to meet Agnes Therapin. Agnes sat sipping coffee from a Thermos cup with her husband in the front seat of a Chevrolet station wagon.

"Felix said he'd drive us," Agnes said.

Mamaw leaned over in the Escort's driver's seat so she could see Felix. "Much obliged, Felix," Mamaw said.

"No trouble," Felix said.

"You want some gas money?" Mamaw said.

"We'll be fine," Agnes said.

Mamaw slipped four twenties into my hand as I got out of the Escort. "Try to get them to let you pay for things," she said low with the back of her head to the Therapins. I nodded and got out of the car.

"You want the front seat?" Agnes asked, but made no move to get out of it. I shook my head and slipped in the back.

The ride to Frankfort was quiet. Agnes fidgeted around like she wanted to talk. She asked me questions, but they were all yes-and-no questions—Are you ready for this? Did you sleep good? Do you want something to eat? I guess I must have been nervous too, because I didn't say nothing in answer to her questions but yes and no.

When we got there, Felix parked in a parking garage and told us he'd wait right there until we got back. Felix told Agnes to remember the letter and the number and the color painted on the big concrete pillar where he was parked.

"You're going to have to help me remember, Dawn," Agnes said when we got away from Felix. "By the time we get out of this meeting, I'll be lucky to even be able to tell what building we're in."

"I will, Agnes."

～～～～～～～～～～

THE GOVERNOR had a woman all smiles and smooth brown hair to take us in his office with its dark blue carpet and shelves full of pictures of people handing stuff to each other. Lawyers covered the dark red leather sofas, ties all stiff and bright with tiny dots and patterns on them. Our lawyer had messed-up hair and old scuffed-up shoes, but he grinned like a boy in a stolen car.

The meeting was a blur of big talk. Our lawyer said, "We will need assurances," and the company's lawyers talked about their unrecoverable losses. "Yes, yes," said the governor, and our lawyer said, "The protections, at least thirty-three hundred feet in elevation, three thousand would be safer . . . future considerations, etc., etc." The governor cleared his throat. "Unique situation, yes, yes." Agnes's eyes went back and forth between the lawyers, and I kept mine on the governor. What makes one person end up this and another end up that? The governor was from a coal-mining county. He went to a high school Hubert said they'd played football against. Same people, rolling in the same mud,

The lawyers went on talking and arguing. You could tell the company lawyers did not want the petition process to play out. If we got our land declared unsuitable for mining, then others might get ideas. And even if we didn't win, the companies didn't want to have to deal with a bunch of these petitions. They needed to make us out a special case, give us something, and get it over with. One of the company's lawyers, he was definitely from Lexington. He had white hair, all swept together in a wad. He was tan as a saddle and talked through his nose and said goddam this and goddam that and stepped out to take a call to work out his UK basketball tickets, right there during a meeting with the governor. You could tell he was getting paid a lot just to be there, win or lose. The rest of us—even the governor—were like Happy Meal toys to that lawyer. He could push us around, feed us to his dog, throw us out the bus window, trade us to his lower arena basketball season ticket friends, and it didn't make no difference.

"When I was a boy," the governor said, and started telling a story. While the governor spoke, dark splotches formed between me and him. The splotches started out far apart and then grew together, spreading like water stains in the ceiling beneath a leaky roof, but not rusty colored—they were darker, like black ink, and the splotches formed themselves into trees, and the trees grew together and then separated themselves so that a road could pass through them. And it was night along the road through the trees, and the headlights from a truck lit the road and lit the trees at the side of the road, and it was summertime and the trees were lush and full like drunk girls from Canard County driving home from the Hazard honky-tonks, and the truck is a twenty-four-foot rental, and my father is driving and I am sitting in the passenger seat and it was not a vision but a memory, and we were headed to North Carolina, the darkness opening in front of us and closing behind us. I am small and have no sense that we are on a line, that life is a line, no sense of that at all, my only sense that of the opening and closing darkness, and I am scared we will never find our way back, scared that North Carolina lies through a hole in the darkness that once closed we will never find again.

I tell my father I am scared. He pulls over as we pass out of the trees and are at a wide place, a river bottom, and there is a gas station, and it is fluorescent and huge but there is still an edge to the light, and my father turns on the light in the cab of the truck and takes the paper map out of the hole in the door and shows me where we are going. He makes a map of the states with our hands—he is Kentucky and Tennessee and I am Virginia and North Carolina—and makes everything fit together. He makes a picture of things and I am OK, because I was a little kid with a map of her own and Daddy said, "Are you all right to go now?" I said I was, and he pulled onto the four-lane and got the truck going fast. After we talked, I was happy to move to North Carolina, down by Daddy's old-timey mother with a garden as big as a football field and a toothy laugh with a gap in the sides.

He got going almost seventy, and I said, "Faster," and he said, "I can't go any faster." I asked why not and he said, "Because the truck won't let me. The truck has a governor on it," and I said, "What's a governor?" and he said, "It's something they put on these rental trucks to limit how fast you can go, something to remind you it's their truck and not yours." And I remember not liking that my father and I were not alone in the wee-hour truck, that this governor was there with us, and I stared into my own face out the truck window, into the forest streaking past as we wound our way out of Tennessee into North Carolina. As the curves got sharper, we didn't need a governor because we were back in the mountains.

We never moved to North Carolina. Momma stalled and Daddy died and then I was at Daddy's funeral, my mother crying, Hubert and them clustered up, glad-handing Sidney Coates, the man that sold the drugs that doped up the man that killed Daddy, me sitting there in the funeral parlor looking at my hands, knowing in my heart they would never be a map again.

I blinked and the dark splotches were gone and I was back in the governor's office. The governor kept talking until a knock came on the door. A state police officer came to the door, same exact uniform, haircut, hat as the troopers who talked to me the night Keith died.

Our lawyer was still smiling. "Governor, if you don't mind," our lawyer said, "we are asking that the land within the permit boundary be declared unsuitable for mining and that it be protected from the surface effects of underground mining, but to suggest that this petition would end all mining on Blue Bear Mountain is alarmist and I fear disingenuous on the part of my colleagues here. Engineering surveys suggest that mining can continue below the elevations designated by the permit boundary."

The Lexington lawyer said, "Boys, let me tell you something. We're going to settle this, but son," and he looked then at our lawyer, "you can't ask these gentlemen to give away the farm."

The governor said, "Let's take a break. We're getting nowhere."

Out in the front room, the governor's woman had set up a table with bags of chips and pop, brownies and cookies.

"It is so nice to see young people involved in the process," the governor's woman said. "You are lucky." Her face was like a breath mint with makeup on.

I rolled my eyes. "The world is old," I said. "It's about to die."

"You have your whole life ahead of you," the governor's woman said.

"That's supposed to cheer me up," I said.

The governor's woman kept setting out pops.

"Things is used up," I said. "Come up and look at Blue Bear Mountain and I'll show you. There aint nothing for me. The world is old and it's made me old."

The governor's woman just kept filling cups with ice. I turned around, turned smack into the governor. I was looking him eye to eye. It made me sad the governor was no taller than I was. I let him look at me. "We won't be much longer," he said to his woman over my shoulder.

"Yes, Governor," she said, and poured him a cup of diet.

The governor looked at me. "Are there a lot like you back in Canard County?"

"I guess," I said.

I don't know why I said that. Yeah, I do. I really did want to know what he cared.

"I don't see too many like you," the governor said, "not in here, anyway."

"Well," I said.

"You know," the governor said, "people been writing in from all over the country about Blue Bear Mountain."

Wadn't nothing to say to that.

"It's a big deal to them that it's the highest mountain in the state. Makes it special to them."

I looked over at Agnes. You could tell she was just listening to see how the story was going to end.

"We're going to protect that mountain." The governor leaned in and took my sweatshirt between his thumb and forefinger. "You reckon you could be up here Christmas Day beside me when I announce it?"

"I reckon," I said.

I looked over at the governor's woman, the one had been handing out the pops. Her eyes were big as fried eggs.

"You reckon," the governor said, "if I had you up there with me you could wear something didn't look quite so rebellious?"

"Like what?" I said.

"Well," the governor said, "I don't know. I suppose Madeline could help you figure something out. Maddy," the governor turned to the pop woman, "you could help her, couldn't you?"

That woman brought her fried-egg eyes back down to normal size quick. She put on a fake smile and said, "Yes, of course we can, Governor." Then she turned her smile on me like she was the sun and I was a tulip bulb in God's own flower box.

When we went back to the meeting, the governor acted like he had somewhere else to be. He said a dollar figure the state would pay for the mining rights on Blue Bear and that the state would then make a nature preserve of the land. No mining, no timbering. He told his man this needed to be done. He said people needed to see that the state had a past, a present, and a future, and nobody was going to say he didn't care about all three.

"Yes, Governor," the governor's man said.

"Yall can live with that, can't you?" the governor said.

And after a little back and forth they all did agree. And the briefcases snapped shut, and there was some handshaking, and when we got out in the hall, Agnes asked our lawyer if it was all right, and he said, "It's the best we can do. Better than I thought we could do." And then we were headed home, all before lunchtime.

~~~~~~~~~~~~

WE STOPPED at a convenience store in Lexington on the way home from the governor's office so that Felix could get gas for the Chevrolet. I called Willett from a pay phone against the brick wall of the store. I figured he would be back at his mother's, and he was.

"Hell-looo," Willett's mother said when she answered the phone. "Bill-sun res-i-dents." It was like a bird call she was doing.

"Is Willett there?" I said.

"Yes, he is," she said, "whom may I say is calling?"

"Dawn, I guess." I had never been called "whom" before.

The wind blew cold through the phone line. "Oh," Willett's mother said, her voice an abandoned bird's nest of sticks and fuzz and bird spit. "I'll see if he can come to the phone."

People rolled through the slush in the parking lot. I should have got the governor to call Willett for me.

"Merrrr-y Christmas!" Willett said when he came on the phone.

"Hey," I said.

Willett asked how it went, and I told him the governor wanted me with him when he announced the protection of Blue Bear.

"I knew he would," Willett said. "Those dudes always want hot women with them when they're doing their serious statesman shit."

I let that one hang in the air. No one cared what we'd done in the parking lot of this one of a million convenience store. A guy walked in telling his friend how excited he was about his new puppy. He'd never had a dog before.

"Um," I said, "when am I going to see you again?"

"Do you want to come down here for Christmas?" Willett said. A truck went by, but I swear I could hear Willett's mother in the background going NO!

"I don't know if I can," I said. "I might get arrested."

"For real?" Willett said. I hadn't told Willett about my brilliant career as a bootlegger. "Geez," he said. "There's no way they can say you wrecked that guy on purpose, right? No way. Besides," Willett said, "you're just a kid."

"Hey, Willett," I said. "I need to ask you something." What I needed to ask him was could he maybe be there when I got home. Crazy to ask. I didn't hardly know Willett. He couldn't drive worth a flip. It was almost Christmas Eve. He wasn't from a family like mine. He was from a family where things went regular, where people could afford to have things happen when they were supposed to happen.

"What is it, my little pudding pop?" Willett said.

The line went quiet.

"Nothing," I said.

Willett said, "Are you sure?"

I said yes, and Willett said he had to go. And I said bye, and he said, "Call me when you get home."

Christmas. Why did all this have to happen at Christmas? It's a stupid question because, like I said, my life don't follow no normal schedule. Nobody works a normal job. My brother Albert, for example, never even knows what day it is. I'm not sure he could even name all the days of the week.

Agnes stood off the curb down in the slush. She wrung her hands, and I knew her feet were getting wet. She said, "Are you ready to go, honey?"

Felix had the car running, staring straight ahead, bent over the steering wheel. The gas station was a big bustle, like Christmas on TV. I had a feeling soon as I was in the Therapins' vehicle things were going to get worse.

"Honey?" Agnes said. "Are you OK?" Agnes knew about Keith and the moonshine rumors, and all the rest. She looked sweet standing there, like a shepherd at the manger.

She smiled, smiled for Christmas, smiled for knowing she wouldn't have to move to her daughter's in South Carolina after all. "Merry Christmas to you," Agnes said, "and a happy new year."

A big yellow truck toting some kind of pop I'd never heard of pulled up at the store. It looked like it might box Felix in to where he couldn't get out. Felix tooted the horn, and Agnes and I got in, and we drove on through the tired winter light of the countryside outside the city, which gave way to the dark and the endless strings of Christmas lights lighting our way home, lighting up trailers and ranch houses and farm houses, a million tiny beacons of steady

living alongside the runaway river of light that was the nighttime southbound
interstate traffic.

~~~~~~~~~~~~~~~

WHEN I got back to Long Ridge, Mamaw was in the kitchen trying to get an
empty jelly jar off the top shelf of the cabinets. She was on her toes, and her
fingers spread out blue-gray-pink and knobby on her walker. She cussed, and I
stepped to her, put one hand on the jelly jar and the other on her shoulder.

"Is it done?" she said. Her eyes were like frog eggs. "Is it done?"

"I reckon," I said, and told her what I could about the details of the deal.

Mamaw nodded and closed her hand on the jelly jar. "They know we're
here, don't they?"

"Yes, ma'am," I said.

Mamaw raised her eyebrow. She ran water in the jelly jar, poured it out.
"Well," she said, "it's not about us anyway." She held the jar to the light. "Is it?"

"I guess not."

She took a carton of vanilla ice cream out of the icebox. She spooned
slow and trembly the ice cream into the jar, packed it in with the back of
the spoon. "What did you think of the governor?" she said, her back to me,
putting her ice cream back.

"Think I don't want to be him."

Mamaw laughed and took a two-liter of store-brand root beer out of the
bottom part of the refrigerator. "That's good," she said. She looked into my
face. "You'd be a good one, though," she said. "Get my vote." She poured the
root beer over the ice cream, stuck an ice tea spoon through the foam and
the pop and the vanilla ice cream, and handed it to me. "Here," she said.

"Let's go out on the porch," she said, "see if we can conjure up spring."

It was too cold for a root beer float on the porch. The wind sliced us, first from one direction and then the other. Someone was cutting up wood in the trees below us. Their saw rang like a crying baby. The smell of mold come up from the plastic cushions when we set down on Mamaw's glider. I set the jar down on the dirty table.

When spring came, Mamaw would move the chairs and the tables off the porch into the front yard. She would spray them with the hose, her dry thumb over the hose end. She would knock the spiderwebs from the porch corners. She would rub oil soap into the wood, and when everything was back in place, light little candles, and maybe we would eat ham sandwiches with lots of pickles on the porch, and maybe a breeze would blow, not quite warm, through the buds and blossoms, the smell of cut grass in the air. Maybe it would be like that. It had been before. But I had trouble conjuring any of that the day I got home from Frankfort. Too cold.

"Well," Mamaw said, "your mother's got religion."

"When?"

"I don't know," she said. "Sometime since that boy died."

I spooned the ice cream into my mouth. The root beer tasted right, made me want to run through the spring woods naked. The leaves on the trees would be yellow-green, and things that would be spiky and sharp later in the summer would still be tender and soft. I wanted to run through sassafras and fall on my face next to a nest of little brown jug, my face buried in the smell of things root beer wished it was, the roots maybe root beer was named after.

"She's all cleaned up," Mamaw said, "her face all plain, hair pulled back."

"Is she going out at the end of the road?"

"No," Mamaw said. "I reckon she's going where Blondie Kelly goes. Up Drop Creek."

I wanted to see my mother sitting up in church. I wanted to see her hand raised, the pale inside of her arm raised towards Jesus, her plain T-shirt falling down her arm. I wanted to see her head thrown back. I wanted to see her eyes barely closed, her lips moving, touched by the Holy Spirit, but I didn't dare go to Blondie Kelly's church. Bad enough Blondie had come to Long Ridge with her brothers to whip me. Untelling what she would do if she had the whole Little Drop Creek Church backing her up.

"Home again, home again, jiggedy-jig," Mamaw said.

I sipped out of my ice cream jar. "Yep," I said.

~~~~~~~~~~~

I STAYED at Mamaw's that night and woke up happy, remembering how the governor said I was the face of Kentucky's future. I went in the bathroom and looked at myself in the mirror. I ran my finger over a pimple, but didn't squeeze it. When I went in the kitchen, Mamaw was on the phone with Momma.

"I don't care what they say," Mamaw said into the phone. "People will say anything. No, I'm not saying she's lying. Yes, I know you go to the church with her." Mamaw drummed her fingers on the counter. "Well, I don't care. She can say whatever she damn well pleases. It's still a free country, Tricia. Yeah. Well. God bless you too."

Mamaw hung up. "God Almighty," she said.

"What?" I said.

"Nothing," Mamaw said. "Nothing but a bunch of idle bullshit."

I said, "She was talking about me, wasn't she? You heard something about Hubert and me."

"Somebody's always talking," Mamaw said.

"Well," I said, "what are they saying?"

"Dawn," Mamaw said, "don't you need to be thinking about what you're going to say up there with the governor?"

"I aint going to be saying anything," I said.

"You don't never know," Mamaw said. "You need to be ready."

I said, "Are they saying I'm going to jail?"

"You aint going to jail," Mamaw said.

"Is Hubert?" I said.

Mamaw said, "I aint studying Hubert."

I said, "He is, aint he?"

"Well," Mamaw said, "don't you think he ought to?" She was staring bullets at me. "Don't you think he belongs in jail?"

My eyes filled up with tears. I was thinking about what he said about Daddy being proud of me. "I don't know, Mamaw."

"Well, I tell you one thing," Mamaw said. "You aint working at that store of his no more. I hear you're over there, I'll come down off this mountain and flail you myself. You'll wish you was in jail when I get ahold of you."

Mamaw didn't talk like that to me. She thought threatening violence was beneath her. I'd seen Mamaw shoot a deer in her garden, seen her cut the throat of a living groundhog hung in a trap. Mamaw didn't threaten violence. She committed it, when she felt like it needed committing. So I knew it was likely fixing to go bad for me if she was talking like that. The phone rang again. It was the woman in the governor's office. She told me she was real sorry, but they had found someone else to be the face of Kentucky's future.

"Why?" Mamaw said when I told her. But we both knew why. Somebody'd told them about me and Hubert.

"I got to go, Mamaw," I said.

"Where you going?" she said. "Sit down right there."

"I'm going to see Papaw," I said.

She looked at me. "You go straight up there," she said after a minute. "Don't go nowhere else."

"I won't," I said.

"Here," she said, and she gave me two oranges. "Give these to Houston."

"Yes, ma'am," I said.

I went outside, stuck the oranges in my sweatshirt pocket. I wasn't going to Houston's. Houston never knew what was going on. I was going to Hubert's and find out what was happening. Christmas Eve at Hubert's, I thought as I started walking between his house and Cora's. Least it would seem like Christmas at Hubert's—fucked-up outlaw hillbilly Christmas, but Christmas all the same. Them women that hung out at Hubert's, they loved wrapping presents. They wrapped them, and then they took them down to the old house, the house where Hubert's daddy Green had lived with all his different wives. It was about the only time anybody stayed at Green's house, was Christmas Eve, and then they'd have their Christmas in the morning.

I wondered where Momma would be. Church, no doubt. I thought about the Christmas presents she would've got for Keith Kelly—the leather jacket and the gorilla perfume or whatever it was.

The trees on either side of the road shrugged at me. I dreaded I might never see them again or might not anyway for a long time. I knew I wasn't likely to go to real jail. But they might send me away somewhere. And now that Momma had gone to Jesus, she wouldn't fight it. She'd want me to suffer. Momma told me later she'd told Mamaw on the phone that morning I should come to church. She said it would be good for me and it would look good to the judge. I walked up the steps to Hubert's. When I crossed the porch, it tripped a laughing Santa with greenlight eyes. It said Ho, ho's in pairs—"HOHO. HOHO. HOHO"—in a demonic way. "SATAN CLAUS," said a sign under it. No matter what holiday, they always found a way to put some Halloween twist on it at Hubert's. The storm door creaked as I went in the house.

# 15

## MAGIC YELLOW POP CAN

HUBERT'S HOUSE smelled of deer meat, tomatoes, onions, and celery cooking in a crockpot. As I came in, Hubert walked into the kitchen wearing three flannel shirts and work pants cut off at the knees, and he waved me to a stool at the counter with his wooden spoon. "Ho, ho," he said, and grumbled into his chili. I sat down and he said, "Did you save the world?"

I said I did and asked him had he heard what was going to happen to us.

"Not yet," Hubert said.

A girl curled up on the couch said, "They gonna bust you Christmas Day, Hubert. That's some Grinchy-ass shit right there."

"Don't make no difference to them," Hubert said. "Everybody loves to fuck Hubert Jewell." Hubert popped a beer and dumped it into the pot. He let the can fall to the floor and popped another, reached it to me. "Merry Christmas," he said. I counted nine beer cans on the kitchen floor.

"Where's Momma?" I said.

Hubert said, "With her new friends."

The girl on the couch raised her beer can and said, "To the eternal salvation of Tricia Jewell" and drained the can, her throat loosening and tightening like the mouse-swallowing snake me and Willett saw in Kingsport. I started down the hall to the back of the house.

"Where you going?" Hubert said.

"Use the phone," I said.

~~~~~~~~~~

"HEY," I said to Willett.

290

"Where are you calling from?" Willett said.

"Hubert's."

"So you're OK?" Willett said.

"Yeah," I said, "pretty much."

"Maybe I should come up there," Willett said.

One time at the lake when I didn't hardly know how to swim, Albert held my head under the water. I figured out the only way to not drown—or worse, be at Albert's mercy—was to relax and slip him. Albert fed off your panic, and when I didn't panic, his super power disappeared.

"I'll be OK," I said to Willett on the phone. Then I said, "Appreciate you offering."

"No problem," Willett said. "Talk to you tomorrow?"

"Christmas," I said.

"Yep," Willett said, and I hung up the phone. Soon as I did, I wished I'd said goodbye.

~~~~~~~~~~~~~

HUBERT WAS gone when I got back in the kitchen. I dropped my beer can on the floor and opened another. There was a brown bag full of spotty yellow apples on the counter. The radio next to the bag played "Takin' Care of Business." It is such a Momma song. I decided to fix a pie. I knew there would be stuff to fix pie at Hubert's because until Jesus got her, Momma loved to get high and bake stuff. That had been her thing before Daddy died—making cakes and pies for money. I took a pack of frozen crusts out of the freezer.

I decided to make fried pies when the girl on the couch volunteered to help me. I laid out all three crusts in the pack, showed her how to cut them in turnover-size pieces, and turned to make the filling. Something came on television she just had to watch—some hip-hop dance thing—"So dope, so gangsta," she said—and I was by myself in the kitchen again.

So I decided to make three apple pies. "Sweet Emotion" by Aerosmith came on the little radio. Momma's favorite song. "Turn that down," the girl on the couch said, but I didn't. I cracked another beer and wiped off a knife and started cutting up apples. "Peel them motherfuckers," I heard my pre-Jesus mother say, but I cut them up with the peel on them, piled them on the counter. I cracked another beer.

Hubert came back in the kitchen. "Tricia Junior," he said. He set a big plastic bottle of vodka with a red-and-silver label down on the counter. Hubert put his hand to my face and said, "Aint so bad." I have no idea what or who he was talking about. I put my apples in a bowl with butter and cinnamon. "Right now," Hubert said. He was real drunk. I was on the edge of being drunk too. Something from Pink Floyd's *The Wall* came on.

"'Run Like Hell,'" Hubert said.

"What?" I said.

"That's the name of that song," Hubert said. "That song sold me a lot of dope when I was in high school. Everybody loved to get high to that song. No dark sarcasm in the high school. Hey, teacher, leave that kid alone."

I took the oranges out of my sweatshirt and held them out to Hubert.

He took the oranges from my hands, cut them into eight pieces with his hawkbill. He gave me three. "Squeeze them in your pies," he said. He squeezed one of the pieces in his vodka cup, air guitared to the Pink Floyd song. I looked in the cabinet for sugar.

"What are you looking for?" Hubert said.

When I told him, he ran out of the room, came back with a fifty-pound sack, flipped it out on the floor. We laughed. Hubert gouged the bag open with his knife, and I scooped out what I needed with a green plastic coffee cup

the color of a lunchroom tray. The fifty-pound sack of sugar sat on the floor
like an old man sent to keep me and Hubert company.

"Get out of here," Hubert said to the girl on the couch when she turned
up the television.

"Shut up, Hubert," she said, "you Scroogy motherfucker."

Hubert got in the gap between the refrigerator and the cabinet and
took the flyswat off its hook and took it to that girl, first to her legs and
then when she wouldn't get up, he swatted her arms and neck. She jumped
up and said, "Get that nasty thing away from me," and when Hubert kept on
flailing her towards the door, she raised her hands up around her head and
said, "What kind of man use a flyswat anyway?" Hubert caught her a good
one right on the back of the neck, but she didn't stop: "Flyswat a woman's
weapon," and about the time she said that, Hubert caught her flush across
the mouth, and she didn't say another word til she was on the other side
of the storm door, where she said, "Merry Christmas, asshole" as Hubert
slammed the door in her face.

"Shit," Hubert said, and turned off the television.

"That wasn't too Christmas spirit-y," I said.

"Her kids be glad to see her," Hubert said. He sat down on the sofa,
twirled the remote like it was a six-shooter. He eyed the vodka bottle on
the counter next to me. "You wouldn't bring that over here, would you?"
Hubert said.

I brought him the bottle and his cup, but Hubert drank straight from the
bottle. I went back to my pies.

"I don't think there will be no more trouble tonight," Hubert said. "No
more trouble," and then he closed his eyes. I put the filling in the pans, then
fitted the crust tops on, pinched them down, cut slits in the top.

"O come, all ye faithful," I sang to myself, and Hubert joined in without
opening his eyes: "Joyful and triumphant, O come ye, O come ye to
Bethlehem," just like he was Perry Como in his white turtleneck and V-neck
sweater on one of those worn-edged albums behind the couch in Cora's
living room. I took the vodka bottle out of Hubert's lap. He stopped singing,
but his lips kept moving. I turned the bottle up. It was too light in my hands,
and I got a whole mouthful of vodka when I just wanted a sip. When I

swallowed, it hit me hard, blew my head up. Hubert grabbed me by the wrist and pulled me into his lap.

"Ho, ho," he said without opening his eyes. "He'll be gone in a minute."

"Who?" I said.

"Santy Claus," Hubert said and fell silent. He wrapped me up in his arms like I was a liquor bottle, like I was a carnival-won stuffed animal. "Ho, ho," he said again.

I tried to pull his locked hands apart, tried to slip out from under him, but he wasn't passed out enough for me to get away. I figured he would be soon enough, and so relaxed in Hubert's arms, put my head on his shoulder. I don't know how long I sat there like that, but when I come to, Hubert's beard was scratching against my forehead and Daddy was sitting in Hubert's TV chair.

"Daddy," I said. I put my hands out towards him.

"What are you doing?" Daddy said like he was mad at me.

"What am I supposed to do?" I said. I stood up. Hubert was passed out. His mirror sunglasses were in my hand. I guess they were his. Maybe they were that girl's. I don't know. I put them on.

"What are you going to be?" Daddy said.

"What am I supposed to be?" I said. "You never got to be, so how do I know what I'm supposed to be?"

Daddy raised his pale finger to me.

"And cause you never got to be," I said, "Momma never got to be what she was supposed to be." I moved past him into the kitchen. I closed my hand on the cinnamon bottle. I looked around for my pies, but they were gone.

"I know what I am, Dawn," Daddy said with his back to me. Daddy turned to the kitchen and pointed to me again. "Let me see your eyes."

I told him no.

Daddy said, "Let me see your eyes, or I'm going."

"Who am I supposed to be?" I said. The veins in my head thrashed like a dropped garden hose. I was sure if I raised my glasses, them veins would burst, everything would go orange. I'd throw up orange. Daddy would be lost again in a flood of orange. "You told me to try to understand Hubert," I said to Daddy. "You told me to try to make it work."

Daddy was eating a piece of my pie. He pressed the back of his fork into the top of the pie. "I didn't tell you to love him," Daddy said. He turned the pie plate over and dumped his pie on the floor. He dropped the plate. "I didn't tell you to get drunk with him, destroy yourself, become your mother."

"Dad," I said.

Daddy stood up, thinned out. "You and Hubert are going to jail," he said.

I raised my glasses, but Dad was gone. Dead and gone. My head gapped open, and I could feel my brain sizzle under the fluorescent light. I fell to the linoleum and rolled to my back. I pressed my hands to my forehead. The cinnamon bottle was still in my hand, and the plastic disk with the holes in it popped off. Cinnamon covered my face, filled my mouth and nose. The side of my head was hot. I coughed cinnamon smoke, snorted like a candy dragon. I closed my eyes and felt myself tumbling head first backwards, my feet above my head, and then I flipped onto my belly.

My mother shook me awake. I was face down on the kitchen floor, and the cinnamon smoke filled the room. My mother coughed. I coughed. We couldn't stop. "What are you doing?" Momma said. She pulled open the stove, and smoke boiled out. The pies were burnt.

"Where's Daddy?" I said. "Where's Uncle Hubert?"

Momma pulled the black slabs out of the oven. "Have you lost your mind?" she said. "You could have burned down the house." Momma opened the doors and windows. Momma moved fast. She didn't act like she had broke ankles.

I said from the floor, "Where's your casts, Momma?"

"Jesus took 'em off," Momma said.

"I'm freezing," I said. The couch was empty. "Where's Hubert?" I said.

"Dawn." Momma grabbed me. "Pray with me." Momma pulled me up to my knees and started praying. She held my head in her arms, mashed me up against her boobs. It was not that comforting, and all I wanted was to be alone in my own bed at Mamaw's house, not praying, not drinking, not seeing things.

"Momma," I said, "let me go. Let me go to sleep." I said it three or four more times, and she prayed right through all my begging and pleading. Jesus. I didn't think she was ever going to finish. When she did, she held me out in front of her to where she could look me in the face.

She said, "Better?"

I nodded that it was. "Can I go back to Mamaw's?" I said, and she took me outside and put me in the Escort. I sat down on her big zip-up Bible, which when she pulled it out from under me, I grabbed the door handle, pushed the door open, and threw up all over the gravel and grass outside Hubert's trailer.

"Oh, Dawn," Momma said.

I sat up, put my head against the headrest, and said more to myself than to Momma:

I WOKE up Christmas morning saying to myself: They know about me and my car stealing. Me and my fighting at school. The governor and them—they know. They are getting a picture in their heads and in it I am dazed and frowning, my hair all fried, holding up a card with a string of numbers and CANARD COUNTY DETENTION CENTER in plastic letters over top of them.

A million things from since I was little run through my mind. Momma and her hundred dollars worth of plants, her and Hubert forehead to forehead planting them. That's when the seed dropped into the ground, the root of all evil. Lying there in the bed, the room darker than dark, I decided to end this story by killing Hubert.

I sat up and turned on the light, thinking I was at Mamaw's. But I wasn't. I was at Houston's. I got out of bed and went in the front room. It was still dark out. I looked out the front window. I seen Houston's truck, his old Cutlass. And I seen June's red Honda car.

"Hey oh," Houston said, way quieter than he usually did. He was sitting in his taped-up chair beside the heater.

"Hey Papaw," I said.

"You didn't stay down long," he said.

"Where's Momma?" I said.

"Don't know," Houston said. "Aint seen her since our big feed."

"Why'd she bring me here?" I said. "I told her I wanted to go to Mamaw's."

Houston said, "Sweetheart, your aunt June brought you here."

I knew Daddy the night before had been in my imagination, but I would have swore Momma was real. "I was with Momma," I said.

"You've had a lot on your mind, youngun," Houston said. "Go back in there and lay down, try and sleep a little more. Give them sugarplum visions one more chance."

I'd gone to Hubert's and got witched. That was the only explanation. "Yeah," I said. "I will." I opened the front door.

"Where you going, sweetheart?" Houston said.

"Clear my head, Papaw."

I was gonna clear my head all right. Clear my head by killing Hubert. I walked over to Hubert's place. Christmas Eve, he didn't stay at Green's. He stayed at his trailer, and there was always a few stayed with him. I walked in and my cousin Jan, the one cut off my hair, sat on the floor in front of the sofa where Hubert was the night before. Her fingers were red from sanding the rust off a tow chain, sanding slowly, lightly, like she had forever to get that chain sanded. I asked where Hubert was, and she acted like she didn't hear me.

She shrugged.

"You don't know where he's at?" I said.

She looked at me like she was going to burn my head to a cinder cause I was trying to make her speak. She scared me. I went down the hall past three different ones of them sitting in different rooms watching different televisions. I asked each where Hubert was, but none had anything to say. The last was Albert, slack-jawed and watching the same wrestling videos he'd been watching since before Dad died.

"So Hubert didn't tell you where he was going? Didn't ask you did you want to go?"

"No," Albert said, then "Yeah, but."

"But what?"

"Leave me alone," Albert said.

Albert held a pillow across his chest. I grabbed his leg and pulled him straight out on the floor. His behind bounced on the rug, rattled everything on the little table next to him. I backed up, braced myself for the fight, but Albert just sat there. He made a face like he knew he ought to have pain from his broken rib, but there was no fight in his eyes. I'm not going to lie to you. It shook me up. I got down in Albert's face and said, "What is the matter with you?" He wouldn't look at me, just kept his eyes on his videos. He stared into the screen and went, "Boom."

"Get up," I said. He acted like he hadn't heard me. I kicked him, and his eyes never came off the television. I stood there with my hands on my hips.

"I'm fine," Albert said. The sound didn't seem to come from his mouth. I went back down the hall looking for what they were using. There were no roaches in the ashtray, no bottles on the counter or the garbage. I went into the bathroom, all through the bedrooms. No sign. I'm fine. No sign. I'm fine. "I'm fine." The way Albert said it made me hope I never felt fine again.

I kicked Albert in the arm covering his broken rib. He barely flinched, just moved slow away from the kick like he was floating in outer space, like a balloon bouncing across the ground light as a dandelion seed.

"I'll be damned," I said, and left Hubert's house. One of my little five-year-old cousins sat shivering in his shirtsleeves on the trailer steps. "Why aint you over at Green's?" I asked him.

"Hubert went to Drop Creek," the boy said.

"Drop Creek?" I said, "Why?"

The little boy said, "He said he was going to bring me a trampoline." The boy played with a shiny silver knife, hand-forged from a railroad spike. A one-legged man from Tennessee lived out Long Ridge for a while made it for Daddy. I asked the little boy how he got it, told him it was mine and to give it to me. He wouldn't, jerked it away, and laid the palm of his hand wide open on the blade. Some stoned woman came walking over from the direction of Green's, kicked the knife off the porch, and started beating the little boy. Blood flew everywhere. The woman cussed me and shoved the boy in a vehicle.

I stood there trying to unwad what the little boy said like it was a crumpled-up paper ball, and all I could think was he was talking about our old trampoline, the one Denny and them had used to catch Momma the day she broke her first ankle. But why, I thought to myself, would Hubert have gone for that? "Why?" I said out loud. The boy broke from the woman and latched onto my leg like a metal clamp holding a hose on a spigot. He tightened down on me, and his blood got all over my pants.

I thought I would take him with me to Drop Creek, but then I remembered I was going to kill Hubert and it would be foolish and unnecessary to take a five-year-old boy with me. So I let the woman pry him off my leg. I thought about taking him to Cora's, but that would slow me down. There would be too many questions, and I would chicken out killing Hubert.

I took off Decent's sweater and wrapped the boy's hand with it. I looked a long time in his face, his eyes brown, green, and yellow, still sparkling and cold, like stones in a creek on a bright sunny day. I took the knife, went back and got Houston's Cutlass, and headed for Drop Creek.

When I got there, I drove past Denny's and parked on the four-wheeler path. I edged through the woods, skirting the hole I spent Thanksgiving night in. I came to the trees at the edge of the clear spot where the trampoline stood. Hubert was on his knees on the trampoline, his back to me. I drew up breath. My plan was to run at him with the silver dagger, an Indian warrior princess, and plunge it in between his shoulder blades.

Hubert stood up and threw a rope over a tree limb fifteen feet off the ground. The other end of the rope was tied to the hitch on his pickup. He grabbed the noose as it fell and put it over his head. He drew it tight around his neck and jumped off the trampoline. He began to dance in the air. I took off running across the clearing, and grabbed him around the legs. He kicked and slapped me in the head. I couldn't tell if he was fighting with me or against me, but I got him worked back over to the trampoline, climbed up there with him, and managed to get my knife over his head and cut the rope. We both collapsed onto our backs. We lay there on the trampoline awhile. I sat up first.

"What the hell?" I said.

Hubert sat up, looked around. He picked up the silver dagger.

I could see his face in the blade. He still had the rope around his neck. I asked him to take it off.

"You sure?" he said.

When I didn't stop staring him in the eye, he took off the noose. The snow came quiet like it always did, and the trampoline squeaked like a girl talking about prom. There was a scrap pile of brick and creek rock near the edge of the clearing. It had been a chimney. Breath wheezed through Hubert's nose and moustaches.

"Your father would set me up for trouble," he said. "Tell me to steal apples, throw a rock at a man's horse, bust a dynamite cap with a hammer."

Hubert pawed the rope. "Then he would either stop me before I did it, or get me out of whatever trouble he'd got me into." Hubert got tobacco out of his shirt pocket, put a wad in his jaw. He unpinned the note from his shirt. "Your father didn't care what people thought of him," Hubert said.

"And you do?" I said.

Hubert ran his thumb down the knife's edge.

"Say," I said.

"It don't matter," Hubert said.

The winter woods smelled of ash and wet snow. "Yeah, it does," I said.

Hubert said, "I don't think I killed Keith. I think he was already dead when I got to him."

I took the knife away from Hubert. I lay the blade against my thigh. I was cold and I missed Decent's sweater. "Will they be able to tell that?" I said.

"Probably," Hubert said.

I turned the blade over and over against my leg.

Hubert set the noose in his lap. "Green didn't understand your daddy. He thought he was soft. He kept wanting me to make him harder." Hubert let the noose drop between his legs, held the loose end where I'd cut it. "Daddy didn't want us at nobody else's mercy."

My eyes filled with tears. So did Hubert's.

"Mercy," Hubert said, and dropped the rope.

A tree branch cracked. Denny and his daddy Fred walked towards us across the clearing. When they got close, they stopped and nodded at us. Denny looked at the ground, and Fred said, "We heard they got Keith's labs back. He was all doped up when he had that wreck." Fred put his hand on the pad at the edge of the trampoline.

Hubert's face was still wet with tears when he looked up at Fred. "How do you know this?"

Fred said, "Sheriff called Houston."

The three of them told me how this meant there probably wouldn't be no charges brought against me and Hubert. At least not over Keith. Then Hubert said, "Doped up on what?"

"I forget what they called it," Fred said. "Something I hadn't heard of before."

It was the first time I ever heard the word. But I found later I had already seen it in action—at that party we went to in Virginia hunting Momma, and at Hubert's that Christmas morning.

Hubert nodded.

"You all right, Dawn?" Denny said.

I nodded. "Merry Christmas," I said.

Denny and Fred smiled. "Merry Christmas," they said. Then they stepped back and left me and Hubert alone.

"Bad medicine," Hubert said.

I took the note Hubert had pinned to himself and read it. In the note Hubert took responsibility for the death of Keith Kelly and everything else anybody might have against me and Momma and Albert.

"I failed your daddy," Hubert said. "And I tried to make it up with you and your brother."

"What about Momma?" I said.

Hubert looked away from me. "I tried to do things different with you. Act like I learned something from Delbert." Hubert shook his head.

"Why didn't you say something before?"

Hubert got down off the trampoline, gathered up the rope, walked to the edge of the highwall, and flung the rope into the pit. I stood beside him as he stared out over the bare yellow ground, at the flat black patches, the dumped barrels and pallets.

Hubert turned and walked back to his truck.

"What are you going to do now, Hubert?" I said.

"I don't know," he said. "Go somewhere."

I asked him where.

Hubert said, "North Pole, maybe. What about you?"

I shook my head.

"You should go back to Cora's," Hubert said. "Try to live normal. You don't have to be a Jewell. It won't hurt my feelings."

Hubert got in his truck and left. That was OK. Nothing else needed to pass between us. I tried to throw Daddy's railroad spike silver dagger off the highwall, send it sailing after Hubert's noose, but I couldn't let go.

I got in Houston's Cutlass and drove back to Long Ridge. There wasn't a soul at Mamaw's. Nobody at Houston's either. I found the Escort and June's Honda all piled up with the clunkers and drug-dealer cars and hiding-from-the-repo-man vehicles down at Green's log house.

I went in and they were all in front of the big-screen TV. Houston and Cora stood side by side with June and Momma. Momma leaned on June, her feet still in casts. All the Jewells—including Albert—were sprawled out on the sofas and on the floor. They watched the governor talk on television about the protections the state was putting in place on the highest elevations of Blue Bear Mountain, and how the state was buying the mineral and timber rights so the companies wouldn't be out no money. Then the governor said they done this for Kentucky's future, and he waved his hand behind him at a gang of Lexington-looking schoolkids all neat and proper, holding up a long piece of butcher paper said, "SAVE BLUE BEAR MOUNTAIN" with signatures all over it.

Then the governor looked dead in the camera and said, "A young woman from Canard County named Dawn Jewell, frustrated that we could not come to agreement, told me this week the world is used up and old, and that the way we so-called leaders acted made her feel hopeless. But I say to her and the rest of the commonwealth's young people that their future, like the top of Blue Bear Mountain, will be there for the rest of their lives."

Everybody in Green's house looked at me. Some clapped.

"Merry Christmas," the governor said, "and God bless the Commonwealth of Kentucky."

I thought about what the governor said. "That don't make no sense," I said, but people slapped me on the back, and somebody turned the TV to a hunting show, and I felt a hand on my shoulder and turned and there was Willett.

"Yay," he said, quiet and sweet.

"Yay," I said back to him, trying to sound the same. We hugged and then everybody ate until there were five huge garbage bags full of red plastic cups, Styrofoam plates, and pop bottles and canned cranberry sauce and gravy smeared everywhere.

Then somebody come running in said Hubert had gone down to the sheriff's office, gave them five copper worms and a truck full of moonshine and turned himself in. That turned Christmas into a funeral for the Jewells. Momma said, "Praise God." Mamaw and Houston and June excused themselves and asked did I want a ride back to the house. I gave Houston back his Cutlass keys and asked Willett did he mind walking. We went outside and June pulled me aside and asked was I OK, and I said I thought I was, and she asked did I hear about Aunt Ohio, and I said I hadn't, and June told me Aunt Ohio died, that she wrapped her Cadillac around a telephone pole in the fog of Christmas Eve.

Albert came up behind us smoking. "And she had some young dude in the car with her," Albert said, "without no britches on." Albert raised his eyebrows.

I looked at June. She nodded. "Her pastor," June said.

"Daggone," I said, and they all nodded and shook their heads and left me and Willett standing there alone. I took Willett by the hand and walked him up to the jumping-off spot. Willett huffed and puffed up the mountainside, his cheeks red as rubber balls. The wind rustled the tree-thick ridge, set off wind chimes, pushed a rattling car along the road somewhere below us. Me and Willett climbed through the empty winter sunshine to the top, and when we got there I pointed out Hubert's store in the valley below. I told him about me sitting on the cliff across the road from the store pouring liquor down the water pipe. I told him about jumping off the mountain all sad and liquored up, and I showed him the ledge where Aunt Ohio saved me from falling off the mountain.

It made me feel old telling him these things because it seemed so long ago, and because Willett kept going, "Gosh," after everything I told him.

I helped Willett lower himself down in a crack between two big rocks where I thought the way to Aunt Ohio's ledge might be, and Willett and I worked our way out there and sat where me and Aunt Ohio had sat. I told Willett how Aunt Ohio told me there should be magic, and he pooched out his lip and nodded his head at that. I stood up and walked out to the edge, like an Indian princess again, looking for game, looking for my lost hunter to come home, and a crow cawed like a courthouse busybody.

Willett said, "I wish we had hot chocolate," and I told him about June telling me one time about this hot chocolate she had in Italy that was rich and thick and tasted like chocolate pudding, and I wished me and Willett were in Italy, even though I'd never been nor even thought much about it.

Willett said, "Look at that," and pointed to an empty dented-in pop can next to the back wall of the overhang. It was the kind of pop in the strange yellow truck I had seen in Lexington on the way home from the governor's.

Willett said, "Man, that's a good kind of pop. That's the kind automatically fills back up if you treat the can right." I felt like maybe Willett was about to play a trick on me, but I let him. He picked the can up and rubbed his thumb across the open hole on top of the can, and the can sealed itself up. Willett shook the can back and forth and told me he had seen this kind of pop when he was in North Carolina. He said this kind of pop was real expensive and when he was in college he never could afford it. As Willett talked, the dent came out of the can. The can filled back up with pop. Willett held the can in front of me and said, "Some pop," and then he opened the can. Willett took a drink out of it and I could hear the pop fizzing in his throat. Willett said, "Open your mouth," and I did and he said, "Bend your head back," and I did and he poured the pop into my mouth, and it was tasty, like ginger ale.

I put my hand up, to tell him to stop pouring, and with my head still tilted back I said, "That's amazing," and I thought, this is Aunt Ohio's magic.

Willett said, "Do you want to know how I did that?"

I thought, no, not really. Willett showed me his thumb and it was black and he said, "Here's the ink I wiped off the top of the can that made it look like it had already been opened." Then he tipped the can and pop squirted out a hole in the side of the can. "Here's where I stuck a tack," Willett said, pointing at the hole in the side of the can where the pop was squirting out, "to let out some of the pop before I come up here. Here," he said, holding up a piece of tape, "is the piece of tape I used to cover the hole while I was packing the can up here."

"And when you shook the can," I said, "the gas in the pop made the can pop back out like it was full again."

"Exactly," Willett said.

"You packed that trick pop all the way up here," I said.

"I did," Willett said.

"Did you know all the time you were going to pull this gag?" I said.

Willett said, "I thought, maybe."

"I'll be damned," I said.

"I've got all kinds of tricks," Willett said, with a gassy baby smile.

"Why explain the trick?" I said. "Why not just let me be amazed?"

"I don't know," Willett said. "It just seemed like more fun if we both knew." Willett took another sip of the pop. "Do you want any more of this?" he said.

I shook my head and Willett finished the magic pop. A pebble fell from above. June stood above us at the overlook. She did not seem to have heard us. Willett didn't see her yet. He was trying to decide whether or not to save his magic pop can. June stood with her hands in her pockets.

"June," I said. She couldn't hear me. I said her name again, yelling it. The sound startled her, and it seemed for a second like she might lose her balance. She looked behind her, and I had to call her name a third time before she figured out where the sound was coming from. When she saw me, she smiled. "Wait there," I said. Willett put his magic pop can in his pants pocket, and we went up to where June was. On the way up there, Willett stopped me.

"You don't need to drink so much," he said. "OK?"

Willett nodded and we walked on up to the top. June sat on a rock and stood up when she saw us. She smiled in the sunshine. She hugged us each when we got close enough. Her hair smelled of the woods. I imagined she had been lying down somewhere on the hillside.

"It's always so good and quiet on Christmas," June said.

Willett looked around, at the trees behind us, at the sweep of mountains below us. He squinted in the light. "Man, it's cold," he said.

I asked June where everybody was. She said the organizer girls had come to Cora's, and they were being happy together about the settlement. "They're wondering where you are," June said to me.

"It sucks the state has to pay the companies for them not to mine," I said. "If it's unsuitable, it's unsuitable. They aint got no God-given right to mine. Why do the taxpayers have to give them all them millions?"

June said, "Eight thousand acres protected, Dawn."

"How many acres is that?" I said, and pointed off the overlook.

"Gosh," Willett said. "A million?"

"Hundreds of thousands," June said.

I don't know why I had turned so sour.

"They're talking about going to your mother's baptizing Sunday," June said.

I asked June was she going. She nodded yes. I asked was it at Lower Drop Creek Church, Blondie Kelly's church. June nodded yes.

"You going?" Willett said, looking at me.

BLONDIE KELLY'S church had carpet on the floor and aluminum siding and padding on the pews and was wide and low with fluorescent lights and a homemade pulpit and lean older men with thinning white hair and plain open-neck shirts and stout younger men with groomed beards and many-colored sweaters sitting on pews behind the preacher, who had cheeks shiny as apples and thick forearms from working in the coal mines all week. A guitar player, drummer, and electric bass player were situated around a long straight-haired woman at a piano, and they played along as she sang, "I've got so much to thank Him for, so much to praise Him for, you kno-oh-o-w, He means so much to me-ee-e."

The Sunday Momma got baptized, Decent Ferguson was there in a pretty skirt on the pew in front of us, and of course Blondie Kelly was there with her brothers and mother. Denny and his daddy Fred and his mother Genevieve, they were there, and so were Albert and Evie and Houston and Cora and June and me and Willett.

The baptizing took place in what looked to me like a humongous hot tub at the front of the church. They had garbage bags held on with duct tape over Momma's bad ankles. Momma in her white robe cried and let the men from the church hold her up. The preacher talked over Momma and asked her questions about being righteous and serving the Lord and such, and then he laid her in the water, and when she came up all the church people came up, wrapped her in pale blue towels, laid their hands on her, and singing started again and kept up for a good while, and all of us cried, at least a little. Albert bawled his eyes out, and went up there and joined the people piled up laying hands on Momma, and I remember being happy for all of them, for all of us, and I remember thinking, people change, I guess. They don't always change the way they want to change, or even in the direction they set out to change in. I looked at Mamaw. She held a stick of gum out to me. It was Juicy Fruit. I took it and gave half to Willett. As he put the gum in his mouth, Willett turned to the back of the church. Then he leaned into my ear and said, "Look."

I turned around and Hubert stood at the back of the church. By this time I didn't trust my own eyes, and I asked Mamaw, "Is that Hubert?" and she said, "I'd heard he got out," and Hubert came up the aisle. He had his hair cut and was all cleaned up. He looked like Daddy. The preacher spread his arms wide, and the people parted. Some people's mouths fell open, and others smiled like ho-hum, another day at church, another miracle. My mother, swaddled up in the pale blue towels, reached out her hand to Hubert, and he took it. Then Hubert said something quiet to the preacher, and the preacher told us another soul wanted to come to Jesus. Then they baptized Hubert, and they hugged on him, too, and Momma stepped down on the floor below Hubert, and she was shaking so somebody put a red blanket on her over the towels, and she looked up at Hubert, and Decent Ferguson turned around in the pew in front of us, with a look on her face I couldn't make sense of, and said, "Aint that something?" I looked at Mamaw, and she looked at me with eyes cool as creek rocks and said, "Good for them." Then Aunt June reached across Willett's lap and took my hand in a way that said, "Hang on," and when I looked at her, her face was the future, and it was full of

A MILLION THINGS NEITHER OF
US KNEW THE NAME FOR.

AUNT OHIO left Mamaw hundreds of thousands of dollars, or as Mamaw put it, "a considerable sum." Aunt Ohio made most of it investing in the coal business, so Mamaw took the money and paid for helicopter rides for journalists—local and state, national and international—to come look at the mining from above. If they can see how bad it is, Mamaw said, and do a decent job telling the story, that will put a stop to it. Mamaw believed this, from the top of her head to the tips of her toes.

On a cold clear day the February after Aunt Ohio died, the first helicopter flew over from Kingsport. Mamaw arranged for a newspaper man from Louisville to take the tour. The helicopter landed in the ballfield next to the community college. Me and Mamaw walked towards the pilot who walked towards us.

"You ready?" he asked.

"Who we're waiting for aint here," Mamaw said. "He's coming from Louisville."

The helicopter pilot had on yellow sunglasses. Mamaw was paying him hundreds of dollars an hour. He looked at a clipboard. After a minute he said, "Is there someplace I could get a cup of coffee?"

Mamaw pointed towards the community college. When the man walked away, Mamaw said, "If that reporter aint here by the time he gets back, I want you to go."

I said, "Me? I don't want to go."

Before he went back to jail, Hubert took me out driving six or seven times, and after that Mamaw let me take her everywhere. When Hubert went back to county, I drove Momma to see him. He didn't say much, just looked out the slit of a window in the detention center visiting room at the brown grass, the dead bushes. When he went off to prison, Hubert wrote me long letters full of stories about my father, and what Hubert said lit up the places they'd been, made their paths and hiding places and battlegrounds glow before my eyes. June kept asking me to come live with her, but when Mamaw stopped asking me when I was leaving, I just stayed.

Mamaw caned her way over to the Escort. She came back with a camera.

"Here," she said, handing me the camera. "Get ready."

When the pilot came back, I looked around for the reporter. The pilot looked at his clipboard again, and then his watch. I waved my hand at him, and we walked to the helicopter. The pilot opened my door, and I climbed in. When he was in his seat, he handed me a pair of headphones. The pilot started the helicopter, and it sat spinning, blowing the grass flat beneath it. The pilot said into my ear, "Are you ready?"

I nodded and the helicopter lifted off the ground. At first it was like looking off the roof of a building, and then we were too high to survive if you jumped. I became something other than human. I was vapor. I was air. I was someone's voice, the words they said when no one was around, their words floating up, up, up, and settling right below the clouds, eventually blown to separate letters by the wind, then chopped into bits and pieces of lines by the blades of passing helicopters.

We moved fast through the air, but the ground was not a blur. It was paths and trails and roads, muddy clearings and ponds and gas wells. Mostly it was the tops of trees. I couldn't take my eyes off the ground. Everything was of a piece. The number of colors shrunk. There were hardly any people. People were scarce, gone inside, and the world had a life of its own, fine without us.

My eyes grew bored with the ground. My gaze drifted towards the horizon. The edge of what I could see was Virginia disappearing into sky. I found Bilson Mountain, the radio tower, the bald where Willett and Kenny's family had their place. Radio waves slid past the helicopter, flowed over under around us like water. My heartbeat quickened. The ground quickened, and I wanted to be on it, feet on its scars, shoulders in its narrow places. I wanted to hear quiet things, trickles and drips, the world's parts scratching against each other.

The helicopter's blades had a beat, and my head began to move to it. It was a fast beat, a punk rock beat. The pilot asked was there anything in particular I wanted to see, and I ignored him. I saw the torn-up land, the towns and the trailers, creeks and ditches, dog lots and garden plots, and everything was just as it is, no better no worse. All of it made, everything made—some by people, some by forces bigger than people, some by a mix of the two. I raised up the camera and took pictures, but when I got back to the house and looked at them, they didn't look like anything. They were more boring than maps—except for one.

When the helicopter came back to the ballfield, there was a big yellow dot next to Mamaw I couldn't figure out until we got closer. The dot was Willett in a yellow track suit made him look like a giant canary, like the magic pop can. And so I took a picture of Willett from the helicopter. And when I got the picture back, there were giant words on the ground beside him, and the words were inside an arrow pointing right at his big yellow dot self. And the words said: YOU ARE HERE.

And I was. And I am.

# Acknowledgments

THE AUTHOR would like to acknowledge the following for their support: Stacey, Will, Will II, Laura, and Barbara Gipe; the genius writing teacher Darnell Arnoult; the Hell Of Our Own writers group, Bobby Amburgey, Wes Browne, Denton Loving, Donna McClanahan, Larry Thacker, Sylvia Woods, Tiffany Williams, and especially ace fellow literary sojourner Carrie Mullins; my Hindman writing family, especially Mike Mullins, Gurney Norman, Jim Minick, Jack Wright, Sharon Hatfield, Pat Beaver, George Brosi, George Singleton, Pam Duncan, Jesse Graves, and Jeanne Marie Hibberd; the editors of the online journal *Still*, Silas House, Jason Howard, and Marianne Worthington, for serializing the early parts of the book; Sandra Ballard for, among other things, introducing me to Gillian Berchowitz; everyone at the Ohio University Press; my Crawdad friends, especially Lauren Adams; my Higher Ground friends, especially Rick and Cindy Brock, and my technical advisor, Rutland Melton; my Southeast Community College friends, especially Larry LaFollette, Ann Schertz, Theresa Osborne, Bruce Ayers, Tony Sweatt, and the Scopa family; my students, especially Johnny Combs, Miranda Moore Payne, Donna Jo Collins, Bonnie Thomas, Lisa Frith, and Danielle Burke McMillian; Tom FitzGerald, Judy Hensley, Hazel King, Roy Silver, Teri Blanton, and the rest of the people involved in the struggle to protect the land and people in east Kentucky; Sue and Harry Orr and the writers in our Sweetwater Extended Novel Workshop; and Dee Davis, Mimi Pickering, Jim Webb, Tom Hansell, Jeff and Stephanie Whetstone, Frances M.O. Dowell, David and Michelle Reynolds, Ann Pancake, David Joy, Crystal Wilkinson and Ron Davis, Erin Fitzgerald, Clifford Pierce, and Watt Childress. Most particularly, I would like to acknowledge Robin Lambert, who has been my friend through it all, told me the truth, and given me good advice and love every step of the way. Thank you all.